GO FULL CIRCLE

SCARLETT FINN

ISBN: 9781914517228

www.scarlettfinn.com

Also by Scarlett Finn

GO NOVELS
GO WITH IT
GO IT ALONE
GO ALL OUT
GO ALL IN
GO FULL CIRCLE

EXILE
HIDE & SEEK
KISS CHASE

WRECK & RUIN
RUIN ME
RUIN HIM

THE BRANDED SERIES
BRANDED
SCARRED
MARKED

FORBIDDEN PREQUEL DUET
ALL. ONLY.
ONLY YOURS

THE FORBIDDEN NOVELS
FORBIDDEN DESIRE
FORBIDDEN WANT
FORBIDDEN WISH
FORBIDDEN NEED
FORBIDDEN BOND

BOMBSHELLS & BILLIONAIRES (ROXIVERSE)
NOTHING TO HIDE
NOTHING TO LOSE
NOTHING IN BETWEEN: ONE
NOTHING TO DECLARE
NOTHING TO US
NOTHING IN BETWEEN: TWO
NOTHING TO SAY
NOTHING TO GAIN
NOTHING IN BETWEEN: THREE
NOTHING TO YOU
NOTHING TO THIS PREQUEL: ONE WILD NIGHT
NOTHING TO THIS
NOTHING IN BETWEEN: FOUR
NOTHING TO DO
NOTHING TO NO ONE
NOTHING TO FEAR
NOTHING TO DENY
NOTHING TO BEAT
NOTHING TO THE WEDDING
NOTHING TO TELL
NOTHING TO IT
NOTHING TO SEE
NOTHING TO WIN
NOTHING TO OFFER
NOTHING TO PROVE

LOVE AGAINST THE ODDS STANDALONE COLLECTION
SWEET SEAS
HEIR'S AFFAIR
RESCUED
MAESTRO'S MUSE
GETTING TRICKY
THIRTEEN
REMEMBER WHEN...
RELUCTANT SUSPICION
XY FACTOR

KINDRED SERIES
RAVEN
SWALLOW
CUCKOO
SWIFT
FALCON
FINCH

MISTAKE DUET
MISTAKE ME NOT
SLEIGHT MISTAKE

LOST & FOUND
LOST
FOUND

THE EXPLICIT SERIES
EXPLICIT INSTRUCTION
EXPLICIT DETAIL
EXPLICIT MEMORY

TO DIE FOR...
TO DIE FOR TRUTH
TO DIE FOR HONOR
TO DIE FOR VIRTUE
TO DIE FOR DUTY
TO DIE FOR LOVE

RISQUÉ & HARROW INTERTWINED
TAKE A RISK
FIGHTING FATE
RISK IT ALL
FIGHTING BACK
GAME OF RISK

ONE

AFTER ALMOST FOUR weeks of being at the beck and call of her mistress, Harlow was used to being barked at and ridiculed. The snide looks and demeaning tasks were commonplace. Sometimes, on rare occasions, Ophelia pretended to be her friend. The duplicity was harder to stomach than the malice.

Wrapped up in the most beautiful of packages, Ophelia Hagan was a bully, pure and simple. There were no other more apt words to describe her. She could simper and compliment with those equal to her or, God forbid, if she found herself in the company of someone who out-snobbed her. But with her underlings—who she saw as less than her in every way—there was always an undertone of contempt or scorn. With Harlow, she usually expressed both.

The last time Harlow had been allowed to attend Windsor's was the night she'd lost her liberty. Since then, she'd existed in Ophelia's apartment, carrying out tasks as ordered.

At that present moment, the woman who'd claimed her was pacing in her living room. Striding back and forth across the width of the fireplace, Ophelia spoke about what would be on her schedule that week.

Harlow's own schedule was clear. Save for her duties to the mistress. She was Ophelia's lackey morning, noon, and night. Really any time her boss wanted to turn the screws. As difficult as it was to take orders and not push back against the subjugation, Harlow often reminded herself that she'd chosen this path. And that it was for the greater good.

Life could be worse. She wasn't beaten, and although she was irritated by almost every person in Ophelia's life, their abuse didn't extend beyond verbal. At least, it hadn't yet. Harlow might be playing the dutiful slave, but she hadn't turned herself off completely. When needed, she didn't shy from putting others in their place if they thought about taking liberties.

"Are you listening, Harlow?" Ophelia asked, pausing mid-pace. "You haven't taken any notes. I don't want mistakes. There is no way you'll be able to remember—"

"Dinners. Corporate drinks. The gym. Breakfast with a girlfriend. Brunch with your family…"

Which was an odd addition given the Hagan family was all dead. Harlow questioned that appointment the previous month. Ophelia explained that once a month, she liked to have brunch and reflect on her family. To appreciate their memories with herself. No one else was invited. Typical that she'd chosen brunch too; God forbid the spoiled brat get up too early to show respect.

"Why are you listing everything I'm doing this week?"

To show she'd been paying attention. Not that playing assistant required a lot of brainpower. For the past month, her life had been nothing but a carousel of these meetings and pandering to Ophelia's needs.

"You want clothes and accessories prepared. You want drinks and food setup. It's my job to make available what you need. All I need to know is the events you have. From there, I can work out what I'm doing," Harlow said. "I really don't need your feelings on every single subject and meeting."

"Aren't you sassy today," Ophelia said, her fingers opening in the ends of her hair. "Time of the month? Maybe not. Seems you're always moody. I don't know how he lived with you."

Ryske.

Even when Harlow had been living with him, and sleeping with him, he hadn't been as constant a feature in her life as he was at Ophelia's. Talking about him, in some respects, was Ophelia's favorite hobby. It was possible Ophelia was so vocal in her obsession because Harlow was around. But she couldn't be a hundred percent sure on that. Maybe the woman had always been this chatty about her infatuation.

Ophelia could find a way to bring him up in the most random of moments. It would be an impressive skill, if it wasn't so conniving and pathetic. Even if she hadn't come to resent her new boss in the way she had, Harlow would still feel the same way.

Everything about Harlow's life was controlled by the woman prattling on about the importance of always being a lady even when one wished to do otherwise. It was amazing that Ophelia could clamber up on that high horse and deliver such a haughty speech in light of what she'd done.

Harlow was half a second away from asking if murder was ladylike when the front door opened. Someone strode in. She didn't even turn around. She didn't have to. Anyone else would've knocked and waited to be invited. Not him.

"Darling, Ryske!" Ophelia exclaimed and opened both arms.

Ryske strode past the couch, where Harlow was sitting, without so much as looking at her sideways. She was used to it, but it still left a bad taste in her mouth. That taste was almost joined by bile when she watched Ryske kiss each of Ophelia's cheeks and then pull her into his arms.

"You look good today, Fi," he said, sliding a hand down her back.

Harlow appreciated that he kept himself angled away from her when he showed Ophelia any kind of interest or affection. Not that his consideration did much to quell her urge to kick his ass. Though the white strip of fabric wrapped around his hand suggested maybe somebody had gotten there before her.

She hadn't seen his face because, knowing he

wouldn't acknowledge her, she hadn't bothered to look up when he passed. But, from what she could see, it definitely appeared his knuckles had been bandaged.

Ophelia laughed. "I always look good," she said, drawing herself to Ryske's side, stroking a hand up and down his chest. "We were just talking about you."

"Always happy to know my name is on those lips," he said, cupping Ophelia's jaw and trying to raise her focus while brushing his thumb across her mouth.

Ophelia was weak and entranced. Her rapture was obvious from the color in her cheeks and the looseness of her body. She couldn't resist being in Ryske's arms and absorbing his compliments. Harlow doubted his motivation even mattered; Ophelia just wanted to be under his focus.

Being ensnared in his spotlight could be intoxicating. In the times Harlow had been under his spell, she'd never cared about his motivation. Sometimes she tried to, but it never lasted. Something about the texture of his fingers and the warmth of his breath coupled with the pound of his heart got through every time. It made her vulnerable to giving him whatever he wanted.

Ryske could control every part of his anatomy. At least, it seemed he could. Even those parts that worked on mechanics rather than choice.

While Ophelia could claim to have known Ryske for longer, Harlow better knew his amour. If he really wanted to be kissing Ophelia, he'd be kissing her. The grip he had on her jaw was intended to imply urgency. Like he meant business. Like he was holding tight. But the force wasn't close to what he would use if he wanted to demand her mouth.

Caught up in the seduction, Ophelia hadn't been aware of Ryske's bandages until the fabric rubbed on her delicate cheek. "Oh, my sweet, what happened?" she asked, taking one of his hands in both of hers. "Did you hurt yourself again?"

"Nothing for you to worry about," he said and retrieved a piece of paper from his back pocket to hand it over. "These are our figures for last week... There's an upward trend."

"Just as we thought," Ophelia said, taking the paper to open it. When she read the numbers, her eyes bulged before she did a double take. "This is enough for the basement renovations."

"Yeah," Ryske said, bobbing his head in agreement.

"Did you look at the plans?"

"I did."

Being evasive wouldn't earn him any points with Ophelia. Though, if there was anyone who could get away with pissing her off, it was Ryske.

As proved when Ophelia laughed and drove a knuckle into his upper arm. "Well, silly, what did you think? Did you call the contractor?"

This time, he shook his head. "Nah, I don't like his plans."

A wide smile spread on Ophelia's face. She moved in closer, pressing her body to his. "If there's anyone I trust to optimize sexual experience, it's you."

His chin dipped, but he didn't crouch, so he wanted to avoid kissing her. Not that she could use her own experience as an honest barometer because Ophelia was taller than her. Maybe if the hostess pushed up, she'd be able to reach him anyway. Instead of a kiss, Ryske did his mesmerized thing, where he treated Ophelia like the only person in the room.

Harlow was the only other one around. Neither Ryske nor Ophelia had any trouble acting like she was invisible. The idea of doing something shocking to throw him off his game was tempting. Considering how he might react if she took off her clothes or crept up behind him to slip her hand into his pants, Harlow giggled to herself. It hadn't been deliberate, but her laugh broke the moment between the couple.

Both turned toward her wearing similar annoyed expressions.

"I'm sorry," Harlow said, her smile still flirting with her face. Leaning back, she crossed her legs and waved an absent hand. "I'm sorry, carry on."

"Is something funny?" Ophelia snapped.

Ryske could get away with being an asshole; Ophelia laughed his rudeness off. In contrast, Harlow's laughter, a happy sound, was met with anger.

"No," Harlow said, shaking her head and curling a finger into the loop of her necklace to pull it side to side. "I was just thinking of something… in my head."

"What?" Ophelia asked, raising her fists to her hips. "What were you thinking of?"

"It's nothing, really," Harlow said. "Really. Carry on."

"I told you to correct your mood today," Ophelia said. "Didn't I?"

Pondering the question for a second, Harlow's eyes rolled upward. "No. You asked if I was on my period because I was sassy… If one caused the other, I'd be menstruating three hundred and sixty-five days a year."

The corner of Ryske's mouth reacted, and she noticed it. Ophelia saw her noticing and turned to him.

Before Ophelia caught sight of it, Ryske flattened his reaction and slid his arms around her again. "Ignore her, Fi," he said. "She's here for a reason, and it's not to entertain us."

Straightening her arms, Ophelia stretched them to his shoulders to drape them around his neck. "I love this new you, Ryske," she said. "Have I told you that recently?"

"Not nearly enough," Ryske said and began to lower.

Sensing the kiss was coming, Harlow tipped her face away to avert her gaze from what would be a hideous sight. One she'd seen before, yes, but never one she relished.

"Miss Hagan."

The interruption was enough to make Ryske forget his trajectory. They all twisted to see Penzance coming from the hallway, looking through the papers in his hands. Harlow grinned. He was good. By all appearances, he was completely oblivious to what he'd just interrupted. But she'd come to know him so much better in the last month. Nothing he did was an accident.

"Oh, Vane," Ophelia said, chastising him, coming across as a petulant child.

Penzance stopped reading and looked up, doing a good job of appearing surprised by what he'd found. "Oh, I didn't realize… Want me to come back?"

But it was too late. Ryske was already withdrawing, putting a foot of space between himself and the woman he'd just been holding. Would he have let her go in the same situation? When they'd been together, he'd never shied from holding her or touching her, no matter who else was in the room.

"You're here now," Ophelia said, tsking at him. "What is it you want?"

"These emails came through," Penzance said, holding them up. "You've got some final figures to approve and your auction is about to end…"

Ophelia glanced at her watch and huffed out a breath before stomping across the room. She grabbed the papers from Penzance who slipped his hands in his pockets and looked over the top of Ophelia's head to make eye contact.

"Thank you," Harlow mouthed over the back of the couch, knowing no one else would see it.

"You slacking, Sweeting?" Penzance asked.

"Much as I can, Vane," she said, lounging in a slouch.

Penzance sauntered past Ophelia. The lady of the manor was distracted, leafing through the sheets he'd handed her.

"I heard a rumor about you," Penzance said, dropping onto the couch beside her.

"A rumor about little me?" Harlow asked, slapping his thigh. "It can't possibly be true…" Despite her assertion, she slanted toward him. "Is it dirty?"

"Little bit," he said, and twisted to cup a hand around her ear so he could whisper. "You never wear panties."

Her eyes slunk toward Ryske at the same time her lips curled. With his hands in his pockets and his eyes on her, her love was trying to remain indifferent. Her salacious smile twitched his brow.

"Who told you that?" she asked.

Penzance straightened. "Doesn't matter, is it true?"

"It matters," Harlow said, but was still grinning when she poked her friend. "You knew that about me already anyway… How could you forget something like that?"

The night they'd met she'd been sans underwear and told him as much. Harlow couldn't be explicit in front of Ophelia. As far as she knew, her boss was unaware she and Penzance met before they both came to work together.

Penzance was smart enough to recall what she was referring to. "I didn't know it was a permanent thing," he said. "I thought it was just that one time… A permanent thing is definitely hotter."

"You're spending too much time with Brash. He's obsessed with my habits. It's rubbing off on you."

"Brash is obsessed with you," Penzance said and slid an arm around her. "I'm more subtle in my approach."

This time it was Ryske's jaw that moved. And, if she wasn't mistaken, that sound was her love grinding his teeth.

"I have to make a phone call," Ophelia said, her voice distracted. "I'll just be a few minutes. Harlow, you remember what I told you about being good. If you behave for the rest of the week, I'll let you come to Windsor's on Friday night… So don't dare think about breaking the rules." The rules had a lot to do with not seducing Ryske. Ophelia had told her not to think of Ryske in that way, but policing someone's thoughts was difficult. Harlow looked over the back of the couch at the same time Ophelia pinned her sights on Penzance. "Vane, you do not leave this room."

That was code for *"don't leave Harlow alone with Ryske."* They knew the setup. No matter how much Ophelia believed Ryske was into her, she still wouldn't let them be left alone. Just what did Ophelia fear? What was it that she was supposed to do to Ryske, against his will, that he couldn't fight off?

TWO

OPHELIA LEFT THE ROOM. Harlow didn't get the chance to turn back around before Ryske rushed the couch.

"Move your fucking ass," Ryske said to Penzance who was already sliding away to give her guy room to sit beside her.

"You know—"

Harlow's words were cut off by Ryske cupping her head beneath her ear to force their mouths together. Just as she'd thought. Not subtle, or playful, or hesitant, he didn't give her an opportunity to refuse his kiss. There was no touching her lips, stroking her, he didn't wait for an invitation and took what he wanted without teasing.

Planting her hands on his chest, Harlow pushed back. Not that her resistance discouraged him. Ryske persisted. With his body looming over hers, there wasn't much space to go anywhere. Especially not while he was using his strong grip on her head to direct her.

"Trink, there's no time for coy," he said, fighting to bring her mouth up again.

"There's no time for that either," she said and pulled a USB from her cleavage to slip it into his pocket. "There are records from the company, financials mostly. I don't know exactly. I don't think everything is there, but if Maze can—"

Ryske kissed her again, driving his tongue so deep she had to gasp for breath.

She pushed harder to separate them, ducking her head down at the same time. "My boss thinks you can't defend yourself against me," Harlow teased, taking Ophelia's order as an aspersion on her scruples not Ryske's. "Just call out for help if I touch your winkie."

"Touch it," he said, letting go of her face to grab her hand to press it against his fly.

"Please don't," Penzance groaned, nauseous.

Harlow stole her hand back and not because of Penzance. "I'm not getting you hard for her," she objected, seizing his fingers to present his bandages between them. "What happened here?" Ryske tugged his hand from hers, but she wouldn't give up so easy and hauled it back. "You're fighting again."

"It's nothing."

"That's what you said to her," Harlow said, touching the graze on his cheekbone just beneath his eye. "I'm not her. Answer me, Crash. Are you fighting again?" He nodded, so she smacked his chest. "Why are you so goddamn angry all the time?"

"Why?" he asked, pushing away from her, his face contorted with rage. "Why?" He flew off the couch to pace to the fireplace and back, thrusting an arm toward the hallway door. "I want to break her fucking neck… You know how easy it would be to—"

"Don't," she said, shooting to her feet. It wasn't easy to argue in these hushed snaps of anger, but she wasn't going to bend or shrink just because he was having a fit. "Don't you dare think about fucking this up."

Ryske got in her face. "You have two choices, babydoll. Either I fuck her or I kill her. Those are your options. Decide."

"No," she said, shoving his arm down. "My options include reminding you that it sickens me to see you touching her. You think it's easy for me to be ignored by you? Do you think I like watching you hold her and kiss her and—"

"Then let me—"

"No," she said, a little louder than maybe she should have, so she lowered her volume again. "You are going to toe the line because it's what we do." She showed him her stars. "Have you ever fucked up a job before?" His lack of response was response enough. "Why start now?" Much as she could match his anger, she also suffered the same frustration. Softening, she touched his jaw. "I know what you feel. I feel it too. I feel it every time she makes a jibe about us or belittles me. I think about how easy it would be to choke her. But transfer of ownership will take maybe as much as another two weeks. I told you, we're playing this straight until then. I will take her crap. I will do my best to gather all the intel I can. *You* will do your best to be attracted to her new powerful side."

"It's never been like this before."

She hated to see him on the edge of defeat. "Because we've never had to do this before," she whispered, moving in closer, sliding her other hand over his stubble. "Not like this... If it's too much, don't come back."

His attention snapped up. "What?"

"If you can't handle this... If seeing me and being nice to her is making you so angry... Go and don't come back... I'll find you when I'm done."

The way he gripped her waist tight betrayed the return of his determination. "I'd rather see you for five minutes once or twice a week, and not be able to touch you, than never see you at all."

They didn't usually have any excuse to touch or kiss. Since leaving the club on the night Ophelia won her, she'd only had the pleasure of his mouth one other time.

"I want to see you too. God, Crash, I miss you so much," she murmured. "It gives me strength to be close to you. You remind me why we're doing this, what I'm doing this for."

He kissed her. Slipping her hand under his tee-shirt, she scratched his abs. Her nails on his tattoos always soothed him; he needed that medicine now.

"Have you been touched?" he asked, searching her gaze. "I need to know you're okay here." He glanced at

Penzance. "Is that fucker looking after you?"

"He does his best."

The suggestion of getting Penzance a job with Ophelia had been hers. The intention was to give her love backup. Yet, he'd ended up protecting her. Penzance was the closest thing she had to an ally on the inside. They'd never worked together before. She hadn't known him well, which meant she'd had no idea if he was reliable or talented.

Harlow was pleased to be surprised, not only by his professionalism, but by his skills. Penzance was good. He knew when to be indifferent, what to pretend to miss, and what to see. He managed to maintain his loyalty to Ophelia without making the woman question it, even though he was obvious about developing a friendship with her.

"If you ever need out, you just walk," Ryske said. "You know we'll find a way to fix it. Your safety—"

"I can take care of myself, Crash. You know I can. Living with Brash is no picnic. Ophelia put me with him so he could watch me."

"Yeah," Ryske said, clenching his jaw. "How often?"

"You have to stop worrying about my body and what's happening to it," she said, cradling his hands in hers to show his bandages. "Worry about yours. Stop fighting, Ryske."

His jaw tightened. "I have to do something," he hissed. "I can't sit there with the acid eating through me… Do you know what it does to me to be kept away from you? Do you know how I drive myself nuts thinking you might need me and I might not be there?"

"It's what you expected me to do when we thought she'd want you," Harlow said. "We thought you'd have to go to her bed and we reconciled ourselves to that."

"Wow," Penzance said, attracting both their attentions. "You guys are fucking solid, aren't you?"

Harlow smiled while Ryske just ignored him. "That's not the same. Do you know what these bastards could do to you?"

"Do I know?" she asked, almost offended by the suggestion she was naïve. "Do I fucking know?" She socked his shoulder. "Want to take off your shirt and I'll give you the rundown on the PTSD I've gotten from your scars? Passing out is easy, Crash. Dying is easy. You did both and I was the one left behind."

"Baby—"

When he tried to touch her face, she blocked his arm and thrust it away. "Do you remember the night you came back to life? Seeing that man force himself between my legs? Do you remember what he tried to do to me?"

The question was rhetorical. If he had forgotten, he couldn't love her as much as he claimed. "Trink—"

"Don't you fucking dare tell me I don't know, don't even imply it. I know exactly what these men are capable of, and I know exactly how to fight for myself."

Ryske lost his softness and got defensive. "And if they drug you? If they beat you? How many guys does Brash know? How many guys could he bring back to—"

"I would beg every single one of them to fuck me before I'd even think about letting down my crew."

He stepped back, his head moving side to side. "Good," he said, still kind of shaking his head. "Thank you for telling me that, baby." She wasn't sure she liked the sinister calm that crept over him. "'Cause it makes it easier to tell you the plan… If you're not out of here within two weeks, I'm moving in… with her."

That came across more like a threat than a plan.

The implication he'd give himself to Ophelia in defiance of what she was doing prickled her anger. "You'll sleep with her?"

The curl of a laugh left the corner of his mouth. "Oh, I'm gonna do more than that, baby," he said, swaggering to her. "I'm going to make love to her like it's my wedding night with you. I'm going to make her fall so goddamn hard that she'll be begging me to put a ring on her finger again. She won't just get the Ryske experience, she'll get me, all of me. Fidelity. Forever."

"Why would you do that?" she asked, angry and heartbroken. "Why would you—"

"Because we all agreed way back when that there were

only two paths out of here. We take her down or we give in."

"Giving in means giving her you."

"She'll never hurt you again; never come near any of you. If she has me, she'll think she's in control, and she'll be happy. That's all she wants."

"All she wants is you," Harlow snapped. "For you to be at her sexual beck and call, remember?"

"It's more than sex," he said. "You told me it was love… There's a difference between the two."

It was cruel to imply she needed to be educated on that.

His jibe just stoked her infuriation. "You can't make yourself fall in love with her, Ryske. That's impossible."

"What I feel is irrelevant," he spat. "You've taught me that just by being here. You've taught me over and over again that my feelings mean nothing."

Her anger left as her mouth opened, hurt took its place. "Crash, how could you—"

"I told you I would take your place… you never listened."

"This isn't about jail."

"No, it's not," he said. "But if you'd listened to me before I died and just stayed with Marlowe—"

"Oh my God," she breathed, then pushed his chest. "You asshole, we are not going all the way back there. I am not the person he wanted me to be. I am not the person you thought I was back then either. Why the hell would you ask me to apologize for loving you? I'm so sorry I ruined your fake death."

"If you'd just done what you were told, what we discussed, you'd be safe now."

"You don't know that."

This conversation would take longer than the time they had. Penzance must have realized the same thing. The couch moved at the back of her legs until the denim of his jeans met her skin. Her ally had shifted back along to his previous position.

"You'd never have gotten involved with Ophelia, or Parratt, or Pothos. You'd never have wound up in jail, or the fire, or the hospital."

Ryske didn't mean if she'd done what she was told. He meant if they'd never met. If they'd never fallen for each other. And he wasn't wrong. If she had never met Ryske, or had returned to Rupert, many things would be different.

Hagan might be alive; the evidence room guard too. The fire might not have happened. Floyd's might be intact. Anwen wouldn't have come out of hiding and she wouldn't have endured the horrific beating at Animal's hands.

Ryske seemed satisfied he'd made his point and turned to walk away.

Harlow's quiet voice broke the silence. "If I had stayed with Rupert, we wouldn't have found each other again or made love in my parents' house either. We wouldn't have seen the potential of what we could be." He moved in an arc until he faced her. With a new fuel in her fire, she raised her arm to show her stars again. "I wouldn't have these. My sister wouldn't have her future secured. My crew would have stayed ripped from their home… Yes, Ryske, lots of shit has happened to us, but I wouldn't trade a second of my time in jail or hospital if it meant sacrificing one that I had with you."

There was only a moment of time for him to respond if he wanted to. Except it seemed he didn't. He said nothing and only became more intense. Harlow dropped onto the couch next to Penzance who put an arm around her. Their position was exactly the same as before, Ryske's too. Like it had been planned, Ophelia returned in that moment.

"That was irritating," Ophelia said, striding across the room to return to Ryske's side. "I'm sorry, sweetie. Forgive me for abandoning you?"

"Yeah, he ignored us underlings," Penzance said. "Har and I made out to pass the time. It's fine."

Ophelia wrapped an arm around Ryske's waist. "My Ryske has time for people from all levels of society. Don't you, honey?"

Her Ryske. God, wasn't it hilarious? The woman didn't have a damn clue who he was. He could be her prince, sure, but he could also be her worst enemy. Harlow knew that from personal experience.

"What a guy," Penzance said in such an ambiguous way that it could be taken as truth or mocking.

Ophelia chose to take it as the first. At least, she didn't care enough to pay attention to him or respond.

"I can make it up to you," Ophelia said, sliding a hand across Ryske's chest and down his torso. "If you want to come through to my bedroom—"

"I've got places to be today," Ryske said, snapping out of whatever trance he'd been in for long enough to kiss the top of Ophelia's head. "Another time."

"Next time?" Ophelia asked, following him when he started for the door.

"Yeah," Ryske said. "Maybe. Take it easy, Fi."

The door slammed and Harlow didn't bother to turn around. He was gone. His departure was far from discreet. She just wished he hadn't left her with this damn anger and all these questions. Could he really give himself to Ophelia? If it saved her life, he could, but this wasn't about life and death. Being there was an inconvenience. Harlow was watched and chaperoned every minute, but she wasn't afraid.

It hadn't been about life and death until he'd said he'd give his life to Ophelia. That was the reality of his suggestion. He didn't mean he'd sacrifice his life, he meant he'd give Ophelia the future he'd once promised her.

THREE

HARLOW WAS STILL getting over what Ryske had said about her returning to Rupert when Ophelia appeared around the end of the couch. Strolling along, she was loose and sighing like a woman in the clutches of new love. Although, in truth, what she was going through was far from new. Ophelia had wanted Ryske for as long as she'd known him.

"I often wonder," Ophelia said, continuing her glide all the way to the fireplace where she traced a finger along the mantel. "How do you feel when you see me with him?"

Harlow looked up just as Ophelia turned to show her subdued, yet curious, smile. Ophelia was great at talking about herself and that was usually the context in which she brought up Ryske. She'd mentioned her feelings, and what she thought of Ryske's, but she'd never been so direct in asking Harlow for her perspective.

"What do you want me to say, Ophe?"

"Do you ache when you see him?"

Harlow knew what answer her boss wanted to hear and imagined it would give Ophelia great pleasure to see her underling broken and begging for mercy.

Instead she muttered, "Yeah, I never did get over that yeast infection."

Penzance laughed, but Ophelia huffed, taking great offense. "You're so rude."

"I'm rude?"

Ophelia sucked in a breath and stormed away, slamming into the hallway, leaving Harlow alone with Penzance. There was no real hurry for either of them to be anywhere. At least, there was none for her to be anywhere. She appreciated Penzance not getting up to run away; he was the only thing she had resembling a friend nearby.

"You are a little bit rude, you know," Penzance muttered out the corner of his mouth.

With a smile, she nudged her elbow into his ribs. "Do you blame me when there are so many assholes around here?" she asked, then rested her head on his arm. "Except you. You're not an asshole."

He slapped a hand to his chest. "Oh, you wound me. I'll just have to keep trying."

"Please don't," she said and closed her eyes.

Dropping her guard wasn't usually an option. Even in spite of her trust in Penzance, Harlow wasn't wild about the idea of him knowing she was gathering herself. It helped that he couldn't see her face in this position. Sometimes she got so tired of being alert all the time. Napping meant giving someone the chance to catch you unaware, so she wouldn't let herself do it.

"Wish I'd got to see more of you two together," he said. "You've got some history. I could tell there was something weird about your relationship the night we met. You were like… connected. Even when he was flirting with Kylie and you weren't even looking at each other, there was an awareness about you… he didn't mean what he said about Marlowe."

Penzance had dated a friend of Harlow's sister. Through that relationship, Penzance learned quite a bit about the Sweetings. Without her telling him, he'd also known her ex-fiancé impregnated Lena, yep, Harlow's sister, one and the same. The wedding was being planned as they spoke. Not that Harlow could be a part of it. She'd missed the festivities while stuck at Ophelia's.

Her new life involved strict rules. Phones and the internet were off-limits. Ophelia's fear, she assumed, was her calling Ryske, or reinforcements. Even ordering food or clothes wasn't straightforward, she wasn't allowed to place the order on her own. She had to write it down and give it to Brash, who enjoyed having power over her life almost as much as Ophelia did.

"It was all planned," she said. "Ryske told me to go back to Rupert and I was going."

"Why?" Penzance asked with genuine incredulity. "I remember Lena talking about how you and Marlowe weren't happy. You left the guy because you didn't love him. Why go back?"

Breathing in, she thought about that time, which felt like so long ago. "Because it was him who helped me when I thought I'd lost Ryske," she said. "Ophelia and I came up with the plan to go in half each on Pothos. It was part of our grander scheme to avenge Ryske, who'd been shot by Animal on Jarvis Hagan's order."

She almost laughed. Back then, rage and resolve coursed through her in equal measure. In retrospect, it seemed incredible. Though, if she found herself in the same position again, she'd probably act the same way.

"How did Marlowe help you?"

"He gave me the money," she said. "A half a million dollars, no questions asked."

"And the bargain was you go back to him?"

Sitting up straight, she smoothed her hands down her skirt. "Yep," she said. "He was good about it and didn't pressure me. The point was to do what I had to do, and then go back to the life he wanted us to have." Her mouth was working without the backup of her brain, shit. Harlow turned quickly to grab his hand. "Lena doesn't know. No one knows, except Ryske and the guys. I—"

"Your secret's safe," Penzance said, touching the end of her chin. "Don't think I'll be talking to Emma again any time soon."

When he put his arm around her to hold her at his side, she got the sense he needed some comfort of his own.

"Do you ever miss her?"

"Em?" he asked. "No more than I ever miss any of them. We weren't… you know."

He'd tell her it wasn't real. Maybe it wasn't. Yet, it seemed there was something more to how the relationship ended than he was letting on.

"Relationships suck, don't they?"

"Not yours. Ryske's just being a guy. He wants to be between you and trouble. While you're here, he can't be… He does love you."

Harlow didn't doubt that, but that didn't mean his words couldn't hurt or that he wouldn't mean them. At the same time Ryske told her to go back to Rupert, he'd been in love with her. Loving her hadn't stopped him faking his death intending to set her on that path.

Breaking her heart was a side-effect; collateral damage to making a unilateral decision about what was best for her. Penzance couldn't know any of that, but he was right about one thing, Ryske was being a guy… a jerk of a guy.

Harlow knew her man. She didn't know how Penzance reached his conclusion.

"How do you know that?" she asked.

"Because I've known Ryske a long time."

"You've known all of them for a long time." Easing their bodies apart, he peeked down at her. "Yes, Ryske and I do talk… I know you're from the neighborhood."

He nestled her to his side again. "Some of the things he told you just amaze me," he said. "Ryske doesn't trust anyone."

"He trusts his crew."

"All of them are suspicious assholes."

"That makes you one too," she said. "You ran with them. Learned with them… That stands for something… Means more than even someone like me."

"What does that mean?"

She sighed. "Sure, Ryske loves me, but his ability to trust me has always been in question."

"If you fucked around on him once—"

"I've never fucked around on him," she said,

releasing some of her bluster to sag. "If I had, maybe I'd understand why he feels it's so necessary to hide things from me. Every time I think I've gotten through to him, I find out something new… I don't know if we'll be able to hold up to it again."

"I guess he feels the same way, which might be why he's telling you about his plan here," Penzance said. "Honey, I can't tell you what's going to happen with your relationship or any of this shit. An old friend of mine used to say something that's helped me out plenty of times. Get what you like and like what you've got. Means—"

"I know what it means," she said and smiled. "It means we're in control of our own actions and that we have to make lemonade no matter what fruit we're given…"

"Dover trusts you too, huh?" Penzance said. "Floyd used to say it all the time when one of us was bitching about something. Sometimes life gives us shit we don't want. But if we've got it, we might as well get used to it and find a way to make the best of it, because it's not going anywhere."

Opening her mouth, she pulled in a breath. "You're right. Dover's right. Floyd's right…" She sat up again and ran her fingers through her hair. Taking some time to compose herself, Harlow got her head back in the right headspace to face the day. "Why can't someone tell Ryske that?"

His smile became a grin as he stood up and grabbed her hands to haul her onto her feet. "Honey, no one changes that much. No one ever told Ryske anything he didn't want to hear."

That was the truth. Harlow could tell him one thing and he'd hear the opposite. Like when she'd told him she wouldn't sleep with him or that they were breaking up. Ryske wasn't fazed, he just contradicted her and let it bounce off.

There was little comfort in that truth. If he was out fighting every night, he wasn't letting it bounce off this time. His rage was controlled, usually. He made a point of it. His father was a violent man and her guy didn't want to follow that example.

This was a difficult time. Knowing she was doing it for her crew helped push her through. In his place, Ryske felt helpless. Harlow could identify. She'd feared being in his position when they believed it was Ophelia's intention to claim him at the card game.

Time dragged while under Ophelia's command, but she had plenty to keep her busy. In contrast, Ryske was at home. Even the refurbishments at Floyd's wouldn't distract him from knowing she was out in the world and possibly in peril.

Harlow needed him to trust her. She was going to do this with his support or not. But at the end, what would remain of the life she'd left behind?

FOUR

LIVING WITH BRASH was a nightmare.

Ophelia would never lower herself to living with her minions. Instead, she leased the apartment directly below her own for her employees. Such proximity meant they could be on hand for anything she needed any minute of the day.

As if just living with the goons wasn't bad enough, Harlow had to put up with Brash's idiot friends too. Most of them also worked for Ophelia; they just lived elsewhere. They liked to come by unannounced on a regular basis and disrupt any modicum of peace she managed to carve out.

That night was no different. Brash and his friends were in the living room, playing cards. Well, that was the cover. As far as she could tell, they were spending more time shouting at the sports game on TV and jeering each other than they were at the table she'd set up for them at Brash's command.

Taking orders from Brash was a kick in the teeth. Ophelia had been clear about the hierarchy and Brash was above her, so she had no choice except to obey. That didn't prevent Harlow from resenting him. Keeping up with chores around the apartment was fine. It wasn't like any of the guys were going to bother. If it was cook and clean or sit around playing social with Brash, she'd take chores any day.

She'd just put a new bowl of potato chips on the card table when someone touched her ass. Touching, she didn't tolerate that. They could leer at her chest and comment on her ass. Neither got a reaction out of her. Looking and speaking, she let go. It gave her a sense of power to ignore and irritate them by being impervious.

Hands making contact with her was a different ballgame. For one thing, these situations could escalate fast. Especially when the men were in a group goading each other on.

Slapping the hand away, she straightened the bowl of chips, then walked away to collect some of the mess strewn around the room. There were peanut shells and empty beer bottles all over the place. It was insane they were happy to live like pigs in this upscale apartment.

"Ah, look at her playing shy," one of the guys said. He could be the one who'd touched her, she didn't know or care. Harlow found it best to just roll her eyes off them, or to ignore them completely. "Thought you said she was a horny bitch, Brash."

Brash snickered. "Maybe you don't got the touch. Minute you guys walk out of here, she'll be all over me."

He wished. Harlow noticed the way he leered at her. Was impossible not to. Almost every time they were together, he made some kind of sexual comment. She had no intention of giving him satisfaction. If it made him feel like more of a man to boast to his ridiculous buddies that he was having sex with a woman who despised him, she wouldn't waste energy protesting. Anyone who mattered would know in a heartbeat that it was a lie.

Penzance didn't hang around with Brash by choice. Their only link was their employer. Harlow had seen them being civil, friendly even. But Penzance always made an excuse when it came to socializing with the asshole and Harlow didn't blame him.

Collecting the trash and dishes, she sighed, signaling, in her own way, that she thought he was pathetic. Without saying a word, she took everything into the kitchen. Separating the trash from the dishes, she didn't look up when the door opened. Assuming someone was coming in for more beer, she kept her head down.

It would be a cold day in hell before Brash would get his own drink. He'd rather holler at her, especially when his buddies were around. But some of the other guys didn't mind snooping in the kitchen.

She leaned over the counter, past the knife block, to reach the discarded food wrappers, intending to clean up.

Someone came up behind her. Pushing his hips into her ass, whoever he was, he liked what he saw. Her lip curled in disgust when he began to grind his proud erection against her.

"What is it you'd do for him… huh?"

Brash's voice was low, but it wasn't seductive. At least, if that's what he was going for, he missed the mark. Someone as evil as him couldn't conceal their true nature, not even in an intimate moment.

"You'll never know," she said.

With her hands on the counter, and her toes barely touching the floor, she wasn't in a great position to fight.

"I heard you like it rough," Brash said, still rubbing himself against her. He snaked both hands around, under her arms to grope her breasts. "Danger turns you on."

She tipped her chin toward her shoulder, but was glad she couldn't quite see him. "I can tell it gets *you* hot," she said. "If you weren't into danger, you wouldn't have your hands on me right now."

He snickered. "You think I'm afraid of him? That fucker is far, far away. He can't save you now."

It sort of amused her that everyone assumed she couldn't take care of herself. She'd completed self-defense classes before moving to the city, and had trained with Costello who taught more than the right way to fight. He taught her to fight dirty as well.

Even without those lessons, it was a mistake to underestimate her sheer will. Despising the man with the audacity to put his hands on her increased her determination. She would rather die fighting than give in to the man who'd put a blade in her love. Though, part of her should be grateful for that wound. If Brash hadn't stabbed Ryske, she may never have met her crew. Still, she wasn't going to express her gratitude in any sexual way.

"I'm not afraid of you, Brash," she said, ignoring his hands kneading her chest and the line of his dick on her ass. It pulsed as he picked up his pace and pushed harder. "But you are afraid of him."

Harlow wouldn't go down without a fight or miss a chance to taunt the man who took such pleasure in taunting her.

He spat out disgust in a burst of laughter. "I don't fucking think so."

"Really?" she asked, craning her head further around. "If you're not afraid of him, why wouldn't you tell him to his face you're fucking me? You're proud to boast about it in front of your Neanderthal friends. Why don't you try this shit in front of him?"

"I took him down once, I'll do it again," he said. "That knife went in real sweet last time. I won't forget to twist next time."

"That's a good tip," she said. "Thanks for that."

Snatching a knife from the block, she thrust around with all her strength. Using the width of her hips to force him back, she twisted to flip around and brought the knife up in an arc, slashing Brash across his cheek.

He screamed out. "You fucking bitch!"

He touched the blood on his cheekbone. When he saw it, he was quick to respond by smacking her across the face, sending her tumbling to the side. Harlow didn't go down. Although her face felt like it was ready to explode, she was grateful to be free of the island he'd pinned her against. He was still between her and the door. Retreating around the island, keeping it between them was an option. Speed and agility were on her side, and she didn't doubt her stamina. The only thing he had on her was strength, and Costello had taught her a few tricks for using that to her advantage.

Her confidence wavered when the kitchen door opened and Animal burst in. Animal was bigger and more insane than Brash. She'd reasoned with him once and had a feeling that was the only pass she'd get from him.

"What the hell?" Animal said, absorbing the scene and registering the thin slice of blood trickling down Brash's cheek. "She fucking did that?"

Animal didn't ask why or even hesitate, he rushed toward her. She turned the knife, praying she'd have the strength to use it on him before he used it on her.

"Stop," Brash said. His order worked on Animal, which shocked her. Altruism wasn't the maniac's motive. That became obvious when he turned his sneer on her. "You're gonna be mine, little girl."

"Never," she spat.

He laughed again. Oh, how she'd come to despise that sound. "You don't even get it. You think Ophelia wants you running her errands and pressing her clothes forever? She doesn't give a damn about you. This is all about him."

Harlow wished her adrenaline would subside enough to let her laugh in his face. The idiot was insane if he thought she didn't know that. Though, it was her mission to gather intelligence, so it made more sense to act surprised. Questioning him could lead to more information.

"What the hell are you talking about?" she asked.

"She wants to break him. Soon as she's got him to heel, you're useless…" He smiled and touched the blood on his cheek while sauntering past Animal who was still ready to pounce. "And when you're useless to her, you're mine… You'll be mine for as long as I want, in any way I want…"

He smudged his blood against her lip. Harlow was quick to swipe it off with the back of her hand, leaping away as she did.

"You can fucking try," she snarled. "I'd put a bullet in my head before I'd ever give you the pleasure of touching me."

Whatever his intention, rape, torture, or murder, she wouldn't let him have the satisfaction. Not if she had a choice, and as far as she was concerned, there was always a choice. As long as she had the ability to take her own life, there was a choice.

Grabbing her arm, Brash thrust her against the fridge. "You're good at that, aren't you?" he hissed. "Putting bullets in people."

Sometimes it was easy to forget that Brash wasn't Ophelia's minion at all. At least, he hadn't started out that way. Ophelia had recruited Brash and Animal to do her dirty work after killing her brother, Jarvis Hagan, their original boss.

Brash and Animal were loyal to Jarvis Hagan and believed they were continuing their work for him by protecting Ophelia. They were ignorant to the fact that Ophelia had pulled the trigger and killed the man they cared for.

Harlow had done time in jail for the crime until the evidence in her case was lost. After that, the charges against her had been dropped. But that wasn't enough for Brash. It wasn't enough for most people.

Being accused of killing a man wasn't an easy mistake to come back from. Harlow hadn't pulled the trigger, but she'd been present when Hagan died. She hadn't gone to the authorities with what she knew either. Both to protect the Pothos operation and her crew who could be implicated in other crimes.

"You're some kind of fool," she said in the back of her throat through her gritted teeth and thrust forward to push him away.

He wasn't holding her tight; he didn't intend to keep her in place. Brash just wanted to throw his weight around in an attempt to intimidate her. That wasn't an easy feat these days.

"You'll think that right up until the moment I pour Pothos down your throat and force you to come around my cock, again and again, over and over."

So rape was what he had in mind. The idea that she could ever enjoy anything he would do to her was sickening. Unfortunately, she wasn't ignorant to what Pothos did. Simply put, the elixir enhanced sexual experience. Magnifying usual sensations to meteoric levels, it wasn't really possible to take the drug and be impervious to the acts being performed.

She'd never taken it and never would voluntarily.

Brash's intention revealed the level of his narcissistic depravity. Most rapists would choose a sedative to subdue their victim, making them easier to manipulate. Brash, on the other hand, didn't want her just to take what he forced upon her, he wanted her to enjoy it too.

"What would your boss say to that?" she asked. "You think he'd like you pleasuring the woman who you believe killed him?"

"Hagan was smart," he said, his attention slithering all over her. "He knew what you were good for. Despised that you kept it for the asshole who ruined his life… Think it's only right we ruin the asshole's woman before we dispose of her, don't you?"

Harlow would accept all forms of torture before she'd choose rape. She supposed that was the point of it. An irrational doubt crept into her mind as she recalled something she'd once said to Ryske about accepting him into her body again if he ever gave himself to Ophelia. His decision would be voluntary while rape wouldn't.

Except she couldn't help but think Ryske would never be able to touch her again if she'd allowed herself to be pleasured by Brash. With Pothos in her system, she couldn't guarantee she wouldn't feel pleasure. That terrified her more than the notion of death.

Projecting confidence, Harlow pushed her shoulders back and smiled up at him. "The trouble is, it's not possible… After being with Ryske, I'm complete. Take whatever you think you can, the memory of him will always put it back."

Turning away, she sashayed past Animal, measuring each step, reminding herself to go slow. Slipping out of the room, she went to her bedroom and closed the door. Her sanctuary was little more than a bed under a fixed pane window. She had a nightstand, with nothing in it, and a vanity beside a dresser.

Sinking onto the stool in front of her vanity, she touched the redness on her face. She didn't have anything to put on it to reduce the swelling. Not in her bedroom. She'd wait until she heard Brash and Animal go back into the living room before considering a return to the kitchen to retrieve ice.

Life was reaching terminal velocity. They'd all put up with each other for long enough; it was becoming too much. Playing it civil had never been easy, but they'd at least managed to keep their hands off each other... until now.

Two more weeks. She didn't know for sure that she'd walk out of Ophelia's then, but Harlow hoped to have the evidence they needed before the deed became final. After that, there wasn't much reason to stick around.

If Ryske was willing to make good on his threat, she had even more reason to work hard. Telling him about Brash's threat could snooker that plan. Her love might be reluctant to hand himself over to Ophelia knowing it would lead to Harlow being thrown to the wolves.

Ophelia couldn't triumph. The damned woman had held the upper hand for too long. One thing was clear, Harlow needed to kick up her efforts. The countdown had just become more real.

FIVE

EACH MORNING, Harlow's first duty was to help Ophelia get ready for the day. An insane process. Something queens in ye olde England probably expected of their ladies-in-waiting.

Even being aware that the task was just another way to demean her, Harlow was growing tired of putting up with the bullshit. Ophelia was capable of putting on her own shoes and selecting her own underwear. Seemed that she'd done it before dragooning her slave, so she should be able to do it after.

When Harlow arrived in her mistress' abode that morning, she'd heard Ophelia in the kitchen, but hadn't bothered to go talk to her. Instead, she went to the bedroom to get on with what she had to do—picking out Ophelia's outfit, as per previous instructions. The bathroom was dry, indicating Ophelia hadn't used the shower that day. Keeping on top of Ophelia's hygiene was just another of her patronizing, ridiculous duties. So after pottering about with accessories, and using some of Ophelia's concealer on her face bruise, Harlow left the bedroom to seek out her overlord.

Approaching the kitchen door, she heard a female voice that didn't belong to her boss.

"You have more patience than I would," the female said.

Flattening herself against the wall, Harlow frowned. That voice was familiar. Who—

"Sometimes I think I should be sainted, An," Ophelia said. "I really do."

Anwen. That was… unexpected. As far as Harlow knew, Anwen was still staying at Floyd's with Ryske and the other guys. At Ophelia's request, Anwen was part of the Pothos operation, had the women become close again?

Being absent from Windsor's on Friday nights meant she missed a lot. On Fridays, Pothos was dispensed to willing, and wealthy, patrons. They had to be rich, one hit cost several thousand dollars. Working women were provided to optimize the experience.

Ophelia was the instigator of the operation. How it all happened was still hazy. What she did know? Her boss brought her brother and Ryske on board. She was also close to Parratt who, in turn, invited Yarker to join. And so their consortium was born. Every man contributed something tangible to the ongoing venture, though, in Harlow's biased opinion, Ryske was the most valuable member.

More so since Ophelia lost the Pothos venue, Windsor's, to Ryske in a card game. Without her name on the deed, the consortium didn't need the heiress anymore. In addition to becoming their host, Ryske was the provider of the escorts entertaining the Pothos-high men.

Parratt and Yarker's roles were supply and logistics; the former linked them to their Pothos supplier in Europe, the latter got the product into the country. Just like everyone else, Ophelia and Harlow invested start-up money. But that was it. That was the sum total of their contribution. What did that mean? Both of them were expendable.

"You should," Anwen said. "I lived with her. I know how awful she can be."

"I don't understand what he ever saw in her."

"Try living with it," Anwen said. "I had to listen to them talking and fooling around… It's sick. It is. I don't know what she has on him."

Ophelia gasped. "Blackmail? Oh, it could be… We should think about that some more."

Harlow's mouth opened. They were talking about her! She and Anwen had never been close, but she didn't think the woman despised her. After hearing the contempt in her tone that misconception was gone. This could be some play by the crew, she couldn't discount that. But it could also be the truth of the woman, and a side she hadn't seen.

There were lots of conflicting reports about Anwen's personality. Jarvis Hagan, once her fiancé, adored her. Ryske had an affair with her for six months and told of Anwen conning him into her bed… But there were times he spoke of her with an affection he wasn't always aware of, she didn't think anyway.

He had hidden the woman away after helping to fake her death. That wasn't something someone would do for a person they had no fondness for. In contrast, since Anwen had been back in their lives, there had been undeniable tension in the air.

Anwen cared for Ryske. In the past, during brief moments of compassion, Harlow pitied her. It was obvious Anwen didn't know how to express her feelings to Ryske or how to reach him. Ophelia loved him too, but she was more proactive in her attempts to gain his attention. Harlow hadn't felt sorry for Ophelia for a long time.

"I am indebted to you," Anwen said, excited and playful. "He's just been a different person since you took her out of our lives."

Ophelia groaned. "I am having fun with her. But it is hard work. You get to have all the fun."

Anwen moaned in a demonstration of pleasure. "My roommate does know how to have the best kind of fun."

"Are you sleeping with him?" Ophelia asked, sounding intrigued rather than shocked.

"God, yes," Anwen said. "Ryske can't be without a woman and when there's a willing one in reach…"

Harlow didn't want to so much as blink while listening to Anwen discuss Ryske being an incredible lover. They'd been together before, which gave credibility to what she was saying. It was that previous carnal knowledge Anwen was drawing on. Harlow didn't doubt the woman was speaking from past, not current, experience.

Yes, it was true that Harlow's relationship with Ryske was in flux, so technically, he could screw anyone he liked. But if Anwen was fulfilling his needs at home, he wouldn't be going out to find himself a fight every night.

Whether they were together or not, either in a physical sense or a relationship, Ryske was focused on her. The only thing that would eclipse his focus on her would be a greater love. If Anwen was that love, she'd have the power to stop him going into the street in a rage. Out there he could get himself killed or arrested.

If Ryske tried to pull that shit while Harlow was home, there would be a lot of screaming arguments and a lot of sex too. No way in hell she'd let him take risks like that. Fighting achieved nothing and probably only raised his frustration levels.

She sighed. Just the idea of having that kind of access to him again fired her yearning. She'd give anything to lie in bed with him again. To be in his arms. To be alone with him. Setting that as an ambition gave her something to shoot for. Even if it was just for a minute, she wanted to lie with him again, at least once.

"He's a man with a high libido," Ophelia said.

"Fifi," Anwen said. "You have no idea… He's insatiable. I just have to tell him I want him and he's ready. It's incredible."

Folding her hands over each other at the small of her back, Harlow wondered if she should interject with her own opinion on how to get Ryske going. It had nothing to do with telling him… or even using words. To get laid when Ryske was around, all she had to do was look at him and he'd know. Though more often than not, he knew what she needed before she did.

Ophelia laughed. "Oh, he's always ready. Have you ever known him not to be on and ready for it? The man's a walking hormone."

Not for her. Oh what she'd give to shout that out-loud. How deluded could one woman be? In Ophelia's mind, she and Ryske were some kind of star-crossed lovers, victims of circumstance. That was how she justified them never having had the chance to be together.

Ophelia blamed Anwen for getting in the way early in the relationship. She seemed to have conveniently forgotten two specific periods of time, both before and after Anwen was a part of his life. Ryske had been single and available before he ever met Anwen and after she'd "died." Instead of starting something with Ophelia, he'd chosen—yes, *chosen*—to move on.

His exit from Ophelia's life wasn't dramatic. He hadn't ousted her in a fit of theatrics or to make a point. It was simply that she'd been so insignificant in his life that he hadn't spared her a passing thought before getting back to his life as it had been before Anwen.

Ophelia seemed to forget that she'd needed to come up with the Pothos plot to get him back in her life. Even then, the wheels of that operation had already been in motion before Anwen, or Harlow, had been a part of his life. If he'd wanted Ophelia, he could've had her then too.

"I'm doing my best to keep up," Anwen said. "I can't say I'm complaining."

The women laughed. "Can't say I would either."

They laughed like girlfriends discussing a new boyfriend. But it couldn't have been more fake. Pushing away from the wall, Harlow tiptoed back to the bedroom to pull the door closed hard like she'd just used it.

Striding down the hallway, Harlow entered the kitchen and came up short, acting surprised to see Anwen.

"I… didn't realize you were coming to visit."

Pretending to be off-kilter, Harlow enjoyed the look of mischief in Ophelia's eyes. The villainess thought she'd surprised her captive. Ryske would get a kick out of her performance.

"Ophelia and I have been building bridges," Anwen said. The two women were sitting at perpendicular sides of the kitchen island. "At the club."

"That's nice," Harlow said, going over to clean up the mess around the coffee machine. "Would you like me to turn on the shower, Ophe?"

Sitting there in her long silk robe, Ophelia liked to project an effortless air. Harlow didn't fall for it. She'd seen the makeup on the vanity. Ophelia wasn't as "just woken" as she'd like to project.

"I think we'll have a bath today," Ophelia said.

"You bathe together?" Anwen asked, raising her coffee cup and her brows at the same time.

"Harlow washes my feet and my hair," Ophelia said. "You know how tiresome these daily tasks can be."

Biting her tongue wasn't easy. Anwen's quick acceptance and nod of understanding was insane. If only she could throw something across the room and knock some sense into her. That wouldn't pass for restraint.

Folding and refolding a kitchen towel, examining Anwen's profile, the bracelet on the beauty's wrist changed everything.

Ryske's bracelet.

Her mouth opened and she took a step forward. Just in the nick of time, she stopped the words from spilling out of her mouth. That bracelet could be a sign he approved of Anwen's presence. Ryske would know she'd notice it given it had been hers, was hers. She'd claimed ownership since his death, minus her jail months.

Anwen shifted and averted her gaze, adjusting the long sleeve of her shirt to cover the bracelet while angling herself away. Well, wasn't that telling. Narrowing her eyes, conclusions came quick. Anwen hadn't wanted her to see the piece. If she wasn't supposed to see it, either Anwen wasn't supposed to have it, or the relationship between Ryske and Anwen was real and extremely powerful.

She knew which she believed.

Pasting on a smile, Harlow put the towel on the counter and headed for the door. "A bath it is. Excuse me."

***

HARLOW TOOK HER time getting Ophelia's bath ready. Not too much time, just enough to let the women in the kitchen relax and forget her intrusion.

Her timing was perfect. After filling the bathtub with bubbles and lighting the oils Ophelia loved, Harlow grabbed a bath sheet and went into the hallway again, her ears pricked.

"It's a process…" Anwen was saying. "You're doing so well. You have to be patient. Don't sell yourself short. You've done a lot of hard work."

How many more platitudes would Anwen spout before shutting up?

"I want it to be a success," Ophelia said. "Pothos might be a game for Gil, but it means something to me."

"It means something to Anthony."

Ophelia huffed. "It means something to Anthony Yarker because I tell him it means something to him. It's easy to manipulate a man into believing anything when you're sucking his dick." The towel almost fell when she clamped a hand over her mouth to hold in a squeal. "This whole palaver only started because he has a loose tongue in bed. Why do you think I said no hookers for investors? God knows what he'd say to them."

"It worked out for you though," Anwen said. The sound of a spoon on the edge of a cup like it was being stirred carried from inside. "If he didn't tell you about Parratt's Pothos contact, you'd never have put this all together… You know I'm still in awe of how you've handled this."

So Ophelia had been having an affair, maybe a relationship, with Yarker. During that he'd let slip about Parratt and his link to Arjan, their Pothos supplier. That conversation sparked the whole operation. Yarker's inability to keep a secret, if it was a secret, had planted the seed, which led to Ophelia's plan.

Thus some of the haze lifted.

Not all of it though.

Some things didn't make sense. Like why were they still keeping the affair secret? Harlow had never even seen any hint of true affection between them. Maybe Ophelia wanted it on the down low so as not to disrupt her potential relationship with Ryske.

The women's chat was intriguing. There was a trust between them Harlow hadn't been aware of when she was last involved in Pothos. If Anwen had known about the affair, she hadn't revealed that knowledge to the group. Not while Harlow was a part of their lives. Something had changed between the women over the course of the last four weeks.

Figuring out how much she should trust Anwen was simple. If Anwen was feeding this information back to the Floyd's crew, Harlow would let herself trust. But if Anwen was hiding things or acting alone, she was a threat to Harlow's family.

The fallout of that level of risk was too high. Where her boys were concerned, Harlow would rather be the overreacting bitch demanding Anwen be ousted than give her the benefit of the doubt. The trouble was, she couldn't contact her crew and had no way of verifying the truth.

The contradictions perplexed her. Anwen's claim of sleeping with Ryske recently was a lie. Was she in competition with Ophelia or had the crew instructed Anwen to mislead her old friend?

Then there was the bracelet. Ryske wouldn't have handed that over unless it was part of the ruse. If that was the case, why had Anwen tried to hide it from her?

Harlow couldn't stand being out of the loop. She wouldn't be able to trust Anwen until she got word from one of her boys that it was safe.

Anwen knew about Ophelia's secret affair with Yarker and how Pothos had come about. She was in the know and had Ophelia's trust—a valuable asset. Was it part of a larger plan or was her crew about to be shafted?

SIX

WHILE STILL TRYING to figure out what was going on and who was loyal to who, Harlow almost missed the kitchen conversation taking an even more shocking turn.

"Bringing you on was the best decision I ever made," Ophelia said. It sounded like she was eating something. "I hoped this would happen. That we'd get this back. I am so pleased we made up."

"Me too, honey," Anwen said. "Though I wouldn't say inviting me on board was the best decision. You made one better one."

The heiress laughed; Anwen joined in. Which decision did they mean?

Ophelia illuminated the truth. "Cutting Jarvis out was more of a necessity than a decision. He had it coming for a long time. He was just lucky I didn't do it sooner. You have no idea how close I came to doing it so many times."

"Oh, I do. I remember you used to talk about it… I never for a second thought you'd really follow through and kill him though."

For a minute, the world went silent. Anwen knew Ophelia was the killer? How could that be?

If her crew had trusted Anwen with that tidbit, a lot

had changed at home. Sickness churned in her belly. Tossing the towel over her shoulder, Harlow needed a hand on the wall for support. This was a huge revelation. Not only was Anwen trusted, she was inside the circle. Sliding an absent hand along her stars, she tried to remind herself of their value, but couldn't quite do it.

If Anwen was one of them, she'd be sticking around. Ryske trusted her in more than just his bed. Giving Anwen her stars meant the crew trusted her with their lives.

Ophelia could have revealed the murderous truth to Anwen, maybe in an argument. Would confessing be worth that risk? It was more likely Ryske told Anwen and instructed her how to coerce the truth from Ophelia without the beauty catching on to the manipulation.

Even if Ophelia had revealed the truth in a fight, Anwen should have told Ryske that she knew. Harlow's hand fell to her side; she balled her fist. Being apart from Ryske and her crew had been frustrating from almost the first minute, but she'd never felt the effects from an intelligence point of view more than she did then.

All she needed was five minutes with any of them. In that time, she'd be able to find out everything she needed to know. Well, five minutes with any of them except Ryske; he'd find another use for any time they got alone.

"Apparently not," Ophelia said. "If you'd believed in me and appreciated what I was capable of, there wouldn't have been any need for Ryske's insane plan. I mean, really, An, you couldn't have stayed in hiding forever."

Talking about Anwen's fake death with such ease suggested the pair had buried the hatchet for real.

"I should've trusted you," Anwen said.

Harlow really believed her. Rather, the tone was genuine. But suspicion rose. Anwen had good reason not to trust Ophelia, the woman had a hair trigger. She was quick with her hands and to jump to conclusions. Ophelia could flip on a person in a heartbeat. It might be coffee and croissants now, but if Anwen crossed her, or Ophelia suspected she'd been crossed, the billionairess could go off like a rocket. There would be no stopping her.

On the flipside, if Anwen was double-crossing Ryske or their crew, Harlow guaranteed no safety net would catch her. Blackmail be damned. She wouldn't let her boys be manipulated again.

"You should have trusted me," Ophelia said. "We'd have been a formidable team."

The following pause drew Harlow closer.

"We still could be, Fi."

Uh oh. That was Harlow's decision made. She would need some real proof before trusting Anwen again.

"Oh, sweetie," Ophelia said, probably coupling her condescending tone with an arm rub or a hand pat. "You know I'm thrilled you and I have reached a truce. Unfortunately, it doesn't change the fact we both have the same goal. I let you dabble with Ryske now, I suppose, as a gift, a sort of farewell. Once he and I are together, I won't want him being with other women." She laughed. "He won't want to be with other women."

Harlow wondered if she'd get her chance to say farewell to him and if Ophelia would approve of their farewell taking fifty to eighty years.

"You can't tie him down like that," Anwen said. "He doesn't respond well to rules."

That was true for the most part. Some rules he didn't mind; like rules made in the bathtub. Anwen, at least, was making some acknowledgement of who Ryske was. To Ophelia, he was just a prize to win. One she would keep to herself. She failed to see the truth and fiber of the man she coveted.

"It won't be a rule," Ophelia said. "It will be what he wants. I'll be enough for him. If he wants to play in the bedroom, I may allow him another, but she would have to be strictly approved."

Meaning not her or Anwen or anyone Ryske might show a preference for.

"Do you love him, Fi?"

With bated breath, Harlow awaited the answer to Anwen's question.

"Yes," Ophelia said. "I love him more than you do."

She sighed. "You and Harlow, you just don't understand what it is that we have. It's complicated."

So much for feigned friendship. Ophelia hadn't changed her opinion on anything, she was just being gracious enough to accommodate Anwen. Could this be keeping enemies closer?

Harlow didn't feel any urge to rush in and defend her relationship with Ryske. As long as she knew what it was, and he did too, she didn't need anyone else to understand it.

"He cares about me too."

"Of course he does," Ophelia said, using her honed ability to patronize. "We won't forget about you. You'll need our patronage. Once Pothos takes off and we expand, we'll need loyal support staff. He and I will be busy, but you can always come to me with any problems."

So it was Ophelia's goal to groom employees for her illegal operation. More and more it seemed that Jarvis Hagan was right about his sister. On the night he died, he'd told Harlow about Ophelia's nature. At the time, the information conflicted with her experience of the woman in many ways. So did the reality of Anwen versus her experience. Until that day, anyway.

People proved time and again that what they projected to the world wasn't always the reality of their character.

"You haven't changed, Fifi," Anwen said like it was a good thing.

"I'll take that as a compliment," Ophelia said, upbeat and optimistic, at least until her next sentence. "Where is that girl?"

That girl, Harlow assumed, was her. Instead of declaring herself, or doing as she had before, Harlow returned to Ophelia's bathroom and sat down to look through the various bottles of scented oil. Better to be caught procrastinating, than to suddenly pop up when Ophelia lost her patience.

Ophelia knew where to find her and would have to dismiss Anwen before she came to bathe anyway. Harlow didn't want to be a part of their fake farewell.

Either Anwen was working for her crew, or she was betraying them. If it was the latter, Harlow would make sure it was the last mistake Anwen ever made.

***

AS EXPECTED, when Ophelia found her in the bathroom, she'd chastised her for wasting time. After that, Ophelia got in the massive tub anyway, expecting Harlow to do her duty.

The deep tub had a sort of padded seat angled in the corner. Ophelia never had to let her delicate body touch the solid base of the tub. There were wide shelves all around it and a wall on two sides. Harlow sat in the corner behind Ophelia with her legs laid along each of the wide edges, her back to the wall.

Harlow followed Ophelia's orders without complaint. She massaged the difficult woman's scalp, trying her hardest to resist the urge to dig her nails in. The debutante could be out of the water, dried and dressed by now. Instead, she preferred to lounge and be pampered.

"I need to know things," Ophelia said, scooping up some of the remaining bubbles.

Know things? Excellent. A novel task… One with potential. Research would require internet access. She started to devise ways to get in touch with Maze. Maybe he could talk her through how to access Ophelia's personal files. The ones they'd so far been unable to touch.

Maybe Ophelia wanted her to hit the streets. Harlow could play investigator, ask around about whatever Ophelia needed, and maybe slip in a visit home… Except, if she did that and Anwen saw her—

"How does he like to be touched?"

All thoughts, and hopes, vanished. Distasteful as it was, it didn't take long to figure out what Ophelia wanted to learn.

"Excuse me?"

"You've been intimate with him… haven't you?"

Even though there was a trace of a question in her voice, it was slightly snide too. Nothing was certain. Everyone still thought she and Ryske had been sleeping together long before they actually had.

"You're asking me if I've had sex with Ryske?"

The question was ridiculous. Not just because of how intimate she and Ryske had been, but because this woman believed there would ever be any circumstances in which Harlow would share carnal knowledge of him.

"I know you have," Ophelia said. "It would be ridiculous of you to deny it."

"Oh, I'm not denying it," Harlow said. "I'm just trying to figure out why you think it's any of your business."

Ophelia raised her chin. "You work for me."

Harlow kept massaging. "That has no connection to my personal life."

The truth was, Harlow wouldn't be there if it wasn't for her personal life. In her opinion, that was a technicality. One didn't give Ophelia the right to the other.

"You must have noticed how he's losing interest in you… Sorry, how he's *lost* interest in you," Ophelia said, washing the bubbles from her hand just to pick them up again. "It's his way. He never keeps one woman forever."

"If you're so sure about that, it amazes me you think you could be any different."

Ophelia smiled. Harlow didn't see it, but she heard it. "I am different. He knew if he gave into his feelings for me that they would overwhelm him… That's why he wanted to be sure he'd sowed all his oats before coming to me… It's almost time and when it is, I want to make sure he gets what he needs."

Ryske didn't come with a manual and if he did, she would refuse to be it. Harlow believed that he enjoyed their intimacy. Not because he told her, although he often did, because she felt it, she knew the truth of her love.

There were no rules on how to be with him either. He didn't *need* a specific act performed to get off. Sure, there were places on his body that got better results than others, but that was between her and her love.

"If you're really the woman for him, you'll know what he needs and how to give it to him."

"I don't see why you won't just answer the question," Ophelia said with an edge of irritation. "You know he's not shy about sex. He'd tell me himself."

"Then ask him," Harlow said. "You ask him what he needs from you in bed. Whatever he wants you to give him, he'll ask for… Like you said, he's not shy."

If Ryske wanted something from her, he demanded it, or he took it. That was the nature of their relationship and their trust. Okay, yeah, they maybe didn't always reveal everything they knew in the first minute, but when it came to physical trust, sexual trust, they had that in spades.

"What's his favorite sexual position?"

Her smile couldn't help but enjoy the gall. Did the heiress think she'd slip up and reveal something by accident? If she did, favorite sexual position wasn't a subtle start.

"He likes us fully clothed on opposite sides of the city," Harlow said and then gasped. "Oh my God, maybe you've been doing it this whole time."

Growling, Ophelia slapped her hands to the side of the tub and thrust up to her feet. "You're an infuriating woman," she said, climbing out and grabbing her robe. "What you have with him isn't special! It's over! Whatever you think you're protecting, you're not. It's a delusion. He's never coming back to you. If he wanted you back, he'd have challenged me." Tying her robe, Ophelia turned in a flourish and opened her arms. "He hasn't even asked."

Because Harlow made him promise not to. On the night Ophelia won her, when she was secreting the bracelet back into his pocket for fear Ophelia would take it, Harlow told him to let her go. She'd made him promise not to make any move to get her back or free her.

He hadn't wanted to promise, but there hadn't been time to argue. He hadn't had much choice.

"What would you like to wear today, mistress?" Harlow asked, using the term to further irritate her boss. Climbing off the tub, she let the water run out and started into the bedroom. "I have laid out a few choices."

Ophelia could stamp her feet as much as she liked, nothing would change. Harlow wouldn't reveal anything of her relationship with Ryske, not even on pain of death. She'd be devastated if Ryske ever shared their intimate secrets. Not because she was ashamed of them, but because they were made more special by the fact they weren't public knowledge.

They'd had sex with others in earshot. They'd had sex with others in the room. But those glances, those touches, those quiet moments, like Ryske had talked about in her childhood bedroom, those moments belonged to her and her man, no one else.

SEVEN

FRIDAY WAS ALWAYS a difficult day of the week. Harlow hated knowing that Ryske was at the club and she wasn't. Maze would be with him, which was a comfort. Penzance was usually at Windsor's as well. Occasionally, he'd come back with a story or two, but her crew still didn't seem to trust him enough to invite him into their circle all the way.

At Brash's, Ophelia's men took it on rotation to stay with her. They were tasked with ensuring she didn't run away or do anything against Ophelia's rules. In Harlow's opinion, it would be more logical to take her to Windsor's. But she wasn't an idiot and understood what Ophelia was trying to do: restrict her input into the Pothos operation and her time near Ryske.

For a month, Harlow endured the distance. Although she didn't place a massive premium on her boss's honor, Ophelia had stated that if she behaved, she would get to go to the club. Her doubts turned out to be valid. Ophelia left hours ago and ordered her back to the apartment she shared with Brash. Either Ophelia never intended to take her, or Harlow hadn't been well-behaved enough.

Lying on her bed, reading a book she'd snagged from Ophelia's closet, the aim was to switch off. While still obsessing over Anwen's visit, it wasn't an easy goal to achieve. How long had Anwen known about Jarvis Hagan's death and Ophelia's affair with Anthony Yarker?

When her bedroom door opened and someone came stalking in, she sat up, surprised but anticipating Ryske. Turned out her imagination was writing checks reality couldn't cash. Disappointment just kept on coming.

"Vane," she said to the man striding in a straight line from her bedroom door to the foot of the bed. "Ever think of knocking? I could've been naked."

"That would've been a lot of fun for me," he said and tossed a bundle of powder-pink fabric onto the bed.

"What's this?"

Unwinding the material to figure it out, it became a loose-fitting dress. With delicate spaghetti straps that crisscrossed at the back of the otherwise backless dress, they reconnected to the skirt just above where her ass would be.

"Put it on," he said, maintaining a severe demeanor that worried her. Until a moment later, he cracked a smile. "You're coming to the party."

Oh, she didn't have to be told twice.

Leaping off the bed, she stripped, without even caring Penzance was there. He was gentleman enough to turn his back… eventually. She'd never changed clothes so fast. Once the dress was on, she ran to the closet to pull out the only pair of heels she had. The ones she'd been wearing the night she got there.

"Did she say why?" Harlow asked, rushing for the door with Penzance in hot pursuit.

"Do you care?" he asked, taking hold of the door above her head when she opened it.

Unable to contain her grin, she didn't even care if she was being setup. Tonight, she had a chance of seeing Ryske.

"No. I don't give a goddamn."

***

THINKING ABOUT RYSKE on the drive to Windsor's, Harlow didn't give a lot of consideration to who else might be around. Not until Penzance turned into the alley at the back of the club and she spotted the wedge of shadow.

"Oh, God," she said and leaped out of the car before Penzance even put it in park.

Rushing across to the shadow, she knew what she'd find there. Who she'd find there.

Diving into the passenger seat, she threw her arms around the man on the driver's side.

"Nightingale!"

"Noon," she said, squeezing him tight. "Oh, honey."

This was probably a bad move. She should be behaving and doing as told. Her opportunity to come to Windsor's again may be linked to her compliance. In fairness, she hadn't been expressly told not to leap into another car and embrace a man. It was only assumption that Ophelia would class it as against the rules.

Harlow was still hugging him when Penzance moved up to the driver's window. To her surprise, he didn't interrupt. He actually stood with his back to the vehicle, blocking anyone's view of what was going on inside.

"What are you doing here?" Noon asked, pulling back to inspect her arms. When he saw the mark on her face, he touched her cheek. "What happened?"

She pulled his hand down. "Forget about that, honey. Tell me everything and talk fast. How is everyone? Dover and Maze? Felipe? Is Tiffy huge? Have you seen Costello?"

"Costello's been around," Noon said, squeezing her hands when they both clutched for each other in unison. "Him, Maze, and Ryske are making all these plans for the pool hall… He says I'll get space, but you know…"

Hearing something so normal—that life was going on—warmed her. Her home was safe. That was more of a comfort than she'd realized it would be.

"What about Felipe? Is he behaving himself?"

"I don't know," Noon said, side-nodding. "Dover had to go pick him up across the neighborhood. He'd been fighting. I don't know what it was about. He's not saying much."

Her positivity faded. "Did Ryske talk to him?"

Noon shook his head. "He's been… in and out a lot." Was his fighting encouraging the youngster to go out and emulate him? "Dover's got Felipe though; he's had him doing more work around the bar. Cleaning up, painting, you know. He said if the kid's so desperate to do something with his hands that there's always chores to do… I think Martina is worried, you know? She doesn't want him getting into the gangs and if he starts fighting, it could provoke Pablo."

"Is he coming home?"

Noon shrugged. "Don't know. She doesn't really talk to us about that shit."

And being guys, they probably didn't think to ask. They wouldn't intrude on the woman's personal life. Since Harlow hired her, Martina had been a staple around the bar. After the guys came back from Anwen's, she'd only taken the occasional shift. Though, of course, the fire had put a stop to anyone earning money there.

Except her information was out of date. Progress must've been made in the renovations.

"Are you open?" she asked, hoping Floyd's was making money again.

Though, she'd be disappointed to miss opening night.

"Not yet."

Whatever the hold up, she didn't have time to get into the details. "Listen, you need to ask Ryske to talk to Felipe. He's not the best role model right now, and I'm sorry he's being… difficult." She knew her guy. "If he's going out to look for fights in the street, he's gone through all of you trying to find one at home."

The heat in her eyes threatened to become tears. Restraining them, she stopped talking and instead stroked his face.

"We miss you," Noon said. Keeping her lips sealed, she nodded. "We all do. You know he's only like this because he wants you back home… We all want you back home."

"I miss all of you too." The way Noon's gaze dropped raised her concern. "What?"

"He's drinking," Noon mumbled like maybe he was revealing a secret he shouldn't be sharing. His tentative eyes met hers through the shadow of the darkened car. "A lot."

Ryske never shied from having a drink; he wasn't teetotal. But he didn't get drunk. Ever. Even though he'd never put words to his reasoning, she knew it was because of his father. Being drunk reminded him of his heritage. He didn't advertise it, but there was a part of him that resented any notion he was like his father or could become like him.

"He gets drunk before he goes out to fight?"

Noon nodded. "Usually. He's making enemies, Har. Enemies we don't know… The neighborhood is looking out for him. Our people know to let him be or bring him home. But if he screws with the wrong person…"

"You don't have to tell me." Her attention drifted toward the windshield. "He could get himself killed."

Noon was quick to defend his friend. "I don't think he wants to really hurt anybody."

Harlow didn't need anyone to justify what Ryske was doing, or to tell her what kind of man he was.

"No, he wants to hurt himself," she murmured. "Intentions don't stop accidents from happening."

Like the evidence room guard. No one meant to kill him. No one had even been fighting him when he fell and hit his head, which ultimately caused his death. But the crime spawned the tragedy. The death would not have happened had the men not gone in to raid the locker, which they only did because of her.

"Yeah," Noon agreed, "and if he does hurt someone and gets himself arrested…"

Ryske could find himself in a similar position. He wouldn't vet the people he fought. Someone could have a medical condition or an existing injury. If the person he confronted had alcohol in their system, they could be sloppy and uncoordinated. All sorts of things could go wrong.

She did not want Ryske in jail for stupidity. She didn't want him in jail at all, but that one would be a particularly tough pill to swallow.

If he wasn't listening to those at home, and she wasn't there to get through to him, there was only one other person she trusted to handle Ryske.

"Bale has to talk to him," she said, hoping the honorary crew member would break through to his brother.

God, if only she could be more helpful. Chances were that although she was being granted permission to attend Windsor's, Ophelia still wouldn't give her the opportunity to be alone with Ryske. His room was private. Ophelia would probably have someone watching it like a hawk to make sure Harlow didn't attempt to go in… There was a bed in there after all.

Noon scoffed. "Ryske's at his place all the time. Who do you think checks out the bruises and the cuts? The doc thought he had internal bleeding a couple of weeks ago, thought he'd cracked a rib. Ryske didn't give a shit, wouldn't go to the hospital."

The idiot. Now she wanted to smack him. If he wanted a fight, she'd step up to the plate. What did he think was the point of getting himself hurt? She'd have no one to go home to if he died for being a fool.

This was another subject she had more to say on, but the flash of headlights out front reminded her of the need for urgency. Sitting out there was risky; anyone could see her with Noon and report back to Ophelia.

"I know I don't know what's going on at home," she said. "You've no idea how sorry I am that I can't be there to share some of the burden."

"We know why you're not, Nightingale. We understand… We just wish there was something we could do to, you know, get you the hell out of there. It must be a fucking nightmare."

"There's less Chinese food and definitely less fun," she said, trying her best to project confidence. "There is one thing you can do. I can't go into details, and I don't know what ops you're running, but I need you to talk to the guys about something for me. You need to be subtle, figure out how to be discreet."

Concern creased his brow. "About what?"

"I want Anwen out," she said. "I don't want her in the apartment anymore."

He considered her for a second, maybe trying to

figure out her thinking. "He's not having sex with her… It can't be easy for you that his ex is living with us. But, far as I know, he hasn't touched her. He might be acting crazy, but he'd give up his life before he'd hurt you like that. You think me and the guys would let him fuck up his relationship with you?"

"Technically," she said, watching her fingers move through his. "We're not in a relationship right now."

"You're not?" She shook her head. "With you guys, it's tough to keep up." Harlow understood that and stroked the back of his hand, appreciating being near a valued friend. "You do… you do still love him though, right?"

Inhaling, she smacked his shoulder with the heel of her hand. "I love him less when he's an idiot," she said, knowing she had to leave Noon even though it pained her. "You can remind him of that when he's getting himself drunk. Remind him I could walk back in any second and I want his equipment to be functional at all times, just in case I need it. If it's drunk, it's useless to me." Noon laughed. She popped open her door but leaned back over the center console to kiss him. "I love you too, Noon, and all the guys. Remind them of that, will you, please?"

He pulled her into a hug. It couldn't last. They had to let each other go. It was tempting to tell him to throw the car in drive and go. She could make a break for it. Penzance would probably cover as long as he could, and Ryske wouldn't force her to go back to Ophelia if she was done.

But Harlow wasn't done and that meant going inside.

EIGHT

PENZANCE TOOK HER through the side door and up the stairs. The guys just inside, guarding the entrance, didn't stop them from going up.

Windsor's main floor was busy. Surprisingly so. Business had picked up, but this was the first time she'd seen it with her own eyes. Every table was occupied. The bar was crowded and there were many more women scattered around the room, with men she assumed were clients.

"You okay?" Penzance asked, laying a hand on her back.

He probably didn't know why she'd stopped dead without saying a word. She was just taking it all in. This operation had been in its infancy when she was last there a month ago. Now it looked like a well-oiled, and successful, machine.

"Yeah," she said, scanning the bar, trying to identify the patrons and where her boss might be.

Her gaze snagged on someone standing behind a customer observing a card game. Though he'd been intent on what he was watching, something made him look up, right at her.

Harlow started to move in sync with him. This was a

riskier meeting than the one she'd had downstairs, but if he was coming to her, she wouldn't hesitate to meet him in the middle.

"Maze," she breathed out and leaped up into his arms.

He took her off the floor, straightening up so her feet dangled. She trusted him to look after her. On the ride over, Ryske had been in her head because she had a better idea what to expect from him. Chances were high he'd ignore her like he'd done at Ophelia's apartment.

Whether it was part of the plan or not, being welcomed by her crew was gratifying.

"God, babe," Maze said, pressing his mouth to the side of her head. "You're a sight for sore eyes."

Her eyes warmed again. She squeezed them shut, fighting to keep her tears at bay. "I missed you," she inhaled, her voice hardly a whisper.

Maze held her tighter. "Come home, babe," he said, putting her back on her feet and brushing her hair away from her face to inspect her. "What happened?"

"Nothing," she said, pushing his hands away. "Nothing. Never mind that."

His concern didn't subside. "Noticed Brash has stitches," he said. Her chin hitched higher; she wasn't going to apologize for defending herself. To her surprise, he breathed out a laugh and smiled. Pulling her up, he bowed to press his mouth to her forehead. "Good girl. You give 'em hell, baby."

"I'm sorry he's been so difficult," she said while Maze's mouth was still on her. "I'm sorry you're going through this with him."

Leaning back, he met her eye. The heels of his hands stayed on her temples; his fingers in her hair. "What about what you're going through? If you come back from this broken, he'll never be the same. He'll never get over it."

"And if he gets himself killed out on the streets?" she asked. "How could you let him go out there?"

"What do you want us to do? Tie him up?"

Harlow crooked a brow, that wouldn't be such a bad

idea. "If you need my permission to chain him to the wall for his own safety, you have it. You tell him I told you to do it. You tell him I'll kick his goddamn ass if he rejects Bale's advice again… If he wants to be an asshole, that's fine by me. But you make sure he knows that for every punch he throws at someone else, he better be willing to land one on me too because that's what it does to me when he hurts himself."

An angry tear slipped from her eye. Seeing Maze soften at the sight of it only pissed her off more. She hated herself for getting upset. Shoving away from his grip, Harlow swiped the tear away.

"Come home, Nightingale," he beseeched her. "Come home to us… You can go right now. Noon's outside. Tell him to take you away from here. Tell him to just drive… We'll find you. Just get away from here."

Harlow shook her head. "I stand with my crew."

He grazed the pad of his thumb across the sensitive bruise on her cheek. If she'd been smart, she'd have put more concealer on. The notion of getting out the apartment had been so overwhelming, she hadn't been thinking straight.

Ducking her head out of his hand, she lowered her chin.

"You think seeing this will make him calmer?" Maze asked, edging closer, curling a hand around the back of her neck.

She shook her head. "I won't be allowed to see him… She won't let me see him and he can't want to either. He's supposed to have lost interest in me."

Grinding his teeth in a display of rage, Maze made it clear Ryske wasn't the only man struggling with the situation.

Sliding her hands onto his chest, she moved against him, trying to offer comfort. "This was how it was supposed to be. We knew it would be like this. The only difference to the original plan is that it's me instead of him. Yes, it's difficult sometimes, but I'm grateful it worked out this way." That confession startled him, though probably not as much as the smile she followed it with. "I can handle being the one more than I could ever handle having him with her."

"You don't know what this is doing to him."

"Don't I?" she asked. "Being apart. Being unable to do anything about it? Wishing something would change so we could touch each other again?" Shaking her head, she almost laughed. "The only difference between this and the first time I went through it is our roles are reversed. At least he knows I'm not dead… We lived through jail. We can live through this."

"They're not out for your blood in jail."

Harlow smiled. "I can tell you've never been to jail," she said, but he wasn't in the mood to tease.

Someone bumped her shoulder and she turned.

Penzance backed up against her. "Ease up," he murmured.

Ophelia was barreling toward them. Moving through clients at such a rate that she was almost knocking them aside, Ophelia was blinkered. Harlow's hands slid down as she tried to back away, but Maze put both arms around her, preventing her from going anywhere.

"Don't you fucking think about it," Maze said, tightening his hold.

Ophelia didn't love Maze, but she wouldn't like Harlow acting without her approval. Still, Harlow wasn't going to fight him. Sliding her arms around his waist, she let herself enjoy these few moments of comfort while she could.

"You're here for a purpose," Ophelia snapped before she'd even reached them. "And it's not that… Is he paying for that privilege?"

Acting on instinct, Maze spun toward Ophelia, pushing Harlow behind him. "You even think about putting her on her back and I'll take you out myself."

"Well, well," Ophelia said, joining them. "Wonder what your friend would think about that?"

"I don't give a damn what he thinks. Man's a fucking asshole."

So Maze understood there was a plan. Ryske had to be over her. Harlow was sorry she'd missed the discussion where the guys got to that conclusion. She'd figured out her crew had decided it was best for him to act like she was invisible; it explained the way he'd been at Ophelia's.

Harlow was no idiot and knew the golden rule: go with it. So when she'd realized he was playing up his interest in Ophelia and down his interest in her, she hadn't panicked that anything major had changed. Ryske was doing it because he thought it would make things better for her.

Seeing it in action with her guys was another thing. It felt like a real choreographed op. They'd made a plan. Her crew had made a plan meant to insulate and protect her even when they couldn't be in her company to shield her body.

"If you have no loyalty to him, you can't have any to her," Ophelia said and tried to reach around him.

Maze blocked the heiress. He wanted to protect her. Whether it was part of the plan or not, he didn't want to move out of Ophelia's way.

"Babe," Harlow said, resting a soothing hand on his arm, trying to ease him aside, except he wouldn't relax. "We don't want a scene here."

It would be catastrophic if Maze started something. For one thing, Ophelia had security at the club. Brash and Animal would probably be in the building too. If she ordered them to take Maze down, Harlow would fight to the last with him and scream bloody murder until Ryske came out to stand with them, plan be damned.

But they didn't want that; they wanted to keep their cool. Maze must have come to the same conclusion because although she could sense his tension, he breathed out and let himself be moved.

Ophelia's triumph was aggravating. "Strange man," she muttered and looped an arm through Harlow's to lead her away from Maze and Penzance.

Harlow didn't dare let herself turn around. If Maze thought for a second she wanted help or needed him to follow, he could change his mind about giving Ophelia what she wanted.

Though, that subject was a little hazy at the moment.

"What do you want, Ophe?" Harlow asked. "You said I was here for a purpose."

"Yes," she said, pulling her closer. "I want you to take a position over here."

"Over here" seemed to be one of the private rooms. Two down from the one she'd known Ryske to be in before. Harlow didn't fixate on his room for long. The last thing she wanted was Ophelia to note her interest.

"I'm not a prostitute, Ophelia," Harlow said when her boss opened the bedroom door and walked them inside.

"Oh, course you're not, sweetie. Whoever suggested you were?"

Ophelia had actually. More than once.

Harlow chose not to remind her. "So what am I doing in here?"

In the corner of the bedroom was a tub chair. Ophelia went over to drag it from the edge of the room to position it in the middle of the space, facing the end of the bed.

Guiding Harlow in front of the chair, Ophelia stood behind it and put both hands on her shoulders to push her down into it. "You are going to sit right here."

"You want me to watch an empty bed?"

Ophelia's laugh was fake and grating. "Wouldn't that be wonderful?"

The wonderful part was that in this position, all she could look at was the door to the left of the nightstand. Each of the bedrooms was linked with adjoining doors. Between that door and the headboard was a button on the wall. A panic button that linked to the room Ryske was stationed in to dispense Pothos.

It wouldn't take any effort to get up and walk over there to push that button. Or she could go through the doors and bedrooms to reach his room. The situation had been infuriating before. It was worse now. She was existing so close to him that she could probably scream loud enough for him to hear. Yet, it didn't matter, they still couldn't have each other.

"As you can probably tell, it's a busy night," Ophelia said, squeezing Harlow's shoulders. "Usually if we have clients who like to be watched, one of the girls will sit in. But they're all occupied tonight and we have a waiting list of clients who wish this experience. So…" Ophelia swatted the top of her head. "You're it."

"You want me to watch people having sex?"

Ophelia was already walking toward the exit. "I'll have someone watch this door to make sure you don't leave. And if I get any negative reports from clients, like you trying to shirk your duties, there will be consequences."

Twisting in the chair, Harlow watched Ophelia retreat further. "You've got to be kidding me."

Ophelia turned with her arms wide. "It's no different than watching porn. You don't have to participate, just watch. Keep your eyes open. That's all you have to do. Sit in a chair and keep your eyes open… Even you should be able to handle that."

If she couldn't, it didn't matter, because Ophelia left the room before she could object anymore. Had Harlow known why she was brought to Windsor's, she might have objected. She'd been sitting in a bedroom at Brash's place, and would have preferred to stay there than come to watch… whatever.

Sex didn't faze her. She'd never watched others have it in person, but it would give her a better appreciation for what her crew endured when she and Ryske got amorous.

Settling back in the chair, she sighed and slid off her shoes. She'd play voyeur for a night, but that was it. Looking, but no talking and no participation.

What a night this was shaping up to be.

NINE

THE FIRST CLIENT came in a minute after Ophelia left. Harlow sat through four of them, watching while trying her best not to look. The fifth was struggling to get up to speed. So far, only one of the clients had spoken to her. Most hadn't uttered a word. The girls offered a smile and were nice to her. Though there wasn't really time for chit-chat; they were on the client's dime after all.

Harlow exhaled. The sound came out louder than she'd intended it to, but she didn't expect anyone to notice. Unfortunately, she was wrong. The client on the bed looked up, catching her eye. She tried to look away in hopes he'd return to what he'd been doing.

"Take your clothes off," the client grunted.

The woman on the bed under him was already naked, so was he. Harlow was the only one in the room with any fabric on her body. He couldn't be talking to anyone else; still, she ignored him. Shaking the leg crossed over her thigh, she kept her eyes on the wall to the side of the room.

Ignoring him was really for his benefit. Acknowledging him would, no doubt, lead to a dangerous fight. She wasn't supposed to act out. Fighting with a naked man, or any man, wasn't high on her agenda for the night.

"Yo, bitch," the client said, crawling over the top of the woman he'd paid for to reach for Harlow's leg. She swiveled her hips, changing position to take herself out of his reach. "I said take your fucking clothes off."

He tried to reach for her again. The poor woman on the bed was trapped under his hairy form. Whatever she was being paid, it wasn't enough.

Closing her eyes, Harlow let them open again only when she could train them on him. "I'm a voyeur."

She wasn't really, but the clients were paying to be watched, so that's what she was doing. Sitting there. Watching. There was nothing sexually satisfying or arousing about what was playing out. But the client had paid for the pleasure. Whatever they paid for, they got.

"I'm telling you to take your fucking clothes off."

"No," Harlow said, as clear as she could muster.

He rose up onto his knees, straddling the woman on the bed. Rather, he was sitting on her chest, which couldn't be a comfortable position; it certainly wasn't an enviable one.

"I'm the fucking client. You want more money, that's fucking fine," the guy said. "I'll pay for two. You take your fucking clothes off and get over here." He worked his dick in his fist. "It's your job to suck a dick when you're ordered."

"Not that one," Harlow said, touching the ring on her necklace.

A frown set on his face. "You make me come get you and it won't be fucking pretty."

"Don't threaten her," the woman under him said. She couldn't help beyond that, he was kneeling on her arms. "Play with me. I'll suck it."

"No, I want her," the guy said. "You take your pretty fucking dress off and get your mouth around this." Harlow shook her head. "You want me to call your boss?"

"No," Harlow said, nonplussed as she rose from the chair. "Let me do it."

Sashaying up the room, Harlow didn't pause to consider how many sirens might be set off. She balled her fist and hit the red panic button next to the bed. Ryske was in charge of these bedrooms and the women in them. If there was a problem, he was the one who'd be called.

There were no sirens or flashing lights, which made sense. Discretion was key in these bedrooms. The alarm was probably silent.

"Renegotiation can't be—"

The woman on the bed was cut off when the door next to the panic button opened. The first thing Ryske saw was her. Any urgency that hurried him increased tenfold when he took in the scene.

Harlow leaned against the wall facing the side of the bed.

"What the fuck is going on in here?" Ryske asked, throwing the door back into its frame.

"He wants to renegotiate," the woman on the bed said, struggling under the weight of the client pinning her down.

"I'm not renegotiating," the client said. "I already paid." He pointed at her. "I told that one to take her clothes off."

Ryske's focus swung to her, but she wasn't stressed about the request. "I refused," Harlow said.

"Yo, bitch," the client barked. "Shut your mouth or suck a dick."

With a loose shrug, Harlow boosted her shoulders off the wall. "Okay."

Instead of going to the bed, she closed the gap between her and Ryske to start unbuckling his belt. The woman on the bed laughed, but Ryske wasn't as amused. He stilled her action and thrust a hand around the side of her head, forcing her to look up.

"Why are you in here?"

"Ophe."

His mouth clamped shut so tight that his lips almost disappeared.

"Yo," the client said. "You want extra for the bitch, I'll pay it. I'll pay top price. That slut won't know what's fucking hit her by the time I'm done with her."

Ryske pushed her aside. In a blur of movement, he strode to the bed and swung hard, catching the client on the side of the head, knocking him out cold.

The woman on the bed pushed the client off and sat up. She felt for a pulse like it was just routine. "He's alive."

"Shame," Ryske said. "Wait 'til he wakes up, tell him he's had his ride, and it was the best of your life. Fucker's drunk anyway."

The girl nodded. "I'll jerk him off, that way he won't be able to get it up again anyway." She grinned. "Thanks, Ryske."

The thanks was genuine.

Ryske went over to touch the young woman's jaw. "This never happened," he said and the girl shook her head. After another moment, which may have included a smile or a wink, Ryske turned to point at her. "You follow."

Harlow was the only other one around, but he hadn't looked straight at her. Still, when he marched away from the bed, in the opposite direction to the one he'd come, Harlow trotted along after him. He opened the door to the next bedroom.

Once they were inside, she was pleased to discover the room was empty. The bed in the new room was in a different position to the last one. In this room, the foot of the bed faced the short hall that led past the restroom and out to the main floor.

Harlow closed the door they'd just come through. Before she could open her mouth to think about saying anything, Ryske spun around to make eye contact.

"Take your clothes off," he said.

Funny. That was exactly what the man in the other room had said and she'd resisted. This time she raised her fingertips to each of the tiny spaghetti straps that hung perilously close to the edge of her shoulders and slipped them down. Letting her hands descend in time with the material that fluttered to the floor, Harlow was naked in an instant.

Ryske's eyes traveled down her figure. He'd seen her naked a hundred times or more. Whenever they were home, they showered together. Whenever they could get away with it, they slept together naked. That he took a minute to himself to appreciate her was beyond flattering.

That minute was over in a flash. Soon, he strode over to sweep both arms around her. One clamped around the small of her back, the other went under her ass to pick her up.

Holding his head, Harlow wrapped her legs around him and stole his mouth, choosing his kiss and his love over everything else in the world.

If it got back to Ophelia that Ryske had come to her rescue, or found her at all, then the hostess would be manic about locating them. She'd check every room. Every corner. Ryske was supposed to be indifferent to her, but if Ophelia learned they were both missing, she'd put the pieces together.

Ryske laid her down on the cushion of the bed and let his hands roam her body. She couldn't remember for sure who freed him from his jeans. Details ceased to matter when he broke their kiss to look into her eyes as he slid himself into her.

Quickly, his pace increased. She wanted him fast and hard. Without her saying it, he'd known. Maybe it was what he needed too.

The good thing about fucking in a brothel was they had plenty of cover for sound. Harlow let herself moan and squeal. She let her hands drive through her hair, matting her locks and scratching her scalp as she arched up to meet each of his powerful thrusts.

Gasping for him, she bit her lip hard when his name threatened her lips. She couldn't take the risk that anyone would hear her calling for him. But, goddamnit, she wanted to, she wanted to scream his name loud. The urge was almost as powerful as her need to have him inside her like this, fast and frantic, desperate and urgent.

They hadn't been intimate for such a long time… At least, it felt that way. Nothing else mattered but this. Watching his body move over hers, feeling the friction between them, experiencing his lips and the texture of his skin, it erased the drama and all the peril. Harlow didn't think about the plan or what they were supposed to be doing. All she could think about was his cock inside her and how badly she needed him.

"Trink," he panted, bracing on his arms and pushing into her, retreating and advancing. "Baby, I can't…"

"Go." Dragging in a breath, she lost her focus. The pressure of need was building between her thighs, in her gut. She could feel the speed of her heart and the weight on her lungs, and knew she was on the cusp of release. "Oh, fuck, Crash! Go, baby!"

Her scream came as she fell into the precipice of orgasm; he followed her with a hard thrust and a deep growl.

Both sated, neither moved. Through the haze of heat and the fog of breath, they found each other's eyes. They didn't say anything, just looked at each other, like they were recalling every time they'd been in this position before.

Coming together again, in this unexpected way, was a relief they both needed. It couldn't have come at a better time either. Ryske was losing his mind and acting like a reckless idiot. Harlow was slipping toward the edge of her control and was beginning to let her discipline slide. But this, she hoped, should get them both back on track.

Ryske rolled away. Though it pained her to be without him, the intimate moment couldn't have lasted.

Sitting up, she was about to slide off the bed when he snatched her wrist. "Where are you going?"

"Ophe will be looking for me."

"That guy still has forty-five minutes," he said, pulling her down to his side. "Which means that's what I've got."

She laughed and drew her nails around his tattoos. "I'm not an escort."

"Could've fooled me," he said, squeezing his arm around her shoulders to pull her up so he could kiss her hair. "Come here."

He took off his shirt and moved up the bed, taking her with him so they could lie on the covers with his head on the pillows. Harlow elected to lay her head on his chest instead. When he put an arm around her, she relaxed and went back to tracing his tattoos.

"You hurt me," she said and his hand stilled on her arm. "You said we should've erased our whole relationship. Has it meant so little to you?"

Harlow knew it didn't mean little to him, but she had to convey how his assertion cut her.

"Do you think it's easy for me to admit that Marlowe would've kept you safer?" he asked. "You know how I feel about the asshole."

Ryske didn't think her ex was an asshole, she knew that. Well, he did, but because of how things had turned out with Lena more than anything else.

"I don't regret any decision I've made. None of them. It hurts to know you don't feel the same way."

Wrapping his arm tight around her, he pulled her higher to kiss her hair. "I regret plenty," he said. "Nothing more than hurting you... It's selfish. The way I feel about you, it's selfish... I wouldn't trade a second we've been together either... But you can't deny you've been hurt."

She flattened a hand on his stomach. "We both have... Doesn't mean we should take it back."

TEN

BOTH OF THEM relaxed, enjoying the silence and the rhythm of their breathing as it slid into sync.

"I made myself a promise," Harlow murmured.

"What promise?"

Closing her eyes, she absorbed the softness of his bedroom voice. She'd missed it so much. Missed him. With only a dim lamp in the corner, this room was designed for intimacy.

"That I'd lie in your arms one more time before I died." Drawing her up higher than before, he showed a frown. When it deepened, it was clear he'd spied the bruise on her cheek. "It's nothing."

She tried to lie back down, but he wouldn't let her. "That's what you say to other people," he said, almost quoting what she'd said to him in Ophelia's apartment. "What happened?"

"Brash," she said. He inhaled so hard, his chest pushed her up. "Don't get yourself in a fizz, I took care of it."

His frown became curious. "The stitches… that was you?"

She nodded. When she next tried to lie down, he let her.

Kissing his chest, she scratched her nails on his stomach. "What if someone wants Pothos and you're in here?"

"Maze is covering," he said. "He said you were here. I didn't know you were… in there."

It was possible Maze and Penzance hadn't seen her go into that room. If they had, it was just as possible she left or went out a different way before clients went in.

"It wasn't a big deal… Ophe wanted me to watch, so I watched. He was the first guy to request extras."

"You shouldn't have been in there," he said. "I didn't know you were the girl watching. I should've been paying fucking attention… All I could think about was ways I might see you… It's fucking crazy that she thinks she can—"

"Crash," Harlow said, dragging her nails on his tattoo. "This might be the only time we have together. We have to use it wisely… I don't want to talk about Ophelia."

"I'm sorry, baby," he said, trailing his fingertips up and down her arm.

She didn't want to talk about Ophelia in the context of her situation because there was nothing to be done about it. But there were things that did need to be cleared up.

Steeling herself, Harlow did her best to gather her strength, knowing she'd need it to keep her cool. "I need to ask you something, and I need you to be honest… Don't worry I'll be upset, whatever the answer is, just tell me the truth."

"I'm not fucking anyone else."

Trust him to go right there. She could've lost her temper over that assumption, but she didn't. "I didn't ask that, did I?"

"No, okay. What is it?"

Rising to hold her head on a fist, she hooked her upper arm over his shoulder, so her elbow was near his ear. God, she'd missed just looking at him, being near to him, admiring him.

Sliding a hand from his temple to his jaw, she drew his mouth around to hers. "I love your mouth," she whispered, sweeping her lips back and forth on his. "I dream about kissing you." She kissed him again. "I love your tongue and your lips—"

"You didn't ask me a question, Trinket."

Stroking his chin and his neck down to his chest, she brushed her fingers over his scar. "Don't think I'm judging. I trust you and the guys completely," she said, letting her fingertips descend his arm to his wrist.

Picking it up, she laid his forearm on his torso and climbed over his leg to lie between them, relaxing her chest low on his abs. His pants were open and low on his hips, she wriggled to switch the buckle of his belt out from under her.

"You trust us," he said, watching her kiss the points of the stars on his arm. "Spill it, what did we do?"

"I love these too," she said, grazing her lips around his stars.

Her arm was parallel to his on his abs and he drew a line down hers and then back, tracing it back and forth. "Yours are attached to something hotter."

"Did Anwen get hers yet?"

Was that subtle?

Nope.

His finger stopped mid-caress. "Get her what?"

"Her stars," she said, trying to be cool.

It wasn't a big deal. No, it was. If the guys decided Anwen deserved them, she'd have to accept not being the only girl on the team.

He raised his arm. "Count 'em," he said. "Read 'em to me."

Pushing higher, she kissed one star. "Dover," she whispered and kissed the next, each in turn with their names. "Maze, Noon… my man."

Tipping up her chin, she let him see her smile before kissing the last star with the thin concentric star around it.

"My girl," he said before she could identify her star. He touched her hair at her temple. "You see any others there?"

Rising to her knees between his thighs, she slid her hands into his jeans to his hips. "Haven't seen all of you, have I?"

He just lifted his head to lock his hands behind his head. "You want the goods, baby. You've got to do the work."

After shuffling backwards down the bed, she unlaced his boots. "Being in here is reckless… but sex…" she said. "We're playing with fire."

It was dangerous enough to have done what they had done. Being naked and wrapped in each other would be impossible to explain away as insignificant or platonic. Unless she admitted to drugging Ryske with Pothos so she could have her way with him. That was a possibility. Although it wasn't true, Harlow would confess to it if Ophelia found them.

"Keep going," Ryske said. "You'll find something else to play with."

Pulling off his boots one at a time, she dropped them to the floor. "Can I keep everything I find?"

"Everything that's here already belongs to you," he said. "Two weeks max and the club will be ours too."

Crawling back up the bed, she kissed his stomach and his stab scar before working his jeans down to pull them off. Once they were on the floor, she laid back down on him, her breasts nestled against his groin.

Closing her eyes, she enjoyed his fingers combing through her hair. "I'm imagining we're at home."

"You should come home with me," he said. "Noon's outside—"

"Maze already made that suggestion," she said and kissed his abs without opening her eyes. "I saw Noon outside. We talked."

"What'd you talk about?"

"Your fighting. You're corrupting Felipe. Will you please tell him you're an idiot so he'll stop copying you?"

"I'm not the one slicing guys up," he said, scratching his fingers in her scalp. "I'd never tell you to stop fighting, baby."

But she didn't see what she'd done as the same as what he'd done. Ryske was going out to seek frivolous violence. Harlow simply defended her honor.

"Brash touched your toys without permission," she said, turning her head to suck his stomach until she was sure it would bruise. "You should know that he and Ophelia have a deal by the way."

"What deal?"

"After you get with her, she's handing me off to Brash…" Propping her chin on his stomach, she blinked up at him. "I'm not trying to start fires. I don't need you to act. I want you to know what my future is after you stick your cock in her."

"Then you better protect it… Just like you're doing now. My dick likes this kind of shield."

"I can tell," she said and shimmied to divert some more of his blood. Laying her cheek on him again, she picked up his hand to fidget with his bracelet. "Don't take this off again."

"How do you know I took it off?"

She smiled, liking that he sounded impressed and incredulous at the same time. "I know things," she said. "Promise me you won't."

"You saw Anwen wearing it," he said. It was pathetic that her heart broke a little. If he knew she was wearing it, that meant he'd authorized it. "Is that why you asked about her? But why would you think she'd get her stars?"

His thoughts were catching up with her questions.

Her heart rate rose, defying her attempts to maintain patience. "I'm not in the loop, Crash," she said, aware of the vibrating strain in her tone. "Whatever decisions you guys are making, I stand behind them all."

"Sounds like you're getting a little amped, babe."

And, he was right, she was.

Bouncing onto her knees, Harlow slapped his thighs. "You know, I just don't understand what I did wrong."

He rose to his elbows, a frown on his face. "You did nothing wrong… Well, you shouldn't have agreed to the stakes that took you away from us, but…"

Telling herself to calm down, she picked at the hair on his thigh. "I think I forget how far back you two go."

"Baby," he said, sitting up to scoop the heels of his hands under her jaw to bring it up. "I don't have a fucking clue what you're talking about."

"You and Anwen," she said, looking into his eyes, fumbling for the bracelet on his wrist. "You guys were together for six months."

"We were never together. We fucked. And I told you how she made it happen," he said. "She's sleeping on the pull out bed in the living room. We figured she's not in danger anymore. I'm not sharing our bed with her."

"What about our secrets? Are you sharing those?"

He scowled. "No fucking chance. You think I rolled on you? Baby—"

"Then how does she know who killed Hagan?" The stern look on his face intensified. "I trust you and the guys and I know it's tough right now because we can't communicate… But when I see her in Ophelia's kitchen wearing this…"

Hooking a finger under it, her gaze fell to the bracelet.

"Trinket, I didn't give it to her. She took it while I was in the shower. You're right, I shouldn't have taken it off. We knew she was going to Ophelia's… She said gaining her trust would help us. But me and the guys, we're not sure. We don't know what's going on there. We were giving her the benefit of the doubt, hoping she'd get useful intel, but she came back with nothing… I ripped her a new one for stealing from you."

Even mad Ryske could provoke her smile. "From me?"

"Yeah, it's yours," he said, turning his wrist. "I'm just holding it for you."

ELEVEN

SO ANWEN HAD taken the bracelet while Ryske was in the shower. Maybe because she knew asking for it wouldn't grant her wish. Ryske wouldn't hand it over willingly. Wearing the accessory gave credibility to her claim of sleeping with Ryske. That would be why she'd stolen it for her Ophelia visit.

Harlow snagged the bullet hanging low on his chest. "You're supposed to be holding this for me too."

Cupping her breasts, he rubbed his thumbs over her nipples. "I'll hold anything you want, baby."

"Seems like your hands are full, Crash," she said, leaning in to kiss him. After a long battle of tongues, she eased back before he could step things up a notch. Bowing her head, her forehead rested on his chin. "I missed this… I feel so much stronger close to you."

He kissed the top of her head. "Come home, baby," he said, not ready to give up. "Just walk out there now and Noon will take you home. The guys and me will fight to the death to keep you safe."

"Don't joke about death," she said, curling her hands over his shoulders, digging her nails in. "And I'm not worried about my life. We're doing this to save you."

"From Ophelia's bed," he said. "I've been in plenty

of women's beds I'd rather have avoided."

"I meant her threat to blame you for Jarvis' death. The only proof we have that it was her is the recording. We can't use that without implicating the rest of us in other crimes."

She could feel his tension. As he grew rigid, she skimmed her hands toward each other across the back of his neck to slide them over her own forearms, clinging tight to him.

"I want you home, Trink," he said, scooping his hands under her to hook her legs over his thighs. "I won't feel right until you're back in our bed… I woke up in your bed without you this morning. That's sure not an experience I want to repeat."

She didn't understand. "My bed?"

"Your mom and Lena have been calling about wedding plans. I went over last night, told them you weren't feeling well, but your mom asked me to stay for dinner. Your dad wanted to talk after. I ended up sleeping there."

She smiled and kissed him, imagining he hadn't put up much of a fight when her mom invited him to stay. Being there might have made him feel closer to her. They'd made memories in that bed.

"What did he want to talk about?" she asked. "He already asked about your intentions."

"This was business, not personal."

"If you take a job at SweSec, your chances of getting me back drop considerably."

He licked her lip and caught it in his teeth. "Getting you back, hmm? Was that your pussy I was just inside?" he asked. "And your titties rubbing all over me?"

"Oh, well if you're complaining," she said and started to withdraw, but he tugged her back.

"Won't ever hear me doing that."

His next kiss felt like a prelude to something. He lifted her, positioning her on top of him, but she pushed back. Losing themselves in sex would be so easy. It was exactly what she'd feared they'd do if they got this chance to reconnect. Tonight was a fluke. They had to take advantage of this time for the sake of the op, not their own animal needs.

"I don't want you to alienate her, be subtle about it… but I think you should move Anwen out of the apartment."

He groaned and tried to kiss her. "Aren't we done talking about that yet?"

Ryske could be impatient because he didn't know he was being played. It was Harlow's responsibility to educate him. "Anwen knows more than she's letting on. No, in fact, if she came back from Ophelia's saying she got no info, she's flat lying… I overheard them. They don't know I did, but… she seemed to be trying to form an alliance with Ophelia."

He stopped trying to seek her mouth. "What did Ophelia say?"

"What she always says. Some variation of, when I'm with Ryske, I won't need anyone else."

Swearing under his breath, he flopped onto his back and rubbed his face with both hands. After a long groan, he threw open his arms, letting them fall out wide on the bed. "I'm so sick of this shit."

"I know," she said, stroking his torso. His head stayed back; she wasn't sure his attention was hers, so she drove her nail into him. "Crash, will you look at me, please?" He lowered his chin to look down his nose at her. "Ophelia is fucking Yarker." His head tilted. "She's been fucking him for a long time… at least since this started. He told her about Parratt's link to Arjan." Their European Pothos contact, their supplier. "I know that we know she orchestrated this, but it's much more contrived than we thought. I don't know if it was Yarker or Ophelia, but some combination of them convinced Parratt to do this… She showed her faith in it by bringing on her brother for money and premises… She knew they'd need someone who could link them to a woman, or group, to facilitate the use of the drug… Ophelia knew they'd need you."

"We knew it was her."

Harlow nodded. "Yes. We did. But I think the affair's still going on, or it's not all the way over. Yes, this all started back then. But you should know the influence she has now. She has him and he has Parratt. You need to start cultivating a relationship with him. We might need it… Ophelia must have manipulated Yarker to convince his good friend to bring you on. I don't think Hagan knew you were coming on until the last minute. I doubt Ophelia cared if the way he acted toward you made him look like a maniac… We know they were competitive and that she's a few sandwiches short of a picnic."

His eyes ascended. "She'd have to be to give a shit about me," he muttered.

Doubling over him, she seized his arms to bend his elbows, pressing all her weight into his forearms, doing a feeble job of pinning him down. "You calling me crazy, lover?" she whispered on his mouth before slipping her tongue between his lips.

Harlow was sure that she could stay like this on top of him forever. Kissing him was the cure for every ache in her body. It might drive her insane, but she'd welcome insanity if it was a side effect of loving him.

When she let him have his mouth back, she kissed his jaw and his throat.

"I'm a fucking mess without you, Trink," he murmured, losing his hands in the mass of her hair when she released his arms. "I'm losing my mind."

"Stop fighting," she whispered, kissing his chest. "Please, my love. Please, stop getting drunk and stop being angry." Rising to look into him, she kissed him once. "I want to come home to you. We just need a little more time. Trust your crew. Trust me… Please, Crash. Trust me."

"I promised I would never leave you again… I feel like that's what I've done. You cursed me for abandoning you once—"

"I abandoned you this time," she said. "It's me. If you have to hate anyone, if you have to be mad at someone, hate me. Be mad at me."

Skimming his hands up her back, they tangled in her hair. "I've never been able to get you out of my blood… You run through my veins, Trink."

She didn't know about the moisture in her eyes until her tear dropped onto his cheek. "Every breath you are is me," she breathed the words. "You are my soul."

"I will bleed my last drop with you."

"For you."

"You ever thought about it?" he asked, pushing her loose hair from between them to hold it against the sides of her head and brush his thumbs under her eyes. "What we'd do if it came to a do or die moment?"

"If I lost you again?" she asked. "If I thought one of us would have to go on without the other?" He nodded. "Die, every time."

Harlow didn't hesitate. The way he didn't blink betrayed he'd come to the same conclusion.

"We should give Bale DNR instructions," he said and she nodded. "Get paperwork for Maze. Leave everything to Dover. We don't want anyone to have cause to investigate or get in their business. It has to be clean."

"Yes," she said and kissed him. "But I can't—"

"I'll do it. I'm still your proxy. I can act and sign for you," he said, pulling her down, tucking her head under his chin, holding her tight, stroking one hand through her hair while his mouth turned down to the top of her head. "I'll take care of everything, Trinket."

This time when she closed her eyes, the tears that escaped didn't surprise her. There wouldn't be any point going on without each other. Vengeance could be left to the crew if there was any need for retribution. But it wouldn't matter to them. All they wanted was to be together, in life and in death.

Pulling his arms away from around her, she sat up on him, sliding down his body until she could rise over his groin. Wrapping her fingers around his shaft, Harlow didn't have to tell him what she needed. He was ready for her; she sank down onto him and began rocking her hips.

Wriggling on him, she guided his hand up to her throat and smiled when he used the other to swipe away her tears. "I love you," he mouthed without making a sound.

"Tighter, Crash," she said and bit her lip.

They could admit to each other there was a chance neither of them were getting out of this. It was a sad notion they might have to give up their lives. But this was their time.

Harlow wanted his memories of her to be positive, especially if there was a chance these could be their last moments alone.

His fingers strengthened, sending a pulse of pleasure through her. His other entitled hand fondled her breasts, erasing any negative memories she had of being caressed by another man. Harlow had asserted to Brash he couldn't take anything from her because Ryske would always put it back, and right there, her love proved her point.

Pushing up, she moved faster, building her rhythm, doing her best to maintain her pace, aiming to bring him to his end. It wasn't easy, she wanted him so much. The way he touched her fired her into a frenzy; she her forgot about stamina and thought only about pleasure.

"My fucking God," Ryske hissed. Her head fell forward, cascading her hair over him. With his hand still around her throat, she leaned further over him, bringing it closer to him while still riding him hard. "How the fuck are you still teasing me?"

He was deep inside her. How he could still feel it wasn't enough or she wasn't giving herself to him, she didn't know. Raising her chin a little, Harlow blinked smoldering eyes through the sections of her dark hair hanging between them. Her teeth in her lip, she winked at him.

Letting go of her throat, he grabbed for her hips, almost trying to slow her like he might be ready to go off at any second.

But neither of them got the chance because the sound of the door opening broke the mood.

Ryske sat up, throwing both arms around her. She twisted to look over her shoulder and saw Penzance striding into the room. The instant he noticed them, he held up a hand that was holding one of her shoes, and turned his head to the side.

"Fuck, you not done yet? Sorry, but you are done. We've got a code red. Miss Thang is less than a minute away from walking in here. Lala is trying to head her off, but that will buy you a few seconds at most."

TWELVE

LEAPING OFF RYSKE and the bed, Harlow tossed her hair back and scrambled to grab up the clothes from the floor. Penzance didn't take his time about turning his back like he had in her bedroom earlier. After witnessing her riding one of his oldest friends, he'd probably got as much of an eyeful as he wanted.

"Can you get back to your room without her seeing you?" Harlow asked, throwing Ryske's pants onto the bed and then running to her dress.

Luckily, all she had to do was step into the circle of fabric and pull the straps back to her shoulders. "Trink—"

"Go, Crash," she said. Although Ryske was still on the bed, he put on his jeans, lying down to drag them over his hips. Rushing back to the bed, she grabbed his chin to force a kiss to his mouth. "I love you."

Leaving him, she went to Penzance and leaped in front of him to drive her fingers into his hair, messing it up.

"Ow," he said, shoving her shoes at her. "What the fuck! I don't know where those hands have been."

Harlow held onto him and hopped into her shoes, one after the other. "Everywhere you think they have," she said, undoing some buttons on his shirt and pulling the tail of his belt from its buckle.

"You want me to take the heat without getting any of the heat," he said. She bobbed her brows and grabbed his hand to drag him toward the door. "You do look just fucked, Har… very fucked."

"That's 'cause I was…" She glanced back at him over her shoulder. "Twice."

Just as they stepped outside, Ophelia came upon them. Literally. The hostess couldn't have been more than ten seconds away from opening the door.

"What the hell are you doing in there?" Ophelia barked. "You were given a job! A task! How dare you think you can…"

Trailing off, Ophelia's anger morphed to curiosity as she examined the couple.

"Miss Hagan…" Penzance said.

Ophelia held up a hand to silence him. "What have we discovered tonight, Harlow?" she asked, a smirk forming on her lips. "Does someone like watching others? Did you maybe like it a little more than you thought you would?" Folding her arms, Ophelia drummed her fingers on her upper arm. "Maybe you should thank me. Being a voyeur wasn't such a terrible experience after all."

Harlow cleared her throat, doing her best to appear embarrassed. The flush in her cheeks had come from a different source, but it would serve her.

"No, I… I guess not."

"You've got to be open to new things," Ophelia said, grinning. "I've got to say… I'm surprised… But it's wonderful."

"Wonderful?" Penzance asked, probably expecting to get his ass kicked.

"Yes," Ophelia said, nodding. "I never wanted bad things for Harlow. But she was holding on to something that was never going to happen. Not ever. She had to come to terms with that and I'm glad that tonight, it seems she has… Didn't take long, did it?" Ophelia took her shoulders, but as she was about to pull her into a hug, she hesitated. "Oh, I… don't suppose you had time for a shower."

"Uh, no," Harlow said, threading her fingers between Penzance's.

There were more eyes on them than just Ophelia's. When Penzance tried to take his hand back, she gripped him tighter. She hadn't had time to wash her hands either; no doubt Penzance was all too aware of that.

Brushing her palms together, Ophelia stepped back. Harlow almost laughed. Penzance wasn't that bad to look at. Few women would recoil from the idea of being intimate with him. The fact that she reeked of sex was probably putting Ophelia off getting too close. Little did the woman with the curled lip know, but the man all over her wasn't the one at her side, it was the one Ophelia had been coveting.

"I thought you two were becoming friends. I had no idea that you were…" Ophelia glanced to the left, a telling sign that she was thinking about Ryske. "I wonder…"

"You…" Harlow started and then sealed her mouth pretending to second-guess herself.

Being hesitant got Ophelia's attention back. "Yes?" she asked. "What were you going to say?"

"We'd rather he didn't know," Penzance said, somehow picking up the same signals from Ophelia, and her signals too. Just another example of the man's impressive skill. "Probably won't make a difference to him, but… we'd rather he didn't."

Ophelia made a sign of buttoning her lips and tossing an invisible key, but she smiled, and then laughed. "Oh, this is wonderful… Isn't this wonderful?"

If Harlow was over Ryske, Ophelia would expect a clear run at him. There was no way on this Earth Ophelia wouldn't tell Ryske; a zero chance of their confidence being respected. Asking her to keep it quiet was a manipulation strategy. It gave credibility to their apparent betrayal and Ophelia got a chance to feel superior.

"We're not too sure about that yet," Penzance said.

Harlow released his hand to put an arm around his waist but didn't pull herself too close. They'd just asked for discretion, being too loved up would contradict the request. It was just so much fun to watch Ophelia's excitement grow with every touch.

"It could be," Ophelia said, pulling a bunch of folded bills from her cleavage. "Don't take anything for granted. You have to work at these things. Stoke the flames of passion."

She shoved a bunch of bills into Penzance's hand; Harlow's smile faltered. Had Ophelia just paid Penzance for screwing her?

"Thanks," Penzance said, putting the money in his pocket. He wouldn't be any kind of grifter if he didn't take money when it was handed to him. "Not a bad night for me."

Yeah, fake sex and a pile of cash, could shape up worse for him.

"Take her out," Ophelia said, optimism bleeding from her.

Harlow lost her urge to laugh, and her jaw swung loose.

Penzance was just shocked. "Uh… what?"

"Drinks," Ophelia said, throwing up her hands. "Take her out for a drink…" She gasped. "And you know what? You should go home with her. Stay in her bedroom at Brash's tonight. Yes. Stay the night. Stay overnight."

"Miss—"

"Thank you, Ophe," Harlow said before Penzance could talk their benefactor out of her generosity.

Of course, Ophelia was only being generous because she knew Ryske's location. While he was at Windsor's, there was no chance Harlow could corrupt him… more than she already had anyway. Ophelia could keep an eye on him to ensure they stayed apart. But Ryske wasn't the only man Harlow could benefit from connecting with.

Ophelia backed away, her arms open. "Go, lovebirds, before I change my mind."

Harlow smiled, showing gratitude, then grabbed Penzance's hand to pull him toward the door before Ophelia did flip. Though Vane was quite a weight to tug along, especially when he wasn't as enthusiastic as she wanted him to be. Harlow didn't let up. She kept dragging him through the club until they got down the stairs and outside.

"Har, we're not really going to—"

"Just go with it," she said, pulling him across the alley, knowing exactly where she was headed, even if the men in her life weren't as quick.

Opening the back door of Noon's car, her startled friend pounced to attention. She shoved Penzance into the back, then ran around the car to leap into the front seat.

"Night—"

"Drive," she said, rolling her seat forward.

Noon didn't ask any questions; he got the car going and drove into the street. "You know what shit I could get for leaving my post? Maze'll tear strips off me."

Pulling down her visor to use the mirror, Harlow tipped her head back to run a hand down her throat, checking the marks her love left on her.

Noon did a double take at what she was doing. "Oh my God, you fucked!"

It was difficult to keep the smile from her lips. Sinking back in her chair, she slid down, exhaling her relief and satisfaction.

"How do you know that?" Penzance asked, sitting on the edge of the backseat to lean between the front seats. "Other than the bliss on her face."

"Ryske chokes her," Noon said, glancing in his mirror. "Nightingale has a thing for breath play… You didn't know?"

Penzance held up his hands. "How the hell would I know that?"

"You probably should know that," Harlow said, opening the glovebox to retrieve a mint. "If we're supposed to be fucking."

"Uh… what?" Noon asked, almost swerving from the road.

"Ophelia gave me the night off because she thinks me and Penzance are having sex."

"Why does she think that?"

Penzance groaned. "Because she was riding your buddy when I went in to warn them they were about to be busted. Ophelia caught us coming out of the room and decided I was her ride."

Noon laughed. "And now I'm your ride."

"Yeah, I'm quite the slut tonight," Harlow said and twisted to address Penzance. "You got paid for the privilege, so, you know, quit complaining."

"Ophelia paid you to have sex with Harlow? I heard the guys talking about what you were into these days," Noon said. "Had no idea you were a gigolo." Harlow laughed, enjoying the look of offense on Penzance's face. Noon wasn't trying to insult him, he was just playing. "Good money in it."

Harlow slid a hand across Noon's thigh. "We are not letting you sell your body," she said. "No way things are that desperate."

"My sex life might be," Noon said. "Though, I've gotta say, picking up women is easier now I'm not competing with Ryske."

Leaning closer, she gave him a squeeze. "When this is over, I'll let him pick up a few for you."

Noon flashed her a grin. "Yeah? Thanks."

"You don't help a guy by giving him bread," Penzance said. "You've gotta teach him how to grow the wheat."

Noon frowned. "What?"

She shifted her shoulder deeper into her chair. "Are you offering to teach him?" she asked. "Because picking up girls will take Ryske a few minutes, those I can spare. But I don't want him taking on a project that will be time consuming. I have other uses for his time."

"Yeah," Penzance said, pushing his fists into his eyes. "The memory is burned into my retinas."

"Try sleeping in the bed beside them," Noon said.

Penzance slapped his shoulder. "I feel for you, man. I do."

"We are not that bad!"

"You're at it like rabbits," Noon said. "Guy can't even go for a slash without hearing you enjoying his buddy's cock one way or another."

She licked her lips and let her eyes trail to her side window. "I prefer another."

Noon laughed, but Penzance shook his head. "You

know, you look like such a good girl on the outside."

Raising Ryske's star to her mouth, she kissed it. "That's 'cause you don't look close enough."

Catching sight of something on Noon's wrist, she grabbed his arm, pulling it away from the wheel to get a closer look. It was exactly what she thought it was: the black flame tattoo. The same one she and Ryske got to show solidarity with Dover after the fire.

Surprised and touched, she blinked up to find him looking at her. Holding in her sentiment, Harlow raised the symbol to her lips and pressed it against her mouth.

After a few seconds, Penzance leaned in closer. "Just a friendly word, buddy… I know where that mouth has been tonight."

Letting Noon go, she swatted for Penzance. He lunged back, laughing, managing to avoid her hand.

"I did not suck his cock," she said, settling in her seat again. "I prefer to do that after he tastes like me."

Both men inhaled sounds of shock and admiration that made her laugh.

"I think I'm beginning to get it," Penzance said. "You're a vixen."

She flopped a hand in his direction. "Oh, you've known that since the night we met."

"So what's the plan, Night?" Noon asked. "Want me to floor it? Get you across the border?"

It was so amazing to be in this safe cocoon. It was only a car, but it was the closest thing she'd had to home in a month. Well, other than her brief interlude with Ryske.

"I remember when Ryske came to me at Bale's," Harlow said. "After the charges were dropped. Do you remember?"

"I remember getting that call," Noon said. "I've never seen a man move so fast. Shit, he thought you'd blown your release. Thought you were going on the run."

She laughed. Her smile widened until her cheeks hurt. "I remember he almost pulled my shoulder from its socket when he told me you were taking us over the border."

"He'll be pissed he's missing this road trip," Noon

said. "Think it will be worth having Maze kick my ass for abandoning them at the club."

"Don't worry," she said, patting his thigh. "We might have to work fast and hard tonight, but we're not going on the run. If all goes to plan, you'll be back at your post before either of them leave the club."

Both Ryske and Maze had told her to take Noon and go; they were willing to get themselves home if it came to it. But she wasn't stealing their ride, just borrowing it for a while.

THIRTEEN

"WHAT'S THE PLAN, Nightingale?" Noon asked.

Right, yeah, a plan. Given she hadn't expected things to go this way, Harlow was still formulating it. "Clyde's," she said. "Can you take me there first?"

He nodded and continued without asking any questions. Harlow hadn't expected to see Ryske tonight. Not only had she seen him, but they'd been intimate. Limited time intimate, but any time together was a gift.

Penzance had been a good sport. Even if he didn't like being used as a beard, Harlow doubted it would change his loyalty to them. Of course, there was still a good chance he was playing them. To what end? No idea. If the chance presented itself, she'd probe more into his motivation.

Their association may have been brief, but she trusted in his heritage with the guys. Ryske seemed to trust him. Maybe not enough to share detailed insider info, but enough that he didn't worry about her safety. None of the guys were wary around Penzance, not like they'd be wary around strangers. If Penzance was going to screw them over, then he was going to screw them over. Nothing about that night would change that.

On arriving at Clyde's, she asked the men to wait in

the car, and slipped out to run up the stairs alone. Her friend may not be home. If he wasn't, she had to weigh the risks of leaving a note. A paper trail meant evidence Ophelia could track.

Relief cascaded when she pushed down Clyde's door handle and it gave. She strode inside, just like Ryske would, and found her friend seated at his dining table surrounded by paperwork.

"You should really lock your doors," she said. "Any crazy could just walk right in."

Clyde's shock gave way to a grin. "Harlow!"

Rushing over, he yanked her into his arms, squeezing her tight.

"Easy, buddy."

"Where have you been?" he asked, hugging and letting her go, only to pull her back into another embrace. When he pushed back again, he sighed. "What's he done this time?"

"This time it's not Ryske," she said, patting his arms and nodding to the couch. "Can we sit? Just for a minute, I'm sort of on a clock."

"Okay," he said, keeping an arm around her as they went to the couch to sit down. "You don't need a place to sleep tonight?"

Tempting as it was to sleep anywhere that wasn't Ophelia's apartment building, Harlow shook her head. "It's a long story, but my life isn't my own at the moment. You can't tell anyone you saw me. Not anyone."

"Not anyone… Not Ryske?"

That question brought her up short. Why would…?

She frowned. "Ryske? Why would you see Ryske?"

"I went over to Floyd's last week… No one told you?" She shook her head. "I was worried about you. I wanted to know what was going on. I didn't see Ryske. To be honest, no one would say much."

"Like I say, it's complicated… I'm not staying there at the moment."

"Where are you staying?"

Her friend meant well, yes, he cared, but there wasn't

time for chit-chat or questions. This was only her first visit, she had other places to be, other people to see.

Ophelia could leave the club any time. An hour was about as much wiggle room as they may have. Even at that, Ophelia wouldn't have a reason to check on her at Brash's, but she wasn't going to take any chances.

"I'm safe, okay?" Harlow said. "And, yes, if you see Ryske, you can tell him anything and everything, I trust him completely." Clyde didn't know quite what was going on. It was all he could do to keep up. "Listen, I came here because I need you to do something for me."

"Name it."

She winced. "Actually, it's a few things. You might want to get some paper."

Leaving the couch, Clyde retrieved his notebook and a pen from the dining table. "Okay, shoot."

"Anything you write down, burn, as soon as you've committed it to memory, okay?"

That just piqued his curiosity further. "Harlow, what are you into? Is it dangerous?"

She smiled. "When is it not? First thing, find out who Jarvis Hagan donated money to. I know he donated to a bunch of city causes, including your department. That's how he got Gina to do his bidding. I need to know if there are any specific officials he donated to, either in a campaign, or to some cause they were affiliated with. I need to know anyone who may have respected him or owed him something."

"Got it," he said, scribbling as she spoke.

"You need to be discreet. You don't want to get caught asking around and definitely don't want to mention my name."

"No, 'cause half the city still thinks you killed him."

She shrugged and sat back. "Well, it's probably more than half. But, yeah, I'm not exactly top of anyone's Christmas card list… Avoid talking about his sister, if you can. Though, it would be helpful to know if Ophelia's name comes up. Note down anything people say about her, or any causes she's donated to. Don't engage her if you can avoid it… And if any scary looking guys approach you or start asking questions, back off."

Much to her surprise, Clyde was grinning when he next looked up. She'd feared this would be asking too much, that he might be afraid to use his access to city systems to do her a favor. No, he wasn't exactly high in the chain of command, but he could move about government buildings and offices. Coming up with an excuse as to why should be easy enough.

"This is exciting," he said. "It's like a mission in a thriller movie."

Keeping her lips still and her eyes open, she nodded. Once, not so long ago, she'd considered this exciting too. Though, that wasn't fair, it was still exciting, the hue of that excitement had just changed a little. There was a thrill, an adrenaline high, when pushing boundaries. But having lost her love and her liberty at different points, the stakes were higher for her. That lessened her desire to grin about them.

"Yeah," she managed to make herself say.

"You want proof to take down the real killer? We have to gather clues and piece together evidence. Do you want me to interview Jarvis Hagan's doorman?"

"No!" she said so quickly that he jumped. Composing herself, she sat up and rested both hands on his leg. "I don't want you to endanger yourself. A job like that needs backup. Ryske can take care of it. He'll take care of anything dangerous. He knows people."

Harlow didn't want anyone near Hagan's building. Her requests were less about his murder and more about the murderess; there was no time to explain that.

Nodding, Clyde seemed to follow. "So you want a list of names, people he donated to, maybe how much. People and departments and causes."

"If you can." She'd crossmatch Clyde's list with that of their Pothos clients at Windsor's. "And if you know anything interesting about those people, let me know."

Clyde knew about Pothos, though he'd never been to the club or seen it in action. But drugs and sex weren't the only ways to take people down. At least, illegal drugs and illegal sex weren't. There were other ways. Some departments were rife with gossip and rumor. If there was anything blackmail-worthy floating around, she wanted to know.

Anything could be useful, any detail.

"Okay, got all that, what's next?"

"Pablo Soto," she said. Some of Clyde's intrigue became a frown. "This one's more personal than business. I heard he might be getting out soon?"

"Yeah," Clyde said. "I've heard that too. I haven't checked if there's a release date though."

"Could you?" she asked. Felipe was on family services radar; Tiffy might be too. Their information would be accessible to Clyde as part of his day job. "Can you get me his prison file?" She wrinkled her nose. "I know it's confidential and you're not supposed to…"

"You care about the family, huh?" She nodded. "You know, we could look into legal guardianship. Martina Soto said she wouldn't let her husband back into the family home. But if you think she's changing her mind, we could have custody of Felipe transferred to you."

That would be a great idea, except she wasn't staying at Floyd's, and they barely had enough space for the people already living there. Oh, yeah, and there was the whole jail-time-for-murder thing. Did that make her a sound bet in the eyes of social work?

If the kid was in danger, she'd take him in, definitely. But Martina might not react well to the implication she wasn't a good mother. Nothing had even happened yet, starting fights in the neighborhood, especially while absent, wasn't a good idea. Anyway, apparently, Ryske had that avenue covered.

Clyde suddenly frowned and looked away.

"What?" she asked.

"Nothing, I… I just realized we'd have to get a judge to approve it… And with your history…"

Yeah, Mr. Two Steps Behind.

"My stay in jail for murder you mean?" she asked and smiled. "Don't worry about it, I know plenty of other people who would make better candidates if it comes to it."

She'd love to put Ryske forward, but Dover would be

a better bet given Floyd's actually belonged to him. He was a respected business owner in the community. That'd be the line they'd sell anyway.

"I just need to know what to expect if he does come back. What's his style? What are his triggers? You know, anything that his notes might tell me. If he's going to be a danger to the family, I need to know how to protect them."

"If Martina thought he was a threat, she wouldn't take him back, right?"

In an ideal world, sure. Clyde should know better.

"How often does it work out like that?"

When she worked for family services herself, she'd read Pablo Soto's jacket. A long time ago. The man wasn't known for his patience. Violence was documented against Martina, and Felipe too. His crimes didn't stop there, he didn't like the word no, and liked to take things that didn't belong to him. What did all his crimes have in common? Violence.

If he was coming up for parole, she wanted to read the latest evaluations. Not that she was expecting him to be born again.

Felipe was older now than when his father went to prison. It wasn't unusual for fathers and sons to butt heads as children grew up. As tough as Felipe liked to think he was—and project to the neighborhood—she knew him as a delicate and sensitive boy with a kind nature. The last thing she wanted was for him to have that grace beaten out of him.

Ryske would take it hard if Pablo raised his hands to Felipe. He had little patience for men who beat on their families. No prizes for guessing why. Protecting Felipe was paramount, but she was protecting Ryske too. Pablo Soto was a strong and dangerous man. While she didn't doubt her love's abilities, she didn't want him and the felon to clash.

"I'll get everything I can," Clyde said.

She gave him a tight hug. "Thank you."

Clyde was always a rock; he'd never let her down. Every time she was there, she vowed to demonstrate she didn't take him for granted. Somehow, life always got in the way of her doing that.

At least he wasn't singled out in that regard. Quality

time with her crew was non-existent and she was supposed to live with them. Life had been constant since Ryske crashed into it. As tiring as it could be, she wouldn't take that moment back. It was worth it. *He* was worth it.

When she tried to pull away, Clyde took her hand. "Harlow," he said. "I know you live this crazy life and I know you can look after yourself… Even if you couldn't, you're with Ryske, and he'd look out for you, but… Are you okay?"

Just like always, he presented her with an opportunity to open up.

"I'm going to be," she said, touching his face. "This is going to be over soon. I promise once it is, I'll come back and we'll hang out. I'll make the time to catch up."

Though hesitant, he let her go. "Okay," he said. "If you're sure. But I'm always here, okay?" She nodded. Making himself smile, he tapped his pen on the pad. "What do you want me to do with this stuff? Bring it to you? Send it somewhere?"

"Just keep hold of it," she said. "I'll come back for it. Keep it handy… But, you know, out of sight."

He pointed the pen at her. "I gotcha."

Leaving the couch, she was already thinking about her next stop. Clyde followed her to the door.

She paused before opening it. "Remember, you never saw me."

He nodded and put a hand to the back of her head, drawing her close to kiss her forehead. "I know," he said. "Look after yourself."

She could tell it wasn't easy for him to send her out into the world without knowing where she was going or what dangers might be waiting. But he trusted her and that was why he let her go.

FOURTEEN

NOON AND PENZANCE were waiting exactly where she'd left them.

"Where to now?" Noon asked when she got back in the car.

"The neighborhood," she said. "I need to see the doctor."

"You sick?" Penzance asked. "Because we have doctors on this side of town."

She turned to look over the shoulder of her seat at him. "Are you scared, Vane?" Though she said the words in jest, she was surprised to see the deep-set scowl on his face. "If you want us to drop you off at Brash's, we can do that. I'm sorry, I... I didn't think about how difficult it would be for you to go back."

If Ryske's tale was accurate, Penzance hadn't been there in a lot of years. The details of why Penzance left were fuzzy. If there had been any sort of trauma, or confrontation, he could have enemies in his old neighborhood, or some kind of regression that could lead him to flip out.

They didn't have time to hedge on this. If he didn't want to come, they had to turn around and take him to Ophelia and Brash's apartment building. They were on a clock and wouldn't have time to turn back later. Offering to drop him at Floyd's would be cruel. Though it was the safest place she knew, and that was even after a shooting and an inferno there, the building might bring back the most potent of his memories.

"I don't need to be dropped off," he said, slouching. "Just don't expect me to jump out and save your ass if you get in trouble."

Noon snorted. "In the neighborhood? Everyone knows Nightingale. No one would lay their hands on her. If there was some stranger who thought about it, he'd have half whatever block we were on beating him to a pulp within minutes."

Strange that such a graphic claim could be so touching. "I don't need help," she said. "You can stay there and keep your head down. No one needs to know you were ever here."

"He knows," Penzance said, nodding to Noon.

"Yes, and Ryske will too," she said. "We don't hide things from our crew. But no one's interested in hurting you."

When he started to mutter to himself, she got more curious. Just like at Clyde's, there wasn't time to probe deeper.

Noon drove fast through the streets, getting them to their side of town in no time. Except… they weren't heading to Bale's apartment.

She got a chill.

"You okay?" Noon asked, spying her tension. "He's at work… If you need me to go in…"

"No." Loosening her shoulders, she sat up straighter at the same time. "I'm fine. I… I'm over all that."

Penzance's head appeared between the seats again. "Over all what?"

The bright lights of the hospital sign lit the inside of the car, mesmerizing her. Slipping into a trance, her psyche languished in a melee of conflicting responses.

"This is where he died," she murmured.

"Where who died?" Penzance asked.

Noon stopped across the street from the entrance. There wasn't supposed to be parking there, but it was late and quiet. If the cops gave him any trouble, there was a diner with parking down the block.

Even those practical thoughts didn't break the hold of the hypnotizing lights.

Noon took her hand. "You were here after the fire, you came to visit Felipe."

"I know," she said. Anxiety didn't respond to reason. "I know that, and that's how I know I'll be fine when I get in there." Tearing her attention from the sign, she forced herself to smile before facing him. "I just… it always comes back to me for a second, you know?"

Noon nodded. "I can go in for you, if you need me to."

"No," she said and opened her door. "Wait here or at the diner, I'll be as quick as I can."

Quick as I can was a relative phrase when talking about locating a specific emergency room doctor in the small hours of a Saturday morning. There weren't as many people as there could be but were plenty of drunks and party-related injuries.

It was almost funny to think these people, and these kinds of injuries, prepared Bale to take care of her and her crew. Those at the admit desk were no help. She checked around the waiting area and loitered, swaying side to side, checking through glass door panels dotted around the department. Still no luck.

Under the guise of seeking a restroom, she read the list of patients on the whiteboard and tried to find his name in the freshest ink. Logging a couple of options, she moseyed down the corridor like she was supposed to be there and tried to figure out how the rooms were numbered.

A door opened and she froze. This was a pretty isolated corner of the department. What was the penalty for wandering? Damn, why didn't she memorize some patient name to ascribe herself to?

Panic ceased when Bale came out talking to a nurse over a chart.

He glanced up and kept talking until the moment he registered her identity.

Silence. "Uh… thanks, I'll catch up," he said to the nurse, who looked between them and walked away. Bale rushed over, crouching to her level, scrutinizing her eyes. "Are you okay? Are you injured? What day is it?"

She swatted his hands away when he tried to take her pulse and feel her temperature. "I think it's Saturday now."

"We'll get you set up in a room. No one has to know you're here."

He took her hand, but they only got a few steps before she dug her heels in, forcing him to stop. "I'm not sick," she said. "But I am on a clock. I need your help and I need it fast."

His expression became sterner and he folded his arms. "Is my brother an idiot?"

Confused, her eyes slipped to the side. "Uh, is that another one of those mental status questions? I thought they were supposed to have static answers, your brother is a moving target."

"Don't I know it," he muttered and slipped an arm around her to guide her out of the hallway and into an exam room. "What do you need?"

"A sedative."

He produced his prescription pad from a pocket. "What kind of sedative?"

Laying a hand over his, she pushed the pad down and stepped closer. "The unofficial kind."

Tilting his head, she could see skepticism creeping over him. "Harlow…"

"I know. I know you don't like breaking the law. Blatantly breaking it. You like the gray area and this is more monochromatic, but—"

He put a hand to her shoulder. "Har, if you need it, you'll get it. But when you ask me for something like this, I get worried. Ryske hasn't been in his right mind this last month. If he's asked you to—"

"He doesn't know," she said, taking his hand and moving against him. "I haven't had a chance to talk to him. To be honest, I didn't think I'd have this opportunity to see you."

In considering how useful it would be to have a few minutes in various places, one of the people she missed was Bale. Lying in the dark in her bedroom in Brash's apartment, she'd craved the doctor's help. She'd craved all her friends.

And there was one thing Bale was especially good at.

Sliding her arms around him, she held her body to his, enjoying his comforting heat.

"You're tired," he said, embracing her. "How much longer can you keep up this pace?"

His worry was reassuring; he felt it for all their crew. But their bond was different. Bale was the first member of Ryske's circle whom she'd trusted.

"I promise when this is done, I'll go on vacation," she said. "You can take me somewhere and we'll drink from coconuts, what do you say?"

There was a laugh in his voice. "You wouldn't rather go with the idiot?"

"He's more likely to get me in trouble," she said. "You'd be quite happy to drink their liquor and lie in the sun. The idiot would want to knock over the liquor store and take pictures of me on a nudist beach or something."

"Get you in trouble? Yeah, that sounds like him."

Time ticked on; she should be moving, yet she couldn't bring herself to leave his arms.

"I need you to keep him together," she whispered. "I know he's a pain in the ass. But I need him in one piece, Bale… please."

"Hey," he said, scooping the hair from her shoulder to ease her head back and look down into her. "He's going to be okay. You always come back to him."

That triggered a memory of her parents' laundry room. Curling her fingers, she grazed the scar on her palm.

"You're the only one capable of loving him as much as I do," she confessed, being able to say to him what she wouldn't dare say to anyone else.

Bale flashed his pearly whites. "Babe, no one is capable of loving him as much as you do." He touched her jaw. "He's a lucky sonofabitch."

"Oh, I know that," she said and they shared a smile.

They were still smiling and holding each other when the door opened and a nurse started to enter. When she spotted them, she paused and backed out, letting the door close again.

Harlow laughed, but Bale groaned. "And there goes months of groundwork on that one."

"Oh, I'm sure she'll understand."

"And which explanation should I give? That, yes, you're the patient she remembers, but it's fine because you're basically my sister-in-law?"

"Are you asking if it's better to be sleeping with a patient or your brother's wife?" she asked and patted his chest, backing off. "It's fine. As soon as I get my hands on Ryske again, I promise to bring him here and we'll get caught doing it in a supply closet or something."

"Great, thanks," he said. "So you're my sister-in-law patient who screws corpses?"

A laugh burst from her. "That's me…" She gave him a light push. "Don't forget, I'm a druggie too."

Linking their hands, she guided him toward the door.

"Right," he said. "No, you wait here. What do you need?"

"Something tasteless. Enough for a woman."

"Ophelia?" he asked. Harlow hesitated, not because she didn't trust him, but because like with Clyde, she wanted to insulate Bale as much as possible. "I need an approximate weight to give the right dose."

She nodded. "And one for Brash too… just in case."

Curling a finger under her jaw, he raised her face to graze the bruise on it. "He give you that?"

"He did, so, you know, just in case."

He kissed her head. "You got it. Wait here, babe."

Doing as she was told, Harlow didn't intend to go anywhere. Waiting in one spot expecting peril from every corner was kind of paranoia-inducing. Pacing, she was about to touch the steel unit by the door when she withdrew her finger, it wouldn't be a good idea to leave fingerprints.

Smiling, she wasn't sure if it was Ryske or jail that conditioned her. One of them had certainly managed it.

She was restless by the time he came back. Rushing to him, Harlow only stopped when he raised two little white packs.

"O and B," he said, showing her the faint initials in the corners of the packs. She was about to take them when he whipped them away. "Don't mix them up."

"Promise," she said and took them, holding onto his arm to pick up her leg so she could slip the papers into her shoe.

"Be careful, Har."

Curling a hand around the back of his neck, she pulled him down and kissed him quick. "Always. Thanks, doc… You never saw me, okay?"

He was smiling when she winked, probably because it was his brother's move.

She dashed from the room before he could give her the after-school special. The moral of the story usually only became clear at the end. Besides, Ryske preferred it if she ignored the morals in favor of doing what needed to be done.

FIFTEEN

NOON'S CAR HADN'T moved. Not until she got in; he started driving before she'd even closed the door.

Penzance rose from his bored slouch and poked his head between the seats. "We going back now?"

"Not yet," Harlow said, touching Noon's arm. "Will you take me to the gym?"

Their driver nodded once.

Penzance slanted deeper into the front. "Are you shitting me? The gym? What the hell?"

"You got it," Noon said.

His love of driving and all things cars made Noon the natural choice for the job of being the crew's driver. He never complained, never questioned, never second guessed. She liked to think his silent faith was an indication of his unwavering trust in her. There was probably an element of that. But it was more likely because other people on the crew were much better at interrogation.

They drove the long way round, avoiding Floyd's though she didn't know if that was for her benefit or Penzance's. It could just be that Noon liked driving so much he couldn't help himself.

The street outside the gym was empty, so Noon had

no problem parking.

Turning toward the interior, Harlow opened her mouth, but it was Penzance's voice that filled the cabin.

"Yeah, yeah, we know: wait here," he said, and dropped into a slump against the backseat. "For the record, this is the shittiest date I have ever been on."

"No!" Harlow protested and hooked both hands over each other on the shoulder of her seat to prop her chin on them. "The shit part comes later when you realize you won't get laid."

Noon was still laughing when she jumped out of the car and ran up the metal staircase that led to a second-floor door.

Knocking, she waited, and hoped her friend was home. A minute later, there was a clunk on the other side of the door. It swung open a few inches to reveal Costello in his underwear.

It wasn't until she noted his heavy eyes and mussed hair that she remembered the time.

Her gasp of apology was masked by his of surprise. "Harlow," he said, opening the door further and grabbing her shoulder to drag her inside. "Shit, I didn't expect you…"

Flicking on the light, he illuminated the small landing at the top of the stairs that led down to the gym. His apartment door was opposite the external one.

As he turned back toward her, the first thing he noticed was the bruise on her cheek. Frowning, he tipped her face toward the bare lightbulb above them.

"Don't overreact."

"Ryske need a posse?" he asked. "Let me grab some clothes."

He started to turn, but she grabbed his forearm to stall him. It took her a minute to speak after he looked at her again.

"You're not going to ask if it was him?"

His smile was brief. "Are you kidding?" he asked. "I've seen that man as mad as a guy can be. I've seen him that angry at you… and at me. You didn't even blink. I know you. I taught you to be braced and prepared at all times… You've got no guard with Ryske. None. Even when he's mad as hell."

The men in her life wanted to overwhelm her, that was sure how it felt. Costello's faith in Ryske, and in her trust in her man, was touching.

"I need your help," she said. "But not for this."

Bobbing his head in understanding, he examined her for a few seconds, probably trying to figure out just how much trouble she was in.

He side-nodded. "Come through."

Pushing open the apartment door, he took her inside the living room that sort of felt a bit like a stoner house, though Costello didn't smoke. It was messy. All the furniture was mismatched and old. But Costello cared about other things, like fitness. Décor wasn't high on his priority list.

He went over to the kitchen that was really just a bunch of units against the far wall to pull out a bottle of bourbon and two glasses.

Harlow dropped onto the couch. Even though her night wasn't over, she was sort of tempted just to lie down and go to sleep. This was the most activity she'd had in weeks.

Costello brought over the glasses and gave her one. They raised a silent toast and drank. Figuring Ophelia had sent her out to drink anyway, she'd be allowed to partake. Not that Harlow would worry about asking permission.

She swallowed the liquor and then cupped the glass on her knee. Her friend wasn't going to say anything, he was waiting for her to talk. Costello had infinite patience, which was probably why he was the best man to do what she was about to ask him to do.

She made herself talk. The situation wouldn't explain itself.

"I shouldn't really be here, so… you know, if anyone asks—"

"Harlow," he said, basically telling her to spit it out.

"You've heard about Ryske?" she asked, stealing a glance at him. "About his mood."

"You mean how he's going around beating people up," Costello said. "Sure. Heard he was doing some enforcing… not something I knew he was into, but he's capable."

Oh, she fumed, so bad that steam might stream from her ears. The bastard hadn't said anything about organized fighting. That was worse. Spontaneous fighting was bad enough, but it could be explained away if anyone came looking for him. Enforcing meant taking someone's side; that wasn't something her crew did. They were on their own side and that was it.

"Yes, he's capable. But he's not fighting for the money or for loyalty. He's fighting because he's frustrated and because he's angry."

"Two of the worst reasons," he said.

The bedroom door opened. They both looked over the back of the couch.

A tired Isla appeared wrapped in a sheet. "You have got to be kidding me," she said, pulling the sheet higher.

Harlow waved. "Hi, Isla," she said, trying her best to be contrite. "I'm sorry, I just need him a minute and then I'll be gone."

"You're not staying over?"

Harlow smiled. "Not this time."

Isla didn't find it funny. Harlow couldn't blame her. The woman had never liked her relationship with Costello, but then she didn't know Ryske.

"Go back to bed, I," Costello said.

Retreating into the bedroom, Isla closed the door probably cursing Harlow's name.

She leaned in. "That's great. You're back together?"

"We're hooking up," he said and scratched his head. "Not sure it's more than that."

"Does she know?"

"I don't know. We don't talk about relationship stuff. She showed up a few weeks back at two in the morning. Since then, every once in a while, she shows up."

"And you have sex?"

Costello shrugged, buying himself time to drink. "I'm a guy and she's hot."

"She's in love with you. Sometimes we women don't make the best choices when we're in love."

Sinking into the corner of the couch, he brought a knee onto the seat and rested his drink on it. "Speaking from experience?"

The need to laugh hit her so hard that she almost spat out her drink. Just managing to hold onto the liquid, she swallowed it down.

"God, yes!" Both of them grinned. "I can't tell you how many times I've had sex with Ryske when doing it was the dumbest possible idea."

"So why did you?"

She wriggled deeper into the couch. "Because I love him, and he's hot, and he's good at it," she said. "Probably all the reasons Isla keeps coming back to you… Though I can't comment on the last one, I know you sure have stamina."

"And that's important," he said, raising the last dribble of his liquor in a toast Harlow reciprocated.

"It sure is."

Each of them tossed back the last of their alcohol. Costello put both glasses on the table before shifting closer to take her hands.

"Ryske," Costello said, bringing her back to the point. "He's fighting for the wrong reasons."

"I'm asking everyone to look after him," she said. "To try their best to stop him."

"If I see him around, I can, but I'm not out after dark much now Floyd's is closed. No one is."

"That won't be for much longer," she said, hoping it wasn't a lie. "And I was thinking something a little more… targeted."

He frowned. "I don't understand."

"You're an amazing teacher and you have so much patience."

"Har, I haven't seen many guys in better shape than him. He doesn't need me to teach him anything… Isn't there a gym in his apartment?"

"Yes," she said. "I don't need you to teach him how to fight. I need you to give him a safe place where he can vent."

"You want me to spar with him?"

She shrugged. "He did say once he wanted to see what you had."

"Yeah, when he wanted to beat the shit out of me 'cause he thought I wanted in your panties."

"We're all over that now and you've been over there talking about starting a business together."

"I'm not saying we're not friends," he said. "But if he's so angry and frustrated, he won't listen to me."

Pouting, she pushed her shoulders back. "That's where your patience and wisdom come in, master."

"Okay," he said, shoving her shoulder and making her grin. "You can turn off the bullshit now, thank you."

"I'm sorry. Look, this is serious. I'm serious. He means something to me and he could mean something to you too. How will you expand if your business partner is dead or in prison?"

"I don't know. You'll probably inherit everything anyway. I'm sure we'd work it out."

He thought he was funny, but she just mock glared. "I could go in there and tell your girlfriend you bought an engagement ring today and really fuck up your life."

His smile fell. "Wow, you're really serious about this, aren't you?"

Leaning back, she folded her arms in triumph. "I'd do anything to keep my man safe."

"Yeah, and what if I fail, huh? What if I just piss him off and he goes out there and gets himself killed anyway? Then who will be to blame?"

"Him," she said. "I know you don't want to be all touchy feely with him." He snorted. "Just tell him I came to you worried, offer him somewhere to work out his frustrations, that's all. Sometimes he needs to get away from home and the guys. He needs to clear his head… Even just let him come in and pound the shit out of one of the bags, anything that's not him on the street."

"You want me to tell him you were in my apartment in the middle of the night?" He looked down at himself and then at her. "I'm in my underwear and you're not wearing much under that scrap."

"I'm wearing nothing under this scrap," she said, other than the scent of Ryske, but she omitted that fact. "But there's also a naked woman in your room."

"Yeah, I'm sure it will appease him to know I had two of you."

"I meant you don't need to fuck me when you've already fucked Isla."

He peered at her. "Why aren't you with Ryske tonight? No one's seen you around and you haven't been over here in like a month. We were beginning to think maybe you'd run off with one of the garbage guys who came to haul all that stuff out the bar."

"It was a short lived affair. He was always putting his trash above me," she said, but he didn't laugh; he wasn't letting her hide the truth with a joke. "I've been around. Not around here, but around."

"The guys make a lot of excuses. You were unwell then you were at your parents helping your sister with her wedding plans... We all knew it was bullshit. We let it slide because, you know, we've heard what they can be into."

Harlow didn't want to ask about rumors because that could lead to being asked. Questions were not her friend.

"Ryske knows where I am and what's going on," she said. "But we can't see each other much and that's why he's so..."

"Frustrated and angry?" he asked and she nodded. After a second of silent pleading, Costello conceded with a long inhale. "Okay, fine. You want me to ask him to come over, I'll do it. I'll open my door to him. But I am not taking responsibility for him."

Overjoyed, she pulled him into a hug. "Oh, thank you. Even I wouldn't take responsibility for him. It means so much to me that you'd try."

"Yeah, well, I wouldn't do it for anyone else." They broke the hug. He tucked her hair back behind her ear and kissed her bruised cheek. "You should get that checked out."

"I've already been to the doctor tonight," she said, jumping to her feet. "And I can't go back... I only have time for one more stop."

She didn't really need a ride to the last stop, but it might be weird to just walk past Noon who was parked, waiting for her. So she got back in the car and tossed her hair from her face.

"Now can we go home?" Penzance griped.

"Yes," she said in a puff of breath and made eye contact with Noon. "Take me home."

SIXTEEN

IT WAS OBVIOUS Penzance was surprised when they drove around the corner, down the block and into the alley behind Floyd's.

He groaned. "Oh, man. This is so not what I meant."

"Oh, hush. Just lay down, no one will see you," Harlow said and opened a hand to Noon. "I need your key."

Seeing Floyd's dead at this time of night was unsettling. Although it was late, there should still be stragglers leaving, or people who'd stayed for an after-hours drink. At the very least, Dover and Lowan should still be around, cleaning up.

But when she opened the side alley door, there wasn't a peep from the bar. No conversation, no music, no lights. Sad as it was, Harlow wasn't there for a drink and couldn't divert her mission.

Slipping off her shoes, she ensured her sedative packets were safe and ran up the stairs. Being as quiet as possible, she opened the door to the apartment and crept inside.

All was dark.

It wouldn't stay dark. When Ryske and Maze came home later with Noon in tow, they'd rouse the building again. They were inconsiderate and the opposite of delicate; the disruption was inevitable. But, for now, it served her purpose that those present were asleep.

Letting the door stay just off its latch, she tiptoed to the right. Keeping an eye on the pull out bed until the curtain she slipped through concealed it, she didn't want to announce her arrival.

The man under the covers of the corner bed was sleeping. She could tell by the rhythm of his breathing. Although it was a shame to disturb him, she'd known waking him was a possibility. So she crawled onto the bed, on top of the covers and lay down with him.

For a few seconds, she just watched him, appreciating his peace. As much as Harlow would love to, she couldn't stay there all night… If she didn't act soon, she'd fall asleep, and that would lead to all kinds of catastrophes. The least of which would be Ryske coming home to find her there.

He wouldn't care that she'd slept with Dover, she'd done that before. But he wouldn't let her leave their home again. No way in hell would he let her walk out. If they fought, they'd both say things they'd end up regretting. On top of that, Anwen would bear witness.

Touching Dover's face with a fingertip, Harlow traced it along his cheekbone and down his jaw. "Hey," she whispered. "Wake up, honey." He did stir but didn't immediately open his eyes. With a light scratch, she moved her nails up and down on his upper arm. "Dover… Dover, honey, please wake up." Giving him a shake, her smile crept up when his eyelids loosened to slide open a few millimeters. "Hey."

It took him a minute to focus, then before his eyes even opened any further, he frowned. "Nightingale?" he croaked and shifted. "Where's Ryske?"

Stroking his face, she rose on an elbow. "He's not here," she whispered. "He's not home yet. It's just me."

No doubt Dover thought Ryske would've been the one to bring her back. "What's going on? You're home?"

His voice was coming back from sleep, so she touched his lips. "Anwen can't know I'm here. Can you meet me downstairs?"

Removing her hand from his mouth so he could lick his lips, he nodded.

With an appreciative smile, she bounced forward to kiss his cheek, then climbed over him to get out of the bed.

Harlow was as quiet about leaving as she had been about entering. When she got to the bottom of the stairs, she put her shoes back on and went into the bar. She hadn't given much thought to how the place would look. When she flicked the light switch, recessed lighting flickered on, illuminating a room that took her aback.

The place looked amazing. Clean and complete. The floor was a dark wood, varnished so it had a sheen to it. A far stretch from the black boards that had been there before. The bar had been finished in a dark wood too though the hue was warmer.

All the furniture was new. The tables and chairs matched unlike before. In place of the pool table was a dance floor. The jukebox was at the back of the room now. Moving around to the front, she didn't expect the bar to be stocked, but it was, with drink and glasses. Lighting was in place; the front door had been replaced. Everything was done.

The more she looked, the less she found unresolved. So when Dover came in clearing his throat and running his fingers through his hair, she opened her arms.

"The place looks amazing."

"Thanks," he said, going around to the back of the bar like it was automatic, because, uh, it was.

Grabbing a glass, he poured her a drink. Harlow went to sit on a stool at the bar, like this was any regular night.

"I don't get it," she said, taking a sip. "Why aren't you open?"

"We're ready any time," he said. And nothing… That was it? She eyed him, trying to prompt him on. That wasn't it, there had to be more. "I won't open those doors to the public until every member of my crew is here."

Lowering the glass to the bar, Harlow was so moved she almost couldn't breathe. "God, you guys are trying to kill me," she whispered and reached over the bar for his hand. "You don't have to wait for me."

"You didn't get a vote in absentia," he said. "It was a unanimous decision among those of us who were here. We're not opening until you're here, Nightingale. I don't care how long it takes."

That just renewed her determination. They had to bring money in. Floyd's was a good way to achieve a steady income. It would never make them rich, but it covered overheads and allowed them to keep the lights on upstairs too.

"I like the dance floor," she said. "I don't think any of you have ever danced with me."

"Yeah, well, don't think we'll be starting."

"Ryske will dance with me," she said, picking up her glass. Dover crooked a brow like he wasn't so sure. Harlow smiled behind the rim of her glass. "If he doesn't, I'll have to dance with other men."

Dover lost his doubt and smiled. "You know what, babe? You're right. He might just dance with you." She took another drink. "You didn't come here to compliment the décor… And if you don't want Anwen to know you're here, I guess you're not staying."

She shook her head. "I don't trust her." His brow lowered. "I asked Noon to float the idea of you guys moving her out."

"What happened?"

Glancing toward the door, could they trust they weren't being listened to? Much as she doubted it, she'd been the eavesdropper, which made her nervous about being on the receiving end.

Lowering her volume, she leaned over the bar. "You know she came to see Ophelia?" He nodded. "She came back here telling you guys that she got nothing. But that's not true. She knows Ophelia is having an ongoing relationship with Anthony Yarker. And she knows who killed Hagan." Surprise deepened his frown. "She also alluded to forming an alliance with Ophelia."

"And so we get to why you're here?"

Licking her lips, she pushed the glass aside. "I need you to move everything. I think she might be trying to locate the weapon."

"The murder weapon? We have it secured."

"Move it. Don't tell anyone where it is. No one… And the recording, do we have that secure? Does Maze have backups?"

"I think so. Maze taped the original to the bottom of the desk."

"I don't know if we'll need it. But…"

"You don't trust her. I understand, and that's all you have to say to me. I'll take care of everything and talk to the guys… We've got you, Nightingale. You don't have to worry about that. You took a risk coming here. You took a risk slipping away. How did you do it?"

"Ophelia let me go to Windsor's," she said, downing her drink and handing him the glass for a refill. "She caught me having sex with Penzance, so now she's over the moon that I've surrendered Ryske to her. Though, you know, his ignoring me and favoring her was already working pretty good."

Dover just looked confused. "You weren't having sex with Penzance."

"No," she said, taking the fresh drink from him. "But *she* doesn't know that."

"Why would she think you were having sex with anyone?"

With her mouth on the edge of the glass, her eyes slunk to the side. "Because… I was having sex with someone."

"Who were you having sex with at…" He trailed off and huffed out a sigh. "Oh my God, Maze is right, that guy is an asshole. He had the chance to get you out of there and chose to have sex with you instead? He couldn't even wait until you got home, he just—"

"He offered," she said. "He told me to go to Noon. That Noon would take me home."

Dover looked left to right. "How did you get here?"

"Noon's out back. He gave me a ride, and I'm hoping he'll take me back."

This whole situation was confusing him. "Why is he

out back?"

It wouldn't make sense for Noon to sit in the car outside if they were just discussing crew business. Their friend could be part of this discussion. That would be just fine, if it wasn't for one small problem.

"He's not alone," she said. "Penzance is with him. Ophelia excused us to go back to Brash's to have sex. So…"

"Instead of doing that you came here."

It wasn't necessary to tell him just how many people she'd visited. "If Ophelia had let me leave with Ryske, I might have followed through, but…" She smiled. "I promise, as soon as I'm done here, we'll go back and act like that's what we were doing the whole time…" Sighing, she hoped he wasn't disappointed in her for taking the risk. "I had to come home, Dover. Just for a minute. I've seen everyone else tonight, I didn't want to miss you the most. Besides, you're the only one I trust to really listen when I talk. The others try, but…"

"Maze is too busy telling you what you're doing wrong. Noon's distracted by your face or your chest, and Ryske is too busy trying to get into your panties…" He held up a hand. "I know, you're not wearing panties. You don't have to say it."

He made her laugh, he always could. Sometimes Dover was like a disapproving brother or a parent at the end of their rope. But, like either of those relatives, even when he was fed up with her, he still listened and did what he had to do for her.

"You know me so well."

"Yeah, probably too well," he muttered. Her smile widened. "How urgent do you think it is to get Anwen out?"

She shrugged. "I don't know. I think you should be subtle about it. I don't want any big confrontation. That will push her closer to Ophelia. And she is helping. You heard about…" Circling her thumb and forefinger around her wrist, she indicated a bracelet, and he nodded. "She was wearing it at Ophelia's. They talked a lot about Ryske. A lot about sex with Ryske."

"And you didn't interrupt? I'd say that's your

specialty." Tossing a beer mat at him that missed, she laughed after he did. "Did you take notes?"

"Yeah, only on how wrong they got so many things," she said. "Who would think a woman had to use words to tell Ryske what she wanted?"

Holding up a hand, he made a cut sign near his neck. "Okay, I love you both, but... I have to hear it in the apartment, I don't want to talk about it too."

Surrendering her palms, she conceded. "I don't need to talk about it," she said, unable to subdue her grin. "I still have something of his inside me."

His expression fell flat and he straightened. "Okay."

Laughing, she had to put a hand to her mouth so as to remind herself not to get too loud. "I'm sorry, I... couldn't resist."

"Try harder," he said and she did her best to erase her smile. Though she knew he was kidding; his sense of humor was dry. They might not like the details, but her crew liked it when she and Ryske were getting along... or more appropriately, getting it on. "So Anwen's selling it to Ophelia that she and Ryske are fucking?" Harlow nodded. "And you're okay with that?"

"It's not fun to know she's saying things about him that are untrue. I don't like to hear her boasting about him. But... I don't know... It is helpful that Ophelia at least thinks she has some competition. Ryske's been doing such a good job of convincing her that he and I are through. After tonight, there's no way she'll keep seeing me as a threat."

"That's good," he said. "We want you safe."

"Yeah, but it leaves Ryske open. Anwen's lie does give some cover."

His chin rose. "You're sure it's a lie?"

Putting down her glass, Harlow licked her lips clean. "Are you asking me if he's sleeping with her or if I believe he's sleeping with her?"

He only thought about it for a second. "Both."

"Neither," she said and raised her glass. "Because it's you and this liquor is good, I won't throw it in your face."

"Didn't mean to offend you, Nightingale."

His smirk was almost proud, but she chose to ignore it and inspect the liquid she had at eye level.

"Lesser women than me may be insulted. But if you believe he isn't utterly besotted with me, you've never seen us together."

"Oh, I've seen you together, Nightingale, and I've seen you apart. And I don't doubt either of you."

"Glad to hear it," she said and turned her glass to move the liquid within it. "I just hope she doesn't start believing her own lies."

"What do you mean?"

"Anwen. If she starts to believe there's something between her and Ryske, it's going to make it more difficult to get her out of here. She could be setting herself up with more problems with Ophelia too. She'll have to recognize when to back off and let Ryske take the lead."

"Take the lead in dealing with Ophelia?"

"You know what I'm like," Harlow said. "I'm bullheaded and don't like to be told what to do…" His head was bobbing. "You don't have to be so quick to agree." He flashed her a smile. "But even I know when Ophelia needs to be dealt with, and I can't be the one to do the dealing."

"Like when you're out on jobs with Ryske and you let him do the whole Lothario thing." She nodded. "You know, I'd love to see that. You'd never dream of bowing to him elsewhere."

Touching the edge of her necklace, her finger slipped inside the central loop that sat over the notch in her throat. "Oh, I don't know… Sometimes I bow to him."

"Didn't I say I didn't want to talk about your sex life?"

Raising a hand in apology, she moved on by taking a drink. "I don't want to think she's evil, you know? Ophelia can bring out the worst in people."

"You ever defended your relationship to her?"

"My relationship with who?"

He almost rolled his eyes. "With Ryske."

Harlow scowled. "Why would I defend my relationship to her? It's mine. It's not hers. I don't give a damn if she believes he loves me, I believe it. Her opinion doesn't matter to me… Maybe if I wasn't so sure about it…" Thinking it out, she began to speculate on why Anwen may be acting the way she was. "I guess it's a competition for them. Anwen wants to mean something to Ryske, but probably fears that she doesn't, or at least that she doesn't mean enough that he'll fight for her."

"He wouldn't fight for her," Dover said. "I thought he told you how they got together. She blackmailed him into bed. He was never there because he wanted to be."

"I know that," she said, watching her drink move in the glass. "But you can't be intimate with someone for six months and not come out of it feeling something."

A single burst of disbelieving laughter left his lips. "That was Ryske's specialty before you. Meaningless sex was his thing. He could fuck a woman, tell her all the right things, and still walk away feeling nothing."

Funny then that when they'd met he'd refused to tell her anything, let alone the right thing. He'd ended up even refusing to sleep with her. By then, Ryske had known she was different. But even Harlow could admit they had no idea just how different their relationship would be.

"Anwen doesn't want him to feel nothing," she said, putting down her glass to draw a finger around the rim.

All this reflection probably wasn't healthy. As secure as she was in the way Ryske felt about her, she did wonder what she'd done to deserve his adoration. These other women were going to all sorts of lengths to gain his affection. Harlow hadn't done anything special to prove herself.

SEVENTEEN

"UH OH," Dover said. "What's with the puppy dog look?"

"What did I do to deserve his love?" Harlow asked. "I wouldn't trade it or give it up for anything, but why me and not them?"

His smile was slow and definitely amused. "You want me to tell you that you're pretty or something?" His eyes narrowed. "I seem to remember calling you beautiful once... beautiful and..."

Though she didn't doubt he remembered, she said it anyway because he was waiting for her to finish the sentence. "Dumb as a box of rocks."

His grin landed on her again. "That's right. Beautiful but dumb as a box of rocks... I stand by that statement... I think I told you at the same time that this whole damn mess was your fault... I stand by that too."

"You know, you're not much of a friend tonight."

"I just tell it like it is, Nightingale," he said and rested his hands on the bar, arms wide. "I'll answer your question if you answer one for me first."

Scooching closer to the edge of her stool, she rested both forearms on the bar. "A game. I like it. Shoot."

"Why do you love Ryske?"

Her mouth closed and her interest cooled. "What?"

"Why do you love him? You could've had Marlowe… Flaxman… Costello if you'd tried at the right time… You could've even had Noon, maybe even Maze."

Nodding in agreement, she considered that and picked up her glass to point at him. "Or you."

Pushing out his lips, he shook his head. "You couldn't have had me."

She narrowed her eyes. "I could've had you."

He shook his head. "Nope."

"I could've." Dover just kept swaying his head side to side. "I could." Her confidence cracked to a smile. "Ah, you're probably no good in bed anyway."

He bent down to retrieve a bottle of beer, which he popped open. "You keep telling yourself that, sister."

"Calling me sister is never a good start for seduction." The twist of his lips intrigued her. After he lowered his bottle, she flattened her hands on the bar, pushing her chest down. "What?"

"Just wonderin' what my boy would think if he knew you were here asking me to seduce you."

"Oh, yeah, right, like that's what I was saying," she said, snatching her drink. "You wouldn't even know where to start with me."

"With you it would start in the shower," he said. Did all the guys know from experience how much she liked having sex in the shower or had Ryske said something to them like he had Rupert? "But you did say my boy left something in you… That's a little too close to get to the guy, even for me."

Yeah, good point. Evidence of their exploits still marred her skin. Good thing Penzance had been there to cover. How else would she have explained the imperfections to Ophelia?

She brushed a finger across the bruise on her cheek. "You didn't ask where I got this."

"Figured Ryske would've taken care of that," he said. "You don't need me beating a drum."

And that was another thing she loved about Dover. "Thank you."

"But you can answer my question. Why do you love him?"

"Why does anyone fall in love with anyone else?" she asked on a shrug. "He's perfect and flawed. Endearing and infuriating. He's a contradiction of a contradiction. He keeps me guessing about everything except the one thing that matters."

"When did you fall in love with him?"

Dover had told her when Ryske fell in love with her; though they could all agree he'd fought the feeling and denied it to himself.

Clasping her glass in both hands, Harlow straightened her arms on the bar. "I've thought about that," she said. "I knew I was attracted to him—"

"We *all* knew you were attracted to him."

Harlow couldn't blame Ryske for denying his feelings when she'd gone a step further and tried to fight her basic attraction to him. "I think I fell in love with him in Bale's bedroom."

"Ha," Dover said and smacked the bar. "We knew you were fucking in there. He denied it, but we knew it!"

Harlow just smiled because the truth was, they hadn't been having sex in Bale's bedroom. Not his original bedroom where Ryske was laid up recovering from the stabbing that brought them together. She'd been thinking of a different, non-sexual, moment. Of the instant when they'd heard gunshots in the apartment and Ryske leaped out of bed to protect her.

Although still injured and under doctor's orders, he'd commanded her to hide in the bathroom and put himself between her and danger. She'd told Ryske once he'd snagged her at Bale's. When he'd opened his eyes and asked about her welfare before his own. Yeah, she'd probably been his then.

The love came after. The love came when she figured out he wasn't just the smooth talking, cocky jerk who could piss her off and charm her with the same sentence. There was substance to him. He had a heart. He cared. That was before learning of the depth of his commitment to his crew and their loyalty to each other.

"Sometimes I miss those days," she said, tracing a line around the edge of one of the new beer taps.

"Of fucking in Bale's bedroom?"

"When he wasn't allowed out," she said, after taking a second to appreciate her friend's joke. "When he was laid up in one place, and I could visit him, and always know he'd be there."

"If he thought you would come here to visit, he'd stay here all the time."

She finished her drink. "I wish he would," she said. "How bad is his drinking?"

"Worse than it's been in a long time."

Harlow appreciated him not softening the blow or coddling her. "And if I told you not to serve him?"

He opened his arms. "There's liquor everywhere. Even if I cleared the bar, it's in the storeroom. And you know he doesn't hear anything he doesn't want to. Saying no to him doesn't make a damned bit of difference. You could tell every liquor store in the neighborhood not to serve him and he'd still find a way… Strong-arming him isn't how you get him to do what you want."

Aggravated, she groaned and let her head fall to her flat hand. Scrunching her hair in a fist, pulling it out was a tempting idea.

"I know that… Do you know how infuriating this is for me? If I was here, I could make a difference. If I was here, I could have the fights with him. I could make him face me. Make him see that he was being self-destructive. If I was here, I'd let him fuck out his frustrations."

"Except, if you were here, he wouldn't need any of that," he said. "Your absence is what's causing this."

"You know it's rich," she said, smacking the bar. "He was happy to waltz off and leave me here when we were sure Ophelia was going to demand him in the card game. I was expected to accept that. But things get flipped around, she picks me, and he thinks he can run off and be an idiot any time he wants? You know, part of the reason Ophelia picked me was to cause this kind of rift between him and those he's closest to."

"Still your fault," Dover said. His teasing was good-natured, meant to stop her from freaking out or losing her temper. To a certain extent, it was working; but she still wished she could do more to support her crew. "If you didn't make him love you as much as he does, he wouldn't even notice you're not here."

"You don't love me as much as he loves me," she said, raising her chin to tease him back. "Do you notice that I'm not here?"

He shrugged. "Paperwork's piling up, so yeah. I notice there's a new fire hazard."

"Did you get the fire marshal's report? Are they sure it was arson?"

"Yeah," he said. "They traced accelerant from the door to the den along the corridor past the restrooms. They think it originated just inside the internal doorway of the stairwell… They're investigating, but…"

"You don't think they'll find anything."

"Don't see how they can. We're not exactly high priority around here—"

"It's not right."

"But it is what it is. We accept it and move on. We got what we like and we like what we got."

It amazed her that he could feel any sense of optimism. The bar did look incredible, so she could understand the hope for the future. But Floyd's was his life. He'd been willing to die attempting to save it when someone tried to tear it down. It infuriated her; she could only imagine what it had done to him.

Yet, he was there in front of her accepting there were things that couldn't be changed.

Harlow took his hand. "Once this crap with Ophelia is done, we'll find out who did this. I promise."

Shaking his head, he took his hand back. "Whoever it was, they wanted to make a point. I'm not going to dignify that by letting them see they got to us."

"A point to make," she said. "That's what Animal said to me the night he was sent after Ryske, the night I met him."

"So?"

"So you don't think... Animal has done just about everything else he could think of to take down Ryske. Why not arson too?"

"Because Jarvis Hagan is dead and Ophelia Hagan is in love with Ryske. She wouldn't endanger him."

"What about the rest of us?" she asked. "It feels strange to me that Ophelia has known where we are all this time, yet she's never tried to approach the bar. She likes to be in the know, and likes others to know that she is... The only reason to stay away is plausible deniability, to assert she's never been here."

He didn't dismiss her and bent to lean on his forearms. "If she's investigated," he said, peering closer. "But why take the risk Ryske might get hurt?"

"She wouldn't believe he'd get hurt. She'd believe he'd get out. He's Superman to her, right? She was probably trying to hurt the rest of us... Even if she thought all of us would get out, if Ryske's home is destroyed, who is he going to turn to...? Where is he going to sleep?"

Dover pondered for a minute. "What was the last thing that happened with her before the fire? Anwen had just moved in, right? It was just after she got beat up."

"Yeah. Ryske went to Ophelia to tell her we were in for Pothos... Maybe he said something during that meeting she didn't like... It's possible she was mad if he said anything in defense of Anwen... or made it clear he was acting under duress."

"We'll need to talk to him about that. See what he remembers."

The reminder she wouldn't be around for that huddle provoked her sigh. "You'll have to talk to him," she said and looked at the clock above him behind the bar. "I won't be here when he gets back."

"Why not stay tonight? Penzance can go back to whatever hole he lives in. You can spend the night with your crew."

She scratched her temple with a single finger. "I'm not sure I could take all of you at once." She feigned a yawn.

"It's been a tiring night."

Dover turned to fill her glass again. "Maybe the other three would take you… You couldn't have me."

This joke wouldn't go anywhere fast. But that was good, she liked having inside jokes with her crew. Especially the ones that might give Ryske cause to pause.

"I guess with Anwen up there, it's moot anyway."

"What's her agenda?" he asked. "To hurt us? To punish Ryske for choosing you?" Widening his eyes, he nodded at her. "Your fault."

Sticking her tongue out at him, she plucked her glass from his fingers. "I don't think it's malice. Maybe I just hope it's not. I think she's volatile, which is why I'm not comfortable with having her around. If she doesn't trust us enough to share, I don't think we should open our home to her."

"Makes sense."

"When she came to my parents to see me, and since then, I… I get more of a sense that she's misguided than anything else. Yeah, I'm pissed at her for lying to us, but I get her position. It can't be a nice place to be. She has no family. Technically, she's dead. Any friends she tries to reconnect with will want to know why she lied to them."

"Ophelia was the only friend she really had, and we saw how that turned out."

Yeah, she got the crap beaten out of her. "Anwen knew who I was when she came back. I think her coming to thank me for offing Hagan was as much a cover for feeling me out as anything. She wanted to know who I was and maybe what Ryske saw in me. Apparently, he mentioned me to her when you guys were staying with her… You know, while he was dead too."

"A lot of that going around."

"As long as Hagan stays dead, I'm fine with it," she said, which was a shame because in the end the man had been more complex than she'd given him credit for.

Maybe it was the false imprisonment and attempted rape that soured her opinion. Still, Jarvis wasn't quite the villain his sister was. The female Hagan was certainly more devious.

"You felt for his pulse yourself."

Which was why she was pretty sure he wasn't still alive. Though, most of that night was a blur.

"Yeah," she said. "But Bale convinced me Ryske was dead by turning off a bunch of machines… Maybe I'm not as savvy as I thought."

"You were young then, babe."

Maybe not much younger in body, but certainly in experience and smarts. "I won't have to worry about that again."

"Him faking his death? No."

That hadn't been what she meant. Tonight, she and Ryske had put words to what they would do if one lost the other. Ryske couldn't take the risk of faking his demise or he'd risk losing her for real.

"Lesson learned, I guess."

"So, if it's not malice, why tell Ophelia she's sleeping with Ryske? Does Anwen know you heard that?"

"No, but she knows I saw the bracelet. I guess she's counting on me not talking to you guys. Maybe she wants me to believe there's something going on between them too. I don't know. She doesn't think I'll be able to check, so whatever's going on, I can't tell Ophelia the truth."

"Well, you could," he said. "You don't need to check with any of us to know it's bullshit. But there wouldn't be any point. Why help her out?"

"Exactly. I don't know if Ophelia believes her, or what's going on. I think they're competing. Anwen had Ryske when Ophelia wanted him. She doesn't want Ophelia to think she's losing her touch."

"So this is all about pride," he said and shook his head. "You know what the sad part is?" Tipping her head back, she asked for the answer. "If either of them actually had him for more than twenty minutes, they'd probably send him back. He's a pain in the ass."

She raised her glass and licked the edge. "Yeah, but he can eat pussy like no other man."

His scowl came with a groan this time. "Have I got

to pay you to not talk like that?"

"What can I say? I've been sex deprived for a month and tonight he switched me back on. A lot of stuff is swirling around in my head. If you could see it, you'd be impressed by my restraint."

"No," he said. "Definitely not impressed."

They enjoyed their drinks and their thoughts for a minute in silence.

"Anything useful on that USB I gave Ryske?"

"Not so far," he said. "Remind me to give you a blank one before you leave. Maze was talking about that. I think he has some somewhere."

"They're in the desk drawer. I'll grab one. There's something I want to do upstairs before I leave anyway." His suspicion narrowed on her. "Not that... not a sex thing... I just want to leave a gift for Ryske..." She paused. "Though, I don't know what he'll use it for."

"He doesn't need anything for the spank bank. You guys have racked up plenty of material for that."

"Thank you, I'm glad he told you." Dover hadn't exactly said that, but it wouldn't be the first time the crew discussed their masturbation habits. "But this, I'm hoping, will have a more soothing effect. It's something to try."

"Guess I can't argue with that."

She got back to business, aware that time was running low. "I have one idea for how to get into Ophelia's private files at the apartment. It's the one place I can't get near. There's always someone around watching me. But if Maze could try maybe getting into her computer..."

"I'll ask. What do you want him to look for?"

"Remember on the recording how Jarvis said his sister was unstable when they were kids?"

"A crackpot, yeah."

"It would be good to have some evidence of that."

His curiosity grew. "Forming a plan, Nightingale?"

"Maybe," she said. "But I can't do anything if I don't have evidence of her... instability."

"He might be able to find that elsewhere if not in her private files... Don't do anything dangerous without backup.

Like you just said, she's a crackpot."

That wasn't her word, but she got his point. A noise at the far side of the bar brought them around. If Anwen discovered them, she could blow the whistle to Ophelia.

Instead, it was Noon who came in. "I have to pee," he said, striding across the bar to head for the restroom.

Wearing a smile, she turned to Dover as she hopped off her stool. "Isn't he adorable?"

"That's one word for him," he said. "Come on, let's get you upstairs to leave that present for Ryske."

Having Dover with her was good cover. He'd take responsibility for any sound she made.

After sneaking into the closet and turning on the lamp, Harlow retrieved the blank USB and pulled a small rubber band from the drawer. Looping it tight around a section of her hair, she cut about four inches.

A lock of hair wasn't much, but she tiptoed to Ryske's bed and kissed it before slipping it beneath his pillow. All she could hope was that when he was feeling low, he'd use the gift as proof she was still with him.

EIGHTEEN

HARLOW HADN'T BEEN prepared for the moment Noon would pull up at the end of Ophelia's block. Going closer would give the doorman intel to report, like the time she and Penzance came back and who'd dropped them off.

There was no point hiding they'd been out late. As for their driver… Noon was dropping them off out of sight of the building so it would seem like they'd walked back. On the return drive, she and Penzance got their story straight about which bars they'd been to and who drank what.

When Noon stopped and they twisted to look at each other, Harlow was filled with a sense of loss. Her friend would go back to Windsor's now and wait to take Ryske and Maze home.

"You be good," she said, leaning over to hug him.

"Call if you ever need a ride," he said, his mouth turned toward her ear, his hand moving through her hair. "I'll come get you anywhere."

Closing her eyes, she breathed him in for a minute before leaning back to kiss him. Penzance was already on the sidewalk and opened her door. Though she wouldn't usually like to be rushed, hurrying her along was necessary. Without the prod, she'd stay in the car all night.

Harlow got out, holding onto Noon's hand for as long as she could, but eventually had to let Penzance pull her away. He kept hold of her, twining their arms together as he guided her down the block.

"You're one busy bee, aren't you?" Penzance asked. "That was an impressive round robin you just did there."

"Yeah, and it all started with getting laid."

Recovering from the farewell blues, a rush of adrenaline boosted her mood. Not only had she seen her man, but she'd seen every member of her crew and her friends too. There hadn't been time to go home and check in with her family, but keeping them out of the loop while she was in harm's way was in their best interest.

"You're welcome," he said like he'd had something to do with it.

Though he hadn't, he had bragging rights and she couldn't do a thing about it.

"Yeah, for covering, I appreciate it."

"You know…" Taking her hand with his furthest one, he slid his other arm around her to pull her close. "Now that we're fucking, we should…"

"You finish that sentence with the word fuck and you won't make it inside another building, let alone another pussy."

He laughed and skimmed his hand down her back to cup her ass. "I'm just saying, your goods are mine now."

That's what Ophelia would think and word would trickle down to the goons. Ophelia had probably already told Ryske what she'd come across. But Ryske would know he'd been in that room and that nothing had happened… with Penzance anyway.

One thing she hadn't thought about was being at Ophelia's with Penzance. They'd have to act like they were an item… and that could mean being amorous in front of Ryske.

Early in their relationship it had been established that she may have to see Ryske with other women. It never occurred to her that she might be the one faking a relationship in front of him.

The proposition was interesting. She would never

follow through in private with Penzance but would feel better getting a chance to discuss it with Ryske. If for no other reason than to get some advice on how to sell the relationship in public. The man did have vast experience in this area. Penzance could offer advice, as he'd done work similar to Ryske, but her trust in the latter outweighed that in the other.

Heading into the apartment building, they rode the elevator to the floor beneath Ophelia's and went into Brash's apartment, where she'd been staying for the last month.

Hers was the guest room. After raiding the liquor cabinet, she walked through to her bedroom with Penzance trailing behind her.

"Are we really gonna do this," he asked when she put the liquor bottle on the floor and went to the closet to take off her shoes.

Standing half in the closet, she blocked what she was doing with the drug pouches and USB secreted in her shoe. Slipping them in a space between a low shelf and the wall, she made sure to move her pile of shirts closer to cover the useful slot she'd discovered while first investigating the room weeks ago.

"Make yourself comfortable," she called over her shoulder.

"You gonna take a shower?"

She heard his shoes hit the floor and turned to see him lying across the width of her bed. "We're not having sex," she said, sliding the closet shut at her back and going across to climb onto the bed.

Kneeling in the middle, she kept her feet hooked off the end of the mattress.

"Ophelia told me to spend the night… I think she's gonna tell me to stay a lot."

When he reached a pointed finger to her knee, she slapped it away. "And you're going to make excuses to stay here as little as possible."

"If I'm here, I can protect you from Brash."

That was a good point. If Penzance was on their crew, if he had their stars, she would beg him to stay with her every night. Backup meant strength in numbers.

"You're asking me to trust you in my bed," she said, moving onto her side, propping her head on a hand above a crooked elbow. "Yet, you have never hinted that you trust me."

The look on his face was one of wry amusement, but she thought he might be a little bit impressed too. "What do you want me to do, honey? Get naked and trust you not to touch my dick?"

Disgust screwed up her face. "I don't want to see your dick, let alone touch it…" Swaying forward, she touched his chest. "I want to see this?"

"How ripped I am?" he asked and rolled onto his back to pull off his tie. "I keep in shape. You're going to love this."

"I guarantee I won't love it."

Tossing his tie over his head, he undid his shirt buttons. "You will. Bet I've got ten pounds on Ryske."

"Wow, that's impressive," she said. "Think about cutting down on the Twinkies." When he scowled, she smiled. "I don't care about your muscles… Have you got tats?"

"Sure," he said and finished unbuttoning his shirt to show her his ink.

While they spent a half hour comparing tattoos and discussing the process, the alcohol on the floor was neglected.

She rolled off the bed to get it. "So I have a question," she said to the shirtless man on her bed as she unscrewed the bottle cap.

"Okay."

Harlow took a swig and went back to kneel on the bed, thrusting the bottle toward him as she did. "What really went down between you and Charnock's granddaughter?"

Groaning, he took the bottle and several long mouthfuls like he was downing water after a run, not hard liquor. "Why do women always want to make drama out of sex?"

"I didn't know you had sex with her." The bottle dropped an inch and he just glared. "Okay, so I figured you had sex with her. But I wasn't asking about drama, just a run down."

"We got hot and heavy, her grandfather thought she was too young to settle down. I started talking marriage… so he paid me to leave. Worked great. I did the gold digger bit in front of him, sweet talked her on the side, and boom, I get a check."

His next drink was as long as the first. Handing her back the bottle when he was done, Penzance flopped onto his back and stared up at the ceiling.

Taking a drink, she tried to see what he was seeing, but there was nothing there. He hadn't moved or spoken for a clear minute, he just lay there, staring.

"You cared about her."

"Hmm?" he asked, his head lolling to look at her. "Em? Yeah, sure, I guess. Much as we care about them all."

"No, not *we*," she said, lying on her side again, her fist around the neck of the open bottle she held between them. "You cared about her… You loved her."

"Not all of us are as easy as your boy," he said and sat up to snatch the bottle. "We don't lose perspective just because a pretty pair of eyes enchants us."

Rolling onto her back, Harlow drew a line from the strap of her dress down the neckline to her cleavage. "It wasn't my eyes that enchanted Ryske," she said. Penzance's gaze dropped to her finger trailing back and forth. "You've been doing this a long time, just like him. Maybe you're ready for something new."

Still distracted by her finger on her breast, it took Penzance a few seconds to snap out of his daze. "Something like settling down? Is that what Ryske told you?"

Those two words weren't exactly Ryske's style. "Ryske has never told me he's ready to settle down."

Even though his plan with the pool hall was a sort of suggestion he wanted to move away from the life he'd had, it had never been put to her like that. Probably because he knew better than to make promises he might not be able to keep.

What other people might consider a dangerous lifestyle was the norm for Ryske. Even if he did slow down and give up the grifting, he'd still never be a white picket fence kind of guy. She couldn't complain about that, he'd never claimed to be. Who the hell wanted a white picket fence anyway?

"I didn't love Emma, not like you're thinking."

She shifted onto her side again. This was the closest she'd come to getting real answers from Penzance. Harlow had the time to probe him… and there was liquor. There might not be an opportunity like this again.

"Then how come you always get this kind of far off look in your eye whenever I talk about it or someone mentions it?"

The way he breathed in suggested he intended to deny it.

His exhale was one of surrender. "Because sometimes life sucks, Har, and that's just the way it goes."

A truth, perhaps, but she didn't see how it was relevant to her question. "I'm sorry, you're going to have to expand on that," she said, sitting up and crossing her legs. "Life sucks all the time. I don't get all quiet and brooding about it."

That wasn't a judgment. Penzance was too warm to get away with brooding anyway. Even when he said nothing, he was approachable.

Still, he was wearing a frown when he grumbled, "No? And I bet Ryske is Mr. Chatty about his shit."

Others might not think so; Anwen wouldn't. Harlow knew a different side to the man who worked hard to shut most people out.

"Ryske is completely honest with me, when he's not lying to me."

It took Penzance a minute to catch up.

Except even after having time to replay it in his head, confusion lingered. "What?"

Sometimes honesty sent people skidding past.

Opening her mouth, Harlow prepared to explain. "Let's get one thing straight, you're not Ryske. And he's also not the only man I have in my life. Every man is different. Every person is different. If I'm worried about someone or I want information from them, I approach them as them, not as some generic entity. You come across as a pretty straight forward kind of guy. So I figure if I want to know something about you, I should just ask, which is what I am doing… Do you recommend another approach?"

Wearing a smirk, he leaned closer. "Why don't you try the Ryske way with me, see how it works out."

Ha, she didn't think he'd like that as much as his expression implied. "You think I blow him to get information?" Hooking her hands on the foot of the bed behind her, she leaned back. "Withholding works better."

He laughed and drank. "No way you could withhold sex from him."

Harlow wasn't discouraged and hitched her chin higher. "Shows what you know," she said. "I am excellent at withholding."

No, she really wasn't, but confidence could cover a multitude of sins. It wasn't like she'd never done it, withheld sex. Not consciously… or even voluntarily sometimes, but there were occasions she and Ryske refrained from doing the dirty. From experience? It was easier to refrain if one of them was dead or in jail.

Except her confidence didn't convince Penzance. "Well, I'm not withholding. Information that is. Being with Emma was fun, being around people, going to parties… schmoozing. There was always something going on, something to get ready for."

Clarity was endearing and heartbreaking. Love didn't suck him into reflection, memories of being part of the circle, any circle, did. With her family, she'd been guilty of resenting the whole process of getting ready, judgment from her mother, piling into cars, being packed off to some glitzy event, blah, blah, blah.

But she took for granted what it meant to belong. It was something she'd always had, whether with family, work, or these days with her crew.

Harlow inhaled. "You're lonely! Oh, Penzance, you…" She paused and tilted her head. "Why do they call you Penzance?"

"Oh, your boyfriend never told you that?" he asked. "I'm pretty sure he's the one who came up with it… It's 'cause

I'm a pirate, that's what they say anyway."

"You rob people on boats?"

"The first part, yeah." His proud grin was joined by a nostalgic laugh. "Though I guess there have been a few antics on the high seas. I like shiny things, loot, I guess. It started when we were kids. I'd hoard my slice of whatever we'd taken… The guys said I should bury my treasure like a pirate."

Hearing him talk of the guys, she sensed fondness there, or maybe it was sentimentality.

"This was when you lived in the neighborhood… Your family are from there?"

"My Aunt Audrey raised me," he said. "She used to sling drinks in Floyd's."

"That's how you got to know Dover and the guys?"

"Yeah. That was our hang out. You know the den in the back?" She nodded. "That was our base of operations. We'd plan shit while Floyd and Audrey were out front… They didn't know half the crap we got up to. Least we liked to think they didn't… We used to sneak out the back window and cut down the alley… We'd get up to all sorts of shit around the neighborhood and then sneak back in."

Floyd and Penzance's aunt probably knew more than they let on. But knowing the guys were together, looking out for each other, the adults could have confidence they'd be okay.

NINETEEN

REFLECTING ON WHAT the ragtag bunch of boys must have been like, Harlow was sorry she hadn't known them then. Though in her neat little uniform with her perfect ponytail and pleated skirt, she wouldn't have known how to handle such a band of ruffians.

Ryske would've liked her though. For different reasons than he liked her now. Harlow was raised to be polite and prim. While she did rebel, she wouldn't in public, not back then. If Ryske and his crew came to ruffle her feathers, she'd have retreated into her manners, and probably amused the hell out of him.

From happy speculation, her mind took a turn that faded her smile. "That window saved our lives."

There was a pause.

"I heard about the fire," he said, obviously figuring out what she meant. "How bad was it?"

Floyd's had been his base through his teenage years. Whatever went wrong between him and his crew, the building wasn't to blame. It seemed he had fond memories of the place.

"Bad enough that Dover had to remodel the whole lower floor," she said like breaking news of a friend's demise.

"Basement?"

"Wiped out for the most part," she said, stealing the bottle and wishing for oblivion.

Harlow was proud of everything Dover achieved in the remodel. But she would never get over the moment she'd realized Ryske was still in the blaze and wasn't coming out.

"Shit."

That didn't quite seem to cover it. "Dover and Ryske saved most of the den though and upstairs made it. We got new furniture."

Her optimistic tone probably wasn't fooling anyone, but she went with it anyway.

"You live there full-time?" Penzance asked.

She raised a hand to the ceiling. Her reality at the moment, wasn't exactly what she'd made it.

"I live here full-time."

That didn't satisfy him. "In the car with Noon, you called it home."

Harlow conceded. "It is home. I love it there... I love being there. I love the way it makes me feel."

"You love the bar, or you love Ryske?"

"Can't it be both?" she asked. Sensing they might be heading into heavy territory, Harlow lightened it up by narrowing one eye and wobbling a flat hand back and forth. "I'd say it's about sixty-forty."

"Toward the man or the building?"

She pointed the bottle at him. "I'll leave that to your discretion."

Harlow was drinking when he spoke again. "I get what he sees in you."

"That's because you've been drinking," she said and leaned back to put the bottle on the floor at the end of the bed. "You don't want to say anything to me that would upset Svetlana."

"Lala? No, we're not... It's not exclusive."

In a singsong voice, Harlow teased. "I think she likes you."

"Svetlana is paid to like men. She's good at what she does. Damn good."

"I'll take your word for that... And you wouldn't

consider…?"

"What's your obsession with my sex life? No, I wouldn't… Way back, when I was a dumb kid, I followed her around for a few months. Promised to take care of her, begged her to stay off the game… I was an idiot. She taught me a lot about relationships… about the cruelty of women."

"We're not cruel… not as a rule."

"Maybe not as a rule, but she was harsh… She was right. Like I said, I was an idiot."

She grinned. "An idiot in love?"

He scowled at her. "I think every person who is in love wants everyone to be in love. It's not that easy. Life is—"

"Shit, yeah, you said that already." Prodding his knee, she clenched her jaw to scold him. "Why didn't you just come home?"

"I swore when I walked out of Floyd's that I would never go back."

"But you were a kid… an idiot kid. What did you know about the world or the way your life would turn out? Why did you even leave?"

"Floyd got my Aunt Audrey pregnant," he said, which made her clamp her mouth closed. He sneered. "Yeah, that shut you up fast, didn't it?"

"I don't get it," she said. "You… he… Dover's dad got your aunt pregnant?" He nodded. "What happened?"

"He wouldn't do right by her. No one even knew they were together. No one knew about the pregnancy 'cept the three of us. I went to him, told him to do the right thing. He tried to calm me down, but I wouldn't listen… I stormed out of there mad and I never went back. My aunt and me blew out of town that night."

"My God," Harlow said.

It was so shocking she almost couldn't grasp its truth. He'd never lie about something so shocking… something she had a feeling Dover would be able to confirm or deny.

"Yeah, so you talk about not trusting you, that's the biggest secret I got… Don't even know which of the guys know it. Don't know if any of them do."

Ryske didn't. If he didn't, Noon definitely didn't. Dover would be more likely to confide in Ryske than Maze, but only by a hair and if there was drink involved…

The more likely truth was Dover had never betrayed his father's confidence and hadn't breathed a word to a soul. Harlow wished she'd known this before seeing him tonight. She just wanted to give him a hug and comfort him, even though the secret was more than a decade old.

"Well, wait a second, where's the child? What happened to your Aunt Audrey?"

"She was in a car wreck six months after we left. She didn't make it."

Harlow was almost afraid to ask, but had to. "And the baby?"

He shrugged, his focus dropping to the bed. "They saved it. It went into the system."

"It?"

Lifting his head, he made eye contact. "Don't even know if it was a boy or a girl. I said I'd step up, but I was in trouble with the law back then. Petty stuff. But with no job, no place to live… I wouldn't have given me a baby either."

"Didn't they track down Floyd?"

Another loose lift of the shoulders. "No idea. I was basically laughed out the room when I suggested stepping up, so I blew town. Never looked back."

Running away seemed to be something he excelled at. It wasn't his fault the authorities wouldn't give him a baby when he was really just a baby himself, probably not much over the age of majority. Just suggesting he'd care for the child was impressive. Not many people would consider something so selfless.

Even if the authorities had known the identity of the child's father, Floyd may not have been deemed a safe bet. Running a bar notorious for its links to crime wouldn't scream stable environment. Floyd may have had priors himself. Dover would've been old enough to voice his opinion and decide where he wanted to live. A baby didn't have that voice.

Courts could be fickle and fathers were often seen as an inferior option, especially back then. And the sad truth was babies, even newborns or premmies, were quick and easy to house. The child had probably been matched with a foster family, maybe even an adoptive family, before he or she left the hospital.

"I can't believe this," she said. When he flinched, she grabbed his hand. "No, I mean, I do believe you. It's just… it's a helluva thing, you know?"

"Maze was in the system, he turned out okay… Noon too, I think, though he's less of an example. Wherever the kid is, I'm sure it's doing better being away from the neighborhood and away from me."

Before volunteering her help, she'd need to discuss the situation with Dover. This was a can of worms that could alter his life… and his opinion of his father.

She'd already offered to help Dover track down the arsonist, if their theories proved to be incorrect. Now she was thinking about an adoption case. Missions stacked up left and right. Though, on the plus side, neither of those should involve women who wanted to pray on Ryske… at least, not yet. He had a way of bringing out that quality in women.

Thinking about her man and how she'd broach the arson theory with him, a cacophony of noise rose in the outer apartment.

Penzance sat straight, but Harlow just sagged. "It's only Brash."

It did sound like he'd brought a few bodies back. That wasn't unusual. Harlow knew the setup. The front door of the apartment, like Ophelia's, opened into a foyer that linked straight into the living room through a square arch.

Everything else in the apartment was accessible from the hallway that led away from the living room. Luckily, there was a solid door linking the two spaces; Brash's friends shouldn't cause them trouble. The restroom and kitchen were the first rooms on either side of that hall. So even if the thugs wanted beer or to pee, they wouldn't need to get as far as her bedroom.

Almost as soon as Penzance relaxed, Harlow tensed. The noise came closer, a voice, someone was in the hallway. It wasn't Brash, it sounded like…

"Shit," she hissed and leaped up to run toward the door to kill the light. "Take your clothes off."

Penzance sat up on the edge of the bed. "What?"

Running back toward him, dropping to her knees in a slide, the carpet burned her skin. She ignored the sting in favor of yanking off his socks and tossing them away.

"Get your belt off," she whispered, sure the voice outside was louder.

"What the hell is going on?"

She stood to force him to his feet. "Ophelia is out there," she whispered. "We're supposed to have been screwing all this time. You know what she's like, she's out there listening in here, waiting for her moment to ambush us."

Catching on, he pulled at his belt while she opened his fly.

"Shouldn't we be making some noise or something if we're supposed to be having sex?"

Opening her mouth, she let out a quick, sharp squeal and then a long moan.

Her voice went back to normal in a snap. "Hurry up."

She let out another moan and shoved him aside while he whisked off his pants to yank the covers down and mess up the sheets.

"Hey, you're good at the faking thing… Did you practice that with Ryske?"

Crawling to the far side of the bed, she slid under the sheet before slipping out of her dress and balling it up to throw it as far toward the door as she could.

She was whining and panting and poking at him when he got in beside her. "Underwear too," she said. He reached under the covers to lift his hips and whip it off. "She'll check what's on the floor and I don't have panties, so it will have to be yours."

"You're damn demanding."

"Make a noise," she said and almost fell out the bed when he bounced on it.

"God, I feel like I'm in a bad nineties romcom," he said, bouncing some more while she kept faking it. "Or a crappy fake porno."

Falling onto her back, she closed her eyes, fearing she'd laugh. When the weight of his body lurched against hers, she opened her eyes to him lying against her side.

"Back off," she hissed, giving him a push.

"We should be doing something." She scowled at him. "Not that, but… something."

"Something like what did you have in mind? You're bouncing, I'm moaning." Over the sheet, he tickled her ribs, provoking her laugh. "Vane!"

She squealed and shoved at his hand, but he kept on. It wasn't easy to fake orgasm at the same time as being tickled.

The door, in a narrow space beyond the closet, opened. Her eyes locked to the still bouncing Vane's. Harlow's next moan was interrupted by Ophelia's gasp.

"Oh, well, I suppose we've found her," the heiress exclaimed.

We? Who the hell was…? Harlow shoved Penzance aside to sit up, clutching the sheet to her chest.

To her absolute horror, Ophelia wasn't alone. All the consortium was there with her. Parratt, Lydia, and Yarker were at her back. Up front, at Ophelia's side, was Ryske.

Ryske.

He'd just seen… and heard.

TWENTY

HARLOW OPENED HER mouth. Penzance chose that moment to lay a hand on her back and sit up at her side, showing everyone he was naked from the waist up at least.

"You've gotta pay for a show," Penzance said, really selling annoyance. Stroking her back, he leaned in to whisper through her hair. "You okay?"

She couldn't tear her eyes away from Ryske. Did he think this was real? That she would even consider betraying him?

Her chest grew tighter. She clung to the sheet trying to show him she did value her modesty. Thunder in his eyes swirled around him. All night she'd made efforts to calm and appease her love. She'd asked her friends for help in keeping him safe and off the streets. Witnessing this gave him prime fodder to take out there.

"Well, I suppose they can miss the party," Ophelia said, turning with open arms to herd everyone out. "We'll be in the living room if you can tear yourselves away from each other."

Under her direction, the group left, even Ryske turned his back and walked away. Ophelia couldn't resist the chance to peek over her shoulder and show a sly smile.

The bitch knew exactly what she'd done. Hundred buck bet the heiress hadn't told Ryske what she'd seen earlier. This was orchestrated so he'd come and find out for himself in full living color and surround sound.

After the bedroom door closed, for a clear minute all she could do was sit there, jaw hanging loose. Penzance's hand on her shoulder snapped her back to reality, forcing her to pull away.

He put his hands up. "Thought you were going to pass out. You okay?"

"Okay? Am I okay?" she asked, twisting left and right, looking for something to wear. Her dress was on the floor all the way across the room. "Did you see his face?"

Spotting Penzance's shirt on the floor by the bed, she tucked the sheet around her back and bent over flat to reach for it.

Penzance just sank onto his back and put a hand behind his head. "Yeah, but, you know, you guys are solid."

"We're solid because we respect each other," she said, whipping his shirt around her head to drive her arms into the sleeves. "That, what just happened, wasn't respectful."

"Don't stress. I'll tell him nothing happened."

It infuriated her that he was so loose and happy to slide deeper into the bed.

Harlow busied herself with fastening buttons. "You think he'll believe you?" she asked, shoving the cuffs over her hands and throwing back the sheet, not even caring she revealed his naked form in the process.

"Why not? It's true. I'll talk to him, tell him—"

"You won't talk to him," she said, storming around the end of the bed, glaring at him as she went. "You'd be best served not to go anywhere near him for a long, long time. I meant you think he'll believe you over me? I don't need you speaking for me. Anything I have to say to Ryske, I'll say myself."

Grabbing his pants from the floor, she flung them at his chest. He hadn't even bothered to cover up. He was just lying there in the middle of her bed completely naked without any modesty. Penzance didn't have anything to be modest about. His body was incredible, but seeing it in her bed angered her.

"What are these for?" he asked, untwisting his pants. "She said we didn't have to go out there."

"Oh, you'd rather stay in here?" she asked, going to the end of the bed to swipe the alcohol from the floor. "Fat chance, buddy. Ryske is out there and if my man is out there, I'm going out there too."

To fix this, that was the idea. Though she didn't have a clue how to go about it with a half dozen or so witnesses.

Gulping from the liquor bottle, she reminded herself her relationship with Ryske was in flux. So, really, she didn't know it was right to refer to him as her man.

"You just told me to avoid the guy, want to make your mind up?"

She had just said that. Damnit, this wasn't on him. He'd saved her ass more than once, taking this out on him wasn't fair. Really, Penzance was irrelevant, she just didn't like the visual of him in her bed. That wasn't his fault either.

"Fine," she said. "You want to stay here? Stay."

Turning around, she headed for the door. What awaited her? Whatever it was, she'd face it. Leaving Ryske out there, picturing what was going on in her bedroom, wasn't an option. It was a miracle he'd held onto his composure at all. If someone had asked what his reaction would be to seeing her in bed with another man, it wouldn't be what went down.

There was no one in the hallway outside her bedroom. While walking past the restroom, she heard voices in the kitchen.

"It's something, isn't it?" Ophelia was saying, unable to hide her taunting glee. "She just wheedles her way in with every man. I've heard the way they talk to each other. The way they flirt. But I had no idea they were... physical with each other. I wonder..." Harlow crept closer. "I wonder how long it's been going on. Have they been fucking for weeks? Maybe it's been going on since they got here."

"Why do you care, Fi?" Ryske asked, hitting indifference.

Turmoil must be churning her love up inside.

Whatever he was thinking, the image of her and Penzance would be burned into his mind.

"I don't. It doesn't matter to me," she said, then squealed. "I just think it's hilarious they've been screwing all this time and we didn't even know it. She's good, isn't she? Good at being discreet. I guess maybe it's because she doesn't feel anything. Maybe she's just using him for sex… I wonder if it's good. Do you think it's good sex, Ryske?" Ophelia's voice became more sultry. "Do you think she likes having him inside her? Do you think she begs him to fuck her? I wonder if she likes it hard or tender. I guess you'd know… Tell me, sweetheart, does she like it rough or gentle?"

Harlow's feet moved before she decided on the smart course. On entering the kitchen, Ryske was propped on the central island, Ophelia angled against him, giving him her weight. The sight sickened her. She didn't like to see another woman propped on Ryske, not that woman anyway, but she folded her arms and didn't comment.

If she was so riled just seeing this, she couldn't begin to imagine how Ryske stayed composed at finding her naked with another man.

"Ophe," Harlow said.

"Ah, we were just talking about you," Ophelia said, slipping both arms around Ryske, resting her head on his chest. "Where's your boyfriend?"

Harlow didn't mean to look at Ryske, not exactly, but she did. Except he wasn't looking back. Hands in his pockets, he stared straight ahead, over the top of Ophelia's head.

"You were out of line, Ophelia. You shouldn't be coming into my bedroom."

Out of line by setting her up so Ryske would find her in flagrante delicto. Not that she could be explicit about that when the play was to make Ophelia think Harlow's relationship with Ryske was over.

"It's not like we've never seen each other naked before," she said. "Though, I have to say, Vane is quite the specimen. Well done snagging him."

"I haven't snagged anything. You don't know what you're talking about."

"No, I don't suppose I do," Ophelia said, being coy while stroking Ryske's upper arm. "I only know what *I've* snagged."

Ophelia wanted a reaction.

She wouldn't give the bitch the satisfaction. "Why would you even be here?" she asked. "Your apartment is one floor up, remember?"

"I own both apartments," Ophelia asserted. "I can go wherever I want... For your information, we came here because we were going to include you in our discussions. But if you'd rather forfeit your voting rights—"

"No, I want to vote," Harlow said. "Though you can bet I'll vote the opposite way to you every time."

Ophelia pushed away from Ryske. "Oh, Harlow, you are so petty," she said. "Don't blame me for your choices. And if you think my Ryske gives a damn about what you do in your bed, you give yourself too much credit." She moved closer, her sinister enjoyment growing with every step. "He is over you. You will never, ever be with him again... Whore yourself to anyone you want; no one here will blink an eye."

Nothing would make Harlow happier right then than to slap Ophelia's smug face. Nothing except Ryske stepping up to contradict the woman. Even though she understood why he couldn't, it did hurt that he stood there saying nothing.

Instead of lashing out, Harlow smiled and sighed. "Oh, Ophelia," she said. "Even if every single word of that is true, I don't see why it should give you such satisfaction... I'm your prisoner, watched every minute, and I still managed to get some... You must be drying up, honey."

Fuming, Ophelia grew rigid and sucked in a long breath through her nose. Expecting a slap, Harlow braced. Before it could come, the door behind her opened and Penzance came sauntering in.

"It's the man of the hour," Ophelia sneered. "Don't you make a cute couple?"

"Less cute when we're interrupted," Penzance said and wandered over to lay an arm across her shoulders. Harlow wanted to shove it off, but Ryske still hadn't looked her way, so she doubted he'd even notice. "Think I'll avoid spending the night if that's what it comes with… Didn't know you wanted to be our audience."

"I promise to never interrupt again," Ophelia said.

No, because she'd done all the necessary damage. As long as Ryske bore witness, Ophelia was fine with giving Harlow and Penzance privacy.

"Not sure that's reassuring," Penzance said.

Stepping back, Ophelia adjusted her angle to look from Ryske to the couple and back. "Is this awkward?" It was sick that Ophelia seemed to be enjoying this so much. "You and Ryske sort of know each other and now you've had the same woman."

"Wouldn't be the first time," Penzance said. "He doesn't care about shit like that."

"Do you?" Ophelia asked and touched her fingertips to her cleavage. "I wonder if Harlow… do you compare your lovers? Now you've had both men, you could offer a comparative critique… wouldn't that be fun?"

"No," Harlow said. "It wouldn't… Though I could compare your depravity to your brother's… Would you like me to do that?"

Ophelia's glee fell. Every time the heiress returned to her joy, Harlow succeeded in pulling the rug out from under her and sending her onto her ass. Good. She'd stand there and do it all night. It was the only chance for pleasure Harlow would get out of this.

"You're a sick bitch," Ophelia sneered and started toward her.

Penzance's hand curled around Harlow's shoulder. He swayed to the side, easing her back to block Ophelia. "Ladies," he said. "There's no need to fight over me. There's plenty of me to go around."

When Penzance reached for Ophelia's face, the woman squawked and leaped back. "Don't you dare touch me!" She scurried back to Ryske and put herself in front of him again. "He tried to touch me, Ryske!"

"Meant no disrespect," Penzance said. "I thought you were interested 'cause you keep talking about it. I'd have been an idiot to ignore a beautiful woman like you."

Harlow hid her grin by turning away. Ophelia didn't know whether to crow or criticize. He conveyed the compliment as genuine. The beauty would want to appear loyal to Ryske, so didn't know whether to act insulted by it.

It wasn't an enviable position. Ophelia probably wanted the same thing Harlow missed, Ryske's defense. Ophelia could request it and get nothing, which would be embarrassing for the woman trying to be queen bee.

"Ryske…" Ophelia started to say, though it sounded like she wasn't sure where the sentence was going.

Lydia poked her head around the door. "Uh, would you like to take the meeting elsewhere? People are getting restless out here."

Resigned, Ophelia pushed up to kiss the corner of Ryske's mouth. And, thank God, he didn't respond.

"I have to go and deal with our guests," the heiress said. "Get your drink and join us, quickly."

Lydia left while Ophelia tried to kiss Ryske again. She still got nothing, so gave up. Walking away from him, Ophelia widened her smile as she passed to leave the room. The woman probably didn't think anything of leaving Harlow with Ryske while Penzance was present. She'd assume the newer boyfriend wouldn't let anything happen, or be said, between the former lovers.

TWENTY-ONE

LEAVING TIME FOR Ophelia to get to the living room, Harlow waited until she heard the hallway door close before shrugging off Penzance's arm and rushing to Ryske.

"Crash," she breathed and planted her hands on his chest to rise onto her tiptoes.

When she sought his mouth, he ducked back and walked away. What should…? How…? She couldn't think; she was speechless. Ryske hadn't moved away from Ophelia when she'd kissed him, and Harlow had been pleased at his lack of response. This, with her, was a step further, a deeper insult. He didn't even pretend to let her near him. He broke her heart and disconnected completely.

Turning around slowly, Harlow found him facing the opposite counter, near the fridge, his hands braced apart on it, head bowed.

"Rejected by my home," she whispered.

"Yo, dude, nothing happened. Don't—"

Ryske's head snapped to the side. Over the angle of his straight arm, he glared at Penzance. "You think I need you to tell me that?" he growled. "You think I need you to tell me what she was doing in there was bullshit? You don't have a goddamn fucking clue about her."

Ryske turned suddenly and grabbed her wrist. Spinning her around, he slammed her against the counter by the fridge.

"The first noise she makes is a breathy little whimper," Ryske said, driving a hand through her hair to clear it from the side of her neck and push her head aside.

Moving in close, he ducked to kiss the sensitive spot behind her ear, just at her hairline. Kissing and nibbling, he did nothing but hold her hair away from his mouth and tease her with barely there touches of his tongue and his lips.

Her body grew heavier. She grabbed for the top of the fridge at her left when her knees buckled and her eyes rolled back. When her lips parted, she did release a breathy whimper but didn't care. Specifics didn't matter. Sensation mattered.

"Crash," she whispered.

His lips slid down an inch. She grabbed for his shoulder, but he snatched her right hand and pressed it onto the counter.

Stealing his mouth from its tormenting, Ryske turned toward Penzance again. "After that comes her second stage."

She was still drifting on the tickles of pleasure left by his mouth when he snaked a hand between the flaps of her shirt to run a finger down to her clit. When she gasped and tried again to grab for him, he diverted her hand back to the counter.

"Crash," she begged, aching with pleasure as he rubbed slow lines and circles over her most sensitive spot. "Oh, God, Crash."

Her eyes closed, her head fell against the upper kitchen cabinet behind, and all she could feel was him.

"She starts to pant," Ryske said.

Instinct curled her leg high around his hip and her lips parted to accommodate shallow breaths. Digging her foot into his ass, she fought to pull him close, pressing her bent knee into his torso so hard it would bruise. Good. She wanted to leave her mark on him.

"Crash," she groaned, tensing her leg.

He was still pleasuring her, moving his finger in

circles and down through her juices to slick his fingertips then sliding them higher to stimulate her again.

"She begs, grits her teeth, hisses at me… She starts to whine, and groan, and asks for what she wants."

"Fuck me, Crash," she whimpered. "Oh, God, fuck me."

Aware he was speaking matter-of-fact words and that he wasn't as engaged as usual, sense struggled. Oh, but what the hell? Fuck, she didn't care when it felt this good.

"What do you want, baby? Huh?" he asked, his breath warming her temple.

Draped across this counter, she struggled to stay upright. Clinging to the top of the fridge and the counter, she pushed her torso back to raise her coiled leg higher.

"I want you inside me…" she begged. "Now, Crash. Oh, God, please…"

Throwing her head back again, she gritted her teeth, fighting for breath through the building urgency of need reaching critical mass.

"Trink, look at me," he said, his voice soft. She brought her chin down, managing to open her eyes a sliver. "Did he touch you?" She blinked, opening her mouth wide when he sped his intimate caress. "Did he?" Forcing herself to shake her head, it rolled on the cabinet door. "I'm not gonna kill him. I'll get close, but I promise not to kill him… Did he touch you?"

"What the fuck, Ryske?" Penzance demanded from across the room. "You're not fucking—"

"You shut the fuck up, I'm talking to my girl." Their eyes hadn't left each other. She read his need and shook her head. "Good girl."

Still massaging her clit with one hand, he used the other to clasp the side of her head to pull her up for the kiss she'd craved. Her guy kept on kissing her, rousing and pleasuring her until the desperate squeak of orgasm tore through her. He masked the sound with his mouth, pushing his tongue deeper when she shook and grabbed for him.

The moment it subsided, he snatched his mouth away, leaving her gasping into the air. "Lover," she said, tightening the grip of her leg when he attempted to step back. Grabbing for his jeans, she reached to unbuckle his belt. Ryske stole her wrists and slammed them back against the cabinet behind her. "Please… I know you want me."

There was no mistaking the reaction he'd had to her. Whether it was touching her, the sight of her, or the sounds she made, she didn't know which sense beckoned him, but that bulge in his jeans spoke for itself.

Leaning in, his mouth hovered over hers. "Always."

"Then fuck me, Crash," she said, desperate to taste his mouth, again, he ducked back. "Fuck me, right here… I'll be quiet."

He smirked. "You can't be quiet, Trink."

"I need you," she whispered, her eyes descending. "I can't send you back to her like that… I can't."

"Then you better do something about it," he murmured and crooked a brow.

Oh, the dirty—she loved it. He winked and loosened his grip on her wrists, letting her slide down his body to her knees.

"Oh, God," Penzance groaned when she unfastened Ryske's jeans. "You're not really gonna… She's not gonna…"

"You can turn around," Ryske said, "keep lookout."

The smug swagger in his voice was enough to tempt her to peek up and smile. Her love had forgiven her the slight but wouldn't miss this opportunity to stake his ownership. Harlow took him into her mouth, sucking him deep, wishing he could feel the depth of her love.

"Welcome to my fucking nightmare," Penzance groaned.

Harlow kept working, pleasing her man, giving every effort. Rolling her eyes upward, she enjoyed him watching her.

"Want to shut up? My girl's concentrating," Ryske said. "You're a good girl, Trink. Oh, that's it, baby. Just like that."

With the side of his fist, Ryske pounded the upper cabinet she'd been leaning on before. The bang wasn't loud but was significant. Just as he knew her, she knew him. Oh, yeah, she did. She knew how long to tease him, how long to suck, to lick, to kiss, exactly how to tongue and tease. She pampered and pleasured him until he grabbed a handful of her hair and thrust himself deep into her throat. He forced her to take him hard as he burst against her tongue, filling her mouth with his seminal gift.

Ryske relaxed and his hand drifted from her hair. "Up," he said. She sprang to her feet to tuck his cock back in his pants and fasten him back up. "Panties at all times."

Her fingers stilled on his belt for a moment. "I don't have panties here," she said and finished buckling him. "You couldn't have told me that before I went home tonight?"

"You were at home tonight?"

Hadn't he got a quick rundown of her antics from their friend?

"Noon didn't tell you?"

"Maze went home with Noon, I haven't spoken to him. I caught a ride with Ophelia."

Wearing a grin, she arched her body against his, and was delighted to feel his fingers in her hair. "Yes, I was home. I left a present for you."

"Oh, yeah?" he asked, scrutinizing his fingers in her locks. "What is it?"

"Wait and see. It's under your pillow."

"Our pillow," he said, bunching up her hair, using his grip on it to pull her head back. "How did this happen?"

"Ophelia caught Penzance and me coming out of the bedroom at the club. She put the pieces together all wrong and thought I'd been riding him."

"You didn't correct her?"

"And tell her what? That I was riding you?" she asked, opening the fridge to take out a beer for him. "It worked out anyway. She was so excited I was having sex with someone other than you that she ordered Penzance to take me out for a drink and to spend the night here."

"She knew you'd be here," he muttered, drinking his beer.

"Yes. She wanted you to see what you saw. I don't know, maybe it was her plan to erase any residual feelings you have for me." Recalling his expression in her room, sorrow filled her. "I'm sorry, baby."

Wrapping her arms around his waist, she leaned back enough to make way for his bottle. He rested an arm around her shoulders, claiming her even while he drank.

When he lowered the bottle, he put it on the counter and scooped a hand around the back of her head to pull her close for a kiss. "You did nothing wrong, Trink. You know I knew that."

"I know," she said, pressing her face to his chest to breathe him in. "Don't suppose you'd consider joining me in my bedroom… maybe staying the night… or the week."

He laughed and kissed the top of her head. "In a heartbeat, babydoll."

"I don't get it," Penzance said, finally leaving his position by the door. "You were stressed out about his mood and he had a face like thunder. No way you believed she'd been faithful."

The shot of tension that went through Ryske tightened her embrace. "Baby," she warned.

"You don't have a fucking clue, asshole," Ryske growled, strengthening his arm around her shoulders, pulling her so hard against him that she couldn't move. "I don't have a goddamn doubt in my girl, not one. But see she thinks you and me are boys, and she trusts my boys… Only I know better, Zance."

"Yeah?" he asked, widening his stance, folding his arms. "And what do you think you know?"

"That you think every woman alive is fair game."

"Is that right?" Penzance asked, his chin rose and his gaze slid to the side. "There was a time plenty would've said the same thing about you."

"Yeah, before Trinket," Ryske said. "Show me your Trinket and I'll chill."

A coolness overcame Penzance who leveled his attention on Ryske. "You don't give her enough credit. Harlow knows a play and recognizes a player when she sees one."

"Damn right she does. She sized me up in a second. Sized you up too… You haven't had to see some of the shit she's been through. I won't let you compromise her."

"She can take care of herself."

"When I'm around, she doesn't have to."

Penzance's head tilted. "'Cept you're not around, are you? I've been watching her tail here. You don't have any idea how much danger she's in every damn minute." He pointed at her. "You saw the bruise on her face, right?"

"Yeah," Ryske snarled. "Proof you can't back up the patter."

"Better than you, no doubt about it."

"Stop it," she said. "Both of you. God, we get ten minutes alone and all you want to do is fight."

Ryske wasn't going to let up just because she got pissy. "Look me in the eye, Zance, and tell me you didn't think about it."

Penzance's upper body slanted forward a fraction. "Excuse me? You're asking if I want to fuck your girlfriend?"

Harlow loosened. "I'm not really his girlfriend right now, I—" Ryske planted a glare on her that shut her up fast. With a sheepish smile, she touched his lip. "I love you."

He drew his eyes back to Penzance. "Did you think about it?"

"Fucking her? Sure!" he said and opened his arms wide. "The woman is hot, Ryske, and she's got spunk. Sorry to tell you, bud. I'm not the only guy who'd shtup her given half a chance."

Ryske pulled away, but she grabbed his ribs to pull him back. "He knows I'm not available. He knows I'm yours. He wouldn't, Crash. He wouldn't."

Penzance wouldn't compromise her. For sure, he wouldn't force himself on her. Even if she was incapacitated, he wouldn't take advantage. Why wouldn't he make that clear to Ryske?

"Sure I would," Penzance said. "I've got no loyalty to him and he's got none to me. That's what we're really saying here, isn't it?"

Ryske had spoken of his time with Penzance in terms of what they had in common. Her love had no idea why Penzance left. From his perspective, it must've been hurtful that his friend just vanished without explanation or farewell.

"This is a bigger discussion," she said, stroking Ryske's chest and eyeing Penzance. "Please don't provoke him. Don't provoke each other."

"I want to punch him in the face," Ryske growled.

She laid her hands flat on him. "I know," Harlow soothed. "I know, baby."

"Oh, come on and try it," Penzance said.

When Ryske tried to move again, she balled her hands, gripping his shirt, using more force to hold him back.

"I thought you two were professionals," she hissed, scolding them both. "This is a job. We each have our role. If you want to go our separate ways after, that's what we'll do." Ryske looked at her again, his brow low. "Not us."

"Hmm," he said in a disapproving way.

She gave him a pat. "You're going to be an uncle and we have a wedding to get to," she muttered.

How the hell she'd get to Lena's wedding with all this crap going on in their lives was a problem for another day.

"If you're dating me, you take me to the wedding," Penzance said.

Ah, and there she got the chance to glare at him. "First off, I'm taking a bunch of people to the wedding, so far you're not on the list. Do you really want to see Emma again while sitting at my table?" That shut him up. "Yeah, I didn't think so, lover boy."

"You see why I don't trust him?" Ryske growled.

Laying a hand on his cheek, she smoothed her thumb along his jaw. "But you trust me, Crash. And I promise, if he ever lays a hand on me in that way… I'll let you kill him."

Accepting the promise, Ryske bowed to touch his lips to hers.

In the moment they met, Penzance called out. "Hey!"

When they turned, he'd backed up to let the door hit him as someone came in, providing the couple a chance to separate. Ryske took his beer to the other end of the island. Harlow opened the fridge to retrieve another one as Penzance stepped forward to let Ophelia inside.

"Just what is going on in here?" the heiress

demanded, growling at Penzance, probably because he hindered her entrance.

"We're having an orgy, Fi, what does it look like?" Ryske asked, sauntering away from his place at the end of the island, acting like he'd been at that spot a while. "Wishing these two well with whatever the fuck is going on between them." When he got to Ophelia, he hooked an arm around her neck. "Come on, let's get this over with."

He took her out of the room, leaving Harlow alone with Penzance. She breathed out a sigh of relief. Ryske was appeased, and he'd control Ophelia, so they could all relax. At least, she could until spying Penzance.

Marching over to him, she thrust the beer at his stomach, then pinched his arm. "What the hell was that? '*Sure I would.*' Why would you say something like that?"

"Because I would," he said, aggravating her more. "Oh, untwist your panties, Har. He deserved it. He's so up his own ass."

"You hurt him."

That claim startled Penzance. For a minute, he didn't say anything. "I… what? No, I didn't."

"You fucked off out of his life. You abandoned him. You guys were close, right?"

"Yeah, but we've seen each other since. Our paths cross once in a while. It's not a big deal."

"That's what he wants you to think," she said, knowing better than to take Ryske at face value.

For a second, he blustered, then settled on a scowl. "How the hell do you know? I just told you what happened tonight."

"Because I know Ryske," she said. "A damn sight better than you ever did apparently." She took his arm. "Now let's get out there and get this over with. I'm ready for this night to be done."

Ophelia probably didn't have much on the agenda. The point had been for Ryske to stumble on her and Penzance, so Ophelia had achieved her goal.

Harlow was tired and didn't want to think about conniving any more tonight. She'd have to stay in game mode for just a little longer. Thankfully, Ryske was there. Without the strength his proximity gave her, she might not make it.

TWENTY-TWO

AS HARLOW EXPECTED, the "party" had been short.

The renovations Ophelia wanted were top of the agenda. She really pushed her ideas and crowed over the success of the changes she'd put in place. No one was enthusiastic. Though, that might have been because of the late hour.

Parratt changed the subject at the first opportunity. Arjan, their Pothos supplier, had the ability to increase supply if the consortium paid to have production facilities expanded. That meant more financial investment on all their parts.

Harlow listened and, as promised, voted against Ophelia both times. It just so happened that each of her votes coincided with Ryske's, which did not go unnoticed.

Once Ophelia's mood soured, she got snide with everyone. Not long after, people made their excuses to leave. Ryske was one of the first. Of course, Ophelia attempted to convince him to stay. Initially, she tried to be discreet with her request, probably because she didn't want to embarrass herself by begging. In the end, there was no other word to describe her pleading.

After Harlow changed out of his shirt, Penzance left too. In contrast to Ophelia's behavior with Ryske, Harlow struggled to muster the energy to appear disappointed while walking him to the door to say goodnight. Ophelia seemed to enjoy her boyfriend cutting out on her. The fact Harlow didn't give two shits about Ophelia's opinion meant it had little impact.

As soon as Penzance was gone, Harlow excused herself from the party. She went to her room, stripped off and climbed into bed. Sliding her hands beneath her pillow, she was surprised to feel something under there. A present. Ryske's underwear.

Smiling to herself, she pulled them on even though Penzance wasn't around. Her man had only excused himself for the restroom once. Now she knew why. He wanted her protected, even if he had to go commando to make it happen.

Vowing to wear his gift every night, Harlow went to sleep reveling in the positive memories of the evening, sidelining those that were not so great.

A renewed sense of purpose joined her through the rest of the week. She wanted to be home with her crew. That would only happen if she did what was necessary and kicked up her urgency. To get home, her mission had to be completed.

In her time under Ophelia's command, Harlow occasionally used the mistress's office computer. Without internet access, of course, Harlow was only allowed to type and such. During those times, she had done her best to access and copy company documents for Maze to analyze.

So far, those files hadn't turned up anything incriminating. They needed to hit closer to home, away from the legitimate businesses Ophelia was in the midst of selling. It was time to get personal.

Ophelia used the second bedroom of her apartment as an office. Gaining access wasn't easy. The door was locked and, in the beauty's apartment, Harlow was always in the company of someone, so sneaking in was near impossible.

Experience was starting to pay off. After living and working for Ophelia for five weeks, the woman's patterns were emerging. That was why she waited for the next Friday to come around before putting her plan into action.

One week after last seeing Ryske, she went through her normal Friday routine. Pressing Ophelia's clothes in Brash's apartment, under supervision. Preparing food for the weekend. Doing chores. Nothing special. Everything normal. Just going through the motions.

Friday morning was one of her favorite times because Ophelia spent it at the spa. The mistress would go out for lunch, then come home to approve, or reject, the clothes Harlow laid out for her. Those clothes were important, very important. Why? They were the ones the heiress would wear at Windsor's… for Ryske.

Every week, after apparel selection, Ophelia would go for a long nap. Getting some rest in the afternoon meant Ophelia could be up all night peddling Pothos.

Usually, after the dress was decided, Ophelia would call down to order whichever minion was in Brash's apartment to come retrieve Harlow. Today, she couldn't let that happen. Not that Friday. Not with the doctor in the house. Okay, so maybe he wasn't right there, but Bale was with her, in spirit, if not in body.

She heard Ophelia before seeing her. That day's minion didn't say much; she preferred them that way. Having hung the dresses on the presentation rail, Harlow told the minion she was going to fix herself a drink.

She'd just stirred the doctor's gift into the drink and washed the spoon to return it to the drawer when Ophelia came bursting into the kitchen.

"I'd say you can't get the staff these days, but you'd never understand," Ophelia declared, stopping to point at the glass Harlow was raising to her lips. "Is that my ice tea?"

"Yes, I was—"

Ophelia lunged forward and snatched the glass from her. "That is so rude, Harlow." The mistress looked left and right. "Where is your guard?"

"In the bedroom, I think."

Ophelia's mouth opened in a gasp of horror. "In the…"

Whirling around, Ophelia marched out of the kitchen. Just as Harlow's smile emerged, the boss poked her head back in.

She scrubbed her face clean. "Yes?"

"You," Ophelia said, still holding the glass. "Follow."

Ophelia disappeared, but she answered anyway. "Yes, mistress."

By the time Harlow had trailed through to the bedroom, Ophelia was reading the minion the riot act. "No, I don't want excuses. You get out of here! You don't work for me anymore! Fired is fired!" Ophelia glanced over her shoulder to watch Harlow enter, but quickly looked back to the minion. "You better leave without any trouble, or you'll have to meet my boyfriend. He's not the type of man you want to cross."

For a second, it looked like the guy considered arguing. But he gave it up and sagged, glowering her way as he plodded out of the bedroom.

Once he was gone, Ophelia sipped her drink and whirled toward the dresses. "Idiot. Why does Brash always hire idiots?"

Harlow wanted to answer it took one to know one; that wouldn't be appreciated. "You could let me do the hiring," she said only to be greeted by a dirty look.

A lot of that going around.

Ophelia drank and pondered the three dresses. "Which would you wear?"

Her? Huh. That was a new question.

Though she picked the dresses from the closet, she didn't contemplate wearing any of them. "Do I get to come tonight?"

"Are you insane? After the way you acted last week? I don't think so."

Exactly the response she expected.

While Ophelia was happy to order Penzance into Harlow's bedroom that first night, the boss hadn't loosened the chain and let them go out again.

To maintain the facade, she and Penzance spent a couple of nights hanging out and he'd slept over, with a wall of pillows between them, just in case.

She'd thought their fake relationship would make

passing notes easier, but Penzance already felt involved enough. He didn't want Floyd's phone number and wouldn't call even if he had it. He'd told her that straight out. She guessed Ryske had no way to get in touch with him, so doubted the men would be talking any time soon.

Svetlana could be the go-between, she'd gotten in touch with Penzance about the first Pothos night. She still didn't know why. Maybe the madam wanted more backup, or wanted a client she would enjoy.

Involving more people was dangerous. The six degrees of separation Ryske had once spoken of wasn't really required just for a simple message. Her crew preferred to keep the circle small anyway. So Harlow chose to work alone and hope her crew would be patient.

"Are you going to answer my question?" Ophelia asked, slipping off her shoes.

Given her boss was over halfway down her drink, she better answer quickly. How fast did the sedative work?

"The middle one," she said. Ophelia narrowed her eyes, suspicious. "The boyfriend you threatened that guy with… it was Ryske, right?"

It never hurt to make herself seem smaller or weaker than Ophelia. The woman would lap up this vulnerable side.

"Yes," Ophelia said.

"Have you… slept with him?"

"Tonight. He's coming home with me."

Ophelia said it with such conviction Harlow wished she'd pushed Penzance harder about passing messages. To be that confident, either Ophelia had a foolproof seduction plan… or Ryske had already agreed to perform for her.

Something drastic must've changed if Ryske was promising to sleep with Ophelia. She didn't like it. Was something wrong?

"Then you'll want to wear the second one," Harlow said, going over to finger the fabric. "He likes short."

Ryske would actually prefer either of the other two. The middle one was the shortest, yes, but the one on the end showed more cleavage and the closest one was sheer. Harlow would go braless with that one, her nipples would drive him nuts all night.

After this mess was over, she'd treat herself to a shopping spree.

Ophelia's yawn interrupted her thoughts.

The drink was finished. Harlow, playing the dutiful maid, took it from her.

"The red platform pumps will set it off," Harlow said, helping Ophelia toward the bed where the mistress was happy to lie down.

"No, the ivory," Ophelia said, laying her head on the pillow.

The ivory would wash out the silvery brocade, but she didn't speak up. Her job was to do as she was told. Ophelia rolled onto her side, eyes already closed, reaching for the phone.

Sitting on the edge of the bed, Harlow intercepted her hand, taking it onto her lap in a friendly gesture. "And diamonds for your accessories, or would you like some color?"

"Diamonds are classic," Ophelia mumbled just before going limp.

The mistress was on her side, breathing even, no concerns about her aspirating. Waiting a moment, she stroked Ophelia's hand, giving her time to drift deeper into sleep. After a minute, she put her hand on the bed and stood up to put away the dresses Ophelia didn't want.

Next was the task of laying out everything the heiress would need for that night, right down to her underwear. Makeup on the vanity, perfume, accessories, everything, she then hung up a robe next to Ophelia's bed.

Everything was just as it should be. If all went well, she'd be out of there and back downstairs before Ophelia woke up. Her boss should just think she'd taken her nap as normal.

She backed out of the bedroom to fetch the office key from its hidey-hole in the kitchen.

The office door opened without any issues and almost silently, not that there was anyone else around to hear it.

Despite the potential risk to her life, she wasn't scared. Ophelia could wake up and snap. What that could mean for her was less important than what would happen to Ryske if she lost her life.

If at any point her life was in danger, she would flee. Leaving would give Ophelia a chance to calm down. After that, if necessary, she'd consider coming back. Risking Ryske just wasn't worth embracing a violent confrontation.

The woman's office was a room equivalent in size to Harlow's bedroom. The c-shaped desk had dainty legs and a desktop computer in the center. There was paperwork in an in-tray and a long drawer underneath containing nothing but stationery.

Harlow was careful not to move anything from its place as she checked the drawer and the in-tray. When she came up with nothing except legitimate paperwork, next up was the computer's welcome screen. It didn't take many guesses to figure out the password was "Ryske'sgrl." As soon as she was in, she plugged the USB into the main terminal to copy all the files.

Knowing that would take time, she searched the filing cabinets for anything useful.

Nothing. Nothing. Nothing. No eureka moment. The USB's progress bar was almost full. She'd been in the office for almost an hour and all she had were invoices, receipts and correspondence for valid transactions with legitimate businesses.

Illegal wasn't essential, she just had to find something that would work for them. Something they could exploit to scare Ophelia off.

Shelving units on the side wall and behind the door were filled with knickknacks. She searched under them and inside, finding that Ophelia wasn't unlike her parents. One of the items had money stashed inside. Granted, there was around a thousand bucks, ten times what her parents had in there, but still, it was good to know.

Inside a padded silk box on the top shelf was what appeared to be a journal filled with Ophelia's ramblings. It might be useful, but she couldn't swipe it; Ophelia might notice that. But if she had the chance, she'd come back and take it before she left.

Returning everything to where it should be, she grabbed the USB to tuck it into her cleavage. Infuriated and frustrated, she considered picking up the phone or sending an email but dismissed the idea. Just because she got nothing didn't mean she should be careless about leaving a trail.

Damn, she'd been so sure she'd find something. So sure. And…

No point in her sticking around to—huh… the heavy drape sat at an odd angle. There was no furniture over there. Something was on the floor; something almost the same color as the vast piece of fabric.

Going over, she moved the drape aside with her foot and gasped at the revelation of a file box tucked behind it. Dropping down, she pulled off the lid. What was it? And why was it separate?

Everything else in the room was neat and in its place. That box had been hidden in the folds of the drape. Either Ophelia thought it would never be found or she had kicked it there in frustration to get it out of her sight.

The more Harlow looked through the items inside, the more she believed it was the latter. These were Jarvis Hagan's things. The man murdered by his own sister, Ophelia.

On top were pictures, both in frames and loose, of the siblings growing up. Some, she assumed, were from school. A couple in other snaps, she guessed, were the Hagan parents. Beneath the pictures was a bottle of cologne and some other junk.

Scent could fire such clear memories. The look on his face, the sound of him hitting the floor, the lack of a pulse when she…

Shrugging off her emotion, she got past the pictures and down to the papers. To her surprise, a bundle of love letters wrapped in a ribbon sat in a corner. It didn't take long to establish they'd been written between the Hagan parents both before and after their children were born when Hagan Senior was traveling for business.

Some were an early generation of sexting and kind of

hot. If she got out of this, she'd write Ryske a sexy letter. A smile contorted her lips at the thought of him innocently opening it only to realize what it was as he read. No laughing. Quiet. She had to be quiet. It would be quite a sight to see him standing in the kitchen, talking to the guys about some BS, opening a letter and...

Once the laugh left her lips, she put the letters away to focus on her work. It wasn't the time to think about sex.

When she met Ryske, he'd told her he was always thinking about sex with her. Turned out to be contagious; the idea of being intimate with Ryske was never far from her thoughts. It could just be that he'd reawakened her need last Friday. The previous week had been tougher to get through than the ones before. All she wanted to do was crawl inside her man and live there forever more.

Before losing her liberty to Ophelia, Harlow discussed with Ryske how their love could be detrimental to other people. They loved each other so much that they would sacrifice anyone and anything to keep each other safe and free.

She didn't know if she'd broken up with him, but she'd definitely put a question mark over their future. With them, that didn't matter. While she'd been at Ophelia's, just like when she'd been in jail, he'd been with her, in her heart, whether they could be together or not.

Her mind wandered as she leafed through the receipts and papers in Hagan's box. Nothing drew her eye, not until she started to put everything back in order. Something fluttered out from between two stapled pages. A receipt.

A receipt bearing a familiar logo.

"SweSec," she whispered, brushing her fingertips over the name of her father's company.

The name and address on the receipt belonged to Jarvis Hagan. The rest of it was just numbers and letters. Even though it was her family's company, she wasn't privy to their inner workings and had no idea what the codes meant.

Wishing she'd paid more attention when Rupert and her father talked, she also cursed data protection and personal security. Those were the reason for this use of codes rather than explicit terms. It meant if people, like her, saw something they weren't supposed to, it still wouldn't make sense.

She sat peering at it for the longest time. Staring wouldn't cause the numbers to magically make sense. Packing everything away, she slid the box back into its hiding spot, using the dent in the carpet as a guide.

Optimism. Yes. She stood and gave the room a once over to ensure nothing was out of place. Everything was as it should've been, so she left and locked the door. After checking on Ophelia and secreting the key back where it belonged, she washed and dried the ice-tea glass. Once it was back in the kitchen cabinet, all evidence of what she'd done was gone.

Ryske returned to her thoughts. Would he be proud?

Tempting as it was to cut and run while she had her freedom, she remained dutiful in slipping out of Ophelia's and returning to the apartment downstairs. She avoided Brash's minions in the kitchen and went into her bedroom to kick off her shoes.

With the USB back in its slot, everything was as it should be. She climbed into her bed, ready to wait. Ophelia would call when she woke up. She just hoped it was to prepare for the night and not to ask what happened.

With SweSec in her mind, Harlow closed her eyes, trying to figure out how she could contact Rupert without Ophelia knowing. It was Friday. SweSec would be closed for the weekend, so she had the next two days to come up with a plan.

Going to her parents wasn't an option. It was too far and would take too much time. Her mind was on overdrive. There would be a way to sneak out. There had to be. She just had to figure it out.

TWENTY-THREE

WHEN OPHELIA CALLED down to summon her, she said nothing about the way she'd fallen asleep and didn't ask how Harlow got back to Brash's. Ophelia must've chosen to gloss over the haze of pre-naptime, maybe out of embarrassment, or it could just be ignorance.

Their usual routine continued. Harlow was escorted to Ophelia's apartment to help her get ready for her night at Windsor's. She listened to Ophelia wax lyrical about how wonderful the night would be. The singing in the shower was an unusual touch. Ophelia displayed a disturbing level of happiness.

Still, she kept her mouth shut and waved Ophelia off with a smile… figuratively speaking.

Just after one a.m., Harlow got a call to go to Ophelia's apartment.

Her craving to see Ryske was at its usual high. Despite that, she dreaded what view may await her. If she walked into Ophelia's bedroom and found the couple naked in bed, there was a good chance she'd have a fit. She didn't rate her ability to keep her cool at witnessing such a horrific sight. It was more likely she'd just vomit right there on the carpet.

Her escort stayed in the open elevator door, watching

her, as he always would, until she went inside. Fearing a scene of seduction, she steeled herself. Would it be Ryske on the couch lit by candles? Maybe a bearskin rug on the floor? Okay, yeah, that was unlikely, but her imagination wasn't playing nice.

With her breath held, she opened the door only to be faced with a far different sight.

Ophelia was pacing up and down in front of the fireplace exuding grief and anger. Penzance sat in the middle of the couch.

Striding across the room, Harlow's alarm level skyrocketed. "What's going on?" she asked Penzance, stopping at the end of the couch, keeping an eye on Ophelia.

Her boss was the one to respond. "I am going to shoot something, I swear I will."

If anyone else said that, Harlow would assume they were exaggerating. With Ophelia, that wouldn't be a safe assumption.

"I don't—"

"He didn't show," Penzance explained. "Maze covered for Ryske tonight."

"He wasn't there?" she asked, skirting the end table to sit by Penzance. "At all?"

"Maze told us Ryske wasn't going to show. Miss Hagan stayed, just in case."

Obviously, Ophelia's stamina ran out. She was home much earlier than normal.

"Did Maze say where Ryske was?"

A part of her wanted to do a happy dance. Ryske must've known Ophelia was going to push her agenda hard this week. Transfer of ownership of the club would be imminent. Was Ophelia questioning her usefulness? The crux of Ophelia's plan involved getting Ryske's attention by being a savvy businesswoman willing to take risks.

Losing the club in the card game hadn't mattered so early in the plan. Now all these weeks had passed and she still wasn't with him, Ophelia had to be pondering what Ryske's ownership of Windsor's would mean for her. Sure, it was insignificant which of them owned the club if they were together. If they weren't, it made a huge difference. Ophelia hadn't banked on failing.

Confident Miss Hagan had believed that Ryske would be hers before ownership transferred. With a fixation on her plot to nab Harlow, she hadn't considered what would happen if her plan failed.

Maybe that's what they were witnessing. The acceptance of reality. If Ophelia was talking about shooting people, she hadn't come to any encouraging conclusions.

"He could be sick," Harlow said.

Even if Ryske was struck down with flu, she wasn't worried. Sure, she'd like to play nursemaid, but with the way his libido responded to her, it was probably best she wasn't around to exacerbate him.

If there was anything more serious wrong with him, the doctor would patch him up. In the eventuality anything serious worried Bale, he'd get word to her, one way or another, no doubt.

Ophelia stopped pacing and thrust her fists to her hips. "Why wouldn't he have sent me a message?"

"What did Maze say?"

"Rowe? That idiot wouldn't say a word, just that we got him instead. What is that? Ryske can't send a ringer. That's insane. It's not allowed."

Allowed? Ryske trusted Maze. Ophelia might not understand how much, but it should be apparent given Ryske made it clear Svetlana and her girls were to be protected. He wouldn't send someone in his stead who'd give any less to their protection than he would.

"It's just one week," Harlow said, sliding deeper into the couch. "I guess he's got other business interests that probably need his attention too."

"Other business interests or other women?" Ophelia let that hang for a minute. "Anwen wasn't there either."

"Anwen wasn't there last week, was she?" Harlow said.

Why hadn't she bothered to find out the reason for that?

"Because I told her not to come," Ophelia said. Ah,

that was an answer. "With the practice we've had, we're more efficient. We don't need much support."

Or because Ophelia was threatened by the woman's proximity to Ryske since learning they were sleeping together again. Apparently. Maybe Ophelia noticed the bracelet on Anwen's wrist and was all kinds of riled by it.

"Did you tell her not to come this week too?" Harlow asked. "Maybe she thought it was an indefinite disinvite. You can be quite harsh, Ophelia. Maybe you hurt her feelings."

Anwen hadn't been around Ophelia's that week. That didn't mean the women hadn't seen, or spoken to, each other. Most days, Ophelia was out and about and made several calls. Harlow didn't track her every move.

The request she'd made to her crew about removing Anwen from the apartment could be the explanation. She'd asked them to be subtle about it. Maybe this was a sign they'd chosen to move on her plea. Except, why would evicting Anwen lead to Ryske not being at Windsor's?

"I didn't hurt her feelings," Ophelia said. "They've run off together or something. They're on some vacation. Off enjoying each other, leaving the rest of us to do their work!"

Pacing again, Ophelia's rage boiled. Even though she shouldn't, Harlow showed Penzance a smile, surprising him.

"You're okay with that?" he asked.

"That Ryske and Anwen are on vacation together?" Harlow asked. "Why wouldn't I be… lover?"

Uh, had he forgotten they were supposed to be screwing around?

"Just checking," he said, covering for his question.

Harlow sucked in a breath. "Now that mystery is solved, I guess it's time for bed," she said and stood up again. "Would you like to shower before bed, Ophe or skip it? Guess you don't need it if you're not getting laid."

Was she playing it smug? Playing with fire more like. Lucky that Angry Ophelia had selective hearing.

"Bed? How can you think about bed?" Ophelia snapped. "We have to do something about this."

Harlow shouldn't have laughed, but she did. It was automatic, so not her fault.

Ophelia stopped to blink at her.

"I'm sorry," Harlow said. "But what's your plan? Even if you could find out where they are, do you think showing up and walking in on them will make him want you? If Ryske's getting some and Anwen's happy, you'll only look like a crazy person injecting yourself into their bliss."

"A crazy person! A crazy person?"

"She's right," Penzance said. "You've gotta eat this one, Miss Hagan. Wherever he is and whatever he's doing, you're not invited." Standing up, Penzance slid an arm around her shoulders to pull her close. "Want to invite me downstairs, lover?"

Excellent idea. Penzance might know more than he was revealing to Ophelia.

Harlow nodded. "Sure, come on."

They barely got one step before Ophelia leaped forward. "I don't think so! I make the rules around here and no one is spending the night with anyone!"

"I don't need to spend the night," Penzance said, squeezing Harlow's shoulder. "I can be done in a half hour."

Wham, bam, indeed.

Harlow drove an elbow into his ribs. "You'll need at least an hour, or I'm not wasting my time."

"I think I can stretch to that," Penzance said, dipping to kiss her cheek.

"I said no," Ophelia said. "No. No. No! Vane leave. Go home. Don't come back until you're summoned."

Uh oh. Harlow didn't say it out loud, but she didn't like the prospect of Penzance being expelled. Judging by his expression, he felt the same.

"What if he hears from Ryske?" Harlow asked, attempting to sway the jailor.

"If he hears from him, he can call me," Ophelia said, raising her chin to peer down her nose. "I doubt Ryske will be in touch with him before he contacts me. I will be calling Ryske myself. As soon as he knows I am upset, he will be at my side."

She shouldn't hold her breath; except Ophelia was deluded enough to believe her ramblings. If after all this time, she wasn't getting the hint Ryske didn't want her, she was gullible enough to believe anything. There was no underestimating the lengths she'd go to either. Ophelia could choose to dangle her minion's safety in front of him, Ryske knew she was a killer. It would betray the truth of their feelings if he rushed over there to save his ex, but what else could he do? He would do anything to keep her safe.

"Then there's nothing to worry about," Harlow said and tried to tug Penzance with her. "Bed time, baby."

Ophelia dashed over and actually pulled the couple apart. "You will not be having sex tonight, Harlow."

If Ophelia wasn't getting any, she didn't want anyone else getting any either. Anyone she had control of anyway. Frustrating as hell attitude. Not for the sex part, that didn't register, she hadn't expected to get laid tonight. But Harlow needed time alone with Penzance to find out if he knew anything.

Penzance had refused to pass messages for her. It was possible Maze was more persuasive or that something dire had happened to cause Penzance to make an exception. They were out of luck. Ophelia was adamant about separating them and took Penzance's arm to drag him toward the door.

"Come on. Really?" Penzance asked, letting himself be led. "If she can't have sex, I can't have sex."

"You're not faithful to her," Ophelia said. "I officially release you from your bond of faithfulness." Opening the front door, Ophelia shoved him out. "Go and cheat on her." She slammed the door, then turned to storm back into the living room. "Ryske would not stand me up."

As usual, it was all about Ophelia… which meant it was all about Ryske. Penzance was forgotten.

"Did you have a date with him planned?" Harlow asked, giving in to the inevitable, Ophelia wanted to rant.

"Every Friday is our date."

"Oh," Harlow said because she hadn't known Ophelia felt that way.

It had to be in Ophelia's head. The idea of Ryske setting a date night quirked her lips. Maybe he had implied to Ophelia he had a different day for different women

"Yes," Ophelia said and pushed Harlow toward the couch again.

She sat down. "But didn't you just say he was off on vacation with Anwen?"

"Maybe he is. Maybe she persuaded him to do something he didn't want to do. You know what she's like. Maybe she blackmailed him."

Ophelia sat down and rested an arm on the back of the couch, eyes moving around like she was speculating. Harlow was too busy losing her own smile to worry about what was in Ophelia's head. Yes, she did know what Anwen was like. She kicked herself for not thinking about it when making demands.

Anwen had blackmailed Ryske into her bed; that's how their affair started. Anwen had valuable information that could hurt Ryske and her too. It was possible Anwen found the murder weapon or the recording before Dover could move them, or maybe she was just taking a chance and had threatened Ryske with the law.

Any number of scenarios rushed through her mind. The possibilities were serious, possibly grave. Anwen blackmailing Ryske into her bed would be bad enough, but that was a better prospect than other things she might have demanded he do. Maybe she'd forced him to go somewhere or to commit a crime that could lead to serious trouble.

In his current mood, with the trajectory of his reckless behavior, Ryske had proved he wasn't thinking straight. It could be that he'd gone too far in doing her bidding. Maybe he was in a police cell.

So much for being sure Bale would get to her if her guy was near death. What if Ryske was already gone? If it happened fast, no one would have time to get to her. Given where she was, her purpose, the guys could've decided not to tell her anything.

Fear became panic. Although she knew Ophelia was talking, Harlow couldn't hear her. Maze. If something happened to Ryske, Maze wouldn't have been handing out Pothos like everything was normal, would he?

Jumping to the worst conclusion was easy. Calming herself was harder. Have faith in the crew like they had faith in her, that's what she had to do. They were out there looking after Ryske. All she could do was trust her love was safe.

If he wasn't, then the worst had already happened. If she got confirmation of that, she'd know how to act.

"You aren't even listening," Ophelia said, lunging forward to jab Harlow's shoulder. "Listen to me!"

"I can't tell you where he is, Ophelia," Harlow snapped. "I'm here! I'm not out there! You have access that I don't... I'm not psychic! I don't know where he is or who he's fucking! I don't know if he's dead or alive! I can't confirm anything for you!"

Apparently, she hadn't succeeded in calming herself as much as she thought. Although she'd shouted, Ophelia wasn't mad and drew a line back and forth on the fabric of the couch.

Probably because the devious mare's mind was elsewhere. "You have access to his people... You could have access..."

The reason for her summoning became clear. Rising to her feet, Harlow flattened her skirt over her thighs.

"There's not a chance in hell I'd use any of my connections to help you," she said, finding her composure. "I sure won't do it just because you're horny... This is your obsession, Ophelia. Your vendetta. Ryske is your fetish."

"He was yours once too."

"Mine?" Harlow said, letting her features relax. "Yes, that's right. He was mine. In a way you'll never understand."

Harlow was too tired to play this game so headed for the door.

Ophelia leaped up to chase after her. "Where are you going? We have to figure this out."

Without hesitating, she opened the front door. "I'm going to bed, Ophelia. You want to sit up all night mooning, you do it. I won't be a part of it."

Asserting herself clearly stunned the heiress who'd worked so hard to break her. That was fine. The gaping gave Harlow the opportunity to make her exit without having to combat further arguments. She had her own worries about Ryske and his safety. The last thing she wanted to do was listen to Ophelia like the woman had some right to fret.

Hadn't she asked Ryske to trust she could look after herself? Paying him the same courtesy was the least she could do. That didn't mean she wouldn't worry. She just had to keep reminding herself of her faith in him. Whatever he was going through, Ryske could handle it.

TWENTY-FOUR

OPHELIA'S MOOD ONLY worsened as the weekend went on. By Monday, Harlow had been relegated to her room and told to stay there. She didn't mind being punished by imprisonment. At least it saved her from listening to Ophelia's paranoid ranting.

Ryske hadn't called Ophelia. Big surprise. He hadn't been in touch with any of the consortium. Ophelia was being vigilant about asking on a regular basis. So far, no one had owned up to hearing from him.

Her staff were the ones to suffer as her anger built. Barking orders and slinging insults, Ophelia was alienating people left and right. Even Brash was at the end of his patience. Harlow heard him griping to one of his minion buddies about their boss. His attitude stank all the time, so Harlow was pleased that in her prison, she got to avoid him too.

All through Monday, she tried to figure out how she might get to SweSec to begin making sense of the receipt she'd found. Problem was, with Ophelia in such a bad mood, it wasn't likely that the mistress would be granting any respite any time soon.

Penzance hadn't been allowed to visit. Harlow asked

for him over the weekend. Their fake relationship gave her a reason to request time with him. Ophelia thought she wanted to get laid. In truth, Harlow only wanted information.

Ophelia was blind to everything that wasn't Ryske. Her need for him seemed to be growing to a fever pitch. In some ways, Harlow could identify. A tiny part of her actually felt sorry for the woman.

Killing her brother, involving herself in the illegal Pothos operation, everything Ophelia had done was intended to win Ryske's favor. She'd had her own best friend beaten, only to bury her resentment of the woman believing it would gain her points with the object of her affection.

Ophelia had orchestrated separating her from Ryske. Although it worked, Ophelia still had to look at the face of a woman who'd had Ryske's love. That couldn't be an easy pill to swallow.

Harlow missed Ryske. Lying on her bed on Tuesday, she gave herself a break from thinking about SweSec and Jarvis Hagan to let thoughts of the man she loved seep in. Their relationship hadn't been smooth sailing. They were both volatile. There was always a chance of them pushing each other's buttons. But she'd do anything for him. Anything in the world.

Did that make her much different from Ophelia or Anwen? Harlow was the lucky one, she had Ryske's love. But if he hadn't fallen for her, would she too be concocting strategies to win him and coming up with ruses that forced them to spend time together?

She was still thinking about him when her bedroom door opened and Brash came in. Sitting up, Harlow was quick to leap off the bed. She wasn't going to give him any opportunity to take advantage of the moment.

"Ophelia wants you upstairs," he said, without venturing further into the room. "Me and the guys are going out, so move."

Good, if he was going out, she didn't have to worry about his mood. Though, it did mean being stuck with Ophelia. Brash stormed out of the bedroom and she grabbed her shoes before running out after him.

Given it was late on a Tuesday afternoon, Harlow expected she'd have to get Ophelia ready for a dinner date or something. After not seeing the woman for almost two days, she was sorry to have to deal with her again.

On the elevator ride up, Harlow wondered if she should've grabbed the other pack of Bale's sedatives. Brash was going out, so she could use them on Ophelia again. Except he'd warned her about the different dosages. The last thing she wanted to do was kill Ophelia and make Bale an accessory to the crime.

At the beginning of her relationship with the doctor, Harlow had promised to keep his association with Ryske's crew a secret. At the time, she hadn't known the truth of that association—that the two men were brothers. Knowing the truth only heightened her need to protect him and all the men on her crew.

Taking a breath as she departed the elevator, she told herself to keep her cool no matter what Ophelia said. Even if she was mean or rude, she wouldn't rise to the bait.

The living room was empty. She took her time about going through the apartment, delaying the moment she'd have to deal with Ophelia again. It came when she opened the bedroom door and found Ophelia seated on the edge of her bed, bent over, buckling a sandal.

"Oh, good, you're here," Ophelia said, more jovial than she'd been since before Friday night. "And you're dressed."

Harlow didn't make a habit of wandering around naked. Given that her nighttime attire consisted of Ryske's underwear, and nothing else, she didn't tend to walk around in pajamas either.

"I am dressed," Harlow said. "Are we going somewhere?"

An excursion could work out for her. If Ophelia wanted to go somewhere in the city, Harlow could find an excuse to slip off, or even a moment when Ophelia was distracted. She could go to SweSec and work fast. If Ophelia noticed her missing, Harlow could make some excuse about being separated and meeting back at the apartment. All she'd have to do was ensure to be back in the building before Ophelia returned.

"Yes," Ophelia said, bouncing up off the bed. "You're going to take me to him."

That statement stalled her optimistic planning. "I'm going to take you to… who?"

Widening her smile, Ophelia came over to lay her hands on Harlow's shoulders. "You're going to take me to Ryske."

Standing in front of Ophelia, absorbing her mistress's glee and anticipation, Harlow waited for the punchline.

When Ophelia didn't come up with one, Harlow smiled and laughed. "I'm sorry, I thought that was a joke. Obviously, I misunderstood what you said. Say it again, explain it to me."

The tension in Ophelia's jaw betrayed her true feelings. She masked her anger by widening her smile. She was asking for something after all; why hurt the person whose help she needed?

"You know where he lives."

"So do you," Harlow said.

It didn't matter that it hadn't been acknowledged. By now, Harlow had no doubt Ophelia knew about Floyd's. If Animal hadn't told her, Anwen would have. It would've earned beaucoup brownie points and cemented her attempts to reconcile the friendship.

"That may be, or not," Ophelia said. Playing coy might work for her with others, but Harlow wasn't buying it. "You know the way in."

"Oh, you want the entrance to the bat cave," Harlow said, folding her arms. "I think I've forgotten the secret code… Yeah, it's definitely slipped my mind."

Breathing out, Ophelia seemed more confident than she should. "We both know you have no choice. You might as well just do it. Ryske is out there somewhere; he may be hurt or need help. He hasn't returned any of my messages. I just don't believe he'd do that to me without good reason."

"Maybe the good reason is he's not interested."

"Or maybe he's in trouble. Maybe Anwen is hurting

him… I know you must be devastated about losing him." Cupping Harlow's face with a condescending hand, Ophelia pushed out her lower lip, pouting in apparent sympathy. "But you did care for him once, didn't you? You can't be happy to know she's manipulating him."

"How is her manipulating him any different from you doing it?" Harlow asked, forgetting what she'd thought outside about keeping her cool.

Ophelia actually had the audacity to appear taken aback. "I… I don't manipulate him."

"He doesn't love you," Harlow said. "Shit, Ophelia, if you had the first clue what he's like when he's in love, you would know that what he is with you isn't it. I'm sorry. I am. I know you really want him to feel for you, but he doesn't." Pushing Ophelia's hands away, she stepped back and clasped her own hands to her chest. "You are a tenacious woman, I will give you that. But you cannot make him fall in love with you."

Offense crackled around Ophelia whose expression tightened. "You don't know. You don't have any idea what we are. You don't know what he says to me in private. You don't know how he touches me."

Raising her brows and her hands, Harlow took one step back. "And I don't want to. But I do know that if he loved you, he would've returned your messages. If he wanted to be with you, or he cared about you, he would never leave you hanging."

Though, she had to admit, she was sort of swinging in the wind at the moment, which contradicted that statement. Still, if Harlow got in touch with Ryske's messaging service, or called the cell number that only she had, he'd pick up. Even in a scenario where he didn't have the phone, he'd find a way to get in touch with her if she reached out.

Ophelia had been calling since Friday night and it was now Tuesday. In that time, Ryske hadn't offered her a crumb of reassurance.

Blinking and maybe a little stunned, Ophelia didn't react for a score of seconds. Eventually, she smiled. "I understand… You're jealous."

"Oh, God," Harlow said, driving her fingers through her hair and giving in by throwing up her arms. "Okay, yes, Ophelia, I'm jealous. I'm crazy out of my mind jealous… Do you think that will make me more or less likely to bring the two of you together?"

"Like I said, you don't have a choice. You will take me to his home."

Ophelia began to cross the bedroom, but Harlow didn't move. "No, I won't." Ophelia stopped. "If you want to go there, you can. You can show up. You won't get in." Because the building would be locked. "You can go and make a fool of yourself, screaming at the windows. I wouldn't recommend it, but I can't stop you… Though, I can tell you Ryske won't take kindly to anyone invading his space like that."

"I'm a concerned friend. It's not an invasion."

"Says you," Harlow said. "Did he give you his address himself? Did he invite you over? If the answer to either of those is no, I'd say it's a mistake to interrupt his life."

Ophelia whirled around to stalk over, her amiable façade disintegrating. "Did he invite you into his home? Did he give you his address? No! You injected yourself into his life!"

For some reason, seeing the woman frayed had a calming effect. "Ryske did take me to his home. He invited me into his life. From that moment, he's refused to let me out of it."

Ophelia took a chance to sneer. "Until I put a stop to that."

"Did you, Ophe?" she asked and leaned in closer when she whispered. "How sure are you about that?"

Letting out a long growl, Ophelia snapped and brought her hand around to slap Harlow's cheek. The stinging pain watered her eye, but the hit was the wake-up call Harlow needed.

Like she'd been wrenched out of a haze, Harlow stepped back and made her own move. Instead of a slap, she threw a punch, just like Costello had taught her. One that sent Ophelia flying to the floor.

The sprawled woman didn't move. After panting through her surprise, Harlow went to check for a pulse. Ophelia was alive but unconscious.

One second to decide, that's all she had. Stay or leave. She needed to get to SweSec. Passing up this opportunity would be insane. And that was her decision made.

Running through to the kitchen, she grabbed the key for the office and seized both Ophelia's journal and the SweSec receipt from the secret box. She also swiped the money that she'd discovered, just for incidentals.

By the time she locked the office, there was groaning coming from the bedroom. Time was running short. Putting the key back, she left Ophelia's apartment and ran down the stairs, thankful Brash and the others were out. Even if Ophelia regained her wits, she'd have no one to call for help. No one who could prevent Harlow from leaving.

Grabbing an empty sports bag from Brash's closet, Harlow went to her bedroom and stuffed all of her things into it, leaving nothing behind. Depending on what happened at SweSec, she might have to come back, but there was an equal chance that she wouldn't.

Her evidence, her drugs, the clothes she'd acquired or been gifted, they could all be important. She wouldn't take the chance of forgetting anything.

TWENTY-FIVE

HARLOW'S MIND RACED with the fear of being intercepted by Ophelia. Fueled by potent adrenaline, her heart hammered faster than it needed to as she departed the apartment building. Facing the woman one on one wasn't a problem, as she'd already proved. But Harlow didn't know if the doormen were in her mistress's pocket or if there were other security men nearby. A gang wouldn't be so easy to take on by herself.

Ophelia wouldn't care what lengths her men had to go to. If Harlow had to be dragged back kicking and screaming, bruised and bloody, Ophelia wouldn't hesitate to issue those orders.

Relief came when the fresh air and daylight flooded her. Even though she'd made it out, Harlow kept her head down and walked fast, aware she could still be spotted. If any of Ophelia's people saw her, they would know she wasn't supposed to be alone and might try to subdue her for brownie points.

With every step she took, she relaxed a little more. By the time she got to SweSec, she was almost giddy. Freedom had never felt so good. Never. Not even after jail. It was important to hold onto the truth that she may not be completely home free. Don't get too excited; it wasn't over yet. If it came to it, Harlow would return to Ophelia's.

Only the need of her crew, or disrupting Ryske's claim to the club, would take her back. Ryske's claim should be legal some time that week, so she couldn't see how it could be stopped or reversed just because Ophelia had a hissy fit.

Going back wasn't a tempting prospect. When being there had a purpose, she could suck it up. But she'd searched every place Ophelia could be stashing anything. Windsor's was almost Ryske's. There was no point to Harlow being at Ophelia's any more.

The SweSec receipt was her last hope. Finding a link to her family in a box of Hagan's possessions was significant. Jarvis Hagan had been at a SweSec function, so she knew that he was aware of the company. But Harlow was ignorant to any business dealings between her father and Hagan.

SweSec was a sanctuary. Harlow had never been so pleased to see the place. The sight of bustling people in the familiarity warmed her. Life had gone on, as it always did, and there was comfort in that.

Harlow knew SweSec like the back of her hand and didn't hesitate to head straight for Rupert's office. His door was open. She tapped a knuckle on it, drawing his attention up from his work.

"Harlow!"

She didn't blame him for taking a second to recognize her, it had been a while. "Hi," she said, moving into the office. "I hope this isn't a bad time."

"No," Rupert said, leaping up from the desk to rush over and greet her, giving her a hug and a kiss. "No, of course not. Wow, it's amazing to see you." With an arm around her, he guided her over to the chair at his desk and sat her down. "Ryske said you were sick… How are you feeling?"

"Oh, I'm over it now," she said, sitting down and holding her bag on her lap while he went around to his side of the desk to seat himself.

Rupert glanced at the door again. "Is he with you?"

"Ryske? No," she said and shook her head. "He's… elsewhere today." Doing what, she had no idea, but he was definitely elsewhere. "How are things? How's Lena?"

"Good," he said, linking his fingers and bobbing his head. "She's really good. Up to her eyeballs in wedding stuff. It's a lot… I thought it was a lot when we did it, but… wow… Things are moving fast."

It wasn't a lot when they did it because her heart hadn't been in it. Harlow had been eager to slow things down as much as possible. Lena was pregnant and no doubt eager to get the wedding planned. With both mother and mother-in-law helping her out, it was probably like a runaway train.

"At least you have plenty of help," Harlow said. "I'm sorry I haven't been around."

He blew out a dismissive breath. "Oh, don't worry. You have been ill; you can't help that." That wasn't exactly true. She didn't like being dishonest, but the truth would be near impossible to explain. Rupert didn't need that burden on his shoulders, not with everything else he had going on. "I did think that maybe Ryske was misleading us… It's not like you to be out of contact for so long."

Misleading them like she'd run off with another man or that he'd slaughtered her and buried her body? Rupert and Ryske weren't the best of friends, so his suspicion was almost expected. She could be offended and demand an apology, but she was about to ask a favor. Ophelia's tack of being amiable seemed the smarter choice.

"I know, I'm sorry. It was awful. Ryske looked after me though, and he can always speak for me on family things. He kept me in the loop."

His smile thinned, but at least it stayed. That was a sign of progress. Rupert was biting his tongue; an improvement over him leaping on the defensive or telling her what to do. Maybe fatherhood, even on its approach, was having a calming effect on him.

"He does seem to be making an effort with the family."

"He is," she said. "It means a lot to me that you all make the effort to include him too." Discussions of her current relationship weren't what brought her to SweSec, but she had to ease in. "And how is my little niece or nephew?"

His smile grew and he leaned back to open a drawer. "Lena knows the gender, but she won't tell anyone. She says she wants it to be a surprise."

Retrieving a small rectangle, he passed it over the desk. Harlow gasped when she saw a more recent scan picture.

"Oh my God," she said, tears springing to her eyes. "Oh, look how big he's gotten... or she."

"Mother and baby are both healthy."

Touching her chest, she smiled at him and examined the picture some more. "Rupe, I am happy for you... This is what you wanted."

Though she didn't really want to, Harlow returned the picture.

He slipped it back into his drawer. "It is... I'm lucky."

His tone made it obvious that the situation wasn't quite what he wanted it to be. That probably had more to do with the way it happened.

"Are you happy, Rupert?" she asked, looking into him. "Seriously, I want to know. Are you happy?"

He thought for a second and then flattened his hands on the desk. "I think so... It's a lot right now," he said. She nodded in understanding. "With the wedding... Oh, and we sold the apartment, so we're staying with your parents at the moment... It's just... constant. There isn't much time to breathe. But... I'm not unhappy and..." His gaze drifted toward the drawer. "There is going to be a prize at the end of the trial."

It made her happy to see him happy. She could understand that it was stressful. Getting married, moving, and having a baby, were stressful things to deal with at the best of times. Rupert was handling all three at once.

Their mothers could be intense, and with Lena in the mix, the poor guy probably wasn't getting a break.

"I know you're going to do great. I know it... I can't wait to meet your little one."

He seemed to appreciate her support.

After a moment of eye contact, he leaned back and straightened up. "Maybe you and Ryske will be next?"

"For which? Marriage, moving, or babies?" she asked.

"It's unlikely to be any of the three any time soon. But you never know, I keep him on his toes."

Rupert's eyebrows moved. "Yes, it's something you do well."

It was nice that they could laugh and tease. There had been a time she'd feared they'd never get their rapport back.

"So…" she said, opening her bag to take out the slip of paper she'd swiped from Ophelia's office. "I was wondering if you could help me out."

"Oh," he said, closing the drawer and pulling himself against the desk again. Holding the receipt toward him, Harlow noted the curiosity in his frown. He read it. "Where did you get this?"

"From a friend," she said. "I was hoping you could help me, you know, figure it out."

He sighed. "I can't discuss clients' accounts with you, Harlow. I can't discuss them with anyone who doesn't have authorization."

Rupert was by the book. He was unlikely to change his mind on following the rules, where work was concerned anyway. At home, in his personal life, when it came to sex, she'd learned he was a little more flexible.

"I know that… Maybe we could talk in broad terms…" Her hopeful smile was greeted by his slow head tilt. "You know… you could tell me, in a general way, what those numbers mean…"

"Yes," he said, putting down the receipt and turning his computer screen away from her before beginning to type. "But you knew Jarvis Hagan."

His name was on the receipt, it wasn't a breach to tell her something stated plain as day.

"He's dead."

Rupert shook his head. "It doesn't matter. His confidentiality remains intact. I don't know why you would have—"

The abrupt stop triggered her curiosity. As Rupert's eyes moved across the screen he'd averted from her gaze, his frown of concentration became more intense.

"Rupert, what is it?"

Putting a hand on the screen, he pushed it toward her. Harlow slid to the front of her seat and looked at him then the screen and back.

"There is only one person authorized on this account and it isn't the deceased." Rupert pointed to a line on the report she was looking at. "It's you."

Her name was there, on the screen. She had full authority. Sinking against the back of her chair, Harlow tried to figure out his game, and why she'd be authorized on anything bearing the Hagan name.

After trying to figure it out for a minute, she looked up. "Is his sister on there?"

Rupert shook his head. "Only you. Jarvis Hagan paid for it, but he didn't even give himself authority on it."

"Okay," she said, grabbing the arms of her chair to push herself up. The bag on her lap got in her way, so she shoved it onto the floor. "So what is it? Money? Savings? Stocks?"

All the businesses and assets had been left to Ophelia; there had been no equivocation on that. Keeping his own name off whatever it was could've been Hagan's way of keeping his sister's hands off the account. If his name had been on it, Ophelia might have a right to challenge Harlow's authority in court.

She couldn't begin to figure out why Hagan would want to leave her anything or why he'd be so sneaky about it.

"No," he said. "It's a safe deposit box."

Oh, that was intriguing. Resting her elbows on the arms of the chair, Harlow steepled her fingers over her mouth.

"Why would..." She didn't want to say too much in front of Rupert. "Why didn't you tell me about this before?"

"I didn't know anything about it. I don't deal with safe deposit boxes. It must have been one of the front office clerks. I imagine they thought you were aware of it... You weren't aware of it?"

Rupert knew her well enough that lying would be pointless, so she shook her head. "No... Why is it still there if he's dead?"

"For all intents and purposes, it's your box. He paid

for five years up front. You would never have learned about it until the lease was up for renewal."

The last thing she'd expected to find on coming to SweSec was a message from beyond. If whatever was in the box was illegal or incriminating, Hagan could be setting her up. Though, if that was the case, it would seem ridiculous to use her own father's company when it could be proved who set up the box and who paid for it.

"Would you like to see it?" Rupert asked.

How long had she been sitting there, staring into nothing? It had probably been a while. Rupert knew to give her space to process. Anyone who didn't know her might just think she'd lost her mind.

"Yes," she said, bouncing to the edge of her chair and grabbing up her bag from the floor. "Can I see it?"

They left his office to go down an internal corridor to a room that Rupert needed a bunch of keys and codes to enter. After putting her in a private room with a table and a chair, Rupert left her alone only to return a minute later with a long shallow silver box.

"We have a spare key here," he said. "It was left with the account."

Putting it in the lock, he turned it. Just as he was about to lift the lid, she put a hand over his. "May I?"

Her request took him aback, rather stopping him probably did. Harlow hadn't intended to hurt him, but she had no idea what would be in the box. While she would trust Ryske to handle whatever it was, she didn't know what questions it may raise with Rupert.

There was also a chance this box could blow up in her face. Literally. If there was a chance of anyone getting hurt, she didn't want Rupert anywhere near it.

"Of course," he said and backed off, clearing his throat. "You know where I am if you need me."

He left and closed the door.

On a deep breath, Harlow sank into the chair and took a quiet minute to look at the box on the table.

Hagan had been a difficult guy to read. Sometimes he'd implied he wanted to hurt her. Though he hadn't when he'd had her imprisoned. Not violently, but the imprisonment was an assault in itself. After that, things had gotten physical between them. Blinded by his hatred for the man she loved, Hagan had attacked her. Yet, just before the end of his life, he'd revealed so much and spoken of their affinity.

One of her most vivid memories of him came at the end. Before his death, he'd said she had to be warned. He hadn't had a chance to explain what he meant.

Maybe this was it. Maybe this box was his warning. It was possible he'd intended to tell her about the box that night. Ophelia had killed him before he'd been able to finish his sentence.

Once, a fleeting thought about how Hagan might get in touch with her from beyond the grave flitted across Harlow's mind. But it had been such an insane thought she'd dismissed it.

But this was it. This was him reaching out. She just didn't know what the message would be.

The truth wouldn't come to her on its own. She had to do something. Holding her breath, she opened the lid with her fingertips, raising it up and guiding it down on its hinge until it was fully open.

The box was full. The first thing she noticed were the bundles of cash at the back of the box. The total was a mystery, but the bundles were stacked from top to bottom with a few more sliding around on what appeared to be a stack of files.

The money wasn't the first thing she touched. Her fingers were drawn to the velvet box on top, nestled amongst the loose money bundles. Popping it open to see what was inside, she gasped at the sight of a gorgeous solitaire ring. Slipping it out of its cushion, she wondered who the ring belonged to or if maybe it was a Hagan heirloom.

The band and setting looked to be custom. It was beautiful. Turning it in the light she spotted an engraving inside, *"To my darling Anwen, forever."* Anwen's engagement ring. It must have been returned to him after her death.

Putting the ring back in its box, it suddenly felt disrespectful that she'd touched it. Setting it aside on the table,

Harlow pushed the money out of the way and lifted the files.

There were various folders. The top one contained Ophelia's school records from her early years before she was pulled and home schooled. It overflowed with reports of erratic and violent behavior that went all the way back to kindergarten. Notes of obsessive behavior, attacking teachers, stealing from the class and other kids, Ophelia had been out of control.

The next file was a juvenile record she probably shouldn't be allowed to see. It held more reports of violence, indecent behavior, vandalism. Kid stuff, there wasn't anything serious. But it did betray how Ophelia liked hurting those weaker than her and breaking things that didn't belong to her.

There was a report at the back that piqued Harlow's interest further; an unsubstantiated report that Ophelia was responsible for a fire at a home. No one was hurt and she wasn't charged, but she had been a person of interest. After reading those documents, she wasn't sure what to think but kept on exploring.

The third file was the thickest and gave her the most clarity. There were pages and pages of psychologist notes as well as lists of doctors' visits and procedures and medication.

Other than acknowledging Ophelia had seen a lot of doctors, she didn't fully understand what conclusions had been reached about what was wrong with her.

Good thing she knew a doctor she could trust, Harlow resolved to talk to him about the medical mumbo-jumbo and moved onto the final file.

Her mind was still wandering; she hadn't been prepared for what was inside. The shocking pictures of charred bodies almost made her close the file straight away. The heading on the paper behind drew her in, it was a fire marshal's report.

The explosion was declared an accident. A leak in a gas line had caused the ignition of the blast that killed the Hagan parents. Apparently.

Harlow was in shock.

Jarvis and Ophelia's parents were killed in a gas explosion. Was it an accident? Why was this file in with all the others?

Absorbing everything she'd read was going to take time. Figuring out how all the pieces fit would take longer. Aware she couldn't stay for too long, she began to pull the bundles of money from the box. They would have to come out before she could return the files to their place. Everything fit inside almost exactly.

It was only after the box was empty that she noticed one last thing she hadn't investigated yet.

TWENTY-SIX

A USB STICK.

Picking it up, Harlow turned it over, looking for something identifying, something that might betray what was on it. The outside was blank. She was going to have to figure it out the old-fashioned way.

The files and the money went back into the box. The engagement ring and the USB went into her bag.

An attendant was standing on the other side of her private room door when she opened it. He helped her return the box to its rightful place in the vault and advised her to take good care of her key.

The employee knew who she was, even though she had no recollection of ever meeting him. But this was her family's company. No doubt many people recognized her. Being the Sweeting who'd gone to jail for murder, she was infamous.

Her mind wasn't exactly in the right place to be social or exchange pleasantries. Harlow thanked the attendant and left to go down the internal hallway alone. One way would take her to the front lobby behind the bullpen. The other led back around to the offices where she'd find Rupert. The latter was her goal.

Returning to Rupert's office, she interrupted his work by just walking in and striding to his desk. "Can I use a computer? A laptop? Anything that isn't connected to the SweSec network?"

"There's a laptop in the lobby. We let customers use it if they have private business." He stood up. "Let me go get it."

Harlow waited in Rupert's office, pacing and clicking her thumbnail on her teeth. Pausing, she glanced at the phone on the desk and thought about calling Ryske. Would he have his cellphone? Probably not. She could call the bar. No one would have time to make it over there before Rupert got back from the lobby. Harlow was too curious to wait.

Rupert came back in with the laptop and handed it over. "I'm going to get some coffee down the block. You want anything?"

His simple smile told her he wasn't going because he wanted coffee; he was giving her privacy.

"Thank you. That would be nice."

He nodded and left. They'd been together six years. It would've been an insult to give him her coffee order or tell him which pastry she liked.

Once the door was closed and she was alone, Harlow ran to the table in the corner and pulled out a chair to sit down. Having a computer that wasn't on the SweSec network was important. If there was a virus on the USB or it was a setup, she didn't want to screw her dad's firm.

Settling herself, she turned on the computer and inserted the USB, anxious about what she'd find on it.

"Maze, where are you when I need you," she whispered to herself before opening the file directory and locating the drive.

It contained one file. Just one. A video file.

Her wish for Maze grew. She laid her hand across her body to touch his star on her arm, taking strength from him, wherever he was, before double clicking the file.

It took a few seconds to load. A few tense, long seconds. When the first image popped onto the screen, she almost fell off her chair. It was Jarvis Hagan, seated on the couch in his living room.

Might be a still, he said nothing and didn't move. All of a sudden, the image sprang to life, and he leaned back.

Harlow wasn't sure she was taking full breaths. For fear what she was seeing might disappear if she closed her eyes, even for a second, she didn't blink.

"Miss Sweeting," Hagan said. The sound of his voice sent a chill down her spine. "I didn't doubt you would find this, though I'm sure you're wondering what lies ahead."

He smiled. The sight drew her closer; she propped her elbows on the table, clasping both hands over her open mouth.

"Oh my God," she whispered.

"Before you get your hopes up, I should tell you that I have no intention of admitting to any crime. You should know by now I'm not that stupid. This also isn't an apology. I am not sorry for anything that has occurred."

Maybe he would've been sorry, if he'd known how it would all turn out. *Our bond gives us an affinity.* He'd told her that on the night he died. *We understand the unique sensation that comes with the clash of love and hatred.*

Sad he'd never known his love wasn't dead at all. Though it may not have comforted him to discover that she was a double crosser, a fake, and a cheat. In life, Jarvis had known Anwen was the last, yet he'd loved her anyway.

Harlow had forgiven Ryske for faking his demise. Hagan may not have been so forgiving with Anwen. Especially if he learned she'd conspired with Ryske, a man Hagan already despised.

Harlow paused the video. Watching it was going to be tough. Hagan wasn't dumb enough to confess he had Ryske stabbed or shot. Figuring out exactly when the video was recorded wouldn't be easy. The receipt's date was in the period after Ryske's resurrection, but before she and Hagan had met in Ophelia's hallway and made plans for what would be their final meeting. His final... anything.

Taking a deep breath, she reached for the computer. "What have you got for me, Hagan?"

Pressing play, she brought him back to life, so to

speak. Hagan was silent. She watched as he picked up a bottle of alcohol and a glass. If she wasn't mistaken, it looked very like the bottle he'd drunk from on the night he died. Shirking her focus from the irrelevant, she shifted it onto him. Any clue could be important, she had to watch for them all.

After Hagan took a drink, he spoke again. "I have a contempt for you that eclipses loathing. You adored a man I despised. I won't ever accept how you could love him and yet, I understand it completely. Heaven knows, my Annie wasn't perfect. She could anger me with a smile and arouse me with a tear… She had a way of playing with me… to me…"

His gaze drifted to the side; a moment of peace.

"You did love her," Harlow murmured.

Even if it was in a sick or obsessive way, he did believe in his own feelings for his fiancée. The woman he'd believed was stolen from him by Ryske.

Inhaling through his nose, Hagan took another drink and looked into the camera. "Do you remember the day we met? You were so… intriguing. I think it's fair to say that we both surprised each other that day. You never stopped surprising me. As loathed as I am to admit it, in the times you're infuriating me, you arouse me, Miss Sweeting. I see what he sees in you…"

His sinister, yet seductive, tone didn't feel good. She hit the keyboard to pause the recording. Being sleazed on wasn't a new phenomenon for most women. That wasn't what affected her. She was more worried about who else would have to endure hearing it.

Rubbing a hand across her mouth, she leaned back. "I have to show this to him," she whispered, hoping the rest of the recording wasn't some sort of salacious love letter.

If Hagan got his cock out, she'd have to make sure Ryske never, ever saw the video under any circumstances. If her love had to witness that, he'd find a way to kill Hagan again.

Harlow could understand being driven to murder; once she'd considered taking Hagan out herself. Hagan didn't have any real love for her. Like he'd said the night he died, he wanted to take Ryske's dignity by taking her. Maybe he'd thought seduction was the way to do it.

These breaks might help her process, but they were risky. She had to watch the whole video. Rupert would be back soon and she couldn't kick him out of his office indefinitely.

She hit play.

"My affinity with you, perhaps clouded by my attraction to your body, has led me to make this video… and to give you this trust.

"I fear you have entered an alliance which may lead to your demise. But you are not the only one to have done so."

Intrigued, Harlow leaned closer. "Keep going," she said to the tape when Hagan paused to take a drink.

"I have to warn you. Someone has to. I am the only one capable of telling you what you need to know. I do this hoping that if the worst should happen, we will both have recourse."

"Recourse for what?" she asked, impatient to discover the truth that had alluded her since the night of his murder. "Tell me, damn it."

Hagan carried on. "Throughout her life, my sister, Ophelia, has shown unstable tendencies. I've included evidence of it in the box where you found this video." So he'd known what he was going to do from the moment he'd made the recording. "She is volatile and I fear that may cause problems for both you and me."

This was the warning. "Oh my God," she said, hoping it wasn't going to become her catchphrase. "I can't… Oh my God."

"Ophelia has threatened my life on many occasions. She has made it her life's work to compete with me. In our newest venture, I fear she may be driven to extremes."

"Pothos," Harlow said, figuring out which venture he meant.

Clueless as to how much he knew of Ophelia's conniving, she hoped to learn what was in his head.

"I compiled everything you see in the safe deposit box for a reason. If something happens to me, I believe the only person who may be left to control her, is you."

It was laughable that he thought anyone could control his sister. From what he was saying, Ophelia had been deranged for a while. Yet, even in the time Harlow had known her, there had been a marked escalation in her lunacy.

"I wish."

"If something happens to me, it will be by Ophelia's hand." Hagan had known how crazy his sister was even before her confrontation with him the night Ryske came back to life. He'd always known. "I need someone to know what she's capable of. I have included her educational and medical history as background. But the real truth is in the file about my parents' death. It wasn't an accident. Ophelia killed our parents; she confessed to me. The maintenance man she was sleeping with gave her instructions on how to rig the gas line. It looked like an accident, but it wasn't. She was tired of them dictating her life and wanted to be in control. That was her justification. My sister is capable of murder. She's done it before and I doubt she'd blink before doing it again if the notion took her. You have to be warned. You believe she is your friend, an ally, but you are in dangerous territory… I've included money that will cover your stake in Pothos. If you find this, and I am gone, I advise you to take the money and run as far away as you can because you're next. She will come for you and she will kill you… If she can do it to her own parents and her own brother… why would she think twice before doing it to you?"

And there was the confirmation that going back to Ophelia's would be a bad idea.

"I hear you," she murmured, resting her chin on her palm.

"If you need leverage against her, use the file on our parents. But be warned, she'll retaliate. You may push her to the edge. Extricate yourself from our project. You won't manage to oust her. She's been having an affair with Anthony Yarker for months. He's infatuated with her and was insanely jealous of Ryske. For a while, I believed his jealousy could cause a rift between them. One that may cause Yarker to hurt my sister… Not in a physical way, he's not the type, but in any other way he could.

"Don't underestimate Gil Parratt either. He's ruthless, but his love for Lydia is real, hence why he too despises Ryske. If you need to get to Parratt, Yarker and Lydia are the only two people in his life he'll listen to. You should also know that his wife has evidence of some deviant sexual practice they used to partake in. I don't know the particulars, but the nature of that evidence is compelling enough to keep them married. Parratt doesn't want the world to know the embarrassing truth, and she wants access to his money."

Taking another drink, he lingered without words.

"What else?" she whispered, lapping up every fact he spilled.

Hagan eventually let his attention sink back to the camera. "You're a unique woman, Harlow Sweeting. You have the ability to make a man hate you and love you at the same time. Don't underestimate yourself. You're capable. You're smart. If you listen to this warning and extricate yourself, you will make it through." On a deep breath, his focus fell to the liquor in his glass. "I told you to avenge him, that it was your job. Ophelia's involvement changes things. She is dangerous. This battle should have been fought between you and I… But now I fear we're caught in a spiral that could be the end of us all… Some days I'm so full of fight and others… all I can think about is joining her." He closed his eyes in a blink. When they opened again, they were on the screen. "Be warned, Miss Sweeting. I love my sister, but I fear her, and you should too. Be safe."

His hand moved though his eyes never left the lens. His focus reminded her of his last moment of life. Their gazes had stayed locked until he'd collapsed and perished.

The screen went black.

Frozen in time with her lips parted an inch, she listened to the echo of silence. There was probably ambient noise from the offices; she didn't hear any of it. All she could feel were Hagan's eyes on her. They were gone from the screen, yet she could still feel them.

Time ceased to matter. A minute or an hour could've passed while she sat still there without saying a word or making a sound.

The door opened and someone came striding in. "There was a helluva line at the coffee shop," Rupert said. "But I got there eventually." He appeared in her peripheral vision when he slid the coffee and pastries onto the table then turned to prop himself against it. She still didn't move. "Harlow, what's wrong?" With a finger under her chin, he raised her attention. Even though he exhaled a laugh and smiled, she could read his concern. "You look like you've seen a ghost."

"I..."

"Harlow?"

"I have something for you," she said. "But I have to send an email first, can I do that?"

"Sure," he said. "Are you sure you're okay?"

"Mm hmm," she said, springing to action. "You don't happen to have a blank USB drive I can have, do you?"

"Yeah, of course."

Harlow sent an email to Maze with the video attached. She didn't know if he'd get it any time soon, but at least he'd have a copy of Hagan's message if anything happened to her. Using the USB drive Rupert gave her, she made a copy to take with her. She tucked it into her bag and then returned the laptop to him.

"Come with me a minute," she said.

They went back to the vault to retrieve the safe deposit box again. Upon returning to the private room, Harlow opened the box, without showing Rupert what was inside, to remove the piles of money.

"Oh my God, Harlow," he said as she stacked the bundles.

When it was all out, she was discreet about slipping the original USB back inside and locking up the box again.

"It's yours," she said. "The money you gave me, I gave it to Hagan and... I guess he never used it."

Although that wasn't a complete truth, it wasn't a malicious lie. Harlow meant to protect him. At least this way, her ex wasn't taking drug money. The provenance of the cash wasn't known, but Hagan wasn't as squeaky clean as most people thought.

Rupert was going to be a father and a husband. She needed him to be clean as a whistle, and completely clueless, if the cops ever questioned him. It was only right. He'd done nothing wrong and shouldn't be implicated in any way.

Harlow regretted ever involving him. Life had changed so much since she'd come to him for help. Her life was so much more dangerous while his was so much more stable.

"This money has… it's been sitting here all this time and you… you didn't know?"

She shook her head. To break the tension of the moment, she grinned and grabbed his hand. "This is perfect! Just when you need it for the house and the wedding and the baby."

"It will take the pressure off but…" He looked at her. "Why did he need it?"

Inhaling, she lost her ease to get serious. "You loaned me money and I have repaid it. That's it."

"That's it," he muttered, reading between the lines. "The money from your half of the apartment sale will come through soon. I'll transfer it as soon as we have it."

"Rupe, you don't have to—"

"I do," he said. "You paid into that place too… How will Ryske feel about you giving me this money?"

Her brow lowered. "What does Ryske have to do with it?"

"Well, you told us to keep the money from our wedding fund and now you're giving me this… won't he want the money?"

Smiling, she wrapped both arms around one of his. "Believe me, he'll be thrilled we've paid this back."

Because it was one thing off his plate. Whatever he'd saved to repay Rupert could be put into his business venture on the other side of town. It wouldn't hurt that they'd no longer be beholden to her ex either.

"I don't trust him, Harlow," he said. Her grip loosened, at least until he sighed. "But… I do think he loves you."

Grinning, she tightened her grip to bring herself

closer. "I think he does too."

"Do you need anything else?" he asked, tucking her hair behind her ear.

"Yes," she said. "I need the paperwork to authorize someone else on this box."

"Someone else who?" It didn't take long for him to guess. "Ryske? You want to authorize him on Jarvis Hagan's box? I thought they didn't like each other."

"That's an understatement."

Rupert went to a drawer in her corner and retrieved a crisp new paper bag to pack the money into. "You want to add him anyway?"

"Yes," Harlow said. "Any string in there?"

Rupert opened a separate drawer and gave her a small ball of twine and a pair of scissors. Harlow cut a short length and tied the key onto the O-ring of her necklace.

"Why do you want to add Ryske?"

"Because if anything happens to me, what's in there can help him."

"Anything happens…" He paused. "Harlow, what do you think will happen to you?"

The potential of what she'd found was sinking in. Hope infused her and joy crept in too. "With that in my arsenal, very little."

He became dubious. "Why do you suddenly look so overjoyed?"

"Because I just caught a break, Rupert," she said, shaking out her arms. "And it's about damn time."

TWENTY-SEVEN

HAVING DECIDED GOING back to Ophelia's wasn't an option, Harlow set off for home. Even though her list of things to do in the city wasn't complete, she was eager to see her crew. Telling them about what she'd found at SweSec was too important to put off.

Using some of the money she'd swiped from Ophelia for cab fare got her back to Floyd's quicker than hoofing it would. She could barely contain her excitement at the prospect of going in and surprising them.

Getting there to find the place empty was something of a letdown.

She should've known no one was there when she had to pick the lock to get in. Knocking would've ruined the surprise and she just assumed they were being safety conscious. If folks in the neighborhood knew that the refurbishment of the bar was finished, they might assume that it was open and saunter in. From the looks of what she found, no one had been drinking in Floyd's. It was still pristine.

She went upstairs and took a shower, then changed into her own clothes and put away the things she'd brought from Ophelia's. Unpacking was symbolic. A gesture that said she was back and wasn't ever returning to Ophelia's service.

Figuring the guys would return eventually, she made coffee and ate. No one showed, so she set about copying the recording she'd made the night Hagan died. Well, not a complete copy, she may have omitted most of the early conversation.

Once she was done, she held up the USB and smiled. It was a weapon. Not a gun or a knife, but it should protect her.

Tucking the secret weapon into her cleavage, she hid the copy of the SweSec recording and went about cleaning the place up. The fact the guys weren't there, and that Ryske hadn't been at the club on Friday, played on her mind.

The longer she was at Floyd's, alone, the more uneasy she became. Something was going on. She wouldn't find out what it was pottering about at home. Given her own list of things to do, she decided to combine two goals. She'd find her crew and neutralize Ophelia at the same time.

Sliding on her pointed full-finger ring, she almost felt like herself again. Almost. Until she had her bracelet on, she wouldn't be whole. Still, fixating on what she didn't have wouldn't get her anywhere. So she filled a gym bag with a few essentials, locked up, and left.

It didn't take long to get to Felipe's. She'd been eager to see the boy and check that he was behaving. Carrying on with her two birds, one stone theme, she checked on Felipe's well-being and took the chance that he'd know where the Floyd's crew were.

He didn't. Neither did Martina or Camila except to say that no one had seen them around since Friday night. The timing suggested they'd gone somewhere right before the Pothos night began. But Maze had been at Windsor's. Why would he have been there while the guys waited around for him? He had to be with them because he sure wasn't at home.

There would be an explanation. Harlow, at least, got some reassurance. No one said anything about injuries or drama. Wherever the crew were, everyone was safe.

She got more good news when Felipe explained that his father wouldn't be coming back to stay with them. While sharing the news Felipe lightened with happiness and she saw glimpses of the glittering innocence of the child he was.

Being free of that fear of his father made such a difference to his personality. She wondered if Ryske had been the same and if maybe that was why he'd chosen Floyd's over his own family.

Felipe volunteered to help Camila with Tiffy; another sign that his mood was better. While they were changing the baby's diaper, Martina explained that family services had basically given her an ultimatum. If Pablo came back, they'd take Felipe into care.

It warmed her that Martina had chosen her son over the man who hurt them. But she didn't expect Martina to tear up and thank her. Through her emotion, Martina explained that Harlow's help and the assistance of the Floyd's guys showed her there was happiness out there. That she didn't have to be dependent on Pablo. That's what had given her the confidence to agree to the parole conditions placed on her now ex. Those conditions stated that he wasn't allowed near the neighborhood, or Martina or Felipe.

After reassuring Martina that she'd talk to Dover about work at the bar and promising the guys would look out for her and Felipe, Harlow was interrupted by Tiffy being put on her lap.

The little one was gorgeous and while Harlow was making Camila promise to bring pictures to the bar so she could put them on the fridge, Tiffy pulled Harlow's arm up to begin sucking on Ryske's star. The guy wasn't even there and Tiffy was choosing him over everyone else.

Light was fading outside, she made her excuses to leave sooner than she wanted to. It was so nice to be among friends. She'd almost forgotten what it was like to relax and enjoy herself. But she couldn't switch off yet, there was work to do.

The night was still young.

***

TO A LOT OF people, going to Windsor's might seem like a crazy idea. The way Harlow saw it, she didn't have a choice.

The man she was looking for hung out there during the week. The danger came in the form of the others related to Pothos. She should be fine. Completely safe… ish.

Some patrons frequented Windsor's for drinks and to gamble. Without Pothos and the hookers, it was more subdued. More like a social club than a drug den or brothel.

A few people milled around Windsor's main floor. No one paid much attention to her. Employees would recognize her as someone affiliated with those who ran the club. Patrons would have seen her around too. So although a few people glanced her way as she crossed the room, no one intercepted her.

Several of Ophelia's minions were seated in the central booth. They were lower down in the ranks; none of them were her target. If they recognized her, they didn't care enough to chase her down. Word of what she'd done to Ophelia probably hadn't reached them yet. Assumption was on her side in more ways than one. Ophelia would never in a million years assume she'd go to Windsor's. That provided a narrow window of exploitable time, and exploitation was exactly the plan.

Long curtains were drawn across the walls during the week. They fastened at the ceiling and floor to cover the doors to the private bedrooms. To anyone who didn't know otherwise, the gathered fabric was just part of the décor. As she was scrutinizing how the sheen in the metallic thread embroidered through the curtains caught the light, someone moved into her peripheral vision.

It wasn't the person she was looking for, but when she turned, the woman was intrigued, probably by her presence. After a moment of eye contact, they moved toward each other and met near the center of the room.

"Harlow."

"Lydia," she said. "This is unexpected."

"This is a good place for Gil and me to meet," Lydia said, wrapping herself in her own embrace and rubbing her upper arms.

Discretion was required because Gil Parratt was married. His wife probably didn't like him to gallivant around with his mistress. Harlow figured the wife knew about the affair, especially if what Hagan said in his recording was accurate. But no woman would want to be humiliated by their husband flaunting their indiscretions around town.

"Is he around?"

Lydia shook her head. "He's running late. He'll be here soon…" She looked past Harlow around the room. "Where's Ophelia? She isn't usually here at this time of the week."

Probably because Ryske wasn't usually there at this time of the week. "I'm supposed to be looking for Vane, have you seen him around?"

That was why she'd come, to seek Penzance. Ophelia wasn't present and hadn't told her to track Vane down. Yet, Harlow hadn't actually lied, she'd just missed out a few pertinent details… Had she been spending too much time with Ryske?

"He was here," Lydia said. "But he left. I think he's coming back later. I don't know."

Damn. She didn't have a clue how to get in touch with Penzance. He'd eventually hear through the grapevine what happened. But he'd made it clear he wouldn't be going back to Floyd's any time soon. Floyd's and Windsor's were the only links they had. She couldn't hang around at Windsor's for too long and she might not be at Floyd's even if he did try to get in touch with her there.

"Thanks anyway."

Harlow was about to turn and walk away when Lydia spoke. "Do you have time for a drink?"

Hanging around might not be a good idea. She'd come to find Penzance, the hope being he'd leave with her. Staying had never been on the cards.

Funny that this place was going to belong to Ryske any day soon and yet, she didn't feel safe. Maybe once his name was official on the deed, she would be more confident about spending time there. Though she imagined that would only happen if Ophelia's people were ejected too. But as long as Pothos was ongoing, evicting anyone was unlikely.

Still, Harlow might have underestimated Lydia's

importance in what was going to play out. She'd asked Ryske to cultivate a relationship with Yarker, and had an opportunity in front of her to nurture a friendship with their other partner.

Harlow smiled. "Sure."

They made their way across to the bar and each of them ordered drinks. At the far end of the bar, furthest from the people in the room, the women seated themselves and sampled their drinks.

"I confess I… I never quite understood you," Lydia said. "I was intimidated by your relationship with Ryske. He's a… a formidable man." She frowned and touched a fingertip to the rim of her glass. "No, that's not what I mean, he's… he's daunting. I… I must admit, I was always a little afraid of him."

What had she got herself into? The purpose of the conversation was… vague, was it going to swing her way? As of yet, Lydia wasn't asking questions. Through her relationship with Parratt, Lydia probably learned not to quiz someone who could take offence.

"He would never hurt a woman," Harlow said.

If Lydia told her that Parratt hurt her, they'd be in a difficult spot. Harlow would want to help if she was being abused, but getting involved in their private business wouldn't endear her to Parratt.

Shaking her head, Lydia laughed. "Oh, I know. I… I didn't mean like that. I… I just have never been confident with men and he's so confident… it's intimidating."

Ryske. Intimidating. Harlow tried to see it. Even when they'd met he'd been so approachable; she'd never feared him. She'd feared her feelings for him and what getting involved with him would do to her, but she'd never been intimidated.

In contrast, Lydia didn't exude confidence. Ryske's cocky persona could easily overshadow the meek.

"Talk to him," Harlow said. "The more you talk to him, the…"

She trailed off and had to turn her lips into her mouth to subdue a smile. Letting her upper lip slide free, she held the lower one in her teeth.

Lydia bowed closer. "You didn't finish."

"I didn't, I…" Inhaling, she let her breath out slowly. "Ryske's mouth can get him into trouble. If he wants to soothe you, he will. But if he wants to be an asshole, he's good at that too."

Lydia smiled. "He's good at a lot of things… He knows things that I…"

Color rose in Lydia's cheeks and no more words were needed. Odd that her skin crawled when she even thought about Ryske being intimate with Ophelia. Yet, seeing this other woman, who had been intimate with him, didn't have the same effect.

"Yeah, he's like that," Harlow said, and gave Lydia time to enjoy her memory. She took another drink and set her glass down again. "Are you tempted?"

Lydia hadn't called her over to ask how to seduce Ryske. No way. Though she wouldn't be the first woman to think that Harlow was pedaling how-to guides.

"Tempted to…" Lydia lost some of that longing and straightened up. "Oh no, I… I couldn't… Ophelia would not be happy if she found out that Ryske and I were…"

It wasn't the resounding no Harlow hoped for, but at least Ophelia was good for something. It was tempting to encourage Lydia to let people think she and Ryske were involved, just to really drive the knife in and twist it in the wench's gut. But that could lead to grave problems for Lydia, so she kept the suggestion to herself.

"Ophelia shouldn't be a reason for you not to do something you want to do," Harlow said. "But you're with Gil, you don't need Ryske."

Shrinking, Lydia glanced toward the bar, showing obvious discomfort in the way she squirmed. "I… I was with Gil when I… when Ryske and I…"

"I know," Harlow said, determined not to let the woman feel shame.

"He can't let it go, he won't. He brings it up all the time and treats Ryske like he did something terrible."

When in truth both Ryske and Lydia had been unmarried when they were intimate. Parratt was the only one of the three bound by vows. Harlow's advice stuck in her throat. She wanted to tell Lydia to remind Parratt of his marriage and to tell him he had no right to belittle her choice as she was free to do whatever she wanted.

Instead she just said, "You and Ryske were consenting adults."

"It was the wildest thing I've ever done," Lydia said. "Ryske was so great about it. He made it so easy, and was so considerate of us… I didn't think it could be like that… Gil asked if I'd… if I'd do it with him, but I… I don't think I want to do it again."

That was one Harlow was happy to confront. "You should never do anything you're uncomfortable with. In bed or anywhere else, and no man should pressure you into anything."

Lydia seemed relieved by the support. "That's just it. With Ryske it didn't feel like pressure, you know? It sounds stupid to say it because I know it's not, but… it felt natural." She deflated. "But Gil just won't let it go. He won't…"

"That's in the past. It's all in the past. Moving forward is important; it's the only way to make progress."

TWENTY-EIGHT

HARLOW WOULD BE the first to admit she sounded like an after-school special. That ceased to matter when Lydia relaxed. The calm acceptance put the woman at ease. A relaxed mark was far more open to talking than a tense one.

Lydia swept her hair from her shoulder. "Now that Ryske's ownership of the club is official, Gil is livid. He says Ryske has too much power."

Ryske's ownership was official? Harlow hadn't known that. As much as she wanted to leap up and punch the air, she couldn't. Playing it cool in the face of finding out something unexpected was Ryske's trade. Harlow had to practice his restraint and bite her tongue.

"Whether Gil likes it or not, Ryske is where he is because of legitimate decisions made by everyone."

Lydia nodded. "Right. Absolutely… Ryske is getting a real tough break recently… Ophelia isn't happy about his relationship with Anwen. She told Anthony that she wanted it to stop, that it wouldn't be good for us… for the consortium."

"Do you think Anwen will influence him?" Harlow asked. "How can she? She doesn't have a vote."

"No," Lydia said. "Neither do I and I said the same thing to Gil. He said we should still be concerned. He pointed out that even though I don't have a vote, my opinion matters to him."

Just like Hagan had warned in his recording. If Harlow wanted to influence Gil, she had to have influence with Lydia.

"To be honest," she said, touching a drop of condensation on the side of her glass. "I think Ophelia is out of line for suggesting Anwen would push her own agenda. Like you said, Anwen's the same as you. You both have influence with your men, but that doesn't mean you would abuse it." Peeking at Lydia, she checked that the woman was listening and processing before she pushed on. "It's especially rich given we both know there are two votes in the consortium who are more than just associates."

Lydia blinked and squirmed again. "You mean two votes who are…"

"Intimate with each other? Yes."

The only votes on the consortium were her, Parratt, Yarker, Ophelia and Ryske. Ryske had secured his vote early. He'd have no reason to offer the service and security he did if he wasn't getting anything in return. Besides, it wasn't his fault he'd been dead when the plans were put in place.

Lydia slid to the edge of her stool, transfixed on Harlow and ignoring how their knees slid together. "I didn't know you knew."

"It's difficult to hide something like that when you live in the woman's pocket," Harlow said, masking her mouth with her glass.

It was better to imply she'd learned about Ophelia's affair with Yarker while living and working with the heiress, even though she'd never seen the man there alone. Ophelia obviously went out to conduct her carnal business. Though, with her renewed interest in Ryske, it was impossible to know how often she and Yarker were seeing each other.

He might be pursuing the relationship for love or with ideas they could have a future. Ophelia wasn't. She was using the man, manipulating him, in favor of her attempts to secure Ryske.

"I was shocked when I heard," Lydia said. "Gil told

me and I was… I didn't see them together; I couldn't picture it. Afterwards, we did socialize. There were times I thought there could be something between them… Gil told me Anthony has feelings for Ophelia, but he doesn't think they're returned… Not with the way she is about Ryske."

Nice to know someone else was paying attention.

Harlow smiled. "I suppose it's their business. As long as you and Gil are secure with each other, you don't have to worry about them."

Sighing, Lydia took a long gulp of alcohol. "He always tells me he loves me," she said. "But he's never faithful."

The statement conjured such conflict that hiding her frown was impossible. Was Lydia talking about Parratt's wife? She couldn't be upset the man was sleeping with his spouse. Surely she'd known that was a possibility when having an affair with a married man. Their whole relationship was built on infidelity. Parratt cheated on the woman he married; it couldn't be a surprise that he screwed around on the mistress too.

"Do you want him to be faithful to you?"

The point of the conversation was to gain some favor with Lydia. Harlow couldn't voice anything that might come across as judgment.

"Doesn't every woman want her man to be faithful to her?" Lydia asked.

Considering the point, Harlow tilted her head. She'd known from the moment she gave herself to Ryske that there was every chance she'd have to share him. Share his physical self anyway. He was always faithful to her in his heart. He would never fall for another woman or prioritize a lover over their relationship.

Seeing other women fawn over him, women other than Ophelia, sometimes bestowed immature superiority. She had him and no matter what those women did to him, he'd still be her man.

Would it be better if Ryske was hers and hers alone? What would it feel like to see him refuse another woman, to stand up and claim her without all the misdirection and subterfuge? Maybe it would be nice. Maybe she would enjoy that too.

"If that's what you want then you have to talk to him," Harlow said. "Tell him that you want to be together."

"Except his wife won't let us be together," Lydia said and sighed. "Oh, it's my fault for getting involved with him in the first place. He wants me to commit to him. He doesn't like me to be independent."

Hence why she was sitting in this club waiting for him like a patient puppy. If this was a unique occurrence, Harlow wouldn't blink an eye. But she had a feeling this was what most of Lydia's life looked like.

"Hey," Harlow said, putting a hand over hers on the bar. "Don't ever lose sight of yourself. Not for anything. If your gut tells you that Gil is the man you want, then you have to do whatever you can to make yourself happy with him. That doesn't mean you have to bow to his will. Don't ever bow to anyone."

Determination kept her eyes locked on Lydia's who seemed to peer into her before smiling. "You're so strong, Harlow… I wonder if there's anything that could ever break you down… I can't imagine that there is."

One thing had. Losing Ryske. If that happened again, if it happened for real, she wouldn't come back from it.

"I've had my knocks and I've been lost too. That's how I can be so sure about this. At the time, walking away from the security I had was terrifying. It went against everything I was being told. But if I hadn't done it, I would never have found this life. I wouldn't have found Ryske."

Lydia frowned. "I didn't think you were together now."

"We're not," Harlow said, her hand sliding away from Lydia's. "That doesn't mean I regret what we had. Whether or not I lost it, I still value it. I wouldn't trade any of the decisions I made, even the scary ones, if it meant I had to give up the memories I made with him."

"I wish I knew my mind as well as you know yours."

"Sometimes it's not your mind you have to know," Harlow said. "It's your heart. You have to follow your gut… Love is difficult and complicated and it's not always like the movies. There isn't always a happily ever after. Sometimes we have to walk away. Sometimes we have to sacrifice. Sometimes we lose."

"Like you lost when you thought Ryske was gone… Like Jarvis lost Anwen… but she came back too."

"It's not always like that," Harlow said. "Sometimes dead is dead."

The sound of a solitary clap made her and Lydia turn. Another followed and another in a slow rhythm. When she saw Brash coming toward them with his arms outstretched, clapping in the ironic applause, she grew rigid and set her jaw. Animal was behind him, stoic, wearing an expression of sinister anticipation that quaked through her.

This was the test. Lydia had said Harlow couldn't be broken. But she had a feeling they were looking at the one man who wanted to give it a shot.

"That's beautiful," Brash said, coming up at her side and picking up her glass to down the rest of its contents. "I couldn't have said it better myself. Sometimes dead is dead." He slammed down the glass but kept his hand on it, between her and Lydia, to lean in and growl. "Sometimes how you get there is worse."

Harlow leaped off her stool. Before she could retreat, he grabbed both her arms and thrust her back against the bar.

Lydia screamed. "Oh my God, let her go!"

"You butt out," Brash said, focused on the woman in his clutches returning his ire.

"Harlow, what should I—"

"Just go, Lydia," Harlow said, glaring into Brash. "I can handle this Neanderthal and his friend."

Lydia only hesitated for half a beat. She obviously figured out there was nothing she could do to help, so quickly scurried off.

"Now it's just the three of us," Brash said, lowering his mouth to breathe against hers. "One happy family."

"I don't think so," Harlow said and tried to pull her arm away, but she didn't get far. "Did she send you to bring me back?"

One corner of his mouth curled; he exhaled a laugh.

"She doesn't give a damn about you anymore. She's given you to me."

Gritting her teeth, she ignored his proximity. If he thought about trying to kiss her or touch her, she'd scream and fight until her last breath.

"I don't belong to anyone."

"You belong to me."

"Because she says so?" Harlow spat. "You don't even know who you're dealing with… You think she's your savior, that you're doing what Jarvis would've wanted. He'd be turning in his grave."

"Don't dare say his name," he said and gave her a shake.

Curling her lips, she laughed. "You're a fool. A fucking idiot. All this time you run her errands and take her shit… You never stopped to ask yourself, why would she let me into her life if I was the one who killed him? If I was brutal enough to take her brother from her, why would she want me in her home?"

"To make you pay for what you did."

She raised her brows. "Is that what she told you? Wow, she must be quite the actress. Look around. If she wanted to make me pay, why would she go into business with me? Why let me earn a crust off a scheme she cooked up? Your boss isn't afraid of me. She doesn't hate me… Well, she does, but only because I used to ride Ryske's cock. But, come on, what woman hasn't?"

His fingers loosened. Although he was still glaring, she was breaking through. He was questioning his assumptions and what he'd been told. The uncertainty was there, behind his eyes.

"What the fuck are you saying?" he asked.

This time when she moved her arm, she got it free of his grip. That gave her the opportunity to slip her pinched fingers into her cleavage to retrieve the USB she'd made at home. Her secret weapon.

"You know I went to see him on the night he died," Harlow said. "Yes, I was there. I can't deny that… What you don't know, what even she doesn't know, is that I got the whole thing on tape."

Stepping back, Brash blinked in shock.

Animal must have been listening in too because he moved close to Brash's side, concern creasing his brow. "What the hell?"

"I won't bore you with the conversation Jarvis and I had… But I wouldn't expect you to take my word for what happened… You hate me because you think I killed him." Leaning toward them, she moistened and plumped her lips before murmuring. "I didn't."

Offering the USB to Brash, she wasn't surprised he was too stunned to move; she shook it at him.

"That's… that's his death?" he asked.

"In audio," she said. "This is a limited time deal. You want to know how it went down? It's on there. You can hear it with your own ears. Why don't you listen to that before you wreak your vengeance on me? Listen and you'll learn I'm not the one who needs to be punished."

Slipping the USB into Brash's shirt pocket, she sidestepped and moved around the pair. They were busy absorbing her unexpected revelation, which gave her time to get out of there.

If they wanted to pursue her and take her down, they could do it later. She figured they should at least know the truth before attacking the wrong person. Ophelia was already mad at her. If the heiress found out she'd revealed her secret to Brash and Animal, her anger would rise until it burst the pressure gauge.

But it was done. She owed the woman nothing.

Keeping her secret was of no benefit where those men were concerned. If there was a chance that revealing it would get them off her ass, then it was a risk worth taking. But it did increase the threat level.

On the recording, Hagan warned her that Ophelia could snap and when she did, it usually had fatal consequences.

This was it. Harlow was in it. For the moment, she was alone. Time was limited. Ophelia would catch up with her eventually. Only two more bases to cover before facing her judgment. But, damn, she wanted the chance to see Ryske one more time before that happened. Except without knowing where he was or what was happening in his life, the chances of that seemed slim.

TWENTY-NINE

HARLOW'S STOP AT Clyde's was short because he was heading out on a call. Before he left, he handed her his stacks of notes in a file, and told her Jarvis Hagan was connected to just about every city department in some way.

She thanked him for his role in securing Felipe's future free of his violent father. Clyde played down his involvement, claiming it was part of his job. But she could tell he'd taken it upon himself to ensure Felipe wouldn't have to live under his father's tyranny ever again.

Tired and light-headed, probably because of the stresses of the day, she'd almost fallen asleep in the cab on her ride back to the neighborhood. Despite the exhaustion, she wasn't going home. Her work wasn't done. Any question over her choice of destination was erased when they drove past Floyd's and there were no signs of light or life.

Seeing the building inert was painful, like the last time it was vacant. This time, she wasn't going to bring it back to life. At least not alone. Her boys were out in the world somewhere; she hated not knowing where.

One friend was her last hope for locating her crew. If he couldn't help her, she'd kiss goodbye to any chance of seeing Ryske again before the inevitable confrontation with Ophelia.

With her crew at her back, she'd be strong, and could lean on them for support. Without them, she wasn't sure she could pull this off alone.

After knocking on Bale's apartment door a few times and receiving no response, she let herself in and checked around. Finding everyone close to her had vanished was too much like a replay of the old days. But after discovering a dirty coffee mug in the sink and water in the shower stall, she guessed Bale was out rather than gone.

There was only one place she'd have left to go after this. Before venturing there, she'd give Bale a chance to come back. Deciding it would be best to have her wits about her, just in case anything did go down, Harlow dumped her gym bag, kicked off her shoes and climbed into his bed.

If Ophelia came looking for her, she might go to Floyd's. Would the heiress think to come to Bale's? No. Not unless Anwen filled her in on the doctor's whereabouts. On the plus side, if she was going to find herself bleeding and in need anywhere, the apartment of a trusted doctor was the best place.

Closing her eyes, she relaxed and let herself fall asleep.

***

IT WAS FULLY DARK out when Harlow felt his hand on her face. Turning into the caress, she smiled and whimpered a sound of appreciation.

"You pop up in the strangest places, Sweeting," Bale's voice broke through the night.

Harlow rolled a little and let her eyes open to find him sitting on the bed at her side. "I was tired."

"I guessed that," he said. "Are you injured?" She shook her head. "Pregnant?"

His hopeful brows made her smile. On a deep breath, she pushed her fists into the mattress and made herself sit. "I don't know the answer to that one." Scooping her hair away from her face, she drew her knees to her chest, hooking her dress over them and hugging her legs tight. "What time is it?"

"Late. You can sleep if you need to, I just wanted to check you were okay… I'll go in the other room."

She snatched his arm before he could rise. "Tell me he's alive."

Concern crept over Bale's expression, hardening it. "He's alive," he said, cupping her face. "Jesus, Harlow, yes, he's alive… Have you been worried all this time that—"

"Not that worried," she said, rubbing her cheek on his palm. Squeezing her eyes closed, she pretended to feel the texture of Ryske's scar. The illusion wasn't enough. "If I'd been that worried, I'd have chased you down at the hospital… I guess it was just… in the back of my mind." While still in the stupor of sleep, her fear had slipped out. "So much has happened, Bale."

He smiled. "It feels like you're always saying that… Did you use the sedatives? Is that how you got out?"

She shook her head. "I used Ophelia's on Friday. I didn't have to use Brash's. I have it with me, you can dispose of it."

His hand fell to his lap. "Or use it on my brother when he gets one of his dumb ideas."

That made her laugh. "Or for that. Yes."

"Ryske told me about Ophelia," he said. "How did you get away?"

"I knocked her out," Harlow said and proceeded to tell him everything about her day.

By the time she was done, Bale was seated beside her on the bed. Both of them were leaning on the headboard, their hands linked between them.

"You did the right thing, babe," he said. "You had to get out of there. But you're in serious danger now."

"I know that."

"If she is what Hagan said, and what you've known she is for a while, then she won't let this go."

"I left all her medical notes in the safe deposit box. Will you translate them?"

"You know I'll do my best," he said, picking up her hand to kiss the back. "It sounds like she has a personality disorder, antisocial or narcissistic, maybe both … I suppose her issues haven't been managed in recent years, certainly since her brother died, because no one's been monitoring her… You said in the recording Hagan states he fears she would be responsible for anything that happened to him. Why can't you take it to the cops?"

"Seeing her behind bars would be the best case scenario. Unfortunately, she knows too much. She could make a deal and testify against all of us to get herself out. It would become a game of he said, she said and I don't trust we'd come out on top."

Especially not now Ryske owned the club, was the contact who'd recruited Svetlana and her girls, and was the one who did the drug deals. The heat could turn on him despite Harlow being the one to set this in motion. She was the one who'd bought in and the person to initially contact Svetlana.

The whole situation was a mess. But knowing that Jarvis Hagan had friends in high places in the city helped.

"The idea is to give Ophelia a choice," Harlow said. "Either she leaves the city of her own accord and never contacts us again, or we reach out to the State's Attorney with what we have. We could agree to make a deal first."

"Ryske will never testify in open court. He just… he wouldn't do it."

"He will if it means me and his crew will be safe. I understand he won't want to and I know the defense would try to attack his credibility. I can testify, I was there. But there are others who know things."

Lydia was sympathetic and could help with Parratt. If Maze could get whatever Parratt's wife had, they would have him on their side.

Ryske should be able to persuade Anwen. He could get Yarker too, she was sure of that, if he could manipulate the man into believing he'd been intimate with Ophelia and that the pair made a mockery of him.

"Others? You think that you can persuade other people to turn on her?"

"I would have faith if I had my crew," she said, wriggling closer to rest her head on his shoulder.

He let go of her hand to raise an arm over her shoulders.

"If Ryske knew you were getting away from Ophelia, he'd have been here. He was going nuts; we were worried about him getting himself hurt. Working with Costello helped, but nothing was going to replace not having you… The guys had an idea to get him out of town. Maze stayed behind because Ryske wanted you to have back-up nearby. I think Maze is at his parents tonight. Ryske wanted all of them to stay for you, but Dover had to go with him. Someone had to be able to step in if he got out of hand. Noon isn't the most persuasive and Ryske outmatches him for strength."

Dover wasn't outmatched by any of the crew; he was the most muscular of them all.

"Out of here to where?"

"Doing your bidding. The task was for you. That was probably the only thing that persuaded him leaving was a good idea. They took Anwen to her old place, they're clearing it out and shutting it down… After that they're going to set her up in her own apartment. They'll be back Friday."

Friday. That could be too late. It was already late Tuesday.

Brash and Animal would have heard the recording; they'd know the identity of the real killer. By now, Ophelia would've figured out her minions hadn't dragged Harlow back. The danger level was increasing every minute.

Without her crew, Harlow couldn't be out in the open and wouldn't be able to coax the consortium to follow her plan. On her own, she wasn't likely to make it through the rest of the week with a pulse.

Twisting out of Bale's half-embrace, she moved ninety degrees to face him, but flattened her hands on his thigh to look at them rather than him.

"Did he talk to you?"

"Ryske," Bale said. "About?" Raising her chin just a fraction, her eyes were at the tops of their sockets when they found his. "Yeah, he did, and I think you're both crazy."

"You don't have to understand it."

He didn't smile. If anything, his expression grew

more severe. "That's exactly what he said." Pushing away from the headboard, he grabbed her hand. "Do you really think he would want anything to happen to you? Do you think he would want you to hurt yourself? Would you want him hurting himself for you?"

Withdrawing her hand, she could feel her palms growing sticky. "You don't know what it is to live without him," she said and her eyes closed. "I don't want him hurt. I want him happy and alive. I want him to have everything in the world… But look at how he's been since I've been at Ophelia's. How would his quality of life be better if he knew I was never coming back?" Bale's lips thinned. "I don't want him hurt. But I know what it is to live without him and I couldn't do that again. I won't do it again. If he feels the same way, who am I to tell him that his feelings aren't valid?" Trying to soothe his frown, she stroked his face and leaned in. "If I'm still here, if I'm not hurt, I expect you to do your damndest to keep him with me."

"And if I can't? What if I'm not there? What if you have kids?"

"I'm not pregnant."

"That's not what you said before. You said you didn't know… Have you had unprotected sex since the last time you did a test?"

"Do you pepper your brother with this many questions?"

"It hasn't been smart to mention your name around him at all recently," Bale said. "And he's not the one I have to worry about getting knocked up."

"Oh," she said, seeing a chance to lighten the mood. Propping straight arms behind her, she leaned back and crooked a brow. "So if I get pregnant, I'm the irresponsible one and…" a thought suddenly hit her. "Wait a minute…" Sitting up, she wagged a finger at him. "It was you."

"What was me?"

But she wasn't buying the innocent act. "He had condoms when he showed up. Those weren't a gift from him, those were a gift from you… You bastard." She socked his shoulder. "You asked if we used condoms when you knew we did."

Now she got a half smile when he caught her wrist and she laughed. "No, I didn't. I knew I gave them to the jerk, but he doesn't keep his head around you... he's too busy being led by the little one."

Sliding toward the end of the bed, she lay down. "I feel like I spend more time talking about having sex with him than actually doing it."

Bale slid down to lie facing her. "Thought you weren't together."

He was sort of trying to sound like he was teasing, but she knew he wanted answers too. "We're not... but we're not... not either. We're in flux."

He laughed. "What does that mean?"

Harlow wanted to growl. "It means, we were talking about whether we should be together or not when all this crap with Ophelia started. We didn't come reach a conclusion and now we can't even talk to each other."

Wearing a look of concern, he raised his temple to his fist, propping an elbow on the bed. "Are you saying you haven't had sex with him for weeks?"

Letting her jaw move her chin, she curled her tongue in her mouth. "No, I didn't quite say that... I said we can't talk, not that we can't fuck."

Groaning, he flopped onto his back, his hands falling on his face. "God, you deserve each other."

Taking her turn to prop her head up, she smiled. "Ryske does that," she said, tracing a nail in the line between his fingers, hoping to tempt them down.

She did and he laid them on his chest. "Does what?"

"Groans and flops away from me thing. He covers his face, talks from behind his hands... I don't know why I didn't notice you were brothers right away."

"You weren't in bed with both of us right away."

"True," she said, picking up his arm and wrapping it around her shoulders as she lay down again, this time putting her head on his chest. They lay in silence for a minute. "Bale?"

"Hmm?"

"You will tell him I love him, won't you? I know he

knows, but with all this flux stuff… if I don't make it to Friday, tell him… remind him…"

"That you love him?"

Closing her eyes, her lips curled. "That he's the goddamn love of my life."

"I will, babe," he said and lifted his head to kiss her hair. "But you're going to make it."

She lost her smile and her eyes opened again. "How can you be so sure?"

"Because I'm your doctor," he said, stroking her hair. "And I haven't lost anyone on your crew yet."

Just that reminder did help her relax. With Bale looking after her, she had the best chance of surviving. If Ophelia got to her in private, and had a weapon, the chances of survival would be nil. In spite of that, Harlow had fought through a lot to get to this point, she wasn't going to stop fighting now.

THIRTY

WAKING UP IN Bale's apartment was great. He brought her coffee in bed and went out to buy breakfast which they ate together in the living room.

He had to work that night and because she thought it best to lay low, Harlow was happy to hang out with him. Enjoying a few hours where life didn't have to be about death and plotting was rejuvenating.

They cooked lunch together and had a nap in the afternoon. Harlow kind of forced him into following his routine. He needed the sleep before his all-night shift at the hospital. If she hadn't been there, he'd have napped. She didn't want to be responsible for him injuring someone or making a mistake. So the compromise was, they napped together.

Harlow had been blow drying her hair with a blow-dryer left behind by one of Bale's ex-girlfriend's—at least that was his excuse for having it—when he came in with the pregnancy test.

She refused to pee on the stick. Instead, she acquiesced to having her blood taken. The doctor's excuse for the blood draw was checking her interlude with Ophelia hadn't had any damaging effect on her body. But she knew he'd do the pregnancy test too. Not that it mattered. She had no reason to believe that she was pregnant. The blood results wouldn't come back fast, so she decided the doctor could have her blood and leave her in peace.

Saying goodbye had been tough. It felt so final. Harlow didn't know what would happen to her over the next few days; there was a chance she wouldn't ever see Bale again.

It was that prospect which drove her to her next destination: her parents' house.

She hadn't been home in weeks. When the cab pulled up outside, she felt more nervous going in than she ever had before. Her family was in there. Her niece or nephew was growing in her sister and there was a possibility she would never meet the little one.

It was a sobering thought and one that made Harlow think about what Bale had said the previous night. If something happened to her, Ryske would take his own life. She didn't want him to be hurt, but understood why he'd make that decision.

Except, what about her niece or nephew. What if they needed the support of an uncle who could get things done? Lena was sweet, not worldly. Rupert wasn't streetwise either. If their child needed someone who'd go to any lengths for them, without her around, Ryske could be their only hope.

Speculating there in her parents' driveway was insane. Asking Ryske to support her niece or nephew would be impossible if she didn't see him again. Even if they did see each other, they would need time to talk things out. If she got as far as Windsor's on Friday, there was zero chance they'd have enough time to communicate everything they needed to.

Coming to her parents gave her a chance to say goodbye. She also wanted to protect her family, who may let Ophelia into their midst without realizing the danger they were in. The danger Harlow put them in.

Venturing forward, she shrugged off her anxiety and strode forward with confidence, channeling Ryske. Opening the front door, she went through the entryway, into the foyer and dumped her bag at the bottom of the stairs while kicking off her shoes.

"Don't panic. It's only me," she said, hearing movement in the dining room.

When she turned toward it, her father was coming out. "Harlow?" he asked. Obviously, her family hadn't been expecting her. Brysen glanced toward the closed front door. "Where's Ryske?"

She grinned. "I'll try not to take that as an insult, that you'd rather see him than me." Going over, she put a hand to his shoulder and boosted herself up to kiss his cheek. "What's for dinner? I'm starving!"

***

DINNER IN THE SWEETING house used to be dominated by the men discussing clients and events and prospects. Only once they were finished with the business news did the women have the chance to chatter about their lives.

These days, that situation had reversed itself. Her mom, Jean, and sister, Lena, ruled the conversation with talk of guest lists and centerpieces and cake tastings.

The wedding was just a matter of weeks away. Lena had picked an empire waist dress just in case her stomach grew larger. She already had a bump. Even in her baggy shirt it was obvious and she wasn't even halfway through the pregnancy. It was going to be a big kid.

Harlow preferred baby talk to wedding talk. The couple was staying at the Sweetings as the apartment had sold. They were still looking for a permanent address, so Rupert's things were in storage.

Although they didn't have a new house, Lena said they were registered for housewarming gifts. They were registered for wedding gifts and baby shower gifts too.

"We thought it would be best to do the baby shower after the wedding," Lena said. "To space things out. But if you want to get my gift before, that's okay. I figure that you and Ryske will want to get one of the big items like the crib or the stroller."

"Oh," Harlow said, glancing around at the expectant

eyes. "Sure. And we know someone in the city who just had a daughter, I can find out if she has any clothes or toys she can hand down."

Lena blinked and looked to Rupert opposite her, in what once had been Ryske's seat. "We actually…" Rupert said. "We wanted everything to be new."

"Oh," Harlow said. "Right… Sure."

Lena relaxed and smiled again. "So which would you like, the crib or the stroller? There's a bassinet on there too, but mom and dad are going to get that."

"We're getting the nursery furniture too," Jean said. "It all matches the crib."

"Okay, then we'll get the crib, if that's what you need." Lena gave Rupert the same look she had before, but Harlow didn't wait for the excuses. "Or the stroller, that's fine too."

Lena smiled. It was funny to watch how she relaxed and tensed depending on what others said. Was this an example of how her sister was going to be as a parent? Looking to Daddy to deliver the discipline when the kids did something Mommy didn't like.

But it was a little scary too. Gone was silly, stressless Lena. Her sister was alert and maybe even a little on edge. Every day had to be a field day for Rupert.

In support and just because, she gave his hand a pat.

"You'll have to be fitted for your dress," Lena said, cutting into her meat.

Harlow stilled. "My… dress?"

"Yes," Jean said on a chuckle, filling in for Lena who was chewing. "Your bridesmaid dress… We wanted you to be maid of honor, but Emma beat you to it. You just haven't been present." Lena appeared disappointed and Harlow didn't want to disappoint her. But she also didn't want to be maid of honor at her ex-fiancé's wedding. "She'll plan a better bachelorette party… It's next weekend… you will be there, won't you?"

Something about her expression must have made her mother doubt it. In truth, Harlow wasn't sure she'd be around then.

"Ryske is coming to the bachelor party," Brysen said. "He didn't tell you?"

"Of course he did!" Not. There hadn't been the time for that kind of wedding talk. "Of course I'll be there," she said and turned to Rupert. "You're okay with Ryske being there?"

Rupert seemed relaxed, which worried her. "Yes. He said he'd bring a few friends, so I won't have to entertain him."

"Oh, God," Harlow said, putting down her fork to press a hand to her décolletage.

Ryske and a few friends meant her crew were going to be at her ex's bachelor party. That could be… interesting. She'd have to make sure he took Bale. The doc was the only one she'd trust to make sure they didn't get too rowdy.

"Would you like to bring a friend to the bachelorette party?" Lena asked.

That perked Harlow up. "I can bring a friend? Can I bring Ryske?"

Everyone at the table laughed. "No, they're on the same night, silly. Besides, it has to be a girlfriend or a gay friend, someone who will appreciate the complexity of the male form."

Lena giggled, but Rupert's fork dropped to his plate.

"Oh, Lena," Jean chastised.

"You're having strippers?" Rupert asked. "I thought we said no strippers."

Paling, Lena twisted a length of hair around her forefinger. "I know, but Emma already paid the deposit."

Rupert blustered. "Well, I… I don't know if Dennis knows how to arrange that sort of thing."

Dennis was the closest thing Rupert had to a friend after her father. Neither man would have a clue how to hire exotic dancers. He worked at SweSec too and was everything she'd come to expect of a finance nerd.

Patting his hand again, Harlow soothed. "Ryske will handle the strippers."

"He… he will?" Rupert asked, probably wondering why Ryske would do him any favors. "He won't mind? Does he know one?"

That startled her. "One?" Harlow's attention darted around to him. "Honey, wherever your friend has reserved, you better ask for a bigger room. Ryske's ratio will be at least two to one… how many guests will be there?"

"Twelve, plus however many Ryske brings."

"So you'll probably need about forty girls."

Lena squawked and Jean was too stunned to even chastise her.

"Forty!" Brysen exclaimed. "That will cost a fortune."

"Not for Ryske," Harlow said, enjoying her food. "He knows people."

Lena got a little lost. "You'd be okay with Ryske being around… that?"

"Bet you're sorry you changed the rules now," Rupert said, almost giddy.

Smiling, Harlow shrugged. "My motto is always the same: if you can steal him, you can have him." She presented a hand to Rupert. "Hence."

"I didn't steal him," Lena said, but shifted in her chair and glanced toward their parents.

"I know, honey. I'm sorry, I didn't mean to imply that, I… I just mean if Ryske can be stolen away then he's not the man for me. But if he was going to be stolen by a scantily clad woman willing to take off her clothes for him, believe me, it would've happened already."

The doorbell rang out. Her father got up to go and answer it. Harlow didn't pay it much attention. The front door was unlocked, she'd walked through it and left it that way. It was only locked by the last person who went to bed each night.

So if it was anyone for her, like Ryske for example, then he'd have walked right in without bothering with the bell.

"How can he know that many?" Lena asked. "You have to be exaggerating."

Something about the way her father backed out the entryway drew Harlow's eye to the dining room door, which gave her a diagonal view across the foyer to the glass door her father was vacating.

As soon as she saw the height of the person with him and the flash of jet-black hair, she stood up, sending her seat clattering backwards.

"Oh, my…"

Rushing away from the table, she ran from the room and barely gave her father a glance as she threw herself up into their guest's arms.

"Maze!"

"You stupid girl," he said, pulling her so close that her feet left the floor. "Why didn't you call me, huh?"

"Oh, you're here," she said, gasping in her desperation. "You came."

"You're damn right I came," he said, setting her on her feet and pushing her hair away from her face. "Are you okay? Are you hurt?"

Shaking her head, she didn't mind that his large hands and long fingers were tangling in her hair as he tried to get it away from her skin to check for contusions.

"How did you find me?"

"Not 'cause you called," he said. "The doc."

So Bale had got in touch with Maze to tell him what was going on. "Did you get my email?"

"This afternoon I did," he said. "Why didn't you use the urgent address?"

"It's not urgent," she said. "And I thought you were at home. I didn't realize you…"

She didn't mean to look around his upper arm toward the entryway, but she did, and he noticed.

"He's not here. I can't get hold of him."

"It's okay," she said, but when her chin sank, he caught it on his curled finger to raise it again.

"It's not okay. You need him."

For her plan to work, she did. But she didn't want to guilt anyone. "He needs to be where he needs to be."

"You think that's away from you?" Maze asked. "We're trying. But we don't have a direct…" She'd looked away, and he must have figured out why. "Give me the number."

"No," she said.

He'd remembered something that most of them probably didn't think about anymore. The cellphone Ryske got when she was in jail. The phone that only she had the number for.

"Does he have it?"

"It's not at home," Harlow said.

"Which means yes. Give me the number."

"No."

"Give me the number… You know I'll get it, so just give it to me."

Folding her arms, she stepped back. "I know you're good, but you can't hack my brain."

His mouth closed; his jaw ticked in frustration. "Damn you two and your privacy. I told him only one person having the number was a bad idea… You know he has it. You can get him here."

"He still has time," Harlow said, leaning in to set her eyes on him. "And I don't call any man to swoop in and rescue me…" Changing the mood because she didn't want to be fighting with him, she looped her arm through his. "Besides, you're the one I need working for me."

"What do you need?"

"We'll talk about that later," she said and smiled at her dad nearby with a sort of dazed look on his face. "Come eat dinner with the family. Mom, we've got one more mouth to feed!"

Leading Maze into the dining room, Harlow almost laughed when both Jean and Rupert thrust to their feet. Lena was chewing, oblivious as always, but she did eye those who'd just leaped up.

"Oh my goodness," Jean exclaimed.

Leaning in, Harlow wrapped her arms further around his. "You're something of a celebrity around here," she whispered to him and then straightened to address the table. "You guys know Aston, right?"

"Rowe," Rupert said, shimmying down and offering a hand. "Yes. Yes, of course."

Maze shook his hand.

Jean came rushing down to grab it in both of hers as

soon as Rupert let him go. "Oh, we're such fans of your family."

"Fans?" he asked, crooking a brow and turning to her, she just shrugged. "Uh… thanks."

"Let me get you something to eat," Jean said, running out of the room.

A series of hissed whispers came from the hall. Were her parents conspiring to oust Ryske? Perhaps. She was enjoying the idea when Lena pointed her fork at Maze.

"You know Ryske, don't you?" Lena asked.

Harlow pulled him around the table and pushed Rupert back into his chair so she could sit down and seat Maze at her other side.

"Ryske? Yes," Maze said, looking around at the table, probably seeking alcohol. "Unfortunately, I do."

"Do you think he knows forty strippers?" Lena asked.

The question made him do a double take. Harlow was smiling when he found her, but she flattened her smile and opened a hand to her sister, forcing Maze to address the question.

"At least forty," he said.

It might have taken him a minute, but Maze was sensing her mood about her family, and didn't mind sinking into the rhythm she'd set. Lena stopped mid-chew. Her eyes bounced back and forth between her sister and Maze.

"I told you," Harlow said. "It's no problem."

Rupert leaned over her to speak direct to Maze. "We're getting married, Lena and I," he said. "In a few weeks. We'd love it if you'd come."

Maze opened his mouth, but Harlow answered. "He's already coming," she said. "He'll be at the bachelor party too."

"I will?" Maze murmured and she nodded, so he shrugged. "Apparently, I will." He turned to Lena. "Congratulations to you both… on the wedding and the baby."

"They're moving too," Harlow said, cutting some of her meat and smudging it in her sauce to offer it to his lips. Maze took it from her fork. "They're staying here until they get their new place… Will you stay over with me?"

Maze swallowed. "Here? Sure… We can go to my mom's if you want."

"No." She'd rather be with her family in case Ophelia showed up. "Ryske doesn't get along with your mom."

"Neither do I, because she'd rather I didn't live where I live or do what I do," he said. "But the house is big enough we don't have to see them."

She gave him some more food from her fork and then took his hand. "I don't want to be that far from you tonight."

He nodded and ran a hand down her hair. "I'm happy wherever you're happy."

"We have two guest rooms," Lena said. "You'll probably want the larger."

Her parents came back into the dining room. Jean carried a generous plate of food over to Maze. As Brysen sat down, Jean retrieved flatware for Maze.

"He doesn't need a guest room, he'll bunk in with me," Harlow said, pouring wine into the glass that her mother had put down for Maze.

The table stopped. After they looked at each other, their gazes settled on her. Most didn't know what, if anything, they should say.

Lena was the first to venture something. "Should… should someone speak up for Ryske?"

"Lena," Jean chastised, shaking off her shock and returning to her seat, though there was a blush in her cheeks.

"Mr. Rowe, I'm sure, you're a wonderful young man," Brysen said. "But my daughter—"

"Oh, please," Harlow said. "Ryske is capable of speaking for himself." Or he would if he was there. "He couldn't care less about me sleeping with other men."

"Sleeping," Maze said, quickly clarifying and tossing her a side-glare before addressing her parents. "I assure you, your daughter's honor is safe around me. Ryske is like a brother and until he steps aside or dies, I would never invade his territory."

Though her family didn't know how to take that, Harlow scoffed and elbowed him. "You just remember our conversation about oral before you start making promises you can't keep."

"Good point," he said and sat back, resting an arm on the back of her chair. "Your daughter's honor is safe from me."

"Ryske would own your ass if you touched me," Harlow said, passing him the rest of her meat. "Eat your food."

Maze sat up to do as he was told. "He'd try. But he'd fail."

"You underestimate how motivated he'd be. And how long it's been since he got any." She noticed her mother and sister looking at her, so she fudged the truth. "Because I've been ill. He didn't want to get, you know, mucus and whatever…"

Maze laughed. "Don't try that shit with me, I know what happened."

Yeah, almost two weeks ago. They'd gone without for longer before, but it felt like an age, maybe because she hadn't seen him since that night.

THIRTY-ONE

THE REST OF the dinner went along at a polite pace. Her family asked Maze about his. Harlow got to hear about Lena's wedding again as she went over everything that had already been discussed. Maze was polite, but she could tell he'd stopped listening a while ago.

"So do you live in the city?" Jean asked.

The doorbell went again. Both she and Maze must have felt the same curl of awareness because they glanced to each other. Bale was working, none of the guys would know where they were. Even if they did, they wouldn't have gotten there so fast.

They hadn't had time to discuss strategy, but if that was Ophelia at the door, Harlow would take her down. She wasn't even sure she'd hesitate.

"Maze lives with me, Mom," Harlow said, distracted by the door.

"I thought you lived with Ryske," Lena said.

"I do."

"The three of you live together?" Lena asked, probably wondering about their weird setup.

There was no time to answer. When Harlow saw who her father was ushering inside, she jumped to her feet again.

"Shit," Harlow said aloud and grabbed Maze's shoulder, giving it a squeeze before skirting the table and running into the hall. "What the hell are you doing here, Zance?"

Neither man had seen her coming, so her question startled them both.

Penzance turned. She didn't like the solemn look on his face. "Is there somewhere we can talk?"

When she'd needed him, she couldn't find him. But that was no more his fault than it was Ryske's for being inaccessible when she'd wanted him near.

"Sure," Harlow said, and gestured him toward the den, but she turned to look in the dining room.

Just making eye contact with Maze was enough to let him know he was needed. He got up to join them.

Once they were in the den, she closed the door and Penzance turned, only to be startled by Maze. "I didn't know you were here."

"Well, I am," Maze said, sliding his hands into his pockets. "What's your problem?"

"She doesn't trust me anymore," Penzance said, opening his arms in a shrug. "So I'm out. But she sent me here with a message."

Harlow moved closer. "She sent you here?" He nodded. Trepidation prompted her to reach back for Maze's hand. He gave it and moved forward, resting the other on her shoulder. "Is she coming here?"

"She says no," Penzance said. "Something went down with Brash, don't know what, but he trashed her whole apartment. Animal put a knife to her throat."

"Shit," she breathed out and her cheek fell to Maze's hand.

"I don't think they're done with her," Penzance said. "Brash said he was coming back for her, that it wasn't over… But he wanted to do it right… whatever 'it' is."

Taking her down, she'd imagine. It might be difficult for him to kill Ophelia given she was Jarvis Hagan's sister. Although she was responsible for his death, would he want her dead? Even Harlow couldn't answer that.

Learning the truth would've been a shock to Brash who had probably taken control of Animal. Animal was easy to control and seemed to like orders. Maybe he needed someone else to guide him, she didn't know, but that didn't lessen how dangerous he was. Animal was a weapon Brash could point and shoot at anyone... including the messenger.

"You came to tell us Brash wants to hurt Ophelia, why—"

"I gave him the recording," she murmured, trying to figure out what to do next.

She was yanked from her verve with a violent tug when Maze whirled her around to grab her shoulders. "Are you crazy?"

"Not all of it," Harlow said. "Just the end. I edited it, so he could hear the truth."

Maze's anger was obvious. "Why?" he asked, giving her a shake. "Why would you—"

"She took his collar off," Harlow snapped back. "I had to do something! We were at the club and he was ready to finish me, Maze! Don't you get it? At the club, with Pothos and bedrooms and—"

"Okay. Okay," he said, holding up his hands and backing off. "I understand... you prepared it before?"

She nodded. "I couldn't go back after I got Hagan's message. I went home and waited for you guys. When you didn't come back, I couldn't just sit around. Brash wanted to hurt me. He's been baying for blood. Ophelia promised to give me to him when Ryske went to her. I didn't know what was going to happen. She's been crazy without Ryske around. She wants to know where he is... This started when she demanded I take her to him... I wasn't going to do that."

Maze took a long breath in and closed his mouth to breathe it out. "You're the only one who can reach him. Har—"

"No," she said. "If I call him—"

"He'll come."

"Yeah, but at what cost? Brash probably still wants him dead too. I cut the start of the recording because I didn't want to renew Brash's hatred for Ryske. But Ryske was being protected by Ophelia. Now Brash doesn't give a damn about Ophelia's orders, how do we know he won't come for Ryske as well?"

"Ryske's old news," Maze said. "He didn't hurt Anwen. She's alive, so—"

"Hagan died thinking she was dead. That's got to jam Brash's craw. His boss never knew that she was out there. Don't forget, Ryske did fuck her, there's no changing that, and that's what caused the hatred in the first place."

"That guy and his damn dick," Maze grumbled.

"You know that's not fair," she said. "You know what happened with Anwen."

"Look, guys," Penzance said, stepping into the fray. "I'm sure this is a great debate, but you need a plan. Ophelia said you have until Friday. She expects you'll show at the club. If you don't, she's coming for you. It's showdown time."

"Oh, yeah," Maze asked, folding his arms with an air of expectation shimmering around him. Harlow wasn't sure he trusted Ophelia's restraint. "What's your plan?"

"You listened to the message, right?" Maze nodded. "You have to find whatever Parratt's wife has."

He became more discerning. "You want to turn the consortium against her."

"I'll give her two options. Either she leaves or all of us turn her in."

"She'll sing."

"Doesn't matter if we put it on her." Harlow raised a finger. "We have her on Jarvis' death. We have the murder weapon and can provide cops with the edited recording. Whether they can use them as evidence or not, they'll at least confirm we're telling the truth. We can edit the Hagan recording, show that he feared his sister was going to hurt him. And we have the evidence of their parents' murder."

Raising a hand, Maze touched the key that was tied to the chain around her neck. "Hard to believe we're trusting him."

"There's evidence, Maze," she said. "It's compelling. The doc says he'll translate the medical notes that prove she has a condition."

"And if Ophelia comes in shooting?" Maze asked.

"I've authorized Ryske on the safe deposit box," she said. "You guys can still use it, even if I'm not around."

That startled him; his hand dropped. "We're not going to let anything happen to you. Doing it at the club, it could be a setup."

"Maybe," she said. "But we have to try something."

"Is there a plan B?"

Unfortunately, there was. "Yes." When she didn't elaborate, he zeroed in on her. "I'll confess to the cops, and Ryske goes to her. That's it."

Blinking, Maze moved away again. This time, he almost stumbled and came to a stop when he hit the high arm of the pull out couch.

He dropped to sit on it. "You'll go back to jail."

"Yeah… Better than going on the run."

"Do you think? Do you think Ryske will think so?"

"It's the only way to control her. He's the only one who can control her. Ryske knew that; he knew that from the beginning. That's why he made the suggestion in the first place. If he's intimate with her, she'll listen to him, she'll believe him. The rest of you will be safe if he's in her bed."

"Then why do you have to go to jail?"

"Because just going to her won't be enough," Harlow said. "She's going to feel like she's been duped too many times. She still wants him, but she'll want to know I'm far away… Anyway, does it matter where I am?"

"It matters to me. It will matter to Ryske."

"It can't matter to him," she said. "If I'm free somewhere in the world, I'll be too much of a distraction, too much of a temptation. He has to make it real with her, as real as it can be."

Over time he could grow to love her and maybe they could be happy. When Ryske wanted to send her to Rupert, he'd known the man didn't make her happy, but with Rupert she was safe. And that was the crux of it. Ophelia might be a crazy person, but she wouldn't hurt Ryske, he'd be safe with her. In fact, Ophelia would go to all sorts of lengths to protect and keep him, so he might even be safer with her than without.

"You can't just give up."

"I don't want to give up," she said. "That's why I want to fight. But you asked for a plan B and I'm sorry, but that's it."

Leaving the couch, he came to take her shoulders again. "It's not. No way. We'll call that Plan C. Plan B is getting you and Ryske the hell out of dodge."

"Yeah?" she asked, her head tipping to the side. "And what about those people through there?" Pointing toward the dining room, she thought about her family. "Ophelia knows they're here. She knows that to hurt me, all she has to do is hurt them."

"We'll pay for protection."

"Forever?" she asked. "My sister is pregnant. I don't want my niece or nephew growing up surrounded by armed guards. How long would it last? How long until she gets to one of them?" Pissed at the angry grief that came with acknowledging how this might turn out, Harlow was losing control. "Do you think I want him with her? Do you think it makes me happy to send the man I love to a psychopath? It makes me sick to think of him touching her let alone…" The idea of Ryske being intimate with Ophelia churned bile in her gut. Controlling the sickness, she couldn't subdue her angry tears. "I need him with her. Don't you get it? I *need* him there. We all do. I'll make him do the one thing he doesn't want to do because it will keep you safe. It will keep our crew safe, and our families safe. Because she won't stop, Maze. She won't fucking stop." Curling her fingers into her palm, Harlow's nails dug deep into her sensitive flesh. "She will pick us off one by one, and the inevitable will happen anyway."

"Nightingale," Maze murmured, stroking her arms.

She didn't want his comfort. Throwing his hands away from her body, she turned to march over to the window that let her see into her parents' side yard.

"You know what makes it worse?" she whispered. "He'll use me… He'll use what he feels for me, and our intimacy to get him through. It's the only way he'll be able to make himself be with her… He'll be with her, thinking of me… How sick is that?"

"He loves you," Maze said. "Only you. He won't be able to do it."

Spinning around, she wanted him to see nothing but confidence. "I'll tell him to."

And that would be enough. Ryske had floated the idea at the beginning, understanding that he had the power to control Ophelia. But they all knew she had that same power over him. Even if he'd changed his mind and decided it wasn't something he wanted to do, if Harlow said she wanted him to, he'd do it, even against his own will.

"He can't be with a woman he isn't attracted to," Penzance said. "After what she's done to you and everyone he cares about, there's no way he—"

"He can," Harlow said, letting her attention drop to the floor. "He will do it."

"There's no way."

She knew her man. He'd use their intimate memories to do what needed to be done. He'd close his eyes and remind himself she'd sent him there. And he'd recall where she was and why she'd gone there, to keep him safe.

Ryske wouldn't want to. But if she told him it was the only thing that would keep her safe, he'd do it. She'd hated the idea every other time he'd brought it up, so if she suddenly authorized it, he'd know they'd reached a point of no return.

"And if she kills you?" Maze asked, displeased with the direction of the conversation and her attitude, but what was she supposed to do? This was their life. "What then?"

"Then, it's moot. Ophelia will leave you guys alone if Ryske and I are out of the picture."

"She won't kill Ryske," Penzance said. "You just said she wanted to be with him and she wants you out of the way. She won't have a problem killing you, I believe that, but Ryske, she won't kill him."

Without blinking, she turned cool eyes to him. "She won't have to."

"Okay," Maze said, raising his hands. "I'm not listening to this anymore. This has gone too far." Looking left and right, he almost expected someone to materialize out of thin air. "Where the hell is Ryske? You've gone fucking crazy."

He believed it. Maze was an exasperated man at the end of his rope.

She smiled. "Bale has instructions."

It was only fair to prepare Maze for what could be inevitable.

He became incredulous, his head bobbing toward her. "You've talked about it? You've talked about…"

She didn't blink and Maze threw up his hands again, this time turning his back on her.

Penzance stepped in front of her. "You're worried about your family, and I think you should be," he said, giving Maze a minute to mutter to himself. "You shouldn't leave them alone tonight. Are they all staying here?"

"Yes," she said with a nod. "Maze and I are staying." He acknowledged that, but she took his hand. "You're staying too."

Startled by her assertion, Penzance would've glanced over his shoulder at Maze if she'd let him turn, but she kept hold of him. "What? Why?"

"Because you just said my family need protection and I know you're capable… It's time you came home, Zance," she said. "You're one of us."

"Wait a second…" Maze said, marching over, pulling Penzance back to break apart their hands, like he was worried she was being infected by him. Taking his glare from Penzance, Maze bowed and leaned close to whisper at her. "Have you talked to Ryske about this?"

"Do I need to talk to Ryske about this?"

Like he couldn't quite believe his ears, Maze blinked a half dozen times then his brows rose. "Yes, you fucking do. Those two were closer than brothers and that one…" He jabbed a thumb back over his shoulder in Penzance's direction. "He fucked off without so much as a thanks for the memories."

"Har, I don't need anyone stepping up for me," Penzance said and backed away.

She pushed Maze aside and took Penzance's hand to pull him toward her. At the same time, she grabbed for Maze's hand, so she was holding them both.

"I am stepping up for you," she said. "You didn't ask me to do a damn thing. I'm telling you you're part of this family… Whether you like it or not."

Maze was muttering again. "Insane," he said. "You've lost your fucking mind."

Harlow just smiled and stepped between them, forcing both to turn toward the door as she put an arm around each of their waists. "That's possible," she said. "It could be withdrawal… it's been a while since Ryske slipped it to me."

Penzance was on the same page and happy to lighten the moment. "There are two right here that—"

"Watch that mouth, Vane," Maze growled. "You wait 'til Ryske gives you permission to talk to her like that."

"Uh, I give him permission," she said, opening the den door. "You two relax, it's time to charm the in-laws. Come on."

THIRTY-TWO

HAVING PENZANCE AT the end of the table was awkward at first. Lena kept staring at him and Rupert kept staring at Lena staring at him. It might have been because Penzance had broken Emma's heart. But Harlow had a feeling, while her trio were having their conference in the den, her parents told Lena not to raise that subject.

By the time dessert was finished, Penzance had her family eating out the palm of his hand. He was good at what he did. Almost as good as Ryske. Not that she'd ever make that assertion out loud.

They stayed up to have a drink and Maze took some time to do some research on the laptop he'd left in the entryway. No one commented on him working. She knew what he was doing, so left him to it.

All retired to bed about the same time. Harlow did feel better to have Penzance in the house, sleeping in the guest room. So if something did go down, she'd have additional backup.

Her and Maze lay in the dark together for a while not saying anything. With her head on his chest, she liked the comfort of his fingers combing through her hair. At some point, they started to talk. She couldn't remember how they got onto the subject, but they reminisced about better times they'd shared since the night Ryske crashed into her.

She drifted off to sleep with a smile on her face and woke up with one too. But it shrank when, just like the previous morning, she reminded herself Ryske wouldn't be a part of the day.

Her father and Rupert went to work. She went shopping with Lena and Jean for baby things, with their two bodyguards in tow, though Harlow didn't let on that's why the men were around. Her mother and sister took her to the dress shop to be fitted for her bridesmaid dress. Mocking her wearing the elegant peach gown seemed to be a uniting experience for the guys.

Before she knew it, they were at the dinner table again. Seated between Maze and Rupert with Penzance at the end of the table, she was supposed to be listening to Lena's story about a parenthood class. Everyone else was listening, but Harlow's mind was wandering.

It was Thursday. Tomorrow, something would change. If she didn't lose her life, she could lose her freedom. She'd been counting on Ryske returning home tomorrow, but she had no idea if he'd come early in the day, or if he'd just show up at the club.

Scraping her fork through her pasta, Harlow couldn't stomach a bite. All she wanted was to look at him, to see him one more time before—

The front door opened.

Everyone heard it. The noise of it bursting open and someone storming through the entryway wasn't quiet. Usually the dining room door was open, that night Jean closed it to trap the scent of the candles inside the room.

Leaping to her feet, her chair clattered over again. "Ryske," she whispered just a fraction before the dining room door opened.

There he was.

His chest rose and fell fast. Not out of breath, he was amped.

Vehement eyes landed on her. "Trinket."

"Crash," she breathed out the word and didn't even

care about the blur of tears obscuring her view.

Half a second away from jumping onto the table and running across it to throw herself at him, adrenaline threatened to take over. Ryske blinked at the others present. Moving forward, he did an amazing job of keeping his composure.

"Brysen," he said, offering her father a handshake and moving around the table to kiss both Jean and Lena. "Marlowe."

The two of them shook hands for a brief second, but Ryske looked past Rupert at her and kept on coming, scooping his hands around her head to pull her closer. Searching her eyes, he seemed content just to look into her, but she wanted more.

"Kiss me, idiot."

The corner of his mouth rose before he pulled her up to unite their lips.

It took all her restraint not to leap up and wrap herself around him. He was there. He'd come. She didn't know how he knew her location or why he'd returned early. She didn't care. His tongue tangled with hers and she coiled her arms around him, eager to give more.

But he broke their kiss and pressed his forehead to hers, holding her head tight in both hands. "You're free," he murmured like he couldn't quite believe it.

"Still too expensive for you," she said, stroking his shoulders and arms. "You came… You came for me."

Opening his eyes, he bent his knees to line up their gazes. "Always, Trink… Every time."

They were trapped between the table and the French windows. Would it be so terrible to drag him outside and have her way with him as she'd threatened to do in a restaurant once?

"You came straight here?" Maze asked.

Her guy. Her man. Busy trying to tempt Ryske's tongue into her mouth, grazing her lips on his, she wanted action, not words. Her love was holding back, though the smile on his face betrayed it wasn't because he wanted to.

"Over a hundred the whole way," Dover said.

Dover? Her friend's voice brought her around fast. Stunned, the last sight she expected to await her was Dover in the doorway with Noon and Anwen.

"We should extend the table," Jean said, sort of overwhelmed by the sight of so many people in her dining room. Leaving her seat, her mother went to the empty head of the table. "Help me pull this out."

Rupert pulled out the top leaf of the table while Jean retrieved chairs from the closet. Ryske righted her chair and sat in it, pulling her onto his lap.

"Ryske?" Lena said.

"Yes, honey?" he asked, scooping up some of Harlow's pasta to fill his mouth.

When was the last time he ate?

Dover, Anwen, and Noon were being set up at the end of the table by Jean who went to retrieve more food.

Harlow took the fork from Ryske to stab some pasta while he and Maze did a fist bump thing. Seemed he'd just noticed how close his friend was.

"You don't really know forty strippers, do you?" Lena asked.

"Male or female?" Ryske said before accepting the food Harlow fed to him.

"Female."

"Sure… You'll have to give them an hour to get here, they don't all live in this neighborhood."

Lena's mouth fell open. "You don't!"

Ryske was still chewing, clearly unsure why this had come up.

Harlow filled him in. "I said you'd take care of the strippers for the bachelor party."

"She said you'd have a ratio of two to one," Lena said.

He swallowed. "At least."

Feeding him some more food, his appetite had to be satisfied. With his mouth full again, she removed his hand from her thigh to reclaim his bracelet. Once off, he took it from her and put it on her wrist, returning it to where it belonged with a kiss.

"Are you going to tell him?" Lena asked.

Harlow reached into Ryske shirt to retrieve the bullet on the leather around his neck. Though he glanced at what she was doing, he didn't question it.

"Tell him what?" Harlow asked, untying the knot in the leather with Ryske intent on what she was doing.

"You know," Lena said, eyeing her and then eyeing Maze.

"I think she means that we slept together," Maze said.

"Oh," Harlow said, putting the loose ends on the table and then untying her key from the loop on her necklace. "I've slept with him too." Harlow nodded at Dover, and then at Anwen. "And her…" Turning to the other end of the table, she nodded at Penzance. "And him." When she leaned back to look at Noon next to Rupert, she frowned. "I don't think I've slept with you… Oh, honey… I'll sleep with you tonight."

"Uh, no you won't," Ryske said. She smiled and turned to kiss him. "We have business to take care of tonight."

Like the fact that it had been almost two weeks since they'd had sex and far longer since they'd spent a night together. Licking his lip, she kissed him again, then nuzzled her mouth against him, before looking behind Rupert at Noon.

"Some other time."

"You've… you've slept with all of them?"

Lena couldn't believe what she was hearing. Her sister was so incredulous that Harlow was almost afraid to look at their mother. Her father was probably close to a coronary.

"I slept with the doctor the night before I got here too," Harlow said, removing the string from the key and threading it onto the leather to join the bullet. "But the only man I've had sex with is the one I'm sitting on." Rupert cleared his throat but didn't take his attention from his plate. She shrugged. "Well, yeah… and… yeah."

Tying the ends of the leather again, she put it back over Ryske's head.

"Thanks," he said. "You get me a present?"

"We have a safe deposit box now."

His brows rose. "No kidding?"

"Yeah," she said, tucking the key and bullet back into Ryske's shirt. "We should talk about it later."

Rupert grew concerned. "That's the only key there is."

She patted it through Ryske's shirt. "And now it's safe."

Rupert didn't seem convinced, but she ignored his incredulity. "It wasn't safe where it was?"

After touching the O-ring on her necklace, her fingertips drifted to her cleavage. "No, that's for something else."

Rupert looked at her necklace and maybe her cleavage too. "What's it for?"

She inhaled to respond. The moment her lips parted, Ryske hooked a finger into it and pulled her down to marry their mouths. Draping her arms around him, she might be happy to just sit making out with him forever. When his hand slid up her thigh, toward the hem of her dress, she remembered her parents were in the audience.

Pulling her mouth from his kiss, she planted a hand on the table. "You know what, Crash? I think we need to go upstairs."

"Harlow!" Jean snapped. The color in her cheeks joined a glance around the table at their guests, most of whom she didn't know. "Really? Control yourself."

"It's my fault, Jean," Ryske said, gliding his fingers deeper between her thighs. "She's hot for me."

Though Harlow narrowed her eyes on him, she didn't duck away fast enough when he darted in to steal another kiss.

She pushed him to the back of the chair. "True or not," she said and then gestured around the table. "I meant *we* have to go upstairs... There are things my group need to discuss."

The chair didn't move when she tried to push back. Ryske took the hint and moved it for her, getting to his feet and taking her hand. His whistle startled her parents, Lena, and Rupert, but the rest of the table stood up, Penzance included.

The whistle was a call for attention and for action,

and if Penzance knew it, Ryske must've been using it for a long time. Penzance went out first with Maze at his back, Harlow and Ryske followed. They traipsed up the stairs, away from the dining room with Noon, Anwen, and Dover behind them.

"Nightingale," Dover said, holding her as soon as the bedroom door was closed.

Noon hugged her too. She and Anwen just looked at each other. There wasn't anger or hatred there, not that Harlow could see, but there was certainly trepidation.

"Go sit over in the window. Damn, it's crowded in here," Ryske said, Harlow started to move with Dover and Noon, but her guy caught her wrist to pull her back. "Not you."

Tipping her head up, Harlow smiled at him, basking in their proximity. Ryske dragged her over to the bed and shoved her down. While her feet were still dangling, she toed off her shoes then climbed on to sit against the headboard, facing the window where Dover and Noon seated themselves.

Ryske got on the bed behind her and guided her back to lean on him. Penzance and Maze took a bottom corner each. Anwen perched on the vanity stool and then there was silence.

"Where should we begin?" Harlow asked, raising her chin to try getting a look at Ryske.

THIRTY-THREE

"WE'RE WAITING FOR you, Trink," Ryske said. "We want every detail."

And what did she want?

Leaning back, she twisted further, sinking down against Ryske to gaze up at him. "Kiss me, Crash."

Tightening the circle of his arms around her, she loved how hard he crushed her against him. When he bowed, she expected a kiss, but he paused before their mouths made contact.

"Talk."

Frustrated by his refusal, she shoved out of his arms and sat up. Straightening out her clothes and hair, she restrained an impulse to curse.

He reached for her, but she swatted his hand away. If he wanted to tease her, she could tease right back.

"Can we trust everyone in the room?" she asked.

If he said yes, she'd accept his faith, but would be honest that she was dubious.

"I don't know," Ryske said, landing a glare on Penzance. "Who invited that fucker?"

"I did," Harlow said.

"They always like this?" Penzance asked from the

corner of his mouth.

Maze shrugged. "They're both sex deprived."

"Not for long," Ryske said, driving a hand between her thighs to yank her leg toward him.

Wrestling the intruder free, she locked her fingers between his to keep his hands from wandering.

"I might be sex deprived… But I hear, Crash, you've been getting yours on a regular basis." Her attention went to the woman on the vanity stool. "Isn't that right, Anwen?"

Tucking her hands under her thighs, Anwen didn't like being the focus of everyone's scrutiny.

"Trink—"

"No," Harlow said. "I want to hear it from her. You lied about the man I love and then you lied to him… Tell me why I shouldn't tear your throat out?"

Her hand drifted from Ryske's when she leaned away to open her nightstand drawer. Needing her pointed ring was a distinct possibility.

"Baby," Ryske said, stroking under her skirt when she settled with her legs bent toward him again.

Harlow slid her ring on and rested her hand over Ryske's, tapping the point of the accessory on his flat hand.

"It was juvenile," Anwen said. "I'm sorry, Harlow. I shouldn't have said that I was sleeping with Ryske."

"She apologized, baby," Ryske said, turning over his hand to open his fingers between hers though their hands remained flat. "Ophelia pushed her buttons… it's like you said about—"

"Stop," Harlow said and looked at him. "You're saying I can trust her? I really don't want to listen to excuses and explanations. She's competitive, I get it. Your cock's not a toy to fight over."

Swagger curved his lips. "You can say that 'cause it's yours to play with any time you want."

"I'm happy to sign over ownership if you want to keep defending her lies," Harlow said, not seeing the funny side. "She knew Ophelia killed her brother. She knew about the Yarker affair. She said nothing."

"I wanted to have a plan… You always have a plan.

You're always so…together," Anwen said. "I knew you didn't kill Jarvis, but I didn't want you to think I wasn't grateful anymore. I didn't want you to think I was angry at you for misleading me either. I understand why you stayed quiet."

"Kind of you."

"Yes, I knew about Yarker too. I thought having Ophelia's trust would help us out in the long run. I just hadn't figured out what to do with it."

Harlow held up her arm to show her bracelet. "And you needed this because…"

Anwen sighed and seemed to shrink. "Like I said, it was juvenile. I wanted Ophelia to be jealous. I wanted to be better than her… I guess I'm no better than her."

"Okay," Harlow said and shifted her focus. "Maze, you know what happened. Will you fill everyone in, please?"

Sliding off the bed, she passed Anwen as she went around the end to get to the door.

"Trinket," Ryske called. "Trink, where are you going?"

She didn't answer him. Leaving the bedroom, she went down the stairs and through the kitchen to the backyard. She was pacing toward the back fence when Ryske caught up to her.

Grabbing her arm, he pulled her around. "Come here," he said, trying to haul her to him.

She resisted. "No, Ryske. Just leave me."

Struggling to twist her hand out of his grip only got him fighting harder to keep hold of her. "Let me kiss you."

"No," she said and kept pulling away. "No, Ryske. I don't want it."

"You don't want what?" he asked, throwing her hand from his grip. "Me? Is that it? Because of some bullshit story Anwen told Ophelia?"

Leaping toward him, she gave up on keeping it together. "I could be dead in twenty-four hours and this is what I spend my last night on earth doing? Do you think I want to be questioning her? I know you didn't have sex with her. This isn't jealousy. I don't trust her and with the way things have played out, I am terrified that any decision I make could lead to someone I love getting killed."

"No one will hurt you," he said, exuding only certainty. "But you want to talk about bad choices? Why in the hell didn't you call me the minute you got out of there?"

"I thought you were home! How was I supposed to know you weren't?"

"The minute you knew I wasn't, you should've called!"

"How was I supposed to call you and tell you this could be the end?"

He faltered. "The end of what? We want it to be the end. The sooner we can get Ophelia out of our lives, the better."

"So much has happened to us, Ryske," she said, softening her voice and moving closer. "I try to be strong. To be sure we'll come out on top." She paused to swallow away some of her worry. "I want you to be proud of me."

His frown grew deeper. "I am. Shit, baby…" Sliding his hands over hers, he locked their digits together. "I am so proud of you… No matter what happens tomorrow, I will still love you. I'll love you more then than I do now. I love you more every minute." When he got no response, he laid his hands on her face, palms on her cheeks, fingers pointing upward. "Baby, if you want to walk out of here right now, we'll go. You before them. Let's just flip."

Raising her attention, she couldn't believe the strength of her love. It filled her so full it almost hurt. "I don't want to let you down. I don't want to lose you."

The trauma of losing him had never gone away. She could squash it down when they were happy, but with this kind of danger on their horizon, that fear swelled.

"You won't," he said, increasing his grip and bowing to brush his mouth over hers.

Blinking, she didn't let the tear on her cheek distract her from confessing. Adrenaline surged until her pulse echoed in her ears.

"I don't want to be in flux anymore," she breathed in a quiet voice.

It took him a few seconds to process her words.

When he did, his lips curled slowly.

"Trinket," he said, pushing her hair back, his hands sliding down under her ears to cup her head. "You want to know when we stopped being in flux?"

Nodding, she didn't know how he could be so amused. That didn't prevent her from basking in his adoration.

"When?"

"The night I came back from the dead," he said, skimming his thumb across her lips. "Standing outside on the corner when you let me kiss you... there's been no flux since then."

They'd been flat broken up for some of the time between then and now. From that moment, somehow, he'd known there was no going back. Yet another example of his arrogance. He'd decided they were going to be together and hadn't heard anything else since, no matter what.

"You remember that kiss?" she asked, drawing a fingernail up his shirt over the location of his tattoo.

"Damn right. Don't you?"

She smiled. "Maybe."

"Maybe?" He scowled like he was offended, but she could tell he was playing. "Fuck. That was some of my best work."

"You need more practice."

"Do I?"

Curling her fingers in his shirt until she had a handful, she pulled him down. "Mm hmm," she said, guiding his mouth to hers.

Their friends would be able to see them through the upstairs window. Her family might be watching from the dining room downstairs. In spite of the possible spectators, Harlow wrapped her arms around him and let the world fade away. They couldn't let their passion consume them, but they could devote their mouths to spoiling each other for a while.

With a groan, he stole his mouth back. "The neighbors are going to talk, baby."

Grabbing his shirt in both hands, she kept him close and grinned up at him. "If our friends weren't watching, I'd give the neighbors a hardcore show."

"Don't let those fuckers stop you," he said, skimming his hands down to cup her breasts. Inhaling hard, his gaze dropped to her cleavage. "Man, you can distract me from anything… You're teasing me, Trink."

He wasn't the only one sunk. They should be talking about their plan. Instead, they were stroking each other in her parents' backyard.

"The problem is all those people in our bedroom. You know they're the only thing standing between you and sex right now."

"Damn those bastards, I never liked any of them." Seizing her hand, he dragged her toward the house. "Let's get rid of 'em."

Trust Ryske to turn her mood around and get her confidence back on track. He led her through the kitchen and back up the stairs, where they found Maze doing as she'd asked. Except Anwen wasn't in the room.

Ryske was about to interrupt when Harlow put a hand to his mouth and tugged him over to sit on the bed again.

"Okay," she said. "I'm sorry. We're ready now."

Penzance glanced at an imaginary watch. "That was like five minutes, dude. That's all she gets after putting up with Ophelia for a month and a half?"

She gasped and flipped over to look at Ryske, startling him enough to forget the snickering Penzance and Maze.

"The club is yours," Harlow said, only just remembering to tell him. "Lydia told me. It's official."

"Ours, Peach Pit," he said, drawing a fingertip down the perimeter of her face. After gazing at her with love for a minute, he looked past her to Dover still sitting in the window. "Hey, we have an empire now."

Dover smiled at that declaration. Maze and Noon laughed.

The absentee concerned her. "Where's Anwen?"

"Restroom," Penzance said. "She went just before you came back."

Ah, a chance! Shoving her guy onto his back, she threw her body across his lap to fumble under the bed.

"Mm," Ryske said, sliding a hand up her skirt to fondle her ass. "I'm appreciating this too much with so many guys in the room."

Damnit, not there. Wait… Hadn't she…?

Clambering over Ryske to get off the bed, she ran into the closet.

"Hey! I'll stop enjoying it," Ryske called. "Come back."

Penzance laughed. She could still hear them while searching her gym bag.

"Maybe she wants you to follow."

"Maybe," Ryske said like he might be interested. No surprise, he was always interested. "We've never done it in that closet."

"But you've done it in others?" Penzance asked, a snicker in his voice.

"Oh, yeah," Ryske bragged.

Yes! Got it!

She pounced out of the closet. Leaving the door open, she turned off the light.

"Catch," she said, tossing the velvet box to Ryske between Penzance and Maze.

"What's…" Sitting up as he popped it open, at the sight of the ring, he frowned, then sighed. "Man, you move fast," he said. "You know I'll say yes, but no finesse? Where's the romance?"

She folded her arms and leaned on the closet doorframe. "I'm not proposing to you."

"Maybe someone proposed to her," Noon said like he'd just answered a question on a game show.

It was hilarious to see how her exuberant friend's exclamation erased Ryske's amusement. His scowl shot from Noon to her.

"Who? I'll rip out his fucking tongue."

"You think it's unbelievable?" she asked.

He straightened up and tossed the ring to Dover for his inspection. "That some bastard would want to take me on for you? Who the fuck thinks they can take you from me?"

"Would you relax and stop shouting," she said,

pushing away from the closet doorframe to cross to him.

Worried Anwen could come back any minute, Harlow put her hands on his thighs and climbed onto the bed, crawling up higher on him until she straddled his hips. He slouched against the headboard, and his hands crept under her skirt, around to her ass. Slipping off her pointed ring to prevent injury, she tossed it on the nightstand before picking up the hem of his shirt to pull it off over his head.

"Whoa, okay, what's happening now?" Penzance asked.

Flattening her hands on Ryske's chest, Harlow slithered down to press her mouth against his tattoo. Scratching her nail around the edge of his ink, their gazes met. Once upon a time, she'd asserted her mouth would never be on his body. He must have been thinking the same thing. His wink betrayed his swagger.

"It's Anwen's," Dover said.

Harlow sat up on Ryske's legs, letting her nails trail to his abs as she twisted to look at the window seat. "Yeah, it was in the safe deposit box," she said. "I didn't know how she'd feel about us returning it to her. Hagan didn't say what he wanted us to do with it… So I thought I'd leave it to Ryske."

"That's the best idea," Dover said and tossed it back to Ryske who caught it with one hand.

"If Ryske pulls out a little velvet box, Anwen's going to think he's proposing to her," Maze said.

"Wait a second," Ryske said. "Someone has to catch me up, what the hell are we talking about?"

The bedroom door opened. Anwen came back in, drawing everyone's attention. Harlow felt a pang of guilt when she noticed the woman's bloodshot eyes. She'd been crying.

"I explained it while you weren't here," Maze said to Ryske. "The safe deposit box was set up by Hagan. He left Harlow a message."

Figuring Anwen's tears weren't caused by her behavior, Harlow offered the woman a smile. "Why don't you sit down while we get Ryske up to speed?"

THIRTY-FOUR

FOR OVER AN hour, Harlow and Maze relayed everything. She explained the safe deposit box though Maze did most of the talking about the Hagan video.

Maze was supportive… ish. He repeated his concerns about her backup plan while she justified its necessity. When they were all argued out, silence descended over the room.

Sitting between Ryske's legs, she curled against him to rest her head on his diaphragm, folding her hands under her cheek and wrapping both legs around one of his.

"Okay, we know what we have to do," Ryske said.

Maze made a sound of shock. "You're just going to accept that? She said she'd hand herself in while you go shack up with your obsessive stalker. Do you want to play house with the Hagan Hag?"

Ryske stroked her hair like some evil Bond villain with her as a pet. "That's not what she said, Mr. Rowe. She said we follow the plan and if we fuck up, that's our fallback. We just won't fuck up. Knowing if we do, we'll be sending Nightingale back to hell is a damn good incentive not to."

"Ryske—"

"This plan hinges on what? A group of people already suspicious of each other turning on an already shady someone.

We worked hard to convince the consortium Jarvis Hagan was crazy, won't take much to convince them his sister is the same. They've seen her behavior. Besides, we hold all the cards and don't need her anymore. Windsor's is mine. Supplies are Parratt and Yarker's side of the deal. Svetlana has the girls under control. Why do we need Fi?"

"Because she could sing," Dover said.

"Yeah," Ryske agreed. "But if we convince the others to threaten to gang up against her, would she take the risk?"

She rolled over to the same position just on her other side with her back to the window. "I'm not being rude, guys," she called out and ran her fingernails around Ryske's lower tattoo. "I'm still listening."

Ryske kept stroking her while her nails worked. Her caress was light, enough to torment him, not enough to hurt.

"It also hinges on you hacking Parratt's wife," Ryske said, she guessed to Maze.

"Yeah," Maze said.

"I have faith you'll find something we can use to blackmail the fucker. But if you don't…" Ryske sighed. "I'll get it from her myself."

"When?" Noon asked. "The meet is tomorrow night at the club."

"I'll have to see Yarker anyway, so I'll go back to the city early."

Tensing, Harlow focused on tracing her fingernails.

"You mean you'll seduce it out of her," Anwen said. "Don't you?"

"Yeah."

"No," Maze said. "You can't fucking do that."

"After all you and Nightingale just went through," Noon said. "You want to do that to her?"

Dover was of the same mind. "You can't, man."

Nice as it was to have their crew defend their relationship, Ryske stiffened, and not in the good way. Their crew's words got under his skin and soured his tone.

"Let Harlow and me worry about Harlow and me. She wants to comment on us, make demands, I'll take my medicine from her… but only from her."

Stilling her hand, she laid it on him and tried to be discreet about kissing his torso.

"She's one of us," Noon said. "You can't screw her around anymore… you'll break her."

Despite being more comfortable in her current position than she'd been for weeks, she forced herself to sit and address the team.

"I guess chilling out with my man gave you all some warped view," she said. One thing they'd require tomorrow night was faith in each other. She couldn't have them believing her to be some weak, artless lamb in need of protection or saving. "If Ryske steps over a line I don't like, I'll open my mouth and tell him." Vehement, she held her frown. "You want to protect me and I appreciate that. But if there's one person in the world I don't need to be protected from, it's this one."

Scanning the crew, her hand drifted down from Ryske's throat to his navel. When it stopped, he picked it up in both of his to kiss her fingertips.

"I'll do it," Penzance droned like he was giving in, surprising everyone. He shrugged and looked at her. "If your buddy here strikes out…" he gave Maze's chest a friendly smack. "I'll seduce Parratt's old lady."

"You think you can do that?" Dover asked. "In less than a day?"

"I know I can," Penzance said to Dover but was only interested in her.

It could be his audition for a place on the team. Throwing his hat in the ring was a good clue he liked this. Vane was accepting the hand of friendship she'd offered in asking him to come home.

"Okay," she said, nodding slowly. "If Maze strikes out, you're up at bat next."

"Baby—"

"You…" Harlow said, flipping her attention a hundred and eighty degrees to pat Ryske's chest. "Have to focus on convincing Yarker that Ophelia is bad news."

"How do you want him to do that?" Noon asked.

"In the way he does, I don't know. Make the man feel

inferior. Maybe Ryske can hint that Ophelia mocked Yarker's sexual prowess or his naïveté. Ryske knows what he's doing. He can make Yarker turn on a woman who's already declared a deeper interest in another man. Shouldn't be that difficult."

"Thanks," Ryske muttered, probably peeved she'd taken the other job off his card.

She stroked him some more and swayed over to give him a quick kiss before focusing on the others.

Harlow pointed at Dover. "You need to grab the doc for us. I want him close by in case anything goes down. Make sure he's supplied with whatever medical stuff he needs. I might need muscle on hand too, so you shouldn't wander off." Dover offered a two fingered salute and she turned to Noon. "You'll have your work cut out for you. Everyone needs to be somewhere tomorrow. Work out the schedule because I want you on lookout watching everyone's back."

Noon nodded. "Yes, ma'am."

Twisting more, she waved a finger between Maze and Penzance. "I need both of you in the field with us tomorrow night. Hang back, but, you know, just in case."

"What are you going to do?" Dover asked.

"We'll have to take the doctor to look at Ophelia's notes. I'll talk to Lydia too. She's sympathetic. She'll hear me."

"What can I do?" Anwen asked.

Everyone looked at her and then their gazes swung around to Harlow. "Agree to testify if it comes to it. I don't know that it will, but when the moment comes that everyone declares their loyalties, you've known Ophelia the longest… You can corroborate what's in those files and what Jarvis thought of his sister."

"Of course I'll stand with you guys, but there must be something useful I can do. Something I can do tomorrow."

If Harlow trusted Anwen, she'd send the woman to Ophelia to coax out a confession. But trust wasn't the only reason for hesitation. Sending anyone to Ophelia would be dangerous. Ophelia was on the edge, that made her more volatile. Trust or not, Harlow didn't want Anwen to be hurt on a mission for the Floyd's crew.

"Let me think on it," Harlow said.

Anwen didn't hide her dejection. Maybe Ryske saw it too. If he did, he didn't say anything.

Her love slapped a hand to his thigh. "Okay, everyone needs to get some rest so we're on form tomorrow night… There are two guest rooms, a pull out in the den and I'll speak to Jean about letting someone sleep in the living room."

"We could go to the hotel," Dover said as everyone began to move. "There's a hotel around here."

Maze spoke up. "With Ophelia on the war path and determined to hurt Nightingale…"

"And her family," Penzance added.

Maze hung back. "I think it's best to have a show of force here, just in case."

"There's a cot in the closet of the big guest room," Harlow said, shimmying to the edge of the bed to stand up. "I'll get it."

Ryske put his hands on her shoulders and pushed her back down. "We'll find it. You aren't leaving this bed." He didn't give her any opportunity to argue. Spinning around, he addressed their crew. "Anwen you take the small guest room. Zance, Maze, you take the big one, with the bed and the cot you'll be fine." He turned a few degrees to point at Dover. "You're on the pull out in the den. Noon's on the couch."

"Why am I on the couch?" Noon whined.

"Because it's at the front of the house. You can listen for hostiles approaching," Dover said, slapping his hands onto Noon's shoulders from behind. "You're always look out."

Mischief danced around Penzance. "Where are you gonna sleep, Ryske?"

Harlow grinned. "Yeah! Oh my God, that's a good point. Where are you going to sleep, Ryske?" She'd flattened her grin by the time he looked at her. Playing dumb, she tapped a finger on her lip. "Hmm, that's a hard one."

Swatting her hand aside, he grabbed her chin. Thrusting her head back as he bent down to get in her face, Ryske wasn't playing. "Take off your clothes and get in that bed. I'll be back to give you the hardest one of your life."

Penzance was laughing as he opened the door. "Three nights, three different guys," he said. "You've got skills, Sweeting."

He sauntered out and the others followed.

Ryske gave her a short kiss. "Stay here and don't fall asleep."

"What if I do?" she asked, trying to keep a straight face. "What if I just pass out?"

"Then I reserve my given right to take advantage of you anyway."

It had been him who'd given her the open-ended invite to take advantage of him whenever he passed out. Still, Harlow didn't argue, she just pushed up to nuzzle her mouth on his.

"Hurry back, Crash."

She hummed out some pleasure and relaxed. The weight of her head sank into the cradle of his hand still wrapped around her chin.

He kissed her again and spoke on her lips. "You fucking little tease."

Letting her go, he stalked out, closing the bedroom door. He'd get their friends settled and then he'd be back.

As instructed, Harlow stripped off and got into bed. If this was her last night on earth, spending it naked with Ryske was a fantasy come to life. For so long they'd missed each other. They didn't have to miss each other anymore.

THIRTY-FIVE

LYING ON HER side, beneath the covers, Harlow kept her eyes closed even after the bedroom door opened and closed. She'd listened to the mumbles of good humor and laughter outside her room as everyone moved around getting set up for bed.

The sounds had died down, suggesting the gang were where they were supposed to be. Though she could still hear some movement in other areas of the house, her focus was listening to the man getting undressed in proximity to her bed.

"You want to know how I know you're faking?" Ryske asked. She did her best not to react. "You're not smiling. You always smile when you sleep with me." The covers rose and the mattress moved as he slid closer. "Guess she wants me to take advantage…"

A shot of instant, abrupt cold on her warm body ejected a startled gasp. She fought to spring away from his hand snaking from her hip to her waist.

She batted at his touch. "Your hands are cold!"

Ryske didn't let her go. He kept going until he had her in his arms. "I brought ice in from the garage for your mom."

His hands were warming up, so she relaxed and

stroked his chest. "Aren't you domesticated?"

Gasping in mock outrage, he tugged her body to his. "Oh no, quick, baby, make me wild again."

Rolling on top of her between her thighs, he kissed her mouth and then descended to kiss her neck.

"Baby, can I ask you a question?" she asked, splaying her fingers around the globes of his shoulders.

Sliding her hands across his delicious skin, she stroked his neck and kept on going until she lost her fingers in his hair.

"Mm," he said, his mouth occupied by her earlobe.

"Do you think we'll disturb Maze and Zance if we screw? Our bed is right against the wall we share with them."

Rising up, he blinked a heavy daze from his eyes. "What? That's your question? I thought it was going to be something profound."

She subdued her desire to giggle. "I know you did."

His brow got heavy. "Will they hear us having sex? Yes. Do I care? No. We'll be having sex at home tomorrow night. They'll get a much clearer audio then. Now shut up and let me make love to you."

His whole body dipped down as he kissed and massaged her breasts.

Mm, she'd missed that mouth. She ran her hands through his hair. "Don't kiss my breasts while we're talking, Crash. It makes me forget that we're talking."

His tongue was still in her cleavage when he spoke. "We're not talking."

"We have to talk about him."

"Who?"

"Vane."

"No, we don't."

"I know things…" she said. "I know things you don't."

"I trust you."

The irritation in his voice only made her smile. "But, Ryske—"

Startling her, he bolted to his knees and grabbed her throat. A rash of heated need raced in every direction throughout her body.

"Now we're not talking," she murmured, her eyes finding his through the night. "Tighter, Crash."

He squeezed so tight, her chin tipped up. Her whole body moved, writhing beneath his, anchored by his fierce possession of her neck.

"This is the reunion sex, baby. Where the hero comes to claim his girl before they live happily ever after. Quit your yapping. Lay there like the grateful little Trinket you are and take my cock like a good girl."

A sharp zap of arousal shimmered across her skin, zeroing in on her enlivened clit.

"Make me take it hard, Crash," she panted spreading her arms to the sides, opening her body to him.

"Oh, you will," he said, snatching himself while still clinging to her neck.

Aligning their bodies, he thrust forward, spearing himself into her so hard she yelped. Keeping her throat in one hand, he planted his other over her mouth, damming her squeals of want and moans of pleasure.

It was the possession in his eyes, that never left hers, which reached into her soul. He was making love to her, but he was fucking her too. Ryske had the ability to be rough and tender at the same time.

His hips worked hard, fucking his cock into her, forcing her to take him deep and fast. His gaze owned her. Not with sentimental love; his fierce stare conveyed he'd use everything he was to keep her safe. That he'd give all of himself to her.

Harlow's eyes flared when orgasm slammed into her. Her body bucked up, her head snapped back, but he didn't let go. He squeezed tighter and fucked harder until his own release filled her up. He flopped onto the bed at her side, their legs twined, their skin sticky, and their breath out of sync with itself.

After they'd had a few minutes to relax, she broke the silence. "I talked to Bale."

Ryske shifted his head to look at her. "You're thinking about my brother?

Still focused on the ceiling, she smiled. "Of course, I always think about your brother when we're having sex. How else would I guarantee myself an orgasm?" Though she knew he'd seen her smile, she flattened her lips and rolled her head toward him, making eye contact. "Should I have kept that to myself?"

He sniffed. "Nah, it's fine. I was thinking about him too."

Laughing, she crawled over to lie on top of him. "I was thinking of how incredible that sex was and how I'd be heartbroken to live without it. Then I thought I wouldn't have to because, you know, of what we discussed… which Bale is outraged about."

Ryske gathered her hair from her face and tucked her head under his chin. "He doesn't understand."

"That's what I said… He asked if…"

He trailed his thumb and forefinger up and down her back. "If what?"

"If we'd still do it if we had kids."

His fingers stopped moving; he stayed silent for a score of tense seconds.

Taking her arms, he eased her onto her back, cradling her against him. "Do we?" he asked. "Have kids?"

"No."

His hand flattened on her stomach. "Baby, this is one thing you can't hide from me. If you're pregnant, you have to tell me."

She tilted her head. "Why? So you can take me out of the field?"

"Yes," he said, not giving a shit when she shoved his chest.

He only swayed back a few inches, then swayed forward again.

"I'm not pregnant. That's not why I asked."

"Why did you ask?"

"Because we're about to have a niece or nephew who—"

"Niece," he said, bringing her up short.

Blinking up at him, she couldn't believe that… "How

do you know? Can you just sense females?"

His lips curled. "Lena told me."

A gasp of offense came out of her mouth when it opened. "I asked her! We all did. She refused to tell anyone."

"Well, she told me," he said, bowing to kiss her. She pushed him back. "What? I promise it wasn't barter for having sex with her."

"I just can't believe that..." Exhaling, she resigned herself. "No, I can believe it. Damnit, baby, you're good."

"Thanks," he said and winked. Lowering, he brushed his lips across hers. "You're pretty good yourself."

"What if the baby needs us?" she asked, skimming her hand across his shoulder to his neck and back. "What if she needs someone capable of doing anything to keep her safe?"

"That's what her parents are for."

Harlow wasn't sure she believed that and gave him an accusatory look that questioned whether he did either.

"Can you see Rupert going as far as you would?" she asked. "Would he even know where to begin? I've protected Lena all our lives. She's always had me to support her. If I wasn't around, you're the only one I'd trust to—"

"She'll always have the guys," Ryske said, his expression becoming a scowl. "We'll make sure they check in on her... Are you saying that you don't want to—"

"I don't want *you* to," she said, catching her lip in her teeth.

"Hold on," he said, sitting up and scrubbing a hand through his hair. "You're saying you're allowed to join me, but I'm not allowed to join you? Why in the hell would you think—"

"Because the guys need you," she said, sitting up fast. "You're the only one I trust to look after my family, because they're your family too. Lena, she needs someone who'll protect her... The baby will be vulnerable and Ophelia won't give up. If—"

"No," he said. "No. I won't let you put fucking doubts in my mind... No."

Trying to touch his face with both hands, Harlow was

thwarted when he caught her wrists and pulled them down. She couldn't stand seeing the scowl on his face. He was mad. But she had to make her point.

"I love you, Crash. I love you so much. I don't want you hurt because of me… for me."

Leaning in, he pinned her hands down to the bed between them, forcing her to bow forward. "You'll be dead. You don't want anything when you're dead."

"Was that your experience?" she whispered, begging him with her gaze.

"That doesn't count," he said, shoving her hands away. Flipping over, he climbed off the opposite side of the bed. "You don't get to fucking do this, Har."

When he ducked to grab his pants, she scrambled over the bed on her hands and knees. "Where are you going?"

Pulling on his jeans, he did all the buttons of the fly except the top one. "If this conversation keeps going, I'll be going out to get very drunk."

"Ryske—"

"If I stay, I'll throttle you."

"Throttle me… please," she murmured, reaching for a belt loop on his jeans to pull him to the edge of the bed.

Skimming her hands up his torso, she curled them around the back of his neck and dragged him down for a kiss. His response started as polite. She needed more. Needed him to surrender. Relaxing, she suspended her weight on her hands at the back of his neck and slipped her tongue between his lips. Need spurred him into action. He grabbed her waist, yanking her body to his. Lifting her higher, he squashed her breasts against him and took possession of the kiss.

Just as she thought he was going to come back to their bed, he let her go, dropping her to the mattress. Harlow lost her balance and fell to her side. She tossed her hair from her face to find he'd paced to the end of the bed.

"No. No. No… fuck."

"Crash?"

Why was he resisting their attraction?

Spinning around, he grabbed the high rail at the top of the bed frame. "You can't do that. You can't distract me with sex."

The objection was so ludicrous that she couldn't stop her lips from ascending. "I think I can," she said, sliding her feet flat up the bed to bend her knees, letting them drop apart to reveal her core to him.

"I'm saying, it's not fair," he said, his voice getting sort of distant.

"I've said what I needed to say," she murmured, cupping her breasts. "We don't have to talk anymore."

He swallowed when she circled her nipples with her thumbs, bringing them to points. Her hands floated down her body, one after the other. She folded both over her pussy to play naughty peek-a-boo with him.

"We do," he said, clearing his throat, forcing himself to drag his eyes upward. She wriggled, ever-moving in the center of the bed they'd just made love in. "Just 'cause you said that doesn't make it true. You can't change the rules."

"You like it when I change the rules," she said, lifting her hips and lowering them, moving against the one hand that stayed in place while the other returned to fondling her breast. "You know what I'm thinking?" She whimpered, pushing her middle finger into her pussy. "It's been too long since I tasted you." Easing her finger out, she took it to her lips and sucked herself clean. "Come, let me taste you."

He smacked both hands to his face and turned his back. "I'm not looking… I'm not watching you."

"Okay," she said, sliding a fingertip over her clit. "I'll just have to keep tasting what you already gave me."

"Fuck."

Harlow smiled and kept rubbing her clit, exaggerating her movement on the bed to ensure he could hear it. Breathing through every whimper and moan, she didn't want him to doubt what she was doing.

"Crash," she gasped. "Oh, fuck, Crash… I need you, Crash."

He didn't relent his stance. Damn his impressive willpower; not that it would discourage her. Slithering onto the floor, she crawled on her hands and knees around to in front of him.

Did he know she was there? One button at a time, she unbuttoned his jeans, knowing he'd be hard. He didn't disappoint.

Tossing her hair to one side, she tipped her head and opened her mouth to suck him into her. His hiss was joined by his hands falling from his face to grab for the metal rail at the foot of the bed, around hip height.

Sucking on his cock, she blinked up to see his head was back, hiding what was in his mind. But he wasn't objecting. Bobbing her head back and forth, she kept going until the throbbing on her tongue betrayed he was close.

Dragging her mouth free, she squeezed her fist around him in slow strokes. "Tell me to stop, baby," she whispered, his head bouncing on her lips as she spoke. "If you don't want me—"

Her words were cut off when he grabbed a handful of her hair and forced himself deep into her throat again. This time when she blinked up, his feral glare was pinned on her.

"Don't you ever fucking dare say that shit again," he said, thrusting his hips forward. "I want you every goddamn second. Need you more than the air I breathe."

Yanking her back, he didn't give her much time to breathe before using his grip on her hair to pull her to her feet. They didn't stay on the floor for long, he spun around, throwing her over the high rail of the bedframe. Grabbing her hips, he pushed her up so her torso was over the bed, and her lower body was just dangling there off the foot rail.

She'd just pushed her hands onto the bed when he plunged two fingers into her. Gasping in surprise, she tried to move, but he pinned a forearm over her hips and smacked her ass hard.

"You wanted it hard," he growled and fucked his fingers into her so fast that she couldn't hold in her scream of climax.

The moment he wrung that first one from her, he pulled his fingers out of her and sank his cock in.

"Crash," she yelped.

But he kept fucking, holding her hips, keeping her in place to meet his thrusts. There was nothing she could do but take it. He didn't let her move, his grip was too powerful. She was helpless beneath his need.

The head of the bed thumped off the wall when his body slammed into hers, punctuating the force of his impact inside her.

"Gonna tell me to stop, baby, huh?" he growled and followed the words with a sinister chuckle. "Want it to stop?"

Gritting her teeth, she hissed out the pressure of overwhelming need. He pushed into her and then laid his body over hers, scooping his hands around to grab and grope her breasts. All the while moving his hips, reminding her how he occupied and owned her.

"Never," she snarled, spitting her hair from her mouth, craving him even as his hands got rougher. "Never stop, you bastard."

He'd taken over her seduction, finished what she started, and proved his wild side never went far. Opening her mouth, she squeaked in response to the tormenting motion of his fingers toying with and tugging on her nipples. Driven by what her man was doing to her body, involuntary and feeble sounds of need proved her dependence on him.

Ryske liked it, and his deep, sinister laugh returned. "That's what I want, pretty little Nightingale... sing for me."

"Crash," she gasped, trying to push her ass up.

Ryske smacked the inside of her elbows, forcing them to buckle, sending her face into the bed. She had no time to recover before he pushed his hands up her back, on either side of her spine, into her hair, dragging it away from the back of her neck, probably revealing her nightingale tattoo.

"Sing for me, Trink," he said, opening his mouth on her back, sucking and licking her flesh before dragging his mouth to the other side to do the same thing. "Fuck, baby, how can there be a heaven better than this?"

Straightening again, he pulled out and then drove himself into her, quickening his pace until she was panting for him again. It was while she was hissing through the vibrations of orgasmic aftershocks that he surged forward and came hard inside her.

They both stayed in the moment for as long as they

could. Eventually, he took himself from her body. Before his hands had even slipped off her hips, Harlow pulled herself forward, using the bedsheets to drag her lower body over the end of the bed. Sated and spent, she slumped in the middle of the mattress.

THIRTY-SIX

HARLOW COULDN'T EVEN bring herself to turn over. She just stayed there on her chest, her cheek deep in the mattress. Her heart struggled to find a regular rhythm. It wasn't happening. Her pulse was all over the place. Her body ached, and her hips were bruised. Her breasts throbbed almost as much as the intimate passage inside her Ryske had just dominated.

"You have the power to make me do anything," Ryske said.

The depth of his profound statement made her lift her head to turn it and let it fall again. Pushing her hair from her face, she revealed the sight of him standing at the side of the bed, his jeans open, hands on his hips.

"You're welcome," she said and smiled.

Ryske didn't. He shook his head and sat down on the edge of the bed. "Not the sex," he said. "You have the power to control everything about me…" With his feet still on the floor, he slanted backwards to prop and elbow on the mattress and ran a finger from the center of her forehead to behind her ear, tucking her hair away. "But don't ever forget who's in charge of this duo."

Snagging the loop at the front of her necklace, he

guided her head onto his lap. He did straighten his arm to lay his upper body on the bed, but she didn't feel like he was all the way with her yet.

"You knew I was alive," she said, drawing a fingertip across his abdomen. "I thought you were dead… I can't live through that again."

"And you think I could?"

"You don't understand the pain," she said, resting a hand on his stomach. "Something leaves you. A space forms inside you and it grows. It grows and grows until you're sure you're being consumed from the inside. I wanted to be a shadow. To be invisible… the only time I felt anything was when I lay in this bed cursing you for leaving me… I wanted to hate you for abandoning me, and I'd scream into the pillow calling you every name under the sun. But my night would always end the same… I'd beg you to come back to me. I'd barter with every God I'd heard of, pleading with them to give you back to me."

His hand moved over her hair, stroking her as she watched her finger move on his stomach. "I came back to you," he said, his gaze locked on the ceiling. "But you know I'd never do that again. So if I'm gone… I'm really gone."

"I know," she said. "That's how I know I won't make it. I just won't be able to make myself breathe anymore."

"If you go anywhere, I'm coming with you. It's as simple as that."

A tear slid from the corner of her eye, but she didn't react to it. "I can't bear to think of this world without you in it, whether I'm in it or not… You have so much life in you, so much potential, this world needs you. You'd find a way to be happy again."

"Without you, there's no happy," Ryske said. "Have you heard about how I tried to tear down the world when you were just stuck across town? I'd go nuclear if something permanent took you from me." Another tear slipped from her eye. She slid her hand flat onto him and he rested his on top. "But, hey, why are we talking like this is a done deal? We have a plan. We're going to beat the bitch."

Rising to rest her upper arm on his lap, she held her

temple on the heel of her hand. "You know you have to keep our people safe," she said. "If I go back to jail—"

"What if you don't?" he asked. "What if we run Fi out of town? Let's make plans for the win."

"We go home, we have sex, we wake up on Saturday morning," she said. "Those are the plans if we win."

"Cool. Simple. Easy to remember... Sex comes after going home, right?"

He winked, making her smile, but she dipped a fingertip into his navel. "Those two could be switched. Downside is, we'll be in the car with a bunch of other people. They might object to sex in the backseat."

"We'll ride shotgun."

Dragging the back of her fingernail up the center of his torso as far as she could reach, she then scratched it back down. "No," she said. "You sit shotgun... I'll ride."

One side of his mouth rose higher than the other. "Works for me, babydoll."

"We do have to talk about Zance."

"Why? What's your hard on for that guy?"

"I know he hurt you," she said, not liking that Ryske was frowning again. "But he told me what happened, everything."

Pushing onto his elbows, he forced her to roll onto her back so her head was on his lap again. "Everything? How the hell did—"

"We were in bed and kinda drunk," she said. "I think he needed to tell someone."

Dropping onto his back, he groaned and flattened his hands on his face. "Man, I love stories that start with you drunk in bed with other guys." After another huff, his arms flopped out to the sides outstretched. "Let me have it. What happened?"

She winced. "I... I want to talk to Dover first."

"First?" he asked, rising onto his elbows to look at her. "What the hell, Trink?"

She put a hand to her cleavage. "I trust you with the story completely. I just think maybe I should find out what Dover knows and what he doesn't... There's a chance I'm going to need your help tracking someone down… if we get through tomorrow and Dover is on board."

"Hmm," he said, his eyes narrow on her. He only peered for a moment before shifting his weight onto one elbow. Grabbing her thigh with the arm he'd freed, he pulled her legs apart.

"What are you…" Harlow's voice faded when he began to circle her clit. "Oh, that's not fair."

"If you want to come, you'll tell me the secret," he said, moving his fingers in a slow stir of her hormones. "Come on, baby, talk to me."

They'd kept their own secrets from the rest of the group before. Ryske hadn't told them when she confessed who killed Hagan. She could tell Ryske anything and he'd never reveal it until she released him from her confidence.

Parting her lips in a whisper of a moan, she rocked her hips against his stimulation. "That's so good."

"I know," he said. "You'll get a big finish soon as you tell me the truth."

"He… he thought he was doing the right thing," she said, opening her mouth wider to yelp at the rising need building between her thighs. "He thought he had no choice."

"Baby, I don't—"

"Floyd knocked up his aunt."

Ryske's fingers stopped moving. Without the stimulation, she was left hanging. Harlow blinked open her eyes to find him staring at the door.

"He…"

This was a shock. She sat up. With her fist on the mattress at the other side of his thighs, she held her weight on a straight arm and kissed his lips.

"There was a baby," she said. His stunned eyes locked onto hers. "Dover has a sibling… that's related to Zance."

"A boy or a girl?"

"He doesn't know," she said. "Audrey was killed before the child was born. They delivered and the little one was put up for adoption… That's all he knows… they wouldn't let him near the baby. He'd just lost his aunt. He was a mess, and a kid alone, something he'd never been before…"

Stroking his face, she kissed him again, but he was still too stunned to respond. "He's been alone since, Ryske."

"He knew where we were."

"He couldn't face Floyd who'd refused to marry Audrey… I don't know how that went down. Maybe Dover does. Maybe he doesn't. I don't know… Zance did what he did for his aunt… He didn't want to leave, but he had to stand with her."

"Fuck," he exhaled, rubbing a hand over his mouth. "I… fuck."

"Let him come home," she said, stroking his arm. "Please."

"How?" he asked. "The guys won't—"

"They will. You were closest to him. If they know you've forgiven him, they will too… But I was thinking, maybe…"

Though he was still processing, he must have sensed her tone of coaxing.

His gaze grew suspicious as his eyes drifted to hers. "What?"

"What you said to Dover about an empire, it's not a bad idea," she said. "I know you were thinking of stripping the club and selling it. But… what if we didn't?"

Dubious, he leaned back to inspect her. "What are you thinking?"

"Get Zance to run it. Then he's part of the team, but not on top of you guys, you know, until things get comfortable."

"You want to keep Pothos and—"

"No," she said. "God, no… I think you should run it as a legitimate nightclub and hotel. I'd get rid of the hoity-toity clientele and make it a regular joint where people can go for fun. Run it legit."

"And all the bedrooms are…"

"Strip them out, knock down some walls, make the place bigger, turn some into party rooms for private functions… You could have different floors for different things. Have a wine bar, maybe a restaurant, if you want. Have dance floors and DJ booths. I don't know… it's just a fun idea. Turn the whole place into a hotel if you want. It's across town, so you couldn't be on the premises all the time while you're running the pool hall at Floyd's. But we have it, it's a business with the infrastructure in place, you could do a floor at a time."

"And we're getting the money for this from where? We still have to pay Marlowe back, I know you won't—" She winced again, which cut him off. "I gave him the money from the safe deposit box." She'd told everyone the money was in there, but not that it was spent. "We're square with him." Ryske's brows rose. She hooked her hands around his neck. "I will get money from the sale of the apartment. I don't know how much, but it will be enough to get us started on something… I promise to tell Rupert to give you the money if, you know, I don't make it."

"Enough with that. You're going to make it," he said, still thinking, though she didn't know if his mind was occupied by the Zance revelations or her suggestion. "I guess we could keep it, see how Zance does… But we'd have to kick out everyone connected to the Hagans and Parratt or Yarker."

"Agreed," she said. "If nothing else, it's an income for a while." She grinned and squeezed herself closer. "I already have an idea of a name."

That surprised him too. "A name?" When she nodded, he laughed. "Okay, give me it. What are we calling our new club?" Holding up her wrist, she showed him the most recent ink Dover had given her. She didn't say anything, but it only took a moment for him to catch on. "Black Flame."

Pulling him forward, she kissed him. "What do you think?"

"I think it's perfect," he said. "Though, I prefer Nightingale's."

She huffed and shook her head, linking her fingers at the back of his neck again. "No, silly." She kissed him. "That's what we're calling the pool hall."

"You…"

Grabbing her waist to flip her onto her back, he leaped on top of her and stole her mouth. The depth of this kiss was enough to make up for the ones he'd missed earlier.

They lay making out on the bed, letting their hands run all over each other until the head of his engorged dick prodded at her belly.

Breaking their kiss, she looked down. "You know there's a chance you'll be the one to kill me, right? Your cock is determined to break me." He smiled. "How will I be tough and menacing tomorrow when we're having our showdown if I can't walk straight or sit down?"

Running a hand from her shoulder to her waist, then down to her hip, he skimmed it around to the back of her thigh. Hooking her legs higher on his body, he edged nearer.

"Stop being so hot then. You quit turning me on and I'll quit taking advantage."

"We should get some rest."

Squeezing her ass, he pulled her closer. "Just let me put it inside you," he murmured, brushing his lips over hers. "See if it goes anywhere."

Despite the pressure she laid on his shoulders, she wasn't really trying to push him away. "It always goes somewhere."

"I love you."

She laughed. "Yes, and you'll love me whether I let you fuck me again or not."

"It'll feel good," he murmured, scooping a hand around her hips, using the other to run the head of his cock through her folds. Rubbing her clit and teasing her entrance, he persisted. "You're already wet... Let's see how it feels, huh?"

She opened her mouth to say something but stopped when he eased his cock an inch into her. A shimmer of anticipation bubbled up through her. He pushed another inch and another, and then before she knew what was happening, he was making love to her.

This time was slow and gentle. They were both tired; they'd likely fall asleep as soon as this union met its crescendo.

On top of her, he moved inside her, but lowered to kiss her hair over her ear and whispered, "Love of my life... of eternity."

Harlow came right there under him, surrendered not

only to the weight of his body, but to his love. They were meant to be together, in this life, and in the next. She just didn't want him to rush after her if this life came to an abrupt end. The truth was, that was likely when Ophelia Hagan was in the mix.

THIRTY-SEVEN

PILING EVERYONE INTO Noon's car had been a farce. It was like a science experiment, or some sketch show skit. Her father and Rupert were at work, while her mom and Lena were shopping. Thank God no one witnessed them figuring it out.

Noon did offer to get another car for them. Given how close they were to her parents' house, she didn't think stealing a vehicle was a good idea.

The first thought was to have Ryske and Harlow in the front seat. But three people in the front would be an obvious red flag to any cruisers they might pass. Dover was too big to be shoehorned in anyway, so he got to sit shotgun. That left Ryske, Maze, and Penzance in the back with Harlow and Anwen on top of them.

It was a squeeze, yes, but she didn't have someone sitting on her, so didn't complain. The experience was something of a throwback to her teen years and sort of fun.

Ryske didn't seem to mind. His dick sure liked it. He got to make out with her whenever he felt like it. For most of the journey, his hand was up her skirt or in her bra, so, overall, not unpleasant for him.

The fun came to an abrupt end when they got back

home and everyone needed to go their separate ways.

Because the doctor's apartment was within walking distance, she and Dover decided to go there first. Penzance and Anwen went to get cellphones and other supplies. Maze stayed at Floyd's to finish his work, confident he'd find what he was looking for.

Noon took Ryske on his trek to Yarker's. Getting him on side was crucial.

Saying goodbye to Ryske was quick. It had to be. On the curb, everyone seemed to lean closer in anticipation of some big emotional farewell between the couple. Instead Ryske just grabbed her ass, hauled her body to his and kissed her until she couldn't breathe. Then he was gone.

Ryske would do his thing, she had faith. Maze would too and Bale would come through for them.

Finding herself alone with Dover was too perfect an opportunity to pass up. Far from eavesdroppers, that was an ideal moment to bring up Penzance's account.

Strolling down the sidewalk, a few seconds passed before she broached the conversation. "How are you doing?" she asked, taking Dover's hand. "Good? Are you good?"

He sighed. "Okay, what's wrong?"

"Nothing. Why would—"

"Just spill it, Night. The doc's isn't that much of a walk."

Her crew really did know her and Dover was right. She'd lose her chance if she didn't spit it out. And if that night went bad, she may never have another opportunity to tell Dover.

"I know this is a lot for you… That you've been through a lot recently…"

"But…?"

Opening her mouth, she took a deep breath. "You know about the whole me and Penzance thing?"

"The fake relationship? Yeah." Dover stopped to land concern on her. "Did he touch you?"

"No!" she said, quick to reassure him. "No, it's just… We had some time to talk alone and he… He told me something that I think you have a right to know. Something about why he and Audrey left the neighborhood."

"You know about Charlize," he said without hesitating or changing his expression.

"Cha... No," she said. "Charlize... is that your sister's name?"

"Idiot can't keep his mouth shut," Dover said and started walking again.

This time it was him who linked their hands.

"Wait a minute, you know?" she asked. "All this time you've known and... you didn't tell the guys?"

He glanced at her. "How do you know I didn't tell them?"

And now was the time to squirm. "I might have... sort of... told Ryske." Dover crooked a brow her way. "He manipulated me with sex, it wasn't completely my fault. How long have you known?"

"Couple of years," he said. "My dad didn't say anything. I wasn't all that sure if he ever knew."

"According to Penzance, he did. In his version, Audrey told Floyd and he refused to do right by her."

"Marry her? Yeah, he would. Dad always swore he'd never get married again."

"But he was so good with you and the guys. Why would he reject another child?"

"I doubt he did. We can't know what really happened."

Dover would be protective of his father's memory, of course he would. It was possible Audrey laid down an ultimatum, marriage or nothing. It was also possible Floyd hadn't known Audrey and Penzance were taking off.

Penzance had said he and Floyd argued about the pregnancy. Penzance might know what Floyd said to him, but both Floyd and Audrey were dead. Their versions of events were lost forever.

"How did you find out?"

"I got a call from an adoption agency," he said. "Didn't know if it was legit at first, so I quizzed the guy. I told him Floyd was dead and that was the last I heard."

"So how did you know her name and..." She put the

pieces together. "Maze knows."

Dover shrugged. "We found out who she was, where she lived… She's still a kid, a teenager, but she's got a good life. Good parents, good grades… She's a good girl."

Walking along in silence, they focused on their own thoughts. Dover's suspicions made sense. It should've been obvious that if he'd told anyone, it would be their resident hacker.

"Did you ever reach out? Talk to her?"

He shook his head and slipped his free hand in his pocket. "Maze and me went out there once, watched her come out of school. Didn't make sense to screw with her life."

"If an adoption agency called, she must have wanted to know about you."

"Her parents wanted to know more about her birth parents, in case Charlize ever asked. According to the guy on the phone, they didn't tell her she was adopted. They were thinking about telling her and wanted to have something to share."

That was a heavy burden. Being adopted was one thing, learning both of your birth parents were dead was another.

"Did they tell her?" He shrugged. "Did you tell the adoption guy that you were her brother?"

"I look out for her," he said, getting defensive. "Maze keeps an eye on her every way he can. If she's ever in trouble, we'll be there."

Harlow thought some more about it. "You should tell Penzance."

"I don't think we want to pull on that thread until we know how tonight goes down."

Dover was right. Introducing more tension and friction into the mix wasn't a good idea. Ryske had been hurt when Penzance disappeared from his life. Having a better idea why that was, she could understand why Dover and Maze hadn't told him about Charlize. That would mean bringing up old grievances. To talk about Charlize, they had to talk about Audrey, which meant talking about Penzance.

Dover was a good guy. Despite knowing about his

half-sister, he hadn't gone crashing into her life. He'd checked her out from a distance and hadn't disrupted her happiness. That couldn't have been an easy decision.

"You know if you ever decide that you want to meet her…"

"I know," he said, letting go of her hand to sling an arm around her. "Floyd always told us to look out for each other. This isn't a great neighborhood for a girl on her own. We didn't have a woman on the crew to soften the blow for her either."

"Now you have me," she said, tipping up her chin to show him a grin.

One side of his mouth curled. "Yeah, I'm not sure you're any better an influence than your boyfriend," he teased and pulled her closer to kiss her head. "One day when she's older, maybe. And if she needs us, we'll be there no matter what."

"But while she's still so young and impressionable, you think it's best she doesn't know she has a thug for a brother?"

He squeezed her. "I think it's best she stays in her nice middle-class neighborhood as long as she can. Look what happened to you after you crossed our path. Death, grief, jail, hospital, servitude… We're tough to take."

"Can't say I didn't give as good as I got."

"That's the truth," he said, swinging her around into Bale's building. "We've gotta let that shit lie for now. We've got bigger things to worry about."

"Yes, sir."

Harlow let him lead her up the stairs to Bale's. Within the crew, it was unusual to have secrets, but she understood why Dover hadn't thrown the issue out for debate. Charlize was happy and safe. A bunch of big, tattooed guys from a rough neighborhood showing up to say they were related to her wouldn't be easy news for the girl to digest.

Their crew had enemies. While Charlize was a secret, she was safe. And how far away did she live? Maybe it wouldn't be possible to have regular contact. Just introducing himself as her brother was one thing, but what would Dover have in common with a middle-class teenage girl?

In the future, if Charlize wanted to meet him, Dover would be open to it. In the meantime, he'd let her live her life in blissful oblivion. A childhood wasn't something the guys of their crew really enjoyed, not an innocent one anyway. Dover was giving his sister a gift but was ready to act if the need arose.

She was proud of him and of Maze for supporting him. Now that Ryske knew, and Penzance was back in their lives, the issue might come up again. But Dover was right, they had to concentrate on Ophelia and couldn't afford to split their attention.

So it was on to the doctor's apartment and then back home to find out how everyone else did on their missions. After they regrouped, they'd get ready for Windsor's. Already the day felt long, but the night would sneak up on them fast.

THIRTY-EIGHT

AND SHE WAS right. Everyone achieved their goals.

With the computer, Maze discovered pictures of Parratt dressed in babygirl clothes being whipped by his mistress. Nice. The woman was in a full body suit with mask, so her identity was concealed. Still, it was primo blackmail material.

Ryske did his thing, gloating and boasting to Yarker. The man was an easy mark. Insecure and timid, Yarker fell for every part of Ryske's ploy. Her love was sure the weak man was festering, dwelling on the ideas and doubts he'd planted.

By reading the files, Bale identified the markers of two personality disorders. He'd noted relevant events and crucial times. It was obvious Ophelia was unstable. Now they had the proof to back that claim up with those who didn't know her.

Despite every part of their plan being in place, nothing was guaranteed as they walked into Windsor's that night. Being cautious was healthy. They couldn't underestimate their opponent.

Ryske held her hand. Maze was at her side carrying two files. Penzance and Anwen were with them as well. Noon was parked just outside. While, in a second vehicle, Dover and the doctor parked in a different alley.

"We should've had sex in the car," Harlow muttered, thinking of how they'd discussed it at her parents.

She tried to pull her hand from Ryske's, but he wouldn't let go. "There's still time."

No, actually, there was no time to waste. They had to show up and soon. Before facing Ophelia, they needed to chat with one more couple.

Living with Ophelia for more than a month came with unseen benefits. Harlow knew the routine and that Ophelia wouldn't be ready to leave her apartment yet. Penzance took advantage of the allies he had on the inside. He'd gained some useful knowledge of his own, like where Ophelia's driver hung out, and that the man owed his bookie big. The driver was more than happy to accept a generous bribe in return for taking the scenic route. The delay would buy them a little more time.

Just before they went through the entrance to Windsor's main floor, she tried again to slip her hand out of Ryske's. He squeezed hard to keep hold of her. So hard that she thought he might crush her bones. Her mouth opened in a silent scream.

Before she could speak, he whipped her around in front of him. "No more hiding," he said, crowding her against the doorframe. "You belong to me, Trinket. Only me."

With the hand he wasn't crushing, she straightened his tie and then smoothed it down his torso. "Actions speak louder than words, Crash," she said, pouting. "You want me? You better come and get me."

Turning around, she shoved into the club, slipping away from him. Glancing back over her shoulder as she strode away, she was excited by the aroused, feral amusement he pinned on her.

He strode in with his posse behind him. The room was filled with people, but she was the only one he saw. Kind of like back in her jail days.

Walking with confidence, one foot in front of the other, shoulders back, she led with her chest. Her breasts were presented in a low cut, skintight dress that clung all the way to her hips and then loosened to a knee length skirt with two slits.

When she got to the central booth, every person there spotted her, or more accurately, her breasts. Bending over, she laid her forearms on the back of the booth between Parratt and Lydia. Plumping her breasts even more for Parratt's visual enjoyment, she widened her smile when she noticed every man at the table was fixated on her chest.

Someone smacked her ass hard. No prizes for guessing who. The sting of painful pleasure spun her around. At the same time, the perpetrator's arm came around her back to seize her hand against her opposite hip.

Ryske just held her there against him but looked over her head at Parratt. "Gotta talk," he said and side nodded.

When he pulled her away, Harlow was quick to steal a glance at Lydia. "You come too," she said and winked.

Still holding Ryske's hand, flanked by Penzance and Maze, Harlow skipped along behind her love. It hadn't been specified that the guys should act as protection, but it sure seemed that was what they were doing.

Behind them, Anwen seemed a little lost. Like it or not, they needed her, and it wasn't nice to see any ally rattled. She extended a hand toward her. Although Anwen was surprised by the gesture, she took advantage of it, and they all trailed across the room in Ryske's wake.

He led them into his Pothos room and sat in the center of the couch. Of course he pulled her down at his side; Harlow swung Anwen around to seat her at Ryske's other side. Penzance dropped into the armchair closest to her while Maze occupied the furthest one, perpendicular to Anwen.

Ryske and Maze exchanged a look of confirmation. Maze had turned on the recorder he was carrying. It was gratifying they took a leaf out of her book. A record would afford them protection and allow Dover and Noon to know exactly how the night played out.

Ryske spread his arms to lay one over her crossed legs and the other across Anwen's in a show of possession.

Parratt noticed, as did Lydia, when they came in together.

Harlow ignored them and leaned in to Ryske, pressing her breasts to his arm. "Can we turn on the porn?"

"Not now, baby," Ryske said, focusing on Parratt.

She pouted and hummed her disappointment. "Oh, I wanted to turn you on."

His heavy-lidded eyes swung around to her and she plumped her pout. "Done."

Grinning like a child receiving a gift, she ran a hand up the inside of his spread thighs. He didn't even stop her when she stroked her palm up over his cock that was already responding to her attention.

"This is not talking," Parratt asserted, blustering. "Did you call us in here to witness this depravity?"

She kept rubbing and brushed her lips down Ryske's jaw. Kissing his stubble, her lips ascended to catch his earlobe.

"No," Ryske said, cocky as ever. "Thought maybe your girl would like to join in."

Harlow smiled against him, dragging her teeth on the angle of his jaw.

"That's outrageous," Parratt said.

No objection from Lydia though.

Acting too enraptured with Ryske to hear another man, she urged her chest against him. "Can I suck it?"

There was a smile in Ryske's voice when he patted her leg. "Later, babydoll. I've got business. Will you ladies excuse us?"

All part of the plan. Unless it was exactly what they needed, Harlow wouldn't be excused for business. Without questioning him, she got up and straightened her skirt with a shimmy before opening a hand to Anwen who took it and stood up. Harlow reached for Lydia's hand as they moved toward her.

Though she didn't quite know what was going on, Lydia accepted her hand and let herself be led into the adjoining bedroom.

Anwen opened the door.

Ryske spoke before they could go through. "Trinket," he said and she turned. "Don't go far."

"I'll be in earshot."

If Ryske needed her, he'd whistle, she knew how it worked. Leading Lydia out, the three women went into the bedroom. Harlow let the other two go inside while she closed the door.

Anwen went over to sit on the bed, kicking off her shoes to lounge against the dozens of pillows propped on the headboard. The night wasn't in full swing yet. Although this was Svetlana's room, she wasn't there, and tonight, she wouldn't be. Ryske had given word to keep the women off the premises.

"You are both with Ryske now?"

"We're whatever he wants," Anwen said, stretching herself out.

Harlow smiled. Anwen was good at this. Lydia was standing near the end of the bed, as skittish as ever. She got on the bed by Anwen, who scooched over to make space for her, though not much.

"You both seem so relaxed," Lydia said, wrapping herself in her own embrace.

The poor girl was wearing a look of fearful worry when she glanced at the door they'd just come through.

"Why do you look so scared?" Anwen asked. "Come lie down with us."

Lydia edged closer, but only perched herself on the bottom corner of the bed. "I think... I think something big will happen tonight."

"Something big?" Harlow said, sitting up and glancing around to make quick eye contact with Anwen. "What do you mean?"

"I don't know," Lydia said, stroking her arms. "Gil and Anthony were fighting... Anthony was saying he was through. I don't know what he was talking about."

"Ophelia, I would guess," Anwen said, startling Harlow with her speed. Lydia jolted too. When Anwen caught them looking, she was startled by their shock. "You know he's fucking her."

Anwen didn't know about Harlow's previous conversation with Lydia. Getting the truth out in the open was good.

Harlow gasped and pointed at Anwen. "That's right… I guess they had a fight."

"Ophelia's been crazy all week," Lydia said. "I can't believe you got away from Brash. He was so mad."

Harlow folded her arms under her breasts. "I'm used to pissing off strong men. I know how to calm them down."

"Yes," Lydia said, slipping off her shoes to fold her legs in front of her. "You and Ryske, I can't believe it. I thought you were over."

Arching and relaxing, she didn't mind looking cocky as she admired her nails. "He can't stay away from me. He's insanely in love with me."

Lydia gasped. "You think he's in love with you?"

"Of course," Harlow declared. "Ryske loves all women."

Anwen scoffed. "All women except Ophelia."

"Difficult to love a woman who doesn't understand the meaning of love," Harlow said.

"True," Anwen agreed. "And I'm the woman who was her best friend for years. I know exactly what she's like. She never gives a damn about anyone. She wants to be worshipped."

"Can she think Ryske would worship her?" Lydia asked. "I didn't think they'd ever slept together… Did they do it recently?"

"You can have love without sex," Harlow said. "But I don't think Ryske will argue with Anthony if he wants to push her out."

Lydia bounced closer. "Really? Gil wanted to keep her on."

"Why?" Anwen asked. "Because he doesn't like Ryske's power? Ophelia is more dangerous. The worst thing Ryske would do is have sex with you. Ophelia would shoot him in the head."

"Or the chest," Harlow said, raising her knees, letting the center panel of her dress fall over her crotch. "She's evil."

"She's more than that," Anwen said. "She's a killer."

"Annie," Harlow soothed and took her hand. "I don't know if we should share." The coy act was a ploy. "But, I suppose, Lydia should know how dangerous Ophelia is."

Eager to know the truth, Lydia was hooked. "I've never enjoyed her company. Ophelia always wanted to take Gil from me… She tried to seduce him away from me. I tried to be her friend, so many times I tried."

"Oh, she doesn't like women," Anwen said, shaking her head. "She wants to be adored, the kind of adoration she gets from men, not women… We're never enough."

"Right," Lydia said, opening a hand to Anwen. "That's it. I always sensed that. The way she talked to me, it was condescending… Though most of the time she acted like I was invisible."

That was truly horrible. "We'll talk to Ryske. Make sure she never belittles you again."

Lydia seemed incredulous. "You know what she's like."

"But you don't," Anwen said. "She told me she killed her brother."

Shocked, Lydia sat stunned for a moment before turning to Harlow who didn't blink. "Oh my God, you spent time in jail for that."

"Yeah."

"Oh my God, but… if you knew that, why didn't you tell the police?"

Harlow gestured around them. "Because of this. She would've turned us all in."

Lydia gasped again. "We'd all go to jail forever!"

Anwen sat up. "Anthony is right. I think we have to get Ophelia out."

Lydia thought for a minute. "We could band together against her. Anthony has no love for her. Gil doesn't want to go to jail… Do you think our word would be enough?"

A loud whistle from the next room put her on her feet. No, she didn't want to imply being trained like a dog, but that sound could mean they had to move fast. If someone was hurt or in trouble, she didn't want to delay.

THIRTY-NINE

OPENING THE DOOR to Ryske's room, she zeroed in on her man in the middle of the couch. Penzance and Maze were in the same positions as before. Parratt was in the corner, but she only looked at Ryske.

"Miss me?" Ryske asked.

Harlow strutted toward him. "Feels like you're punishing me when you send me away."

He smacked his thighs. "Come tell me what you want for Christmas."

Skirting the small table in front of the couch, she climbed on to straddle his lap. He slid a hand into each of the slits in her dress to snake his hands around to her ass.

Leaning in, she kissed his mouth, then trailed her lips to his ear. "She's with us," she whispered.

His mouth was lost in her hair. "We own him."

One of Ryske's hands stayed under her dress, slithering around to press her lower back, holding her body to his. The other came out of her dress to cup the back of her head to guide their mouths together.

Rocking her hips on his, she gained pace and let the fury of their mouths increase. She'd said they should've had sex in the car, but seemed to have forgotten there was a bed in the room.

Without breaking the kiss, she squeezed her hands between them to unbuckle his belt. God, she wanted him. This could be their last chance. She eased their mouths apart to make eye contact, to check he was going to consent.

The light of daring desire in his eyes betrayed his curiosity. He wasn't going to back down, wasn't going to stop her. Seizing a handful of her hair, he yanked her head back and bowed to suck on the swell of her breast until the nip of his suction made her yelp.

Stretching his arms along the back of the couch, he didn't disguise how proud he was of marking her. As the tingle of pain went through her, she glanced down to see her marred skin. Instead of offense or anger, a shot of feral need surged through her.

Grabbing his face, she joined their mouths, pushing her tongue into his, wishing she could fill him with the same pounding hunger he instilled in her.

"You have one helluva nerve."

Ophelia's voice was probably the only thing that could interrupt this moment. Taking her mouth from his, Harlow locked her eyes onto Ryske's. They shared a moment, silently telling each other they were ready.

"How nice of you to join us?" Maze said. "I think there was about to be a vote. Wasn't there? Ryske?"

"I think there was about to be a federal crime," Ophelia said.

Harlow brushed her lips over Ryske's and then slithered down his body to sit on the floor between his feet.

"Look around you, Fi," Ryske said. "This whole place is a federal crime and you know it... You orchestrated the whole damn thing and recruited every member... I've got to give it to you, you've got some chutzpah."

Laying a hand on her head, Ryske stroked Harlow's hair. She wrapped both arms around his leg and rested her head against it.

"I suppose this sight means my brilliant plan didn't work," Ophelia said. "Unless she's poured a few doses of my product down your throat."

"Ha," Ryske said, still stroking her hair. "Harlow is my drug, Fi… Haven't you figured it out yet?" He slowed his words. "I love her."

"You're a fool. She's not the right woman for you. She's using you."

"As long as I get to take her home every night, what do I care?"

"Maybe we should leave the jealous woman talk for after the vote," Penzance suggested.

"Yes," Ophelia said. "I vote to get rid of Harlow."

Stepping forward, Ophelia opened her purse and pulled out a paper bag that she dumped on the table.

Ryske tapped Harlow's head, so she let him go to reach over and get the bag. She handed it back to him.

He opened up the bag to look inside as she returned to her place embracing his leg.

"Her initial investment?" Ryske said, scrunching the top of the bag again. "Half a million dollars."

"That's right," Ophelia said, reeking of smugness. "Now she has no need to be here." She looked around. "Where's Anthony? Someone get him in here for a vote."

"We should get him in here, yeah," Ryske said. "But we don't need a vote. We accept."

Ophelia's arrogance faltered. "Wha… we?"

"Yes," Ryske said. "I was here acting as Harlow's agent. We were both coerced and manipulated by you… Everyone here was. I think you're right, I don't think we need our place in this consortium anymore… So we'll expect all of you to withdraw this evening. Our premises will no longer be accessible to any of you or used to facilitate your operation… Same goes for our contractors."

"The hookers," Penzance said and hissed in a breath. "No premises and no staff. That's gotta hurt."

"Any employees on their payroll can go too. The locks on every access point are being changed as we speak."

Dover's talents seemed to know no bounds. The man was skilled in many trades. Noon usually reserved his locksmith skills for vehicles, but he wasn't averse to branching out for a good cause.

"You can't do this," Ophelia asserted but turned her glare down to Harlow. "How are you doing this? How did you do this to him?"

"It has a lot to do with her personality…" Ryske said, "and the fact she isn't you."

Parratt murmured something to Lydia who scurried out of the room.

Ophelia was fuming and didn't see the woman go. "Oh, I will ruin all of you for this," she growled. "You'll regret crossing me."

"You might want to think carefully about that," Harlow said, skimming a hand up Ryske's leg, then turning her attention to Ophelia. "You're going to be too busy running to think about payback."

"What? What are you talking about?"

Maze tossed one of his folders onto the table. It spun around and came to a stop in front of Ophelia. Taken aback, while trying to maintain her confidence, Ophelia bent down and picked up the folder to leaf through it.

Harlow could almost see each of the pages register as the certainty drained out of Ophelia. There was a snippet transcribed from the night of Jarvis' murder. Pages from her medical and educational report, and evidence from the investigation of her parents' death.

Curling her hands over Ryske's knees, Harlow boosted herself onto her feet.

"Where did you get this?" Ophelia asked. "It's lies. All lies!"

"That's just a sample of what we have," Harlow said, skirting the table. "We have evidence of everything, of exactly what you're like, of who you are. If you force us to use it, we will."

Ophelia tossed the folder down. "This proves nothing. You know nothing."

"I know I was there," Harlow murmured. "I know I saw you do it. I took the rap to protect the people in this room from you… But now these people are smart enough to see what you did."

The curtain over the entry hallway moved. Yarker

came in with Lydia behind him.

"Anthony," Ophelia declared, rushing over to him. "Do you know what's going on in here? What they're accusing me of?"

"You orchestrated this whole thing and I let you," Yarker said, pushing her hand away when she tried to reach for him. "You never loved me. You manipulated me. You forced me and my best friend to get involved with something that could cost us both our freedoms… I told you Gil got the offer and refused because we didn't want to be involved in anything illegal like this… I thought it cost your brother his life. Now I learn it was you who took it. You killed your own brother… You're a monster."

Grabbing Lydia, Yarker pulled her away from Ophelia and across to Parratt like he was protecting her.

"No," Ophelia said, searching the room and her thoughts. "No, this isn't right… this isn't how it's supposed to be."

"That's the way life goes," Harlow said. "You've got to learn to go with it."

Fury clenched Ophelia's jaw and her fists. "You've ruined everything!"

The heiress stalked across the room toward her. Even when the beauty's hand went into her purse, Harlow held her ground. Gasps echoed when Ophelia produced a gun.

Harlow's blood chilled. This was the way Hagan had gone and he hadn't seen it coming. What was her excuse? This was how it was supposed to end, she'd known that. Still, shock tensed her muscles.

Before Ophelia could reach her, a shadow crossed between them, then Ryske's body was in front of hers. Though she tried to push him aside, he just wrapped both arms around his back and held her against his spine.

"You want to use that…" Ryske said, "you better take me down first."

"No, Crash," Harlow said, fighting to wrestle out of his grip, but he was too strong. "Crash, let her have me."

She couldn't do it. She couldn't go through the torture of losing him again. With his height and breadth, she couldn't see around him. Damnit, fuck, she resented him for putting her in this position.

"Every person in this room is willing to testify that this was your operation," Ryske said. "The cops will buy it because your plan was the only thing you brought to the table… You can leave now, get out the city with all the money you raised selling your brother's life's work… Sorry, your murder victim's life's work… or you can start shooting… But that's a six shooter. Even if you use every shot to kill someone, there will still be witnesses… Think about all those clients out there with cellphones and the drugs behind that curtain. You bet your ass you'll be going to jail. Oh, and that evidence we have, it will find its way to the cops even if we're dead. That's the benefit of having a crew… something that comes with loyalty."

"And compassion," Penzance said, leaving his chair to put himself in front of Ryske.

To her amazement, Maze got up too. "And dedication," he said, standing shoulder to shoulder with Penzance.

"Ryske isn't the only one who'll stand up for Harlow," Penzance said.

"No, he's not," Anwen said. To Harlow's amazement, Anwen came over to stand with the guys. "It's over, Fi. You're being given a chance Jarvis would never have given you… Think about it, Brash and Animal know the truth. They know you killed Jarvis. They'll be out for your blood. It would be smart to get out of dodge anyway."

"Leave town, Ophelia," Parratt said, though he, Lydia, and Yarker stayed in their corner. "Never speak of any of this to anyone and none of us will. Force our hand and you will be pinned as responsible."

"Because you are," Lydia said. It was nice to hear the woman stand up for herself.

Tension hung in the air as everyone waited to see what Ophelia would do next.

"All of you deserve to burn," Ophelia spat. "If I'd set that fire myself in your precious bar, instead of hiring someone to do it, maybe you'd have got what you deserved!"

In the same second Ryske's muscles clenched to lunge, she threw her arms around his waist to pull him back. In an instant reversal, now she was holding him where he didn't want to be.

"Don't, baby," she said, dropping her weight back to hold him.

"Get the fuck out of here, Ophelia!" Maze shouted, something he didn't often do. "If you don't leave now, I'll take you down myself."

"You're all ungrateful, ignorant swines," Ophelia said. "To hell with you all."

Harlow heard movement and then the sound of the curtain. A moment of silence followed before Ryske began to relax.

"Check she's really gone," Ryske said.

"On it," Penzance replied.

After a few more seconds, Ryske eased her arms from around him. Her love turned toward Parratt who was coming their way. Penzance and Maze strode out of the room.

"I hope our paths never cross again," Parratt was saying to Ryske when he and Yarker reached their position.

"Oh," Lydia made a sound of disappointment. "I was going to ask Harlow to lunch."

Harlow smiled.

"Absolutely not," Parratt said.

Leaning to the side, Harlow peeked around Ryske to see Lydia. "I'll call you."

Lydia grinned, but Parratt was blustering.

Ryske ignored him to address Yarker. "Get your people out of here, Ophelia's too."

"Within the hour," Yarker said and helped Lydia drag Parratt out of the room.

Ryske turned to Anwen, but she just raised a hand. "I'll go help Maze," she said, smiling as she left.

"That went as well as it could have," Ryske said, turning to face her. "No one even got hurt."

Before he'd stopped turning, she brought her hand across his face in a hard slap. "You asshole! Don't you ever do that to me again!"

His hand was on his face until she tried to move.

He seized her arms, hauling her back to him. "I will always put myself between you and danger," he asserted, shaking her. "Always!"

"What would I have done if I'd lost you?"

He lost some of his anger and slid a hand up to cup the side of her head. "The same thing I would've done."

Pulling her up, he kissed her hard. Though she objected at first, she melted and surrendered until she was loose in his embrace.

He ripped his mouth free of hers too soon. "Don't leave this room. I'm packing up Pothos for Parratt and then we're clearing this place… It's ours now, baby. Just ours… Told you we were going to own the world. This is just the first step."

"What's next?"

"Home, sex, wake up tomorrow," he said, nuzzling her mouth. "All part of your plan."

"Dover should open Floyd's tomorrow."

"He should."

"And we should go to my parents for dinner Sunday."

"You're getting good at this planning for the future stuff."

Coiling her arms around his neck, she pulled herself to her tiptoes. "Crash?"

"Hmm?" he asked, licking her lips.

"Tell me I belong to you."

Easing back, he met her eye, an intrigued smile on his face. "You do belong to me, Trinket… You have since that very first night."

"Crash?"

"Yes, baby," he said, tucking her hair back from her face.

"Tell me I'm going to marry you one day. That I'm going to bear your children and we're going to be together forever."

"We are."

Mesmerized by his mouth, she rocked on her tiptoes, eager to taste him again. "No, I need you to say it."

He laughed. "Why?"

"Because every time I resisted, you fought, and you've been right every time. You are my soul, Ryske. The love of my life. My blood… If you say it, you believe it, and you'll make it happen."

Taking her face in both hands, he bent his knees to align their eyes. "You're going to be mine forever, Harlow Sweeting. I told you you'd share my name and you will bear my children. But happy?" He scowled. "Happy is for wimps. We don't do things by halves, baby. Happy ever after? No. This is our deliriously, ecstatic, orgasmic ever after, because even when you hate me, you love me, Trink."

She smiled and curled her fingers to drag her nails over the area of his tattoo. "I do."

"You do," he said, guiding her mouth to his.

"I do."

Harlow hadn't anticipated the love of her life would crash into her in the middle of the night and almost bleed to death in her lap. Even in spite of all they'd endured to get to the place they were at, she was grateful for it, for him.

The taxing adventure wasn't over yet. With Ryske at her side, backing her up, she was ready for whatever the world could throw at her.

If there was one thing she'd learned, it was that going it alone didn't work. Going all in had almost cost Harlow her freedom. She'd had to go all out to get it back.

No matter what, Ryske would never have let her stay lost. Her Crash knew how the world worked. He lived by the most valuable piece of advice she'd ever received.

Trust was vital and no matter what happened, the best plan was always to go with it.

Thank you for reading this tale!
If you can, please take the time to review.

~

Ask your local library for more Scarlett Finn
novels!

~

For all things Scarlett Finn
check out:

www.scarlettfinn.com

Check out the Roxiverse: